HIGH
THE WAY OF AN EAGLE

Charlene Quiram

This book is a work of fiction. Names, characters, and events herein derive from the author's imagination or are used fictitiously.

Copyright © 2013 by Charlene Quiram
All rights reserved. Published by Keytree Press
P.O. Box 6503, Yorktown, VA 23690

Summary: Sixteen-year-old Verona flies like an eagle out of her classroom, witnesses maiming and murder, falls for a devilishly handsome boy and discovers she is part of an ancient mystical group charged with thwarting a demon-infested killer.

Cover and cover art is designed by Lady Symphonia.

Printed in the United States of America
10 9 8 7 6 5 4 3 2 1

Library of Congress Control Number 2013912467
Quiram, Charlene 1960-

High: The Way of an Eagle: a novel/by Charlene Quiram

ISBN: 978-09895145-0-7
ISBN(ebook): 978-09895145-1-4

This book is dedicated to Dale Richards, who lost his physical body in 2010. In the words of Jeremiah Cleveland, *Save us a seat at the banquet, friend.*

There are three things that are
too amazing for me,
Four that I do not understand;
The way of an eagle in the sky,
The way of a snake on a rock,
The way of a ship on the high seas,
And the way of a man with a maiden.

Proverbs 30:18-19 (NIV)

Eagle Perspective

Friday, September 11th
688 Days to Home Free

TODAY MARKS THE ANNIVERSARY of the most infamous attack on American soil; but here at Colonial High in Jamestown, Virginia—two hours south of the Pentagon—you'd never know it. No one has said anything all day.

No moment of silence, no memorial. Nothing. Nada. Zilch.

Back at East Side High, my old school in Manhattan, we would've had a half-day assembly starting with the band playing John Philip Sousa's *Stars and Stripes Forever* and ending with a speech from some firefighter to impress on us the day's significance.

Honestly, we don't need any more of an impression; most of us have wounds from the day. They aren't open and obvious and on the outside, like a torn-off leg or shrapnel scars. For most of us, these wounds are buried, languishing in the chasm between heart and soul. Oh, they bubble to the surface for some people—like the razor cuts Laura Flannery hides beneath jeans and long sleeves, or the stuttering problem Kyle Price developed after his father's funeral. But for me, for most of us, really, you'll never see them. I'd never *let* you see them.

I remember how the cherubic face of my third-grade teacher, Miss Goldstein, segued from disbelief to horror, from horror to anger, and after her eyes swept over us, to fear. When they sent us home, I caught my dad on his knees, praying to the TV news. I'd never seen Dad pray before, not even when Boston was hammering the Yankees.

I remember how every September 11th afterwards, we would pat Laura Flannery and Kyle Price on the shoulder and say something like, "How you holding up?" And every year my family—my mom, Dad, Danny and me—would take the D-Line to Bensonhurst to comfort Aunt Gina with stories about her husband, my Uncle Jimmy, the funniest *and hairiest* Cookie Monster imitator in the world. He also happened to be a New York firefighter killed under the North Tower.

Today Mom and I won't be going. But I know Dad and my nine-year-old brother Danny will catch the subway to Brooklyn and eat mounds of Grandma Mima's fettuccine alfredo.

I kiss the silver cross around my neck, a gift from Uncle Jimmy and Aunt Gina the Christmas before everything changed. Meanwhile, the kids sitting around me agonize over our chemistry quiz; the girl behind me lets loose a jagged moan. For the millionth time in the last five months, I can't believe I'm here. I can't believe how different I am from these kids, these mostly *southern* kids. How out of place. In New York, no teacher would ever *think* of scheduling a quiz on September 11th.

I check my quiz answers, then stare at the minute hand of the clock over Mr. Zeke's head, willing it to move, willing the bell to signal the end of another week away from home, and marking one week closer to freedom. Freedom means rooming with Luka at NYU. New York University—where people won't laugh whenever I say *tawk* and *sawsage*. In 688 days, Luka and I will decorate our apartment with pink hippie beads and vintage Woodstock memorabilia, including an authentic poster of a young, yet-to-be-discovered Carlos Santana that Dad bought me off Craigslist for a going-away present.

That's what I'm thinking when, for some reason, the taste of burnt charcoal attacks my mouth. Like licking a barbecue briquette, but without the burn. So now I'm thinking I need to get rid of my gum—quick. I tear off a corner from the quiz's back page. Mr. Zeke hears the page rip, and looks up from his book. Wrapping the gum into the paper, I swallow the vile taste. Bad idea. My stomach likes it even less than my mouth does.

I will myself not to lose my lunch all over the girl in front of me; a tragic-looking emoticon who took a razor blade to her purple Hello Kitty shirt. It looks like Hello Kitty lost a cat fight to Calvin's tiger, Hobbes. The thought of these two cartoon cats fighting makes me smile, and to my relief, I don't throw up. But then something more frightening, frightening and unexpected, happens. I *pop* up and out of my body, up to the ceiling, like my body is an iridescent bubble holding my thoughts and feelings hostage. The *pop* is muffled; it's actually more of a *poof*.

Up near the ceiling, I hover next to the clock. Its hands are spinning round and round like time is moving at warp speed, and at the same time, my mouth fills with the salty taste of the ocean. I would've preferred chocolate or mango, but the ocean flavor is pleasant; it reminds me of buttery steamed clams, and it's infinitely better than burnt charcoal.

My teacher, Mr. Zeke, hovers up by the ceiling with me. Only now he doesn't look anything like Mr. Zeke—for one thing, he's an eagle. Seriously, an eagle. No black-rimmed reading glasses, no suit, just feathers. A sweet bald eagle with butterscotch eyes set in a white head. And he's sporting a killer wingspan.

And then—hoping that if I look at myself and will it, I'll return to my body—I make the mistake of looking down. Below us, kids hunch over their quizzes. Except for me, Verona Louise Lamberti. Hands hugging my stomach, I'm bent over, with my chin jutting out, staring straight ahead like some B-movie zombie. Two incorrigible brown curls loop over one eye, and my tie-dyed T-shirt climbs up my back, covered by my hair. From up here, it almost looks like I'm not wearing a shirt.

I will myself to go back, to reconnect with my body, so at the very least, I can pull my shirt down. But that works as well as willing my parents not to divorce, or willing today's class to end.

Am I dead? If I died, I'd have fallen over into the aisle, right? You can't die and sit up straight at the same time. But then, if I'd fallen over in class, I'm pretty sure I would have died of embarrassment, regardless of whether I'd been dead in the first place.

Before I can figure out if I am, in fact, dead, Mr. Zeke tells me to follow him outside. Wordlessly. No…stranger than that—telepathically. I *feel* him tell me, "Follow the way."

"No! I don't want to. Put me back!" I'm not really sure if I'm yelling at the chemistry teacher Mr. Zeke, or the eagle Mr. Zeke, or some other entity in control; but it doesn't matter, because my new out-of-body body has a mind of its own, and it's following the eagle.

We race toward the window. I close my eyes, expecting the glass to shatter—but it doesn't. It moves for us, permeable and rippling, like the clear surface of a pool that happens to be vertical. Cool air splashes my face, smelling of fresh-cut grass and distant bonfires, yet more distinct. Somehow I can tell the grass is a fescue and clover blend, and the wood being burned is a mixture of white oak and maple. *How do I know that?*

And, as if tasting burnt charcoal, popping out of your body and flying isn't enough weirdness packed into the span of two minutes, today's sunny afternoon has somehow spun into twilight. But this twilight is different. Instead of the usual milky-gray bridge between sunlight and streetlight, this twilight is a Coney Island frantic mix of colors, colors that fill all my senses. Greener-than-green viburnum leaves twinkle like xylophone whispers. Bluer-than-blue hydrangeas smell like salt-water taffy, and browner-than-brown tree trunks evoke relaxation, like reading in a hammock on a beach.

We fly over the faculty parking lot adjacent to the tennis courts. Both are empty. At a fast clip we head straight for the back of the football stadium bleachers. I shut my eyes and scream, bracing myself for pain, and quickly lose the reading-in-a-hammock calm I was feeling moments ago. Seconds before impact, we arc straight up into creamy sapphire with the honeysuckle flecks of evening stars. I exhale.

Mr. Zeke's whiter-than-white tail feathers level over the stadium lights, with me trailing in their wake, trailing and relieved not to have whacked into the posts. Relieved and amazed.

Amazed! Astonished! Both flabber and gasted! I am flying, *flying*, an emerald floating high in a jewel-encrusted sky. Make that *real* high. Normally, I hate high; but here I am, three hundred feet over the football stadium, and I'm loving it. It's everything I've ever loved all at once—Christmas, ice cream, Zeppelin, the Hudson River Painters, Newma's peppermint hugs and chocolate chip cookies, Danny's goofy, freckled laugh— and it's making me feel more alive than I've ever felt in my entire life, infinitely more alive than I was feeling in chemistry.

A quick glance over my shoulder alerts me to the fact that I am not an emerald, but like Mr. Zeke, I have wings. Whatever this funky thing is, whatever is happening to me, I am an eagle too. Hmm. I do feel a twinge of concern. I wonder if the Buddhists have been right all along and I've reincarnated as an eagle; but decide that the Buddhists are irrelevant compared to what I'm feeling. *Irrelevant*—my mom's trump word in any argument: *What all the other kids do is irrelevant!* Even the fact that I'm an eagle is irrelevant. 'Cause… I. Am. *Flying*!

To my right, a sliver of apricot lines the horizon. To my left, the bluer-than-blue arch of Busch Garden's Griffin rollercoaster rises above the tree tops—the same coaster Danny guilted me into riding last spring because Dad wasn't there, and there was no way he was going to get Mom on it. The picture they took at the first drop is taped to Danny's bedpost. His trophy, my humiliation: Danny's still-chubby hands and cantaloupe-colored hair are sticking straight up, his mouth and eyes three round "O"s, and me, my dark hair swimming up where my face would have been if I hadn't been curled into the fetal position, wondering if an otherwise healthy sixteen-year-old can die of a heart attack from fear alone.

Mr. Zeke veers left, over the auto shop building beyond the visitor bleachers, and crosses over Memorial Drive to the student parking lot, with eagle me in his wake. A group of popular kids—the elite of Colonial High—huddle in the section most obscured by trees, drinking beer and laughing. Some of the guys wear Cougar football jerseys, the same ones they're wearing today in school. Assuming this still *is* today.

My eagle body leaves Mr. Zeke's eagle body circling the dusky sky and dives down, straight down, kamikaze-fast toward the kids. Somehow, and with the same sort of *poof* as before, I land inside the head of a cheerleader as she passes a half-empty Bud Light to Alex Chortov, her boyfriend, and the star quarterback on Colonial's football team.

Inside. Kind of like the old-school movie *Invasion of the Body Snatchers.* Or a warped version of *Freaky Friday,* where I invade the cheerleader's body, but she doesn't have to find out what it's like to be the loser new-girl at school. And not just any cheerleader, but Angie Jett, the bad-girl head cheerleader, founding member of the "Jett Set" and everyone's pick for homecoming queen. A white feather floats in front of Alex Chortov's face. His gargantuan fist grabs all that's left of my eagle body.

Angie burps loudly. They say New Yorkers have no manners, and true to form, everyone laughs. Except me. I'm busy hiding somewhere inside Angie's head, like a bad dream, or a brain tumor.

"That's my angel—such a lady." Alex Chortov tickles Angie's face with the feather, *my* feather. I feel it, too. We pull away.

Overhead, the streetlight buzzes, flickers, and pops on.

"Hey Genghis, let's move this party down to the river before the cops come nosing around." Clyde Baker grabs the beer from

Alex, nicknamed Genghis Khan for his Russian Tartar heritage and fierce reputation on the football field.

"What do you say?" Alex turns to face me. He presses into the car on either side of me, sandwiching me between his massive arms and Schwarzenegger chest. I know he's seeing his beautiful Asian girlfriend, but I'm seeing and feeling his body leaning over me, with my back butted against the door of a kiwi-green VW Beetle. Trapped like a voyeuristic creeper in someone else's love life, I inhale the heat wafting up from under his jersey. He smells of fruity drug-store cologne and, when he opens his mouth, onions. "You want to hang down by the river?"

With eyes just inches from mine, Alex Chortov is, without a doubt, *the* hottest guy I've ever seen this close up. His identical twin brother, Ben, sits a few seats behind me in chemistry class, but I've been too intimidated to throw him more than a glance. Both brothers share the same muscle-bound frame and football-enhanced popularity, and by that I mean both brothers are googols out of my league.

I wiggle out from under his embrace. "Sure. It's boring here." I feel these words emerge from my mouth; my throat tightens and vibrates to form them—but they're all Angie.

"Give me a kiss for the ride, baby." Alex holds his arms out wide.

I dangle a set of keys in front of his face. "If you beat me to the river, I'll give you more than a kiss."

Wait a minute! No! I can't be stuck in here when you do whatever constitutes more than a kiss! I'm screaming inside her head, but Angie doesn't hear me at all. I feel everything she feels, but apparently she doesn't have a clue that she has company.

"Really? You think there's a chance you can take me in *this* thing?" He backhands the VW. "You're crazy, Angel. But, you got it!" Alex winks, then rushes around his Impala. The other kids fall back to avoid being plowed over. I yank open the VW door, slide in, turn the key, and fasten the belt.

Leanne Morris presses against the passenger-side window, long copper locks blowing back from her face. "Don't drive, Angie. Don't you think y'all drank too much?" Her brow wrinkles.

"Back off, Leanne!" I say between gritted teeth. Of course, it isn't really me—it just *feels* like me. The VW reverses so fast Leanne falls into Clyde Baker, who drops his beer to catch her.

I try to control the wheel, stop the car—every effort a colossal fail.

We slide in front of Alex's Impala, tires squealing. My heart pounds so loud I can hear it as we skid out of the parking lot and onto Memorial. Angie guns the accelerator.

Alex catches up on the straightaway, then passes us in the left turn lane. The light at the Monroe Highway intersection turns yellow. Both cars speed up.

I feel Angie's determination in every clenched muscle. I try to move her foot to the left, to step on the brakes, to wait at the light. A redder-than-red light. But it's useless. Alex's Impala slips under the light inches ahead of the VW.

A low warning growl broadcasts the truck before I see it. Its headlights, blindingly orange-yellow, and its low threatening horn bear down on us like a giant fire-breathing chimera. Angie gives up, goes completely limp, too stunned or drunk or scared to do anything.

God, please don't let me die! The words are whispered in Angie's voice—not mine. God is the last thing I'm worried about. Getting out of the monster truck's way tops my list—if we don't get over quick, we're dead. I mash the brake pedal to the floor but the pedal slogs like a drenched sponge. Yanking the wheel hard to the right, I steer away from the lights and the blaring horn.

The truck just skims the back bumper of the VW. Directly in front of us, a massive tree lights up like it's been hit by lightning. Tires screech on dry pavement, metal rips, and glass explodes in the space of a second.

Something punches me in the head and chest. My lungs crush inward, and darkness blankets the car. I gasp for air—a high-pitched whistle sound. Noxious gas fumes burn my throat. Rubber presses my nostrils shut and yet it all reeks of explosives and plastic. Inexplicably, staples jam into my right cheek in rapid succession. Metal clamps down on my legs, trapping them—but they don't hurt. I can't feel anything below my knees.

The truck's horn blast fades to obnoxious buzzing that filters through my ears and whirls through my head. I gasp for air. The plastic falls away, and withered-edged rose petals fall around me like fat, bloody snowflakes. A white light flickers in front of my eyes. Once again, I wonder if I'm dead.

Slow and murky, the rose petals melt away, and I realize I'm back. Back in my human, featherless, mostly H_2O body. Back in chemistry, where the buzzing noise turns out to be the final school bell of the week. Where white quiz papers shake in front of my face. I grasp the sides of my desk, fighting to steady my breathing.

"*Hello?* Anybody home?" The flaxen blonde from behind waves a handful of quizzes in my face to pass up to the front. "It's not like you haven't been finished for, like, *ever*."

"Sorry." I pass the papers to the blurry hand in front of me and pull my wayward shirt down over the top of my jeans. The kids in class retrieve their cell phones, talking about the weekend. Compared to the world I just came back from, everything looks so drab, so washed out. So retro.

I feel around for my glasses, but they've gone missing. Thinking they may have fallen off my desk, I stand up… to the unmistakable crunch of yet another optical casualty. My third pair of glasses this year.

With one hand I finger-comb locks over my right eye, and with the other hand I adjust the broken glasses on my face. Mr. Zeke leans on the front edge of his desk, shuffling quizzes. What kind of weird subconscious would turn this middle-aged black man into an eagle? His hair is turning white at the edges, but that's where any similarity ends.

"Verona, please wait. I'd like to talk to you." When my shoulders slump, Mr. Zeke quickly adds, "You're not in trouble."

He doesn't know I'm cringing because he said my name out loud. Baritone-loud, and in front of everyone. All my life I've put up with the story of my parents' honeymoon in Italy, and my first appearance into the world nine months later. Verona, the city of Romeo and Juliet fame. When I complained about this to my mother, she laughed and said I should be grateful I wasn't conceived in Assisi. Maybe so, but I hate my name, and all that romantic nonsense it conjures up. The day I turn eighteen, I'm changing it. I will not answer to *Verona* at NYU. Possibly something cool like Joplin or China, but probably something normal—like Emma, Brittany, or Natalie.

I stuff my cell phone into my jeans pocket, all the while pulling more hair over the eye with the broken lens. I could kiss Mr. Zeke for pretending not to notice the lopsided glasses on my face.

"What happened to you?"

"What? I took the quiz and—" Now I wish he hadn't noticed me at all.

"For a few seconds it looked like you fell asleep with your eyes open. When I started to walk over to check on you, the bell rang and you snapped out of it. Is it possible you had a seizure?"

"A what? Seizure?" I shake my head *no*. I was going to say, "Stepped on my glasses again," but the impact of what he's asking kicks in. Aunt Gina has had seizures ever since she hit her head ice-skating. She's never been allowed to get her driver's license. Seizures mean you can't drive. I'd be stuck at home—not my real home in New York where my MetroCard pretty much guarantees me unlimited freedom; but here, where public transportation is synonymous with bumming a ride with a friend. And since I haven't made one friend in the five months since my mom and I moved here, I'd be stuck, trapped. I shake my head back and forth vigorously.

"Have you ever had a seizure?"

"No. Never." I glance at the clock above his head like I have somewhere to go, hoping he'll let up. The clock's hands are moving normal now. It's 2:28 p.m.

"What happened, then?" he continued to press.

"I don't know. I mean, I was thinking of something." I'm trying to reassure myself as much as him. "You know, daydreaming. I do it all the time."

While that last part is technically true, I know for a fact that the first part was something completely different from a daydream. The problem is, I don't know what to call it, and I'm not ready to admit that to anyone but Luka. And I need to leave so I can tell her.

Mr. Zeke narrows his eyes at me, takes a breath, and pats the manila envelope I'd left with him before class. "I'll get to your reference as soon as possible."

THE STUDENT PARKING LOT IS CLOGGED with cars trying to escape for the weekend, except for the section in back where the Jett Set hangs out. Wondering how it would feel to really *be* the cheerleader, to be wildly popular, totally *in,* and adored by everyone, I sneak a look in their direction.

Angie, enthroned on the hood of a restored Impala, whispers in Alex's ear. She catches me staring, pulls back, and narrows her eyes in a question, or a threat; I can't tell which. When Alex turns toward me, Angie grasps his face in her hands and brings it to hers for a kiss. And then—because I'm a complete klutz, destined to be friendless for the next almost-two years—I trip over a curb. So instead of kissing Alex Chortov, I'm about to kiss the pavement. *In front of everyone.*

Only I don't. A strong hand grabs my arm above my elbow and lifts me upright. Before I know what's happening, before I can mutter a meager "thanks," Ben Chortov has advanced several feet toward the Jett Set. I march to the Rover, head down and stomach churning.

I climb into the "gently worn" Land Rover my mother bought me as a consolation prize for moving me four hundred miles from home, rest my head on the wheel, and text my best friend back in New York:

Me: U there?
Luka: yeah?

Me: eagle flew out window body-snatch car wreck

How can I relay what happened in a text?

My Beatles "Come Together" ring tone lets me know Luka is calling. I tell her everything—starting with the eagle flight above the school grounds, the risk-taking cheerleader body-snatch and car wreck, and end with needing to be propped up like an old lady crossing the street. Then I wait for her opinion on what happened. And wait. And look to see if we still have a connection.

"Texting with talons would bite." Luka giggles, a lame attempt to get me to relax. She's been doing that a lot lately. "But the whole flying thing would be cool—don't you think?"

"Girl, you are so not funny. And *cool?* That's it? I just had the weirdest experience of my life, and you're making jokes?" If we were walking home from school together like we should've been right now—I would punch her for that. In a punch-buggy sort of way.

"Maybe your PCQ vision is a funky, subconscious reaction to the fact that today's 9/11—you know, like a post-traumatic stress thing."

"My first 9/11 away from New York. Wait, what's PCQ?"

"Post-chemistry quiz."

"PCQ vision a reaction to PTSD? I thought you wanted to be a medical doctor—not a shrink."

"I don't need to be a shrink to see what kind of year you've had—your parents' divorce, a new home, new school, new everything…"

I bang my head against the steering wheel. Luka has a point. It could be connected to all the change. No wonder I'm having creepy visions of eagles and car wrecks.

I can't help a sarcastic attempt at perspective. "Yeah, but only 688 days until we're at NYU together."

And Luka, being Luka, can't help her optimism. "Yeah, but only *seven* days until I get to see your new home."

"Temporary living quarters," I remind her. But Luka's impending visit does cheer me up. I look forward to renting scary movies, eating Moose Tracks ice cream and popcorn, and catching up on the gossip from my old school. As I start the Rover, I utter, "Fuggedaboutit," in my dad's Brooklynese.

Saturday, September 12th
687 Days to Home Free

JAMESTOWN, VIRGINIA'S BIG CLAIM TO FAME is that it's the first permanent English settlement in America. It's also known for its "hot" list of things to do on weekends—but only if you're a card-carrying member of AARP. So the scorching highlight this Saturday is taking our sheepdog Max for a stroll through the Farmer's Market in Merchant's Square.

Merchant's Square is pretty much what it says it is—it's a square brick plaza in what used to be a street with rows of quaint-looking stores on two sides. My mother loves Williams Sonoma and Talbots, and I love Wythe Candy and the College Book Store.

Merchant's Square works like a buffer between the College of William and Mary, where my mother works, and Colonial Williamsburg, a living history museum where spooky-looking interpreter-people in seventeenth century dresses and wigs show you how life was back then. I'm up early anyway, because I need to drop my mother off at the college, where she teaches in the English Department on weekdays, and now, apparently, on weekends as well. "A writing workshop," she tells me.

At the open market, Max tugs me toward the spicy pork-barbecue and is rewarded with a treat by an amiable man in a burnt-sienna-splattered apron. I watch some of the local artists at work. Back home my weekends were filled with art, canvassing the latest art exhibits at the Met (New York's Louvre) or the MoMA (Museum of Modern Art), or exploring the funky galleries down in SoHo and the Village. My heart is set on becoming a brilliantly gifted painter, the next Frederick Church or Claude Monet; but in the event that doesn't pan out, plan B is museum curator or gallery owner. In New York.

The aroma of chocolate-covered donuts wafts into my nostrils and through my brain to my ears, whispering, "Verona, eat me—you know you want to," from a booth claiming Devine Donuts. I dig through my jeans pocket for the ten bucks I brought along. This sugarcoated temptation costs almost four bucks, but I figure I need one to soak up the water in my mouth.

The Devine Donuts sales woman, so thin you could see the bones around her eyes—probably *not* a farmer or even a farmer's wife, since she's wearing a long fuchsia dress, fuchsia necklace and earrings, fuchsia high-heeled sandals, and shiny fuchsia blush and reminding me of a gigantic version of Luka's favorite lip gloss—hands me the donut like it's some sort of confectionary masterpiece. She nods at Max. "You want one for your dog?"

"No, thanks. He just had a treat." I smile, but only one side of the woman's fuchsia lip curls up. Max growls low, threateningly, and pulls back while I wait for my change. That's when the burnt charcoal flavor seeps into my mouth again, tasting as putrid as it had yesterday in class.

I stare at the woman's back while she takes forever counting the change from her little gray box. Meanwhile, Max's leash tugs at my wrist, and the disgusting taste turns my stomach. I spit my gum into the pastry's paper napkin and brace myself for another out-of-body flight, when the woman turns around.

Her face holograms into a grotesque skull, the fuchsia lipstick and all traces of skin replaced by rotting flesh, pink and gray and bloody, with slimy see-through worms munching to the bone. Her mawkish eyes, like the bottom of a cesspool, grope at me, try to pull me in. She wants my money—for some reason she thinks I'm rich—my looks, my future, my family. In fact, it's like she covets all of me, my life, my essence, everything that makes me, me.

Her eyes lock me in place, forcing me to watch movie reels of memories, one memory movie after the other and overlapping so that, in a mere two seconds, I know her past and present way better than I'd ever want to. In one memory, she's stealing a new watch from a sleeping girl in the Romanian orphanage where she grew up. In another, she fights with her roommate over a pair of donated boots. They're painfully tight on her, but she doesn't want the other girl to have them anyway.

In another reel, she's sitting on the stoop, making a show of eating candy, when a small boy, dirty and disheveled, creeps up to her, licking his lips and staring at the candy. She throws a rock at him, then laughs as pink, blood-tinged tears run down his face and turn to rose petals drifting to the ground.

I recoil as the change falls onto my outstretched palm. My fist clutches the bills. The coins scatter on the pavement, but I don't stop to pick them up. Max pulls me to the opposite corner and across the street, where, having lost my appetite, I dunk the pastry into a garbage bin and slide into the William and Mary College Book Store.

Safely inside, I peek through the door window. A passerby picks up my coins and hands them to the woman, whose mouth has reverted to its normal fuchsia snarl. I turn and swallow, relieved that the burnt charcoal taste has dissipated. My heart is pounding uncontrollably, and this time I know it won't be possible to *fuggedaboutit* so easily.

"Hey, you can't have a dog in here!" a bearded man behind the cash register yells at me. All the shoppers between us look at him, then at Max.

Pretending not to hear him, I weave through a swell of people up the stairs to the coffee shop. After setting Max under an empty table in the back, I rest my head in my hands while my thumbs massage my temples. *What is wrong with me?*

Wait. I hit my head with the palm of my hand. I know. Somehow, someone must have laced my gum with some kind of hallucinogenic—like angel dust or LSD. Only hallucinogenics can take you to a psychedelic place where time can stand still, or stretch forward and back like the movies. I unzip the outside pocket of my backpack. Max's ears perk up.

"You just had a treat," I remind him.

Max tilts his head in an adorable rapscallion look.

"Oh, okay." I secret him a Milk-Bone dog biscuit from my backpack, then plop my turquoise pack of wintermint-flavored Orbit gum on the table like it is hot from the oven.

I peer around the room to see if anyone's noticed me—the rogue girl with the forbidden dog and the drugged chewing gum. Everyone is otherwise engaged—conversing over mocha lattes, reading books, newspapers, and magazines. The students working the counter are occupied with a swarm of customers fidgeting around the dessert display.

I sniff at the gum lying there in its package. It doesn't smell like burnt charcoal—in fact, mixed with the aromas in this room, it reminds me of coffee-mint-chocolate chip ice cream. Maybe I should nix the Moose Tracks, and get coffee and mint chocolate chip ice cream instead. *Does Luka even like mint chocolate chip?*

Maybe I'll order a Mocha Latte, daydream about Luka's visit, and "Fuggedaboutit,"—it being the second burnt charcoal vision. But, no that would be too easy, too sissified. I open the pack and start analyzing.

Five pieces left in this pack, which means I've already chomped on nine. Only two morphed into burnt charcoal—but not at first. Before the PCQ vision, I'd chewed the same piece all of third period art and most of chemistry, before the grill-licking taste hit.

This morning I popped a piece in my mouth when we were stopped at a red light, since my mom was in the car and would've thrown a fit if I did anything but drive while driving. But still, even today the wintergreen passed to gum-flavor-heaven long before the burnt charcoal appeared with all its nasty Romanian orphanage hallucinations.

I know that some drugs have a delayed release, but since when are criminals that sophisticated? I mean, really, a headline appearing in my mom's old newspaper: *Today's Junkies Demand Delayed-release High*. As my mom would say, *ludicrous*.

Since this pack of twenty had come sealed in a plastic wrapper, part of a three-pack sealed in another plastic wrapper, there are only two viable explanations:

1. Some sicko removed my gum from my backpack without my knowledge, drugged a few pieces and then wrapped them up carefully so I wouldn't know, or;

2. Some moron at the Orbit chewing gum factory is lacing random pieces early in the packaging process.

If I report #2 to the police, maybe the FBI will place a hidden camera at the factory, catch "Orbit's Wintermint Tamperer" and I'll get a reward, and an interview on Oprah's network…where I'll probably embarrass myself in some irredeemable way and have to move to Ireland and live with my grandmother. Note to self: Ask Newma if OWN broadcasts in Ireland.

Pulling a piece between my forefinger and thumb, I sniff it, do another quick scan of the room, and wonder if I'll get arrested if someone else discovers my gum is drugged.

It doesn't smell like burnt charcoal.

Removing the gum from the white wrapper with the gray circles, I look for evidence of tampering. The piece is white, with columns of the letter V carved into it. I never noticed those before. *Suspicious.*

The next piece—identical. All the remaining pieces have the same little Vs.

I hold a piece under the table in front of Max's nose to see if he goes berserk like the K-9 dogs on TV. He sniffs, but when he opens his mouth to swallow, I pull it away.

The last thing I need is a dog that thinks he can fly.

The man with dark, slicked-backed rock-and-roll hair who's been reading with his back to me gets up, stretches, and wrestles into his black trench coat. When he turns around, I cover the gum and wrappers with my arms, and pretend to be interested in the picture on the wall—a black and white photograph of the Christopher Wren building taken in 1815.

He bends down to pet Max, scratching under his ears. Max's tail beats against the base of the table.

"Sheepdog?" His accent is definitely *not* Southern. It sounds somewhat similar to my Newma's Irish brogue, but different. Maybe British or Scottish or Australian.

I nod.

"We have a lot of sheep where I'm from."

I nod again, wondering where that is, but not wanting to start a conversation. My last conversation with a stranger didn't go so well. I'm afraid to look into his eyes. Afraid he might turn into some anime freak with a history full of stealing things and hurting people.

He smiles and walks away, when I notice his book is still on the table.

"Hey! You left your book."

He turns. I point at the book and he shrugs, waves his hand like he wants me to have it. "I'm done with it." Then he disappears down the stairs.

"Stay," I whisper to Max. I lean over the adjacent table and slide the thin volume to the end, where it flips over in my hands. The cover makes me jump and drop the book, but in an uncharacteristic moment of agility, I catch it before it hits the floor.

A massive bald eagle with wings as wide as the page hangs in the sky, with talons curled like they're going to attack. The book's title, *The Way of an Eagle*, is embossed over it.

What? This time I do drop it, rub my eyes under my glasses, and look again. But the book with the eagle spread over the cover still stares back at me. *The Way of an Eagle*, by Kendrick MacLeod.

What are the chances? Some guy leaves a book at the table next to me, a book which contains two elements of my weird PCQ vision right in its title: Mr. Zeke's *Follow the Way* imperative, on top of the fact that we were both eagles at the time.

I dart over to the balcony, searching for the man with the rock-and-roll hair and black trench coat, but he's dissolved into the crowd downstairs.

Max jumps out from his nook under the table and barks twice, leaving all eyes on the forbidden dog, and by default, me.

One of the girls at the counter gives me a look that says, and not in a good way, "No dogs allowed."

I loop Max's leash over my wrist, shove the book into my backpack and scoop up the gum and the wrappers. Throwing the gum and wrappers in the garbage at the top of the stairs, I run down and out the front door before anyone can scold me again.

While I don't technically steal the book— the rock-and-roll haired guy said he was done with it—I'm afraid everyone might think I did. Who would understand why I want it? Or for that matter, why do I think I *should* have it? What are the chances that this is a coincidence? One in a gazillion? Maybe, despite everything I've been taught, there is such a thing as providence— maybe things do happen for a reason. Besides, I'm hoping this book might teach me something, since what I know about eagles I can count on the fingers of one hand:

They fly.

For some reason they are one of our national symbols.

They eat rodents and fish (okay, I'm not a hundred percent sure about the diet, but don't all birds of prey?).

I know they were endangered at one time, but I think they're fine now.

YouTube has a riveting video of an eagle picking up a baby that looks to be about one year old, all bundled in winter clothes. Assuming it's real, I guess eagles are pretty strong.

Okay, I google-cheat to get that last one. If you haven't seen it, Google *eagle picks up baby*. If you don't want to get sidetracked surfing the internet, but you're wondering—spoiler alert!—the baby is okay in the end. Looks like the winter clothing cushioned his fall.

Still, four out of five isn't too bad for a city girl. I don't remember seeing any bald eagles at the zoo in Central Park. In fact, I've never actually seen a real bald eagle except on TV or YouTube.

Later I use something I gleaned from my eagle book for my art homework: the Chinese symbols for The Way of an Eagle.

Sunday, September 13th
686 Days to Home Free

"YOUR FOOTBALL TEAM WON." My mother folds the newspaper, then sips her coffee.

I grab a Diet Coke from the fridge. "They're not *my* football—"

"What happened to your other glasses? Don't tell me—"

"I stepped on the tortoiseshells."

"In your messy room, right?" My mother glares over her reading glasses.

I roll my eyes. "No, Mother. In chemistry."

My mother ignores the eye rolling. "What about contacts? Your eyes are a particularly striking shade of green—it's a shame to hide them. Plus, contacts would be harder to break."

"Here's the thing about contacts: First, I'd probably poke my eye out trying to get the stupid things in. Second, I'd be forever losing them, 'cause without my glasses, I can't see tiny, transparent things.

"*Be*-cause—you could give them a try. And you should try going to a football game, too. It's part of the whole high school experience you would've never gotten in the city."

"I've been to more than my share of football games with Dad. And I don't recall you ever jumping at the chance to go to one."

"That is *irrelevant*, Verona Louise. Those were professional games, and your father was working—high school is different. I went to football games at all three of my high schools. You should try it. Make some friends here."

My mother, the army brat, is a walking dichotomy. In some ways she can be smothering—hounding me to make friends, clean my room, and care more about my appearance. In other ways she gives me a lot more freedom than the parents of the other kids I know back in New York. When I was in the fifth grade, I was the only kid in my class with an Express MetroCard. I was allowed to ride around the city, so long as I told her or Dad where I was going and when I'd be home. I got to be a free-range kid before it became cool.

Monday, September 14th
685 Days to Home Free

ON THE DRIVE TO SCHOOL I try to cheer myself up listening to the Beatles' "Here Comes the Sun." I need cheering up for several reasons:
1. It's a Monday—enough reason for most people.
2. I woke up stuck in Virginia as opposed to New York.
3. Last night I got so into reading *The Way of an Eagle* I forgot to put my clothes in the dryer, which leads us to number 4.

Today I'm sporting the grunge look with dirty, wrinkled jeans, and by wrinkled, I mean several degrees past the built-in wrinkles that make you look cool. On the upside, I'm so invisible, who'll notice?

Turning right off the Monroe Highway onto Memorial Drive, I glance left to where Friday's PCQ vision crash took place, expecting nothing. I'd be cool with nothing. But no, there *is* something. And this *something* makes the hairs on my neck bristle.

The monstrous oak on that far corner has been hit, its trunk charred black where its bark splinters upward in a sinister grin. Broken glass decorates its roots, glistening in the sun like a diamond necklace—on the exact spot where Angie's crash took place in my hallucination. But wait, if that was a drug-induced hallucination—it couldn't really happen, right? With my head peering over my left shoulder, I start to swerve into the oncoming lane. A gold minivan honks an obnoxious, albeit necessary, warning.

I jerk the Rover back into my lane a millimeter from scraping the van. But I overcompensate, and my right front tire hits the curb. The Rover shakes and makes a deep metal-grinding-metal sound. Needless to say, it shakes me up, too. And I'm not alone.

On the sidewalk behind the curb, a gangly boy hidden under a black hoodie jumps back and flips me the bird, like I planned all that just to scare him. My hands tremble too much to return the salute.

Somehow I manage to steer the car to an empty spot in the farthest recess of student parking. Dropping my head against the wheel, I work to calm my breathing—focus on the Beatles tune and force myself to think, not feel, which would undoubtedly lead to panic.

Think. The gash in the tree and the broken glass were probably there last week and I just didn't notice. That would be typical. Luka says I wouldn't notice a shirtless Justin Timberlake on the subway seat across from me—I'm that pathetically unobservant. As for Angie Jett, she's probably chewing on Alex Chortov's bottom lip in the hallway, or holding court in the ladies room, or whatever the popular girls do before school.

A rap on the car window shakes me from my rationalizations. It's Leanne Morris, noted as "Everyone's Best Friend" by the yearbook committee, and one of only a handful of people at Colonial High who has ever bothered to so much as ask my name. She wears the same wrinkled brow as in my PCQ vision when she tried to stop Angie from driving. I take a deep cleansing breath like Luka taught me the time she was into yoga. Mouth closed, teeth apart, stomach out.

"Y'all all right?" Leanne yells above the Beatles belting out, "It's all right." I punch the stereo power button off, nod, grab my backpack, and swing the door open. When a handful of pens and loose change escapes from an open backpack pocket all over the concrete, she helps me retrieve them.

"I'm such a klutz!" I mutter under my breath.

"I drop stuff all the time," Leanne assures me, with a slow protracted drawl that makes her sound, well, slow—as in dim-witted, though rumor has it she's in the running for Colonial's valedictorian. I sling my backpack over my shoulder, take another cleansing breath, and we head toward the school entrance.

"I thought you might be upset about the accident." She motions toward the intersection, and I have to bend down a bit to hear her as the top of her mane of curly red hair only comes up to my shoulder. "It's gonna be hard (pronounced *haahd*) to make it through the day without cryin'."

I whip my head toward the intersection at Memorial and Monroe Highway and back to her. I swallow, and cough out, "Accident?"

Leanne squints up at me as if I'd grown another nose. "New purple glasses. Nice." Then she takes a deep breath—a lot of breathing going on! Luka would be proud—and her eyebrows wrinkle again. "After the game on Saturday, a bunch of us were hanging out here." She pauses as if she wants to add something, but shakes her head. "Anyways, Angie decided to race Alex to the river. Then this monster dump truck came barreling toward her, and she crashed her car into that tree." She tilts her head in the direction of the scarred oak as we wait to cross Memorial Drive.

"Is she all right?" My arm crosses over my chest, remembering the force of the airbag's punch. I work to steady my breathing. As we cross Memorial, I can literally smell plastic and explosives.

"She didn't die, if that's what you mean; but I hear she wants to, bless her heart. They had to amputate her leg to get her out of the car. It was...*horrible*." Ribbons of tears stream down Leanne's face, which she wipes with the sleeve of her jean jacket. "I *told* her she shouldn't drive. If I had only been more forceful, maybe this wouldn't have happened." So much for getting through the day without crying—she didn't make it to the front door.

I put my hand on Leanne's arm, as much to steady my weak knees as to reassure her. "I'm sure you did everything you could. At least she survived, right?" My stomach is a bumblebee hive pressing on my throat. I want, no *need*, to get alone to figure this thing out. Maybe I can find an empty bathroom before first block to think, to calm down, to make sense of it all. Nope. Over the front door, crackling loudspeakers direct everyone to the auditorium, ruining my chance to get away.

"I'll bet this is about Angie," Leanne whispers. Teachers, stationed along the front corridor, corral us toward the auditorium. We are good little sheep converging through the large open doors.

The cheerleaders gather exclusively in the back row, engaged in cupped conversations or crying into each other's shoulders.

The football players fill several rows to the front of the cheerleaders, doing their best to look cooler than the rest of us, aloof.

The Chortov twins, both star football players, flank either end of the second row from the back, easily identifiable by their shoulders spilling over the kids next to them, and their blue-black hair. Not that they're fat or anything, but I can picture "oversized load" signs affixed to their backs. Instead of flashing escort cars, they have flashy cheerleaders surrounding them at all times. With a few exceptions, like Clyde Baker—the only other player I know by name—the other guys on the team look puny in comparison.

Whichever Chortov brother slouches in the aisle seat closest to us looks up at Leanne as we pass, his face a blank mask. I glance away, and the tips of my fingers start to numb. Leanne sighs, but continues down to a middle row. I tag behind her; grateful that she doesn't choose to sit with the popular kids in the back.

Teachers and guidance staff line the walls of the auditorium, whispering to each other or casting the stink eye at the usual troublemakers. Unlike the juniors who've been here since ninth grade, I know only a few of the adults by name, and even fewer know me.

In a skirt designed for a woman twenty years younger, my snarky geometry teacher from last semester, Mrs. Cadella, balances on tiptoes, whispering to Coach Chortov—father of the football stars. He bends over, rubbing the back of his shaved head.

I've seen Coach Chortov in the hallway a couple of times, but his auto shop class has its own building behind the stadium. As disconnected as I am with Colonial High mythology, even *I* have overheard the rumor about his connection with the Russian Mafia before immigrating to the United States. But I seriously doubt it's true. Lately, it seems like every popular action movie has Russian bad guys.

Growing up in Brooklyn, Dad and Uncle Jim played baseball with a few *paisanos* connected to crime families. And when opposing crime families sat on bleachers rooting for their kids, you can bet baseball became thrilling, and you can also bet none of these guys ended up teaching high school auto mechanics. According to my dad, most of them ended up in jail or dead before they reached the ripe old age of thirty.

Arms crossed and eyes squinting, the obviously older-than-thirty and probably pushing the far side-of-forty Chortov leans back against the wall, scanning the rows of students in front of him. Aside from his muscular build, Coach Chortov bears no resemblance to his richly tanned, high-cheek-boned sons. With arctic eyes and an imposing stance, he looks like the sinister Russian KGB agents from the movies. This probably explains why rumors about his former life circulate around school faster than the latest hook-ups. He smiles at something Mrs. Cadella says. When she leans over a seat to talk to a student, Coach Chortov's eyes fixate on her ample bottom aimed right at him.

"I don't know what to think about Alex," Leanne confides softly to me. "I mean, I thought he really *liked* Angie. But he never came back to see if she was alright." She pauses, lowers her voice and puts a hand on my leg. "Which, the good Lord knows, she wasn't."

"Maybe he didn't know she'd crashed."

"No." Leanne shakes her head. "He had to know. His car was right in front of hers. The crash sounded like a loud—like nothing I've ever heard before… And then no one showed up down by the river." Leanne wipes away a tear. "So even if he went completely deaf for the time and drove the two miles to the beach, you think he would've come back to see why no one followed him."

"Why do you think he didn't?" I watch Coach Chortov feign fascination with the overhead lighting when Mrs. Cadella returns to the opening next to him.

Leanne exhales. "I've racked my brain trying to excuse him, but I can't think of anything that makes sense. Unless he was afraid she was dead." She digs in her backpack pocket for a Kleenex. "I hope he's riddled with guilt!" Leanne blots her eyes, and then twists the tissue around her fingers.

I glance over my shoulder to the back of the room where cheerleader Amber Claussen leans forward to whisper in Alex's ear. "Me too," I say with a sigh.

A spotlight draws the crowd's attention to the stage. Mr. Sams, our principal, climbs the side steps and marches to the podium. His real name is Samuel English, but everyone—students, staff, and faculty—call him Mr. Sams. There's instant female chatter around the room. Half the girls at Colonial High have a secret—and, sometimes, not so secret—crush on the principal, who possesses a strong resemblance to actor Liam Neeson. The noise subsides quickly when Mr. Sams grabs the microphone and scans the room. His face looks both fierce and pained, as if he wants to punch someone, but can't. The room falls silent.

"Students, teachers, and staff. Today I have some sad news to deliver about one of our most gifted students. Saturday night, Angelina Jett was involved in a serious car accident at the intersection of Monroe and Memorial."

There's a simultaneous intake of breath from the large number of students who haven't heard. Angelina Jett is the girl everyone knows is *all that and then some*. Her flawless Asian features, in combination with her sassy, fearless attitude, give her a presence that compels attention. Her notoriety is enhanced by her position front and center of the cheerleading squad at every football and basketball game. It's hard to imagine that anything as inconsequential as a hangnail would ever befall this charmed beauty—much less a severe car accident.

"I talked with Mrs. Jett, and she wanted me to share the news with you. Angelina is in serious, but stable, condition at the VCU Medical Center in Richmond, and will live. However, she had to undergo a traumatic amputation of one of her legs, and the other is badly broken. The doctors are unsure whether she will retain that leg." Several gasps fill the room, and many hands reach up to cover mouths. I bite the inside of my thumb at the memory of the steel trap around my legs. One of my legs begins to shake, so I clasp it still with my hand.

"Despite suffering this amputation, a severe concussion and broken ribs, Angelina is scheduled to be moved from ICU later today to a standard care floor. This is encouraging—it means her doctors feel she is out of imminent danger. As you can imagine, Angelina and her family are devastated. They need our prayers and support during this time."

At this point, many of the girls start sobbing.

Mr. Sams pauses. He scans the back of the room. "The question has been raised as to whether illegal substances contributed to this event." His clenched fist pounds the podium. "Beer bottles were found in the school parking lot."

He looks down at the podium, and then clutches the end until we can see the whites of his knuckles. He looks up again, focuses toward the back of the room, and belts out in a voice that thunders through auditorium: "Be warned, that if I catch even the faintest sniff of alcohol or drugs being consumed on school grounds, the culprits will be sought out and I will personally make sure that they are prosecuted to the fullest extent of the law!"

He pauses, and looks down again. All talking has ceased. The only noises in the room are muffled sobs and sniffles. The heaviness makes it hard to breathe.

"If you have any questions, please ask a counselor. I am keeping them apprised of Angelina's condition as I receive updates. Proceed to your first block."

On the way to first block, I try to process all this. Mr. Sams' admonition about alcohol and drugs on school property makes me glad I threw the hallucinogenic gum in the bookstore trash.

Wait a second. Certain drugs can make you hallucinate—everyone knows that. But can they make your hallucinations come true? Probably not, right? Doesn't that throw a king-size monkey wrench into my Orbit gum-tampering theory? Goodbye, Oprah, hello Dr. Phil, or some other *psycho* analyst.

Leanne touches my arm, startling me back into reality. "I'll see y'all at lunch, Verona," she says, as she joins a group of girls headed the other way.

"See you," I call after her. I cheer that someone in school has called me by my actual name—as much as I hate it—and wants to see me later. Then I berate myself for being so absorbed in my own thoughts that I completely forgot that Leanne was walking next to me.

ENCAMPED IN AN UNOBTRUSIVE SPOT in a corner of the cafeteria, I dig through my backpack for my lunch bag and chemistry book, which I flip open on the table in an attempt to appear busy, not merely friendless.

"These seats taken?" Leanne sets her tray on the table in front of me. She isn't alone.

"Help yourself." I nod to her, masking my surprise that she actually wants to sit with me instead of with the cool kids at the other end of the room.

Tall, caramel-skinned Nicholas Chase has corn-rowed hair tied with chrome lug nuts that ting different notes whenever he shakes his head, sounding like a wind chime. He sits next to me in Mr. Zeke's class.

When he sees my open book, he sputters, "Chemistry," like the word tastes bad. "How do you think you did on Friday's quiz?" Friday's quiz on the periodic table was our first of the year. I'm pretty sure I got a perfect score, but I don't want to brag.

So I lie. "I don't know, it was pretty hard."

"I expected worse. Everyone says Mr. Zeke's the toughest science teacher in the school—maybe even the toughest teacher at Colonial. But I think the quiz was fair." Nicky waves his fork for emphasis. "He told us what would be on it, and he kept his word."

"It was torture. I didn't even get to the last three questions." The straightening-rod-thin flaxen blond, the *impatient* straightening-rod-thin flaxen blond who sits behind me in chemistry, plops her tray on the table across from Nicky. She glares at me. "And you finished in like, five minutes." Her tone makes it clear I've flunked some major coolness test. Like chemistry is *supposed* to be hard.

Flaxen blond is part of a gaggle of girls—friends of Leanne's—whose trays soon cover the rest of the table.

A bob-haired brunette, with cheeks so big and round her eyes disappear when she smiles, speaks first: "Can you believe that about Angie?" She looks directly at Leanne—probably waiting to be filled in on all that was omitted from the morning assembly. I recognize her from third-block art class. She pokes fun at our teacher, Mr. Keats, but he never seems to mind.

"I know. It's crazy." Leanne looks down, refusing to give up any juicy details.

Then she remembers her southern manners, and turns to me. "Verona Lamberti, meet Caitlin Prescott, Susan Wythe, and Paris Johnson."

Caitlin is the flaxen blond with the attitude. I've heard Nicky call her *Pringles* in chemistry, after the potato chip—he says she's thin, blond, and salty. Susie is the bob-haired brunette from art. With round eyes, deep cocoa skin, and hair done up in a confusing array of braids circling her head, Paris reminds me of Nefertiti, the Egyptian queen.

Leanne waves her hand at Nicky. "Of course, y'all already know Nicky Chase."

Caitlin and Susie taunt in unison, "Everyone knows *Chaser*."

Caitlin leans over, puts the back of her hand to the outside of her mouth. "He chases anything in a skirt!" she says, in a stage whisper.

Paris turns away and acts blasé, but I get the sense that she's not crazy about Nicky's nickname.

"Thank you, adoring fans." Nicky performs a bow over his food, causing his hair to rattle and the lug nuts to hit the back of his head. I wonder if it hurts. He winks at me conspiratorially, but says loudly enough for the others to hear, "They all want my hot body and are jealous 'cause I'm saving it for you."

While I quickly squeeze my nose to keep from snorting out my soda, the other girls erupt in screams, scrambling to throw straws, spoons, and French fries at him.

"Ladies, please, some control here!" He raises his hands like he's holding them back. Again, he turns to me: "Verona, tell us about your *fine* self." Naturally, I'm in mid-chew of my PB and J sandwich—the peanut butter sticking to the roof of my mouth. I reach for my Diet Coke.

"Like, where are you from? Did you move to Jamestown this summer?" Susie buys me time as I figure out where to start.

I swallow, and swipe my teeth with my tongue to remove peanut butter residue. "My mother and I moved down from New York last semester." Hopefully that will satisfy the curious.

"New York *City*?" Caitlin lifts her eyebrows.

"The Upper East Side. My mom got a job at William and Mary—so here I am." I shrug like it's no big deal to be relocated from the world's coolest city to this place.

"I love New York." Paris sings it like the old New York jingle, snaps her fingers, and sways in her seat.

"When have you ever been to New York?" Caitlin rolls her eyes. I mentally add *crispy* to Nicky's Pringles analogy.

"I haven't been yet, but I've read all about it, and I may get to go this summer." Paris leans toward me. "Were you there for 9/11?"

"Not Benghazi. She means the original 9/11," Caitlin adds.

"Pringles, that was obvious to anyone with half a brain." Nicky rolls his eyes.

I nod, swallow again, and think, *I guess they have heard of 9/11 here.* All eyes are on me expectantly. "Yes. I was in the third grade. They sent us to the gym while they tried to figure out what to do with us. My teacher was in a panic 'cause her husband worked a few blocks from the World Trade Center. Someone told us about the planes hitting, but I didn't really understand until I got home and saw it on TV."

Everyone stares at me in silence, expecting more, so I continue, "We'd eaten at *Windows on the World* a few times, so I was sad when my parents explained that we couldn't go back there. I was too young to get why it was such a big deal."

I don't tell them about my Aunt Gina and how she wears black every day to mourn the man she had worn white for two years before. Or how a body falling from the North Tower crushed him.

I don't tell them how Aunt Gina married her brother's best friend and her brother is my dad.

I don't tell them how, because they didn't have children yet, Uncle Jimmy treated me like his daughter, always buying me popcorn and candy at the games when my dad was down on the field or in the locker-room interviewing players.

I don't tell them how, one week after his father's funeral, Kyle Price came back to school with a stuttering problem.

I don't tell them about all the kids that never *came* back to school because their parents moved them to New Jersey or Westchester or across the country.

And while I think about all the things I'm not telling them, Susie explains that *Windows on the World* was the restaurant that had been at the top of the North Tower of the World Trade Center.

"The bombing at the Boston Marathon reminded me of 9/11. That we're vulnerable, even when we think we're not," Paris said.

"Angie's accident reminds me of that. It's closer to home, and it's much more common to be killed in a car accident than by a terrorist." Leanne touches my arm. "Did you know anyone who was killed that day?"

I gulp down a memory of my parents' hugging and crying late into that night and trying their best to hide all this from me. "My dad played baseball with a firefighter who was killed when someone landed on him." That's all I tell them. I don't want to be known all over Jamestown as the girl whose uncle died on 9/11.

"Oh, my God! That's so gross." Caitlin wrinkles her nose at her ketchup-smeared French fry, but then pops it into her mouth. *Yeah*, I think, *especially for his family.* But I don't say it. I don't say anything, just look down and hope someone else will take over the conversation.

"How do you like Jamestown? I bet what happened with Angie happens all the time in New York." Paris smiles nervously at me. "Driving in New York is crazy!"

"No, not really. I mean, it could happen anywhere."

"Yeah, but bad stuff like that usually happens to normal kids like us, not the popular ones, like Angie Jett." Caitlin nods toward the end of the lunchroom where the football players and cheerleaders camp every day.

"Who you callin' *normal*, child?" Nicky crosses his arms in mock annoyance at the perceived slight.

"Bless your heart, Nicky. You're nothing like normal." Leanne pokes him with her fork. Everyone laughs, even Nicky.

"Speaking of not normal… Who do you think Alex will take to homecoming now? I doubt Angie will be able to go." Caitlin's eyes dart around the cafeteria.

We all try to inconspicuously scan the football table. Alex is straddling the back of his seat, bent close to the same cheerleader from the assembly.

"Three guesses." Susie frowns and rolls her eyes.

"Amber Claussen," Caitlin, Nicky, and Paris say at once, scowling.

"That boy didn't waste no time." Paris crosses her arms.

"Claussen is a popularity bloodsucker." Caitlin's fingers curl in a clawing motion. She attaches her claws to Nicky, but looks at me. "Like a leech, she sucks the coolness out of whoever will put up with her. Alex is her latest target, now that Angie's removed from the competition."

Leanne scoots her chair back and gets up to leave. She motions for me to come with her. As we walk past the popular kids, a few of the football players look up. "Hey Leanne," one of them says to get her attention. Some of the cheerleaders wave to her. I wonder why she's hanging out with me—the new kid. She grabs my arm and leads me over to their table.

"Hey, y'all. I want to introduce you to Verona Lamberti. She's from New York. Her mother works at the college." Leanne announces my awful name to the whole section. Now I'm cringing and I can feel my cheeks turning red. Some of the players look up, smile, and nod, but quickly return to their discussions.

Alex Chortov never turns my way. He continues his conversation with Amber Claussen, who swings her platinum head around Alex's torso and gives me a cursory once-over. Her smile raises just one side of her glossy pink mouth. Seemingly content that I will never pose a threat to her new position as queen bee, she bends closer to Alex.

A boy with wavy umber hair and blue-lagoon eyes flashes me a wide grin. "Welcome to Colonial, Verona. I'm Ross."

I smile back. "Hi." I tug against Leanne's arm that we should leave.

When we reach the hallway Leanne turns to me. "What are you so afraid of?"

"Making a complete fool of myself," I answer with unexpected—by me, at least— openness.

"What? They don't do foolish things? Drink beer in the parking lot. Drive cars into trees. That's why I don't like to talk bad about anyone; we're all humans who sometimes do foolish things." Leanne looks up at me. "What Caitlin said about Amber may be sorta true, but it's not nice to say."

"Yeah, you're right." I smile. *A girl who doesn't gossip?* Maybe I can make friends in this place after all.

"Leanne, who's the boy who smiled at me back there?"

"Cute, isn't he? That's Ross Georgeson. He's the superintendent's son. He also kicks for the football team. Ross doesn't usually sit with those guys, but I think his best friend isn't in school today." I raise my eyebrows and tilt my head at Leanne.

"No." She chuckles, reading my mind. "His friend isn't a girl. I don't think he dates anyone right now. Ross usually keeps a low profile. Maybe he likes you."

I ENTER CHEMISTRY EARLY, hoping to talk to the teacher. Mr. Curtis Ezekiel—Mr. Zeke to the students, but never to his face—isn't in yet.

The manila envelope lies on his desk exactly where he'd put it Friday after I gave it to him. I requested a reference for my application to the National Honors Society. Most of the work was done in New York, but my guidance counselor suggested I get a few references from Colonial as well.

I think the whole Honors Society thing is dumb—I don't see how it'll help. My mom pressured me by saying that anything that might help me get a scholarship for college is worth the effort. Since I have my heart set on going to NYU and know it will be expensive to rent an apartment in Greenwich Village, I went along with it. Maybe if Mr. Zeke comes in and sees me sitting here, it will prompt him to fill out the form.

Hanging my backpack on the chair, I gaze absentmindedly toward the bookshelf in the back corner. I gasp and hold my breath. It must've been there the whole time. Only now, the eagle sculpture, with its wide wingspan and open mouth, freaks me out. Could this be the cause of the PCQ vision? Could my subconscious register what my conscious mind never notices? I'm hopeful for a second, until I realize that it still wouldn't explain Angie's car wreck.

Taking my seat, I remove my glasses and rub my eyes. Peering out the window to the football stadium, I try to recreate each phase of Friday's vision: the rush of air against my face and the intense grass smell, the swerve over Memorial Drive, and my vertical dive into Angie Jett's body. I grab my right knee, remembering the numbness following the accident. It's like I was there. And yet, it didn't happen until several hours later.

The buzz of the second bell brings me back to the present. I feel around for my glasses. Out of the corner of my eye I catch a blurry Nicky gesticulating crazily. "Where's my seeing eye dog?" His voice is high and all sing-songy, the voice boys always use to sound like girls. The kids around us laugh, but I'm not amused.

"Give them back." I karate chop his arm slightly. Nicky feigns a war wound from the impact. But at least he hands me my glasses.

Mr. Zeke, passing out Friday's quizzes, pauses beside our desks. "Nick, Verona, I want to talk to you after class."

I glare at Nicky. He shrugs. When my quiz comes back with a perfect score, I'm tempted to let him see it just to gloat. Thinking better of it, I stuff it into my notebook.

Nicky's gyrating in his seat with his quiz paper grasped between two hands flashing his score for all to see—a whopping eighty-two. Behind me, Caitlin is swearing under her breath.

Still fuming about getting called out in class, I ignore Nicky. I hope this won't cause Mr. Zeke to refuse my request for a recommendation. That would be humiliating, as he's the first teacher at Colonial to whom I've said more than two sentences, and the one I respect the most. He's also the only one who asked if I was adjusting well to my new school. I sense that under his strict all-business exterior, he really cares about us. Maybe that's why he was the one who showed up in Friday's vision. I study him up at the whiteboard as he goes over the test questions most kids got wrong.

Mr. Zeke always wears a neatly pressed suit and tie. In my mind, his appearance commands respect; the majority of teachers at Colonial, and even my teachers in New York, have taken what used to be *casual Friday* to mean TGIF every day. I like to dress differently each day, depending on how I feel—ripped jeans, a tee, and high tops, or a maxi skirt and bracelets jingling on my arm, different colored polish on each finger and toenail. The kids at my old school called me *hippie chick* because I love Woodstock and own about fourteen T-shirts from that era and oodles of peace sign jewelry. Today it's paint-stained blue jeans and a seriously wrinkled peasant smock that I wore last week and discovered sticking out from under my bed. It's just my luck that today, the day I look like a homeless hippie, is the day I finally meet people.

I spend most of the class dreading the tongue-lashing I'm destined to receive at the end of class. As a rule, I rejoice at the sound of the last bell of the day, but today I slump lower in my chair, stare straight ahead, and wait for the rest of the kids to clear out.

Nicky jumps out of his seat. "Don't worry, sugar; Zeke's not a bad guy."

"Don't call me sugar," I say, between gritted teeth.

"Uh-oh, the dame's got a temper."

Ben Chortov maneuvers in front of us, waiting for Mr. Zeke. When there are only three of us left, Mr. Zeke turns around, setting the whiteboard eraser back on its ledge. He peers around Ben's mountainous shoulders, and asks Nicky and me to please wait outside.

Nicky closes the door. "What do you think he's going to do?"

"Chew us out, obviously." I cross my arms. If this is what Southern friends are like, I can do without them.

"Look, Verona, I'm sorry. Will you forgive me?" His lips pout and his face tilts to the side, reminding me of Max. *Pathetic.*

I roll my eyes. "I guess so."

"Thanks." A wide smile covers his caramel face. The door swings open, and Ben Chortov bumps into Nicky.

"Sorry," Ben murmurs. Then he looks directly at me. "Can I talk to you…after?"

Mr. Zeke holds the door for us.

"Okay," I murmur, as I enter the classroom. Why would Ben Chortov—whom I've never met—want to talk to me?

Mr. Zeke closes the door, crosses the room, and sits on the edge of his desk. "You're probably wondering why I asked you to stay after."

"If it's about the glasses and the clowning, it's my bad, and I'm sorry." Nicky looks at Mr. Zeke, then the ground.

Mr. Zeke snorts, dismissing Nicky's admission with a wave of his hand. "I think Verona is more upset by your tomfoolery than I am." He takes a deep breath, puts his hands on his thighs and leans forward. "I know you both were at the assembly this morning and heard what happened to Angelina Jett."

We nod, wondering what this has to do with chemistry.

"This Saturday, I would like it very much if you would come with me to visit her." Mr. Zeke pauses, looking back and forth at our confused faces.

My mouth drops open. Okay, back up. Refuse to write the stupid recommendation. Give me the tongue-lashing. A week's detention. Anything but...

"At the hospital? But——" Nicky looks at me and back at Mr. Zeke, and then voices my own thoughts exactly. "Wouldn't she rather see her own friends?"

"Do you think her old friends really care? From what I hear, her so-called boyfriend hung out at the river the whole time she was being extracted from the car." Mr. Zeke crosses his arms.

First I picture Amber whispering in Alex's ear at the assembly, then chumming up to him at lunch. "He's right," I say to Nicky. "But what makes you think she'll want to see *us*, Mr. Ezekiel?"

"I've been talking with her mother. Angie's in a bad way, as you can imagine. The only one calling to talk to her is Leanne Morris. I noticed you sitting with Leanne at lunch, and thought perhaps you two could be the friends she needs right now to get back on her ... to get well." He corrects himself quickly, but Nicky can't resist a quick smile at the faux pas. I elbow him.

"I'll go." *Did I say that?* I've never said one word to this girl before, and now I am volunteering to see her right after she's lost her leg, her boyfriend, her entire world. Then again, that eagle vision makes me feel pulled to her like there's some wispy connection in our completely opposite lives. Maybe feeling stuck inside someone's head at the worst moment of her life will do that.

Nicky looks at me sideways and creases his forehead, but he says, "I'll come too."

"Okay, we'll meet in the student parking lot at 12:30. I drive a silver Mercedes." Mr. Zeke dismisses us with a somber nod.

We both exhale as we cross the threshold. When he notices Ben leaning against some lockers, Nicky takes off in the other direction.

I hesitate, wondering which way I should go, but Ben waves for me to join him. I step in his direction. "My name is Ben Chortov. You're Verona," he half-asks, half-tells me as he saunters over. All cool. All confident. Funny, it's not so cringe-worthy to hear my name spoken by a hot guy.

"Verona Lamberti." Everyone knows the Chortov brothers by their full names; I figure he should know mine.

"How'd you do on the chemistry quiz, Verona *Lamberti*?" The corner of his mouth goes up like he's teasing me, sort of chuckling.

"Okay, I guess." I push up my glasses.

"Only okay? I heard you aced it." He stops. I feel the heat of his eyes on me. Glancing up at his face, my eyes ask how he knows my grade. All the while my mind screams at me, "He's gorgeous." I look down quickly.

"Listen, Verona *Lamberti*, I did not ace it." He crashes against the lockers, sending aluminum echoes down the corridor and causing me to jump. "In fact, I flunked it. When I asked Mr. Zeke for help, he said I should ask you to tutor me. He said it would help you earn leadership points or something. If I don't bring up my grade on the unit test, I'll get suspended from the team."

"Isn't your dad the coach?" I begin feeling more and more uncomfortable as I drink in his musky aroma, how good his body looks in blue jeans and a black leather jacket.

"Yeah, but there are rules he's got to follow. Trust me, Coach is the last person who'd ever show favoritism. Having him as our coach actually works against us most of the time." He smiles at me. "I'd really appreciate it. I need to pass this class." His cocoa eyes have tiny marshmallow flecks in them, tempting me under the cold florescent lights.

"I don't know. I work after school most days." This can't be happening to me! A guy this hot is asking me to spend time alone with him. "Say yes, say yes, say yes!" a voice inside me cheers. Not surprisingly, the voice sounds an awful lot like Luka.

"I have practice after school every day. We could meet in the evenings a couple of days a week. You pick the place—I'll meet you anywhere."

"I don't know," I say again. My heart pounds a percussive rhythm I'm sure he can hear. But then his pleading eyes tear up any resolve I'm hanging on to. "Okay." I exhale.

So, within the span of five minutes I've made not one—but two—commitments packed with infinite embarrassment potential.

I START THE ROVER. Shifting into drive, I notice an ivory envelope, like a wedding invitation, under the driver-side wiper. I look around student parking while shifting back to park. Most of the kids have left. A lone turkey vulture peers at me from the white horse fence along Memorial. I step out of the car to retrieve the envelope, wondering who might've left it.

I pull out the note card. Three withered rose petals flutter down to the ground. A poem typed in a chilling red font sucks the breath out of me: *Roses are red. Violets are blue. You'd better watch out. I can see you.*

My stomach churns. I've met so many people in just this one day—obnoxious Nicky Chase, Caitlin Prescott—aka Pringles, Susie Wythe from art class, Paris Johnson with Egyptian goddess hair, Ben Chortov—the hottie football player with cocoa eyes, Ross Georgeson—adorable turquoise eyes and friendly smile. Why would any of them want to scare me?

AFTER SCHOOL AND SOMETIMES ON SATURDAYS, I work at The Aquila Art Emporium, Jamestown's one and only artist's supply store. This job keeps me in gas money, and I can buy art supplies at cost—not that I've picked up my paintbrushes since my parents' split last April.

Through text messages sent between waiting on customers, I relay the day's events to Luka, who reacts with the appropriate pyrotechnic expletives. When I recount how Ross smiled at me, Luka suggests I dress grunge every day. She squeals (a long "EEEEEEEE!!!" in our texting world) when I tell her about Ben. I squeal back, and in my excitement, I inadvertently let out a real squeal when I push SEND.

My boss, Mr. Stanworth, who seriously has a turtle's neck with a penguin body, sticks his head out of his shell—oops! I mean his back office. "Miss Lamberti, are you alright?" For some reason, Mr. Stanworth always calls me Miss Lamberti. He says it real slow and nasally, enunciating each syllable—Miss Lam-bert-ti. I never say anything, since it's better than my first name.

"There was this really gross bug, but it ran under the counter," I lie, shoving my cell into my jeans. Mr. Stanworth mutters something about exterminators.

After putting the order away, helping a few customers, and taking some phone calls, I read some of *The Way of the Eagle* book. It talks about the perspective eagles have when they're soaring. I can't help but connect it to the PCQ vision.

II

Eagle Preparation

Tuesday, September 15th
684 Days to Home Free

MOST EVERYONE AT COLONIAL buys the cafeteria lunch, but I've seen the cuisine and I'm not impressed. At the jock table, Alex Chortov scarfs down a mega-sized burger—at least I assume it's Alex and not Ben. I have never seen twins look so much alike.

I figure it must be Alex because Amber Claussen sits next to him, her left hand resting on his leg, while her right hand plays with her fries. He wears a diamond stud in his left ear. I can't remember if Ben wears an earring, but I can find out in chemistry later.

Leanne and Nicky jostle for a seat near me, but before all the girls join our table, Ross Georgeson and a redheaded boy sit at the far end, across from each other. I recognize the redhead from last semester's English. He never said two words to anyone. I can relate.

Ross mouths, "Hello," his baby blues all lit up.

"Hi." I will my face not to redden and start rooting in my lunch bag like I have misplaced something really important, like a gallon of ice cream.

"Verona, this is my friend, Craig Hamilton—a.k.a.—the *Red Fox*."

I look up just in time to see Ross throw a French fry across the table. It splatters into the Red Fox's soup.

Craig turns his freckled face to me and forces a quick "Hi," with no smile behind it.

"Hi." I sigh. I've forgotten my napkin, and I am a triple napkin user. Leanne notices my dilemma and hands me an extra from her tray.

"Y'all going to the game Friday?" Nicky mimics Leanne's southern drawl.

"Wouldn't miss it." Leanne flutters her fingers in front of her like a snake charmer.

Nicky nods at me.

"I don't think so," I say, as quietly as possible, hoping Ross won't hear and be offended. When everyone turns to me with questioning expressions, I feel obliged to explain: "My girlfriend is coming from New York and I'm not sure when her train gets in." This is technically true, because while I knew what time Luka is scheduled to arrive, Amtrak is notoriously late.

Nicky leans his elbow on the table. "Hey, Kicka, who we playin' Friday night?"

Ross—obviously Nicky's "Kicka" for his position as Colonial's kicker—glances over. "Monticello."

"Aw, easy win. The Mice have been crushed by everyone this year." Nicky smacks his hand on the table. The table vibrates and doesn't stop.

Ross tilts his head, his blue eyes smiling toward our end of the table. "Hope so."

The table starts shaking.

"When are we playin' Harrison?" Nicky holds a French fry in the air like a pointer. "Now *that's* gonna be a game!" He throws the French fry at Craig. "Hamilton, stop kickin' the table! You're spillin' my Red Bull." The quaking ceases.

Ignoring the preceding exchange, Ross grins. "Two weeks from Saturday. I sure hope we stomp on them this year."

"I don't know, Kicka." Nicky shakes his head. "They've got that Megatron linebacker—what's his name? I'd hate to be Chortov and have that guy tackling me."

"Ty Blanchard's big alright, but he's only come up against the small weights. Genghis is the toughest quarterback in the league."

I lean in to Leanne. "Who's Harrison?" I whisper softly.

"Who's *Harrison*?" Nicky's voice booms.

Not softly enough. I slump down in my chair, feeing all eyes within a fifty-foot radius bearing into me, the stupid new girl.

Leanne rolls her eyes at Nicky, and throwing back an intractable strand of ginger hair from her face, says, "Harrison High is our biggest rival. Somehow they managed to beat us last year. So this year, the pressure's on."

"They only won last year because Cal was sick and Kub was suspended. We were down two of our best players." I admire how Ross defends his team. "Still, Harrison is doing well this year. It could be close."

"Kub?" I whisper to Leanne, more softly than before.

"Kublai Khan—you know, Ben Chortov." Leanne touches my arm like she understands that I'm not expected to know everything. I knew Alex was called Genghis, but I've never heard Ben referred to as Genghis's grandson—the one that founded the Yuan dynasty in China.

I think about what I know of Kublai Khan. One of my favorite poems is about Kublai Khan, and I love the classic rock song, "Xanadu," by the band Rush that references the poem. But naturally, I don't say anything. It would be like announcing that I'm a nerd. What's the chance of even one of these kids knowing either the poem *or* any song by Rush? Kids my age like Lady Gaga and Usher, and do most of their reading on Facebook and Twitter.

Susie squats down at the end of the table and addresses all of us: "Hey, did you hear about the party at my house this weekend?

Tons of Tex-Mex. Nucleus will be *jamming.*" She looks straight at me. "You'll love my brother's band." She hits the table. "My house. Seven o'clock. Saturday night. Got it?" Then she launches on to the next table.

Leanne nudges me. "You don't want to miss one of Susie's parties. They're awesome." I don't tell her that Luka is all the entertainment I need, and Leanne doesn't ask if I plan to go. Still, it is flattering to be invited. While I don't feel *in* exactly, I'm beginning to feel less like an outsider, like maybe I've etched out a niche where I can wait out the next six hundred and eighty-four days. But then I remember yesterday's lovely note on my windshield, and now I think, *or maybe not.*

ART HAS ALWAYS AND FOREVER been my favorite class, but when my third-block teacher tells us that for our next project we are going to graffiti our desks, he promotes it to an even higher level of cool.

Mr. Keats looks like a grown-up Frodo, with curly hair and big feet. A cool Frodo. He lets us listen to our iPods while we work on our projects, and he also allows us to eat and drink in class—the ultimate taboo of all my other teachers.

I show him the design I worked on over the weekend. He gives me the go-ahead to start painting one mean-looking eagle, with New York skyscrapers in the background, and Chinese characters for *The Way of an Eagle* in the foreground. I flip open the top of my Diet Coke can—gotta love that sound—fetch my ruler and pencil, and begin outlining the eagle, buildings, and sky.

Outside the classroom, the real sky turns black. One of these crazy-violent Southern storms has rolled in. Mr. Keats takes this opportunity to hang by the window with the kids, playing a game where they rate the thunderclap: "1" for *lame as a lightning bug* and a "10-strike" for *hide under your desk.* They call it, *Bowling for Thunder.*

From where I'm hunched over my desk, I hear kids yell, "a 9—no 10!" that's followed by a crash of thunder that rattles the building. I taste burnt charcoal for the third time. Since I've taken a sabbatical from chewing Orbit—all gum, actually—I now know for a fact that this can't be drug-induced. For a nanosecond I wonder if I've been hit by lightning. Before I can ponder this, I *poof* out of my body.

    I look around to see if Mr. Keats will morph into an eagle and join me like Mr. Zeke did in the PCQ vision, but he and the rest of the class stay huddled by the rain-striped window; the very window my eagle body sails through.

    Outside, my wings propel me into the storm. I'm taken for a wild ride above the woods at the south end of Memorial Drive, out over the churning James River. I never actually feel wet, and while the sheets of rain cause poor visibility, I still can see much better than I can with my glasses. All my senses are on high alert. I can smell the rain. See the wind. Hear the lightening crackle before the boom. Skimming the brackish, cymbal-clashing waves, I taste the vastness, the length, and the depth of the river.

    Fierce gusts of wind hurl me back across the northern shoreline. I twirl down from the sky into the arms of a large tree, and tumble through the leaves until my talons lock around a branch. My wings struggle to set me upright. The entire tree whips back and forth like it's purposely trying to throw me, but my talons cling tight. In a single lightning flash everything stills, while the rain rolls up into a gray cloud scroll.

    I look up from my talons to find that I'm perched in the scarred oak across from Colonial High—the same tree that bit off Angie Jett's leg last weekend. There's no sound. No vehicles. No animals. No other birds in the tree with me. And, like in the last vision, it's night, or almost night, with only a hint of pale blue lining the western sky.

    The intersection is littered with shards of glass that reflect the light from the streetlamp on the opposite corner. Each iridescent shard looks alive somehow—each has a tiny eye inside. And they can see. Worse, they can see *me*. Rather they see *into* me. And not just the eagle me.

A breeze carrying the smell of honeysuckle and rain swishes past me, and forms a powerful mini-tornado in the intersection below. I stare, mesmerized, as two wings, opaline and miniscule, sprout from each shard and lift it from the ground, higher and higher inside the funnel, until it all meshes together into a lighted ball, or an orb, or a really bright Chinese lantern, or a small sun. That's it; it becomes a star.

The star is white, brighter than a lightning flash—even a *10 strike*. I am feeling frightened, but intrigued. I pull back, attempting to jump to a safer inside branch, but my stubborn talons won't loosen their grip.

"Don't be afraid," a female voice from inside the star reassures me. *Too late*, I think. In my world, tiny pieces of glass do not fuse together to create a star, and talk like some Tinker Bell wannabe. Then again, this isn't my world anymore.

"Come with me. You must see this. I'm sorry if it disturbs you." The last part is said—telepathically—in a voice resonating with such compassion that the sport in me decides to toughen up and face whatever this star with a gazillion eyes says I must see.

She ascends over the trees lining Memorial Drive. The streetlights appear dimmer than normal, but maybe that's in comparison to the, uh, *Star Lady*, for lack of a better word.

Star Lady leads me over the faculty parking lot and stadium, much like the time I followed Mr. Zeke's eagle; but instead of arcing higher around a circumference, she descends over a corner of the auto shop's tin roof. On the roof's edge, I attach my talons to a rusted gutter.

At this time of night the parking lot would normally be very dark in the shadow made by the stadium, with the only streetlight around the other side of the auto shop; but with Star Lady's glow, it's lit up brighter than day. Below us, a sedan idles, with a gray rubber tube looping from underneath into the back window. A hulking figure, dressed all in black with a hood covering his head, faces the driver's window, his back to us.

From behind, it looks like he's gesturing to someone in the driver seat with his right hand, which I can't see behind his thick torso. And then, like the Times Square images that change in a blink of an eye, the black hooded guy transforms into a leathery giant with bloody, elephant-like feet. He's wearing a gold crown with two horns on the sides, and a gold robe. He has a shawl around his shoulders, like something an old-school king or emperor would wear. And then, the image changes back into the man-sized, but still ominous-looking, hooded guy.

I fly closer, using a slight wing motion, akin to treading water, and hover directly over the hooded figure. A blotchy face peers out from the driver's window.

Ross Georgeson's blue eyes are red-rimmed and tearing. He mouth appears to be pleading with the person on the other side of the window, who keeps switching back and forth from the giant leathery emperor to the black-hooded guy. The hooded-guy points to an object toward the edge of the door. Maybe he's telling Ross to come out. No, the man would have to move back a step for the door to be able to open. Ross's face falls as the lock button on the door shrinks down.

The closed doors, the idling car, the tube running exhaust through the back window. The realization of what I'm witnessing hits me. The man in the black hood is trying to kill Ross and make it look like a suicide. I swoop at the man's head.

"Wait!" Star Lady warns—too late.

I dig my talons into the thick material covering the back of the killer's head and scrape the flesh covering the scalp. The figure swings around, swiping at me with a hard metal object—a pistol. At the same time he morphs back into the monster. The face is hideous. The fleshy green-gray surface festers with oozing pustules and raging eyes, bleary and blood-soaked.

I jump back, just missing being struck by his beefy hand. It feels like I've seen death personified. And it's ten times worse than I could ever have imagined.

"He is Mammon." Star Lady urges me away. We fly over a discarded backpack. "One of the seven princes of hell. The greedy one."

Somehow I know this creature isn't just motivated by greed. It *is* greed. The instant its angry eyes meet mine, I know that it wants *me* dead, too. My wings beat faster and my breathing accelerates.

"Verona! Watch out!"

And pop. I'm back in art class, clutching the edge of my desk, shivering, and out of breath, like I've just run a mile in P.E.

Susie Wythe taps my arm and says, "You knocked your soda on the floor." She scoops up the Diet Coke before it empties completely.

Amy Sedgwick, a sprite-like sophomore wearing braces and a neon-pink sweatshirt, races over with the roll of paper towels from the sink. I glance around to see if Mr. Keats has noticed either transgression—my flight out the window or the spilled soda, but he's busy in a far corner, conversing with a group of girls who've merged their desks together to paint a graffiti mural. Outside, blue sky pokes holes in the clouds. *How long was I out this time?*

"Are you okay?" Susie puts her hand on my arm. I look at her, put my hand up, and bend down by Amy, who's already begun to wipe up my mess.

"I can get that." I peel some paper towels off the roll.

"I don't mind. I've got a little brother. He spills stuff all the time." Amy's face lights up.

"Thanks. I do, too . . . have a little brother . . . and spill stuff all the time." My brother, Danny, has inherited my dad's coordination, and hasn't spilled anything since he was a baby.

Susie touches my arm again, and looks into my eyes. "You zoned out."

I look at the floor. "It's okay. Sometimes I get like that when I'm working on stuff." Or after I finish a particularly easy chemistry quiz. Or—*what is happening to me?*

I am not, in fact, sure that everything's okay. And yet I'm certainly not prepared to admit that to anyone here. What kind of person zones out so far in third block that they witness a kid they just ate lunch with being murdered by some kind of demon? A *specific* demon! Well, maybe the kids who skip lunch to get high in the woods behind the auto shop—but I seriously doubt they're posing in eagle bodies at the time.

ON THE WAY TO CHEMISTRY, I pop two peppermint Altoids in my mouth, not because I still taste charcoal, but because I read somewhere that mint is soothing. I need soothing. Soothing is good. I try to calm the conflicting voices hounding me. Then I remember my mother telling me that I have a choice in how I feel: *To worry, or not to worry?*

I decide to postpone worrying about the eagle vision thing now. It's just too huge to figure out by myself, and my one piece of intel is not particularly helpful: The visions are not caused by drug-laced chewing gum. So what *is* causing them? *Am I schizophrenic?* Note to self: Google schizophrenia when you get home.

Presently, I have something more important to worry about. Well, if not something more important, at least more imminent. Ben Chortov. Ben Chortov is the most popular, most stunning guy who's ever talked to me *in my life*. Still, I need to get a grip. Obviously, he only wants to pick my nerdy brain so he can keep playing football.

I hide my surprise that Ben has switched seats with Caitlin. His long legs trail out on either side of my desk like a dare. He bends one so I can get through. I catch him smiling out of my peripheral vision as I rummage through my backpack for my notebook and pen. A glance at his ear confirms my earlier hypothesis—no sparkly earring. He is going over the homework from last night and, from upside down, I already spot a wrong answer.

"I'm not getting this," he whispers when I sit down. I nod and turn right in my seat to look back at him. But as luck would have it, Mr. Zeke begins teaching, so I face forward. I shake my hair out of its ponytail in case the tag on my shirt is sticking out.

When Mr. Zeke turns to write an example on the board, a piece of paper lands on my desk. I jump, which incites a chortle from Ben. Second note to self: work on that obnoxious startle reflex.

As inconspicuously as possible, I unfold the note:

Verona,
Are we still on for today? Can we meet at 6:00? Even though you're indecisive, you pick the place. Ben

Indecisive? Big word for a jock. What makes him think I'm indecisive? Then my mind takes me back to our little talk in the hallway, the two times I blurted out, "I don't know," when he asked if I'd tutor him. I'm not always indecisive, am I?

As quietly as I can, I tear out a fresh scrap of paper from my notebook. I keep his note to show Luka next weekend. It's my first note from a boy. Well, actually my second. The first note came from Tony Rubowski, a crooked-nosed, bow-legged kid who's had an annoying crush on me since fifth grade.

By middle school, Tony Rubowski stalked me like a Coney Island hawker. In the cafeteria, in the hallway, and even once in Central Park, I'd get this feeling ants were crawling up my neck and when I'd look around, there he was—ogling me.

Luka told me I should have been flattered, but at the time, all I felt was uncomfortable, disgusted, repulsed. In eighth grade, when he handed me a note in the hallway before homeroom, I read it, shredded it, then walked away so I could pretend not to notice his body deflate like the Pink Panther balloon stabbed by police at the Macy's Thanksgiving Day Parade.

After that, Luka and I always hummed the Pink Panther theme music to each other when he was around: *Da, dun, da, dun…da, dun…da, dun, da, dun, da, dun, da, dun, da, dahh…da, da, da, dun.* We thought we were so cool—but looking back now, I feel bad for what we, by *we* I really mean *me*, or maybe it's *I*, did. Yes, it's definitely, *I did.* I shouldn't have made fun of his crush, even if he didn't have a clue what we were making fun of.

But Ben is no Pink Panther. I find my hand is shaking a little when I write:

> *Ben,*
> *Indecisive? Where did you get that? As for where to meet—oh, I don't know.*
> *Just kidding. My house. 6:00. Got it? Verona*

When Mr. Zeke turns back to the board, I pass the note back with my left hand. Naturally, with my keen coordination, it misses Ben's desk entirely, and falls to the floor.

After a few seconds, I hear a quick exhale, like a short laugh. Good, he gets my quirky sense of humor.

I wait to see if another note will come, but instead I hear his deep voice call out from behind me, "Mr. Ezekiel, could you explain the last question on the homework?"

"Would anyone else like me to explain the solution to the question on Avogadro's constant?" Several hands go up. As soon as Mr. Zeke returns to the board, a note sails past my face. I slap it down with my hand before it slides off my desk.

> *V, Your house is cool. Where is it? B*

Duh. The address would help. I write my address as clearly as possible with directions from school, but can't pass it back because Mr. Zeke is done explaining Avogadro on the board, and is now perched on top of his desk teaching the next lesson.

Mr. Zeke's class is the only one where we have to deposit our phones on a table up front before class, and then retrieve them on the way out. He says this will do two things: cut down on distractions, and improve grades. I have to admit he's probably right—based on the amount of text messaging that goes on behind the desks in other classes.

The first day of class he did something no teacher has ever done before; he had us write our cell numbers on an index card along with what we're most afraid of. I wrote that I'm most afraid of embarrassing myself. I'm glad I was honest, because now Mr. Zeke goes out of his way not to call on me. I wonder what Ben has written on his card. It doesn't seem like someone his size would be afraid of much.

With my new focus on the guy sitting behind me, class drags on. I try concentrating on what Mr. Zeke's saying, but my mind keeps wandering back to Ben.

When the bell rings, I hand Ben the note with my address.

He reads it right in front of me. "You live in Jefferson Village? It must be cool to be near everything."

My mom rents a townhouse in Jefferson Village, a brick-filled, nouveau-urban neighborhood that boasts the best shopping in Jamestown, the Jefferson Village Cinema *(JV* to locals) and several ethnic restaurants. She says it would be the least traumatic environment for me, since I love the city so much. Contrary to my mother's hopes, this purposefully planned community strikes me as a fabrication—like a Hollywood movie set. It makes me miss New York more because it's trying so hard. Still, it is convenient to walk three minutes to a coffee shop, the art supply store where I work, or the one pitiful art gallery.

But if Ben thinks Jefferson Village is cool, score one for Mom.

"Yeah. I like it." Talk about fabrication. At least I manage to smile when I lie.

I TRY ON PRACTICALLY EVERY ARTICLE of clothing in my closet, settling on a clean pair of jeans and a fuzzy guacamole-colored sweater that my mom says accentuates my eyes. I toggle between the purple-framed glasses and the newly fixed tortoiseshells, finally deciding that the purple contrasts well with the sweater. I brush my teeth again, even though I was too nervous to eat one of the frozen dinners I usually microwave when my mom works late.

The evening chill makes me want to turn on the gas fireplace, but I don't want Ben to get the idea that I'm trying to stage a romantic scene. I play with the fireplace remote—turning it on, then off, then on again, until I hear a knock at the door.

He's here! I accidentally drop the remote—okay, the fire's staying on. I wipe my hands on my jeans, push my glasses up, take a deep breath, and open the door to find Ben looking down at his scuffed-up cowboy boots.

"Hey," we both say at the same time. His smile melts me. It showcases perfect teeth between perfect lips on a perfectly tanned face. I lead him to the table in the living room and offer him a Coke as he hangs his jacket on the back of the chair.

"No thanks. I brought this." He pulls out a Monster Energy Drink from his backpack, along with his chemistry text and notebook.

"Okay, I'll be right back." I swing the kitchen door shut and lean against it. I inhale deeply and tell myself: He's just a boy. *A boy who only wants you for your brains.*

I return with a caffeine-free Diet Coke and gesture at his drink. "Won't you have trouble sleeping with all that caffeine?"

"Not after practice. Most nights I can't stay awake long to get my homework done without it." Ben peers at a watercolor of the ruins of an abbey nestled in the Irish countryside on the fireplace mantel, walks over to get a closer look, and then fingers the books that line the shelves on either side. "This looks more like a library than a living room. Emerson. Aristotle. Shakespeare. Tolstoy. Have you read these?"

"I've read some of them." What a nerd, geek, loser—I can practically *hear* his thoughts. "My mother is an English professor at the college." Ben returns to the table where I'm now seated, sipping my soda.

"That explains a lot." He grins.

"What do you mean?" Is he going to tell me I'm a nerd, because it's one thing if *I* think it, and completely another if *he* says it out loud.

"Nothing bad. It's just that your house is kind of funky—different. Like you."

"I'm different?" I narrow my eyes. "Like crazy different? Weird different? Or plain old nerdy different?" He may be the most handsome guy in the universe, but he isn't going to get away with making fun of me to my face.

He shows me his palms in surrender. "Calm down, Verona. I like that you're different. It's cool. You don't try to fit into the same old Jamestown mold. I've known most of the girls in this town since grade school. After a while, they all start to seem the same. And *same* can get boring fast."

Ben flops down, smelling like cinnamon, and stares at me.

My breathing quickens. "Show me what you need help with." I decide we'd best get down to business before my brain stops working completely.

Ben exhales hard. "Okay. Let's start on page one, and proceed from there."

"All of it?" My eyes widen, and I drop my chin to look at him over my glasses, then realize I'm doing just what my mother would do, and push them back up my nose.

"Yeah, pretty much. I mean, I know some of the periodic table that we were supposed to learn the first week, but after that, it all gets…" He shakes his pencil like the word eludes him.

"Okay. A lot of chemistry is simple memorizing." I point to a question at the end of the first chapter. "How would you do this one?"

Ben attempts to figure it out. He has the process right, but his figuring is wrong. Resting my cheek on my hand, I glance at him out of the corner of my eyes. "How would you execute a play if you didn't know the names of all the positions on the field?"

"Pretty badly, I suppose." He shrugs and twirls the pen in his hand. "But that's different. I grew up eating, drinking, and sleeping football. My father's idea of a good time is watching football replays over and over until we can recite each move by heart. After a while, it becomes automatic." He flips through the pages. "How am I expected to learn all this in such a short time?" He slaps his book, his brows crunching together in a way I try not to find adorable.

"I'll show you." I hand him a stack of index cards. "The game is chemistry. The elements are the positions. Once you learn them, you'll graduate to learning the plays."

"Huh? Plays?"

"The plays. You know, the formulas."

I instruct him to copy down the key points, and only memorize a few cards at a time until he knows the whole stack. The process takes over three hours, but he's diligent. I pretend to be studying from my text, but mostly I sneak glances at him—trying to collect delicious details to fill Luka in on later: the way he taps the pencil head against the page when he's concentrating, the way he rakes his hand through his hair when he's frustrated, and how he smells like a tantalizing combination of cinnamon and musk.

He pats the growing pile of cards he's memorized. "You're tricky." His dark eyes narrow, but crinkle at the corners in a smile.

"You're learning it, aren't you?" I cross my arms, shrug.

"Yeah, I guess it's not hopeless after all." His stomach growls and he rubs it.

"I'll get some chips." I stand up. At the same time, a key rattles in the door.

My mother backs into the foyer, shaking her umbrella on the porch outside. "Hi, honey," she calls, her head still behind the door. "It's a good thing I keep an umbrella in my brief—"

She jumps back when she sees Ben sitting at the table beside me. He rises up from his chair. My mother's eyes follow him up, her eyes registering surprise at how big he is.

"Hi, Mom." I wipe my hands on my jeans. "This is Ben Chortov, from school. We're studying chemistry."

She collects herself and moves toward him. "Hello, Ben Chortov from school. I'm Verona's mother, Cheryl Newman."

Ben shakes her hand. "It's nice to meet you, ma'am."

"Nice to meet you, too. But please don't call me ma'am—it makes me feel old." She carries her briefcase into the kitchen and turns at the door. "Verona, would you come here a moment?"

"Uh, sure." I shrug my shoulders to Ben. "I'll get those chips."

Ben shakes his head no. "I'm good."

I close the door. Removing her raincoat, my mother whispers, "Who is he?"

"I'll tell you later." Can't she see this isn't a good time?

"He's a jock." My mother's tone infers that *jock* is synonymous with serial killer.

"So?" I hold my hands up and shake my head. My mother sighs and rolls her eyes. Since when does my mother have something against jocks? My father's a jock. And she *married* him. Oh...

"He's a kid in my chemistry class who needs some help. Mr. Ezekiel suggested I help him." I jerk my head toward the living room. "Look, can we talk about this later?"

"You betcha, we will. I don't like the idea of a boy in the house when I'm not here."

"That's a new one."

Mom lets her shoulders down, exhaling slowly. "I guess this is new for both of us. We can talk when he's gone. I'm going to pour a glass of wine and take a bath."

"Fine." I retreat through the door to the living room.

"Sorry about that." I nod to the kitchen. Ben swings his backpack onto his back.

"Do you mind if we do this again on Thursday?" Ben's eyes scan my face and hair like he's noticing my appearance for the first time.

"Sure." I'll figure out a way, even if my newly overprotective mother forbids it.

"You know, you look like your mom." He stretches his massive arms out to the sides and I hate myself for wondering what it would feel like to be held in them. "And that's a *good* thing."

Wednesday, September 16th
683 Days to Home Free

ROSS—ALIVE AND LOOKING WELL, not at all scared and upset like in yesterday's vision—and his best bud Craig claim the two seats at the far end of the table while I remove my sandwich from its baggie.

"Hello, Verona." Ross's Caribbean eyes are as enticing as a travel poster.

"Hi, Ross." I'm palpably relieved nothing has come from my vision this time.

"And hello, Craig—I mean, *Red Fox*." I force a smile. Craig looks down, his pallid face changing slowly, chameleon-like, to match his Hawaiian Punch hair. I can't tell if he's angry or embarrassed.

Nicky drops his tray in mock anger. "You steppin' out on me, woman? Gotta watch you every minute!"

I exhale, sensing Ross' eyes on me. I can feel my cheeks redden like Craig's.

"Shut up, Chaser!" Susie, Caitlin, and Leanne collapse into the seats across from us.

"Verona doesn't like you," Caitlin chirps in a singsong voice. Nicky feigns surprise. Then she gives me a quizzical look. "What kind of name is Verona?"

All eyes turn to me. I swallow. I really don't want to explain it again. Before I can open my mouth, Nicky comes to the rescue. "Verona is Veronica without the 'ick'." Everyone laughs, but not in a mean way.

During most lunch periods, a rocket could launch from the kitchen at 180 decibels and no one would notice the additional noise. It's that loud. But when Mr. Sams storms through the door, it gets so quiet you can hear kids sweating.

Everyone knows Mr. Sams avoids the cafeteria, delegating any high-level announcements to the assistant principal, Mrs. Hale. So today, jaws drop when Mr. Sams walks in, taps Alex Chortov on the back, and heads for the exit. Alex stands up, his face a thin mask of bravado, and clenching and unclenching his fists, follows him out the door.

"Hey Ross, what's going on with Genghis?" Nicky seems to think that if you're on the football team, you automatically know everything about every other player.

"How would I know?" Ross looks at Craig and they laugh, seemingly at an inside joke.

"I saw an unmarked police car out by Officer Morris' cruiser when I got back from the dentist. It was the end of second block." Susie massages her slackened jaw.

"I bet it has to do with Angie's accident." Leanne says this under her breath, but when the rest of the table leans in, she sighs. "Angie insists her brakes gave out that night. On Friday, she'd brought it in for a tune-up. The accident was the first time she drove it after that."

"Maybe Mr. Sams is conducting his own investigation." Nicky waves his fork. "He looked pretty upset at the assembly."

Craig joins in the conversation for the first time. "Chortov is probably in trouble for parking in the faculty lot. He thinks he's so cool he can park anywhere."

"Yeah, but Officer Morris would handle something like that." Caitlin rolls her eyes.

"I expect we'll know by the end of the day." Leanne winks at me. Her comments placate the curious, so the conversation at our end of the table falls back to the usual complaints about homework, teachers, and parents.

Thursday, September 17th
682 Days to Home Free

NEW NEWMAN RULE #1: "No boys in the house when Mom's not there" leaves me in a quandary. After what is probably a typical heated exchange between a girl striving for independence, but not yet possessing the means to make it a reality, and a parent who finds herself completely in charge for the first time, my mother suggests an alternative setting—the Swem Library at the College of William and Mary.

Ben agrees. He did say he'd *meet me anywhere* when he first asked me to tutor him. I force myself to stop imagining all the places I'd love to meet him—a candlelit dinner, a secluded lagoon, a—enough already! Replace that last thought with admonition to self: *Do not to read too much into what Ben said when he needed you to help him not get suspended.*

Perched on the hood of his '73 Ford pickup, backpack on the ground below his cowboy boots, Ben twirls a pocketknife in his right hand. When he jumps off—looking like he only uses abdominal muscles—I admire how his faded Levi's fit him like they were made for his body. I remind myself once again—he's just a boy. I sigh. *Just a boy.*

We stroll through the library's automatic doors. Although neither of us has been here before, Ben leads me through a room full of college kids camped in front of computers. The room smells of coffee, chocolate, and stress. We take the stairs to a quieter level, where an empty table at the end of a row of books makes for a cozy study area.

"Before we start," I plop my backpack on the table for emphasis, "I have a question."

Ben raises his eyes. Do I catch a scintilla of fear in them? The hair on the back of my neck stands up. *What does he have to be afraid of?*

"Did you know that Mr. Sams grabbed your brother from first lunch today?"

"I heard." Ben exhales in a way that seems to say, *"That's all it is,"* and searches for a pen. When he notices me waiting for more of an explanation, he adds, "They were asking questions about the shop. Like if he knew who was working on student cars last Friday."

I nod as if I understand what he means, as well as the relevance of it, and keep nodding for him to continue. "Alex was there, but Clyde Baker was the one in charge of repairs."

"Why would Mr. Sams care about that?"

"Angie Jett's car was in the shop on Friday. I guess it's just part of the investigation."

That's what Leanne said, too. "I see. And since Angie's brakes didn't work that night, they want to be—"

"Her brakes didn't work? Really? She's blaming the wreck on her brakes?" Ben glances at the ceiling as though debating whether to say anything further. "Since middle school, Angie Jett's been getting her kicks by pushing her horse to the edge of the cliff. It was just a matter of time before she went over with it. Honestly, she's lucky she's not dead. She's reckless. Crazy. I don't understand the hold she had over Alex—really, the hold she *still* has on Alex." He says this with a tinge of resentment in his voice, his massive fist tightening, threatening to snap the pen in two.

I feel small and vulnerable. For the first time I realize how little I know the hulk sitting across from me. I wonder if Ben catches the fear in my eyes, for he instantly relaxes, running his fingers through his straight black hair.

I am stunned as I take in what he's just said. From outward appearances, Alex is long over Angie. "What about Amber Claussen? It looks like Alex has a thing for…"

"Theoism Number 22: Appearances are deceitful.… Alex doesn't really like Amber; he just takes the path of least resistance. She's made it obvious that she's available to him."

"Theoism? I've never heard of that. Is it like Taoism?" I scribble a yin/yang symbol on my notebook paper. "You know—an Eastern way of thinking?" I think of my new book with the Chinese letters. *The Way of an Eagle.*

Ben laughs. "If you consider Russia 'eastern' compared to here, I guess it is."

"I've never heard of that one." I tilt my head, wondering if there was a Russian Lao Tse I've never read about.

Ben's eyes light up. "After Alex and I got to America and we learned English, we noticed that Coach, you know, our father, Theodor Alexandrovich Chortov, always had these—I don't know—words of wisdom, I guess you'd call them. At one point, we started giving them reference numbers."

"So a Theoism is stuff your father says?" I ask. "Idioms. Like, 'Ignore your teeth and they'll go away'? *My* father thinks that one's hilarious." Uh, oh. I'm not expecting that heart pang just mentioning my father—but there it is. I swipe my cheek to brush the feeling away.

"Yeah—idioms." Ben writes the word down on one of his cards. "Anyway, the Coach would say something in Russian, and then translate it into English. I've got a list of them in a notebook under my bed. It's funny when the translation makes no sense. Alex and I compete to rattle one off before he finishes. Drives him crazy."

"It sounds like you and Alex are pretty close?"

"Yeah, we are. I guess it's more like we *were*, sort of—lately, he's been interested in things I'm just not interested in."

"Like?"

"Like partying." Ben frowns. "I don't get what Alex is thinking. He tests better than me, but always takes the easy courses. I guess he's just lazy." Ben crosses his arms.

I try not to notice the muscles in his arm tighten.

"Football is the exception. He completely bought into Coach's goal for us to go pro after making a name for ourselves in college."

Ben flashes me a lopsided, somewhat embarrassed smile. His eyes look at me, and then quickly look away.

I find myself wondering what it would be like to be the girlfriend of a football player, not to mention a football player this hot. Gorgeous. Adorable. I swallow and fiddle through our textbook to the homework chapter before I say or do something embarrassing. Because for the first time, I actually know what it is to *fawn*—or at least feel like fawning—and I don't like it.

I quiz Ben on the questions we've been given for homework the last few days. He is getting it, studying his note cards. We work for over two hours. Focusing on chemistry helps me cope with the intoxicating effect of his proximity. By the evening's end, I'm surprised to find I'm relaxed—well, almost.

Under a canopy of crepe myrtle blooms that cover our two vehicles, Ben holds my door. "Are you coming to the game tomorrow night?"

That question catches me so completely off-guard, I feel like I've been sacked. I freeze for a second, then shrug my shoulders. "I don't know." That's all I can think of to say? *I don't know!?*

When the truth is this: watching football with my best friend in town strikes me as a colossal waste of time. And yet, I certainly can't—couldn't ever—admit that to him.

Ben stares into my eyes for a second, but like before, it's only for a second, until he looks away. "Okay, see you in chemistry."

Friday, September 18th
681 Days to Home Free

A DRAFT OF WARM SEPTEMBER rustles up from the south as my mom and I pace the platform—the only platform in this rinky-dink train station. It is laughable to try to compare it to Grand Central, which boasts over a hundred platforms.

"Verona, have things gotten better at school this semester? You don't seem as lugubrious as you were last spring." My mother often uses words like *lugubrious*—gloomy, doleful, melancholy—expecting me to know what they mean. And to my never-ending shame—I usually do. Ever since I uttered my first syllable, she's been turning me into a walking thesaurus.

"Actually, I've made some new friends," I tell her, neglecting to add *just this week*.

"The football player?" One auburn eyebrow arches. At least she doesn't use the *jock* label this time.

"Ben's alright." I do a little right-sided shoulder shrug. Mom raises both her eyebrows. I ignore it. "I've made other friends at school besides him. A girl named Leanne Morris, and her friends, Susie, Caitlin, and Paris. And an annoying kid named Nicky. I was even invited to a party tomorrow night at Susie's house."

"That's great, honey." She pauses, expecting me to fill in the details.

"I'm not going."

"Why not?"

"Because I'd rather hang out with Luka." All I want to do this weekend is watch movies, eat popcorn, coffee and mint-chocolate chip ice cream, and catch up on the latest New York news.

Both our heads spin toward the brassy trumpet-whistle from the far end of the tracks.

"Luka might want to meet your new friends. She's a lot more outgoing than you, you know!" Mom shouts over the rumble of the oncoming engine and the relentless horn.

And than you, I think. My mother always pushes me to mingle with people, despite the fact that she loves nothing more than cozying up with a good book by the fire. Why can't she accept the fact that her daughter is just like she is?

The train brakes screech, then a low puff of air fills the tracks. I search the windows of the front passenger car for Luka, watching the people stepping off the train. A poke on the back of my shoulder startles me. When I turn around, my best friend in the whole world embraces me. I look down the tracks and see people descending from a car at the other end.

Fastening our seatbelts, my mother turns to face Luka, where she sits next to me in the back seat. "You hungry? We can grab a bite to eat on the way home."

"Not really. I've been munching on Fritos the whole way."

"You look like you've grown another six inches since I saw you last spring." My mother pulls the Rover out of the lot. Luka stands just under six feet tall, with ebony hair, long and straightened, and glistening chocolate skin, designer clothes, model-worthy make-up, and infectious sass. Nevertheless, she's been as much of a misfit at our old school as I was. She intimidates everyone with her looks—my mother says she's pulchritudinous, which I took for an insult until I looked it up—and her sharp tongue. Me? I'm a misfit because of my eclectic ideas, fashion, vocabulary, and interests.

We really don't *want* to fit in, either. There is too much to conform to. The cliques might as well wear uniforms, their clothes as so similar. Plus, in addition to what they wear, they all have their own rules about how to behave, what to eat, what music to listen to—even how to sound stupid. *Oh my Gawd!*

Take the Fitches—our name for the girls who look like they popped out of Seventeen wearing Abercrombie tees and skin-tight jeans— they go overboard to make everyone who doesn't fit into their tight mold feel like gutter scum.

The CBC guys—Cute, But Clueless—wear Yankee hats, death metal tee shirts, and saggy jeans with boxers hanging out, and play either baseball or hockey. For Mickey Silver, Luka changes it slightly to: Cute Butt, But Still Clueless. The Fitches and CBCs pretty much only date each other.

Of course there are other groups: the Emos, Goths, the Band Geeks, the Nerds, and then everyone else. We are part of the *everyone else* crowd. The uncategorized misfits. Now I get to be a misfit in another school that has these same sort of divisions, with minor variations.

"I've left ol' Shorty here in the dust." Luka elbows me.

"Five-foot-five is not short." I elbow her back.

"We can always grab a hot dog at the game, Doctor Newman." Ever since my mom earned her doctorate, Luka loves to tease her with the *doctor* title.

"What game?" My mom and I ask simultaneously.

"You don't think I came all this way to play Barbie, do you? Especially when all I've heard about this entire week is a hunky football player." Luka drops her chin to look at me through the tops of her perfectly made-up eyes.

"He's *alright*," my mom mimics me under her breath.

I, of course, ignore her. "Luka, I don't know." I look out the window, thinking how stupid it was for me to tell her about Ben asking if I was going to the game. *Stupidly stupid!*

"Girlfriend, he asked you to go. Don't you think he might like you?" Luka circles her finger in the air around her ear.

"He didn't *ask* me to go." I swat at her hand. "He asked me *if* I was going. Big difference."

"Same thing." She flicks the back of her hand to dismiss my retort. We play girl-fight, swatting our hands with limp wrists until we're both laughing so hard we fall into a hug.

"You girls should go. You've never been to a high school football game." My mother's eyes lock with mine in the rear view mirror.

I pause, trying to think of a way out. "But—"

"I want to see your new school… and your new boyfriend. Let's go Colonial!" Luka does a lame cheerleading move next to me.

"I guess we could go for a while." I kiss the popcorn, ice cream, and Channing Tatum movie goodbye for now. There's always tomorrow night. "If it's too boring, we'll leave at halftime . . . and he's *not* my boyfriend."

"It won't be boring." Luka hums. "Mmmm—all those hot guys in tight pants."

My mother grunts.

CROWDS NEVER BOTHER ME MUCH. I love the bustle of the streets of New York, the energy of the anonymous throng. But at an event like this, I enter an arena with Vast Embarrassing Mishap Potential (VEMP)—the prospects of which play on my brain like an unending horror movie.

If I trip and fall down the bleachers (like when I was six years old), spill soda on the person seated next to me (like when I was ten), or root for a player not presently on the field (this led to the discovery that I was half-blind at eleven), my sorry face can't fade into the obscurity of the Big Apple. I will have to see these people in school on Monday, and for the remaining 681 days I'm stuck here. The thought sends shivers down my spine.

I resolve to: 1. Not drink anything, 2. Not say anything louder than a whisper—and even then, only to Luka, and 3. Sit as close to the deck as possible.

We follow a group of noisy freshmen clad in Colonial's navy and white, including their hair. As we pass, the dazzling band uniforms catch my eye. Leanne winks at me from behind a clarinet. Clarinet! That's what the snake charmer thing she did with her fingers meant. She's in the band! A band geek accepted by everyone. I never would've imagined such a thing could exist.

I point her out to Luka. Leanne waves her clarinet in midnote, trying not to be detected by the energetic drum major circling his hands like a madman in front of her.

Luka points to a few empty seats about three rows from the top, and starts climbing.

I scowl, keeping my gaze on the steps, determined not to fall. "This is too high up," I whine.

"C'mon, V. Eagle girls aren't afraid of falling, right? Look, there are hardly any seats left on this side." The bleachers are packed tight with Colonial fans of all ages. I look around to see if any of my new friends are sitting near us. Thankfully, they're not. Luka will not give up. "So, where's your boyfriend?" I'm sure everyone within a three-row radius hears her. "What's his number?"

"I don't know," I whisper, trying to quiet her. "He's down there somewhere." I motion toward the blue uniforms surrounding the coach. Then I elbow her and say between gritted teeth, "Stop calling him my boyfriend. We're study partners."

"And his number?" Again, *Luka-loud*, ignoring my plea for quiet.

"I told you, I don't know." I look down, pulling dark locks of hair over my face.

She sighs dramatically. "Well then, what position does he play?" I shrug. She scowls at me as if I had just made some outlandish proclamation. "Do I have to teach you everything about being a girl?"

"He looks exactly like the quarterback, minus the earring."

It doesn't take long for Luka to figure out which position Ben plays. She listens to the announcer calling the plays. Ten minutes into the first quarter, we hear amid the crackling over the loudspeakers: "Colonial junior Ben Chortov makes his first sack of the game." Ben helps the opposing quarterback back to his feet.

"Number fifty-five," Luka shouts, while elbowing me. "Big and broad. *That's the way, uh huh, uh huh, I like it, uh huh, uh huh.*"

I hold my head, thankful for two things: First, that the band's rendition of KC and the Sunshine Band's song drowns out most of Luka's outburst; and second, none of the kids from my classes are sitting anywhere near us.

Luka's eyes are pinned on the game; mine examine the western sky—the same apricot patina I saw during last week's flight over the stadium. My mind goes back to the first part of the visions, the good parts—the exhilaration of flying. The perspective from that high up was mind-boggling, greater-than-groovy, awesome. Not awesome like everyone always says it. *New haircut? Awesome.* But really awe-some: Invoking awe, reverence, wonder.

I'm caught completely off-guard when everyone around us jumps up and hollers, "Booo!" I follow them to my feet, trying to ascertain why the Colonial fans are so upset.

"The other team scored," Luka says, sensing my cluelessness.

"Way to go, Colonial." I twirl my finger in the air.

Luka exhales. "It's almost halftime. I'm hungry. Let's go get a hot dog before the line gets too long."

"Sure, Miss *I munched on Fritos the whole way.*"

At least I manage to make it down to the deck, down the stairs to the concession booth and back up to the deck without tripping.

Hot dog in one hand and soda in the other, we head toward our seats. Nicky jumps from his seat immediately in front of me, causing me to splash soda on my hand. Paris and Caitlin pop up behind him.

"Verona! I didn't think you were coming. Who is this goddess?" Nicky gestures at Luka.

"Lukeisha Williams, Nicky Chase." I use my sticky soda hand as a pointer, and then wipe it on the side of my jeans.

They nod at each other, while the girls chime in stereo, "Chaser!"

I introduce them. "And Luka, this is Paris and Caitlin." The girls give a quick wave and head over to concessions.

"I insist that you sit with me." Nicky points to the space vacated by Paris and Caitlin.

"Thank you." Luka sits down like it's understood. I sit next to her, grateful not to have to climb to the top of the bleachers balancing a soda and hot dog, but inwardly begging Luka not to embarrass me.

"You must be Verona's friend from New York." Nicky places his hand on my knee as he leans across my legs to talk to Luka. I swipe off his hand and he pulls back, acting all confused. Luka nods while chewing her hot dog, absorbed in the action on the field. Nicky leans over me again. "Verona's in love with me. She just doesn't know it yet." I roll my eyes while Luka chuckles.

At this point, the crowd jumps up with unrestrained cheering. We rise to our feet, which causes me to drop my soda. Nicky catches it the second before it lands on his feet.

This time the crowd is jubilant. "Way to go Colonial!" Fans whistle amid a victory tune from the band.

"Colonial scored." I shove Luka to let her know I'm not a complete football moron.

She reaches in front of me to tap Nicky's arm. "Did you know Verona's father writes a sports column for a big New York newspaper, and yet she doesn't know the first thing about football?"

"Well, she's perfect in every other way." Nicky grins. Then he looks at the scoreboard and scowls. "The score's tied and it's almost halftime. This wasn't supposed to happen with the Monticello Mice." The other team's mascot is a moose, but everyone calls them 'the mice.'

"Georgeson's up next." Nicky cups his hands around his mouth. "Kicka!"

"Ross Georgeson sits at our lunch table," I inform Luka, like she hasn't heard me talk about him for days. The kick shoots up, and then dribbles off at an angle. It is scooped up by the front line of the opposing team.

"Oh, Ross!" Nicky groans. We stand up to get a clear view of Monticello's player sprinting down the sidelines. Our defense misses tackling him by a breath, and he crosses into the end zone.

A steady roar streams from the stands across the field. On our side, even the bleachers moan as spectators rush to climb down. "Ross is never going to hear the end of that one!"

"It's just a game," I say.

"Not to Coach Chortov." Nicky looks at me. "He's ruthless with players when they make mistakes. Even his own boys. *Especially* his boys." Nicky's head drops. Then he turns back to the press box on top of the bleachers. "See that man standing by Mr. Sams?" I strain to look back though the glass, but only see a shadow in the reflection of the lights from over the field.

"Yeah?" I pretend to see him.

"That's Ross's father. Reginald Georgeson is the superintendent. That man is mean. He's just mean." Nicky tugs up the zipper of his hoodie like he has a chill. "I wouldn't want to be Georgeson tonight. He'd better not choke in the second half, that's all I'm gonna say." And that *is* all Nicky says, because when a cluster of sophomores parades by, he trails after them.

Watching the players file into the locker room, I wonder how Ben is taking the first-half loss.

"Hey, thanks for bringing me. Nicky's a trip. Can we stay a bit longer to see if your school comes back after halftime?" Luka asks.

"Sure. Why not?" I haven't embarrassed myself so far, the warm breeze feels delicious, and besides that, the excitement is starting to rub off on me. I'm not ready to admit I like watching Ben play. Yet, somewhere inside, I sense that reason buttressing all the others.

"Verona, I was hoping you'd be here." The familiar baritone jolts me out of my thoughts. Mr. Zeke, in blue jeans and charcoal windbreaker with pockets he's using to warm his hands, claims Nicky's spot. Without his jacket and tie, he looks so *casual.*

"You're going up to the hospital with us tomorrow, aren't you? I forgot to remind you in class today."

"Oh, yeah," I lie. No! *The trip to Richmond to see Angie.* In anticipation of Luka's visit and all the tutoring with Ben, I have completely forgotten about it. "Um, Mr. Ze—Ezekiel. I, uh…" I try to formulate a plausible excuse, but instead, I stammer on like a fool.

Luka reaches across me with her hand out. "Hello, Mr. Zeke. I'm Luka Williams, Verona's friend from New York. Verona would love to go with you to visit the girl in the hospital. She told me about the whole sorry thing. I've got a paper to write, so I'll have plenty to keep me busy tomorrow. Right, Verona?"

I shoot a fierce look in her direction before turning to Mr. Zeke. "What time should I be there?"

"Twelve thirty in the student lot. I'll drive." I nod. He stands up, takes a couple of steps, and then turns back. "I'll get to that reference soon. I don't want you to think I've forgotten about it."

When Mr. Zeke is out of hearing range, I scold Luka. "Why did you do that?"

"Because when your teacher first asked you, you told him you'd go. Just because your brain is all muddled with number fifty-five doesn't mean you can back out."

"But *you're* here!"

"Yeah—*so?* I can entertain myself for an afternoon. I really *do* have a paper to write. I started it on the train, but I was too pumped to focus. Besides, that cheerleader was in your PCQ vision last week. Aren't you a little curious to find out more about her?"

Now I feel miserable. Normally, I would have worried every waking moment about this new opportunity to put my foot in my mouth. I hate awkward, and meeting Angie Jett minus her leg is going to be mega-awkward. Serious VEMP.

On his return, Nicky completely misreads the reason for my frown. "Don't worry, Verona. Colonial always pulls through in the second half."

"Did Mr. Zeke talk to you?" I ask him.

"He reminded me about tomorrow—you know, seeing Angie." Nicky doesn't seem bothered by it at all.

The second half starts. Nicky punches his fist into his other hand. "I heard Chortov took Kicka out. He's replacing him with Robbie Aigle. And Aigle is only a freshman!"

Ross, or as Nicky calls him, Kicka, slumps on the bench, with his helmet dangling between his legs. The rest of the players stand on the sidelines. The day Leanne introduced me to the kids at the popular table, Ross was the only one who made an effort to welcome me. He doesn't deserve this—not for one mistake.

A younger, squatter man in a blue polo pats him on the back. "Who's that guy?" I ask Nicky.

"That's Coach Grimes. He teaches health and P.E. You never had him?"

I shake my head.

"Good guy. I'll bet Georgeson's dad is hopping mad. Coach Chortov's sure to hear about this." I look over at him. "Sorry," he says. "I can get carried away."

"Why aren't you out there if you like the game so much?"

"Are you kidding? I can barely fight the women off me now. I'd never have *any* peace as a football star."

"Right." Luka and I exchange smiles.

"Ruh-roh. Here comes trouble," Nicky says, sounding a lot like Scooby-Doo.

Leanne pokes through the crowd, holding her flume-topped hat in one hand and an orange soda in the other. At her side, a cute guy with spiky brown hair and a scruff of stubble on his chin regards us with a smile. He wears black jeans and the pointiest shoes I've ever seen outside of New York. Definitely *not* from Colonial. Older. *Has Leanne been holding out on us about an older boyfriend?*

"I have someone I want y'all to meet." She tilts her hat toward the pointy-shoed guy. "This is Nicolai, the Chortovs' cousin from Russia. He just started at William and Mary."

"Nic, I'm Nick." Nicky shakes his hand, then looks at Luka and me. "And these bombshells sitting next to me are Verona and Luka."

"They all call him Kolya for some reason," Leanne says.

"Nice to meet you." Kolya speaks with a thick accent. "What is boomshell?"

We laugh. Luka punches Nicky lightly on the arm. "It's just Nicky trying to give us a compliment in his own weird way."

Kolya looks at Luka, perplexed. "You speak funny. I don't understand."

"I *tawk* funny?" Luka's New York attitude accelerates to full throttle.

We all laugh. Kolya gives up trying to understand us and takes a seat next to Luka. Leanne squeezes to my left, forcing Nicky over.

I almost choke on my Diet Coke when Kolya turns to Luka and asks, "Can I touch you?"

"What?" Luka leans way back, shooting him a dangerous look.

"I can explain." Kolya's face reddens. "At home, in our little village, I never see a brown person except in television. In airport, I saw man with brown skin. He——" Kolya hangs his head in frustration. "In America, many people with brown skin. I never touch it. I think you beautiful."

Luka pulls up her sweater sleeve. "Okay, Russkie, you can touch me here." She points to a specific spot on her forearm, adding, "If you touch me anywhere else, I'll deck you."

Kolya wrinkles his brow, probably wondering what she means, but then places his whole hand on her forearm for a few seconds with his eyes closed. "Same." He nods and removes his hand.

"What did you think? I'd be cold? Cold like a vampire or something?" Luka asks, slowly, and with surprisingly clear diction.

"Vampire? No. Hot, like fire." Kolya eyes widen.

That sends us laughing again.

A loud roar explodes from the fans in the seats around us. We all jump to our feet, look at the field, where a pass has just been completed a few yards from the end zone. The next play sends off a flurry of "Ooohs!" when the Mice push our runner behind the line by another yard.

Alex Chortov throws a pass. The receiver, who just missed getting his hands around it, knocks the ball out of the end zone. Third down is equally disappointing—we only get inches closer to a touchdown.

The freshman kicker, Robbie Aigle, runs onto the field. Ross walks up to the sideline, still a considerable distance from the others. The field goal is good.

The crowd cheers wildly, while the cheerleaders shout out a victory chant. We head into the last quarter with a four-point disadvantage.

Ross looks happy for the team before he returns to his lonely position on the bench. I look at the scoreboard and the kids around me. Except for feeling bad for Ross, I am having fun. I actually want us to win. I can't remember the last time I actually cared about the outcome of a football game.

"I need to get back with the band." Leanne pins her hat strap under her chin. "Okay if I leave Kolya with y'all?"

Luka nods. Nicky slides next to me when Leanne gets up.

Colonial's defense manages to keep Monticello from reaching field goal range, thanks to excellent defensive coverage on our part. *Yay, Ben!* Colonial's defense repeatedly frustrates the other team's passes, and we quickly regain possession of the ball.

"Their punt was long, but look what Genghis' golden hands can do." Nicky points to our offensive line. His prediction is true: Colonial does advance down the field quickly.

Luka cheers louder than the short-skirted girls on the field, continuously yelling directives at the players and referees. This entertains Kolya, who has never been to an American football game before. He confides his confusion over why we call it football when we spend so little time actually kicking the ball. In Russia, he explains, soccer is called football. I have to admit that it seems to make more sense.

Alex hands the ball back to a runner, who leaps over the goal line and falls into the end zone. The crowd erupts, and the band plays louder than it has the whole game.

There are still four minutes left on the game clock, but with Colonial ahead, the stands are clearing out steadily. Luka's tremendous effort to speak clearly to Kolya amuses me. In Luka's dictionary, the word *Patience* comes somewhere between *Non-existent* and *Zilch*. It takes a really cute guy to cause it to move all the way back to *Considerable*.

Watching them interact, I completely miss the action on the field that brings Monticello within scoring range. It's third down, and the Mice's quarterback passes to a receiver, who is dragged to the ground only one yard from the goal line.

With only seconds to spare, the center hikes and the quarterback moves back for a pass. The distinct sound of silence fills our side of the bleachers when the crowd holds its breath. If this pass reaches the open player in the end zone, the game will be over and Colonial will lose. I look down at Ross. *Will he think it's his fault if they lose?*

I think of Ben, and my heart hurts. But before Monticello's quarterback can get his footing to execute the throw, number fifty-five, who seems to appear out of nowhere, plows him down.

I jump up and down like an eighties punk rocker, and exchange double high-fives with Luka, Nicky, Kolya and even the kids sitting behind us. As the buzzer sounds, the rest of the team rushes onto the field, hoisting Ben into the air while the band plays a crazy-loud version of another old-school Kool and the Gang song, "Celebration".

Luka whispers in my ear, "Your boy, fifty-five, saved the game."

I snicker at the *your boy* reference.

When everyone tires of jumping and screaming, we all make our way to the exit, melding into the crowd. As we pass beneath the band and I look around for Leanne, someone calls my name. Luka nudges my side, points below the fence to the field where number fifty-five, helmet in hand, smiles up at me.

I see, for the first time, one darling dimple in his left cheek. "Verona, you came. Did you like the game?" He wipes sweat from his forehead with the hem of his jersey.

"Yeah. It was fun—especially the end." He chuckles at that, still trying to catch his breath. I can't believe he's talking to me in front of everyone after what just happened. I weave around to the side fence so we can talk without impeding the mass of bodies lumbering to the exit. Luka and Kolya lean on the fence next to me.

"This must be the famous Luka… I'm Ben." He winks at Kolya.

I want to hit her when she replies, "So I've heard."

His gorgeous grin nearly paralyzes me. "Did you hear about the party tomorrow night?"

Luka taps my collarbone with her finger. "You holding out on me, girlfriend?"

"Y'all should come to the party," Leanne says, like there couldn't be any reason we wouldn't love to come. Ben and Kolya nod in unison.

"I'll work on her," Luka yells down to Ben.

Saturday, September 19th
680 Days to Home Free

LUKA AND I STAY UP past three in the morning, updating each other on the intimate tidbits that can't be communicated by phone or text message—vital, global-impact information like: 1) a certain CBC making goo-goo eyes at Luka in health class, resulting in his Fitch girlfriend dumping him, even though Luka never even hinted that she might like him, 2) the sudden loss of my invisibility cloak's power, and 3) the fact that the PCQ vision came true, and now what if the ACV (art class vision) comes true, and Ross Georgeson is killed by some gun-toting demon?

Luka is all for telling Dr. Newman about the visions. Easy for her—she's not the one who'll end up on some psych's couch week after week reliving the breakup of her family and trying to connect that loss to these crazy visions.

So when I pull into the student lot five minutes early to meet Mr. Zeke and Nicky, I'm all baggy-eyed and jittery, and want more than anything to be told that the whole thing's a joke—we really don't have to drive an hour each way with our chemistry teacher to visit a girl whose leg was sawed off last week.

Nicky parks his rusty maroon Taurus next to the Rover. "Nice ride," he mouths.

Mr. Zeke pulls in on the other side of Nicky's car. I am so not in the mood for several hours of Nicky's inane banter. When Nicky beats me into the back seat of the Mercedes, I shoot him a mean look. Adjusting my seat belt in the front passenger seat, I feel light-headed and claustrophobic in this enclosed space, stuck with two people I barely know.

Mr. Zeke's spidey sense must've picked up on our anxiety, because when he pulls out of the parking lot, he says, "I realize this probably feels uncomfortable for you, because neither of you know Angie very well."

"You got that right," Nicky agrees out loud. I swallow.

"Well, let me give you the latest on her status, so you won't be shocked when you see her." *Shocked?* Not a word I want to hear. "The first couple of days, Angie remained on heavy doses of pain killers and antibiotics, because her right leg was amputated at the scene. It was pinned tightly, almost severed, in the wreckage. Removing it was the only way to extract her from the car. In medical parlance, it's known as a traumatic amputation. I don't think she was fully aware at the time."

You don't *think* she was fully aware? My mind flashes back to a scene from last Christmas, back before my life was severed: my father slicing the leg of lamb with the electric carving knife. I stood by, hoping to steal a piece before we sat down to dinner. I picture the carving knife coming to remove my leg and wrap my arms around my stomach.

"She has a couple fractured ribs and a badly fractured tibia—the bone below the knee on her left leg," Mr. Zeke continued. "Thankfully, the surgeons at MCV were able to insert a rod that's allowed her to keep her left leg. She's suffered a concussion. On Friday, the doctors closed up the stump wound." He pauses. I choke my breakfast back down my esophagus, willing my mind to focus on the different greens of the foliage, and find myself wondering which shade most resembles the color of my face right now.

"When do you think she'll be able to go home?" I pull on the seat belt, feeling like I can't breathe.

"Her mother said if all goes well, maybe next weekend. If there are any complications, there's no telling."

"How is she doing . . . otherwise?" I look over at Mr. Zeke, fumbling for the right word.

"Emotionally?"

"Yes."

"When I visited her on Thursday, she was having a difficult time adjusting to everything that's happened. Angelina is well aware her life has taken a detour. It's going to take weeks, probably months, for her to be able to walk, depending on how quickly the broken leg heals. She won't be fitted for a prosthetic for several months. All told, this once-healthy, fit, and independent girl will be confined to a bed, then a wheelchair, and in time, may walk again."

He takes a deep breath. "Mrs. Jett told me Angie is really down. Understandably. She thinks having friends visit might help get her mind off of things."

"What can we possibly say that will cheer her up?" Heading straight for an emotional shipwreck, I'm hoping Mr. Zeke might throw us some sort of life jacket.

"My advice to you is to play it by ear. Listen. Listen with your heart. That's usually what folks who are hurting need the most—someone to listen."

"Thanks, Mr. Ezekiel. I'm really nervous about this." I let go of the seat belt.

"I am too," Nicky adds. To my surprise, he sounds completely serious—for once.

I glance back.

He winks at me, then changes the subject. "Mr. Ezekiel, what are they paying teachers these days that you can afford a Benz? Did I miss your episode on *Pimp My Ride,* or do you have a side job?"

My breath catches in my throat, fully expecting Mr. Zeke to give Nicky a verbal thrashing. How he can afford a Mercedes is *so* none of Nicky's business! Instead, Mr. Zeke just laughs. "Esther here's a beauty, but she was a gift. I didn't earn her or win her. My wife bought her for me on my birthday, shortly before she died. She knew I'd always dreamed of driving a Benz, but that I'd never buy her myself. She told me to use the life insurance money to pay off the loan after she died. It was such a gift of love."

"Why do you call her Esther? Was that your wife's name?"

"No. We decided to call the car Esther after a beautiful queen in the Old Testament. She risked her life to save her people."

I wonder about the uncertainty of life as the Richmond skyline comes into view—piddly compared to Manhattan's, but, unlike Jamestown, at least Richmond *has* a skyline. Our lives could permanently change at any time without warning: death, divorce, and dismemberment on the downside, life-long dreams-come-true on the upside. Even a skyline could change dramatically in just a few hours.

At the hospital, Mr. Zeke asks us to wait outside Angie's door. The hallway reeks of burnt microwave popcorn, causing me to rethink the popcorn part of the movie plans for later. My stomach tightens as I calculate the high-voltage VEMP this imminent encounter holds. Nicky taps his foot in time with a patient's snoring from an adjacent room, attempting to get me to relax.

Finally, Mr. Zeke comes to the door with a reassuring look that doesn't extend to his eyes. And nothing he said in the car prepares us for what we see when we cross the threshold.

The vivacious teenager we're used to seeing shouting down the hall is a broken doll in an oversized bed—her cherubic face swollen, purple and yellow, like a grossly distorted Easter egg.

Black stitches pepper her right cheek under blotchy red marks that make it look like she'd been crying for the entire week. A plastic line drips liquid into a port in her arm. It takes all my willpower to not back out of the room. I catch my gasp and gulp it down, then force my lips to the side in a lame facsimile of a smile.

Nicky doesn't have the self-control. "My Lord, woman, what happened to you? Looks like you went ten rounds with a prize-fighter!" Nicky's pathetic attempt at humor does not go over well. Angie buries her head deeper into the pillow, like she's trying to escape from us.

Mrs. Jett, her whole face sagging like she's been in the ring with her daughter, whispers to us, "Y'all need to understand; Angie's not herself. She would normally laugh at that, you know." She pats Angie's arm. The slow-speaking Southern-accented woman sounds drugged. And she's definitely not Asian. Not with her frizzy blond hair and see-through skin.

Mr. Zeke comes along her other side and holds Angie's free hand in his.

"I do appreciate y'all making the long drive up to Richmond. Angie's received lots of flowers—" Mrs. Jett stops there and turns to Mr. Zeke. "Curtis, would you mind if we went down to the café and got a cup of coffee. I'm asleep on my feet." Her slow drawn-out *asssleeep* sounds like she really is close to passing out.

"Sure. I'm buying." He gives us an encouraging smile, and steps out of the room with Mrs. Jett.

Nicky and I stand at the foot of the bed, trying not to look at the spot where Angie's other leg would be tunneling under the sheets. At least I assume Nicky is trying not to look. He isn't saying anything, and that is so not like him.

Angie turns to me. Our eyes meet. "Hi," I say after an awkward moment, my eyes darting around.

"I know you." Her voice sounds fragile and yet, somehow enticing, like a tinkling wind chime. You just want to hear more of it.

"You do?" My arms cross. I feel my body from rocking back

and forth like a mental patient, and work at stopping, standing still. I think I understand why they do it. It's soothing.

"Yeah, you're Verona Lamb-something."

"Lamberti." My fingernails poke deep ridges in my arms.

"You came from New York last spring," Angie says, while Nicky—the coward—pretends to smell the sunflower and carnation bouquets cramming the windowsill. I move a step closer to Angie, but keep eye contact so I won't be tempted to look at the flat space under the covers where her right leg should be, but isn't.

"How did you know? I don't remember having any classes together."

She stops me with her hand. "Nick, would you do me a favor?"

That lily-livered fraidy-cat jumps at any excuse to escape the awkwardness. He spins around, saluting. "I'd do anything for you, dear, *anything*," Nicky recites, almost sings really, like the street urchin in *Oliver Twist*. I roll my eyes.

Angie doesn't seem to mind. She holds up a small pitcher. "Would you go down to the nurse's station and fill this with water. My throat is really dry." Through the straw, she slurps up the last bit of water in her cup.

"I'd be happy to." Nicky, the cravenly deserter, actually performs a bow. Grabbing the pitcher from Angie, Nicky runs out the door so fast you'd think the room was on fire.

We shake our heads simultaneously. "That should take care of him for a few minutes." Angie wriggles higher on the pillows so she's almost sitting. It must take a tremendous amount of strength, given all the gadgets and wires tangling out of her body.

"Last semester I had art right after you. I admired your paintings as they were drying—we all did. Some kids joked that you were Colonial's newest Picasso—but I thought your style was more Monet. You have a great eye for color contrast. My stuff always looked flatter."

Is *the* Angelina Jett, queen of the Colonial Cougars, complimenting me? I am dumbstruck.

"The other thing that I want to tell you is really weird. I don't want you to tell anyone." She scans my face, then closes her eyes, as if trying to decide something. When she opens them, I see raw determination. "Don't freak out. But right after the accident, when I was in and out of consciousness, I dreamed about you. Well, not *about* you, exactly. It was like you were there with me. Like you were telling me it was all going to be all right in the end. I should just hold on."

I cover my mouth in disbelief.

"I told you it was weird." She eases back down onto the pillow.

"No." I wave my hands like a crazy Italian New Yorker, which I guess, in truth, I am. "I mean—yes, it's weird—but I had this weird vision on Friday afternoon where I saw you crash, and I was with you." There's no way I'm going to tell her that I'd invaded her brain. That would be too freaky. "That vision haunted me all weekend. Then, on Monday, when I found out the accident really happened—"

"Did my brakes work? 'Cause they sure bombed that night." Angie's tone turns fierce. Her eyes pierce through me as she lifts her head.

I back up, but then something prickles at the edge of my mind. "Wait." I think back to the part of the vision I've most wanted to forget. "I remember thinking, it was like pushing down on a sponge."

"I was thinking the same thing. Actually, I was thinking wet newspapers—but sponge describes it better." She wrinkles her brow, easing back down. "We must be connected in some crazy way." A smile forms in the corner of her mouth.

"I don't know. I mean, I guess so—"

"Anyway, most of the time I just want to die, but there's a tiny voice holding out hope in here." Angie's hand covers her heart. "Maybe it's yours." She looks out the window. "And now you're here. Go figure."

I nod. I don't tell her that Mr. Zeke asked me to come (while holding my Honor Society reference hostage). The multi-colored floral arrangements she seems to be looking at catch my eye.

"Have you thought about painting?" I turn and watch her grimace as she tries to move to her side a bit.

"Are you kidding? Look at me." She waves a hand down her body. "I'm a mess." I look, seeing the empty spot where her blanket lays flat. I look at all of her. It isn't as frightening as I expected. Either that, or I'm getting used to it.

"You still have your hands." Oh. My. God. I gasp and turn away. Did that just happen? Did I just blurt out something so incredibly, unbelievably insensitive it could win an award? If they gave out awards for putting your foot in your mouth, that one would be a shoe-in. *Foot in mouth!* I shut my eyes. Even my *thoughts* are insensitive! Why did I come? Can I just evaporate right here, right now? Where's the burnt charcoal when you actually *want* to poof away?

A tiny giggle intensifies almost to a laugh behind my back. "That's something I would've said." I look back to her shiny eyes. They are wet and smiling, even if her face isn't able to.

And I breathe relief.

Nicky saunters in, not like the sniveling, betraying, turncoat he is for leaving me, but like a ridiculously flamboyant waiter, and carries the water in one hand and a plate of warm oatmeal raisin cookies in the other, all of which he places on the tray next to Angie's bed. "Madame, if you're still languishing in this five-star hotel next week, I'm taking you out for lunch and a shopping spree. The boutique on the first floor is fabulous." Nicky pours water in Angie's cup. We look at him like he's lost his mind. Ignoring us, he continues, "I got these puppies right from the café, fresh out of the oven. Oh, and your mom and Mr. Zeke say they'll be right up."

Angie manages a weak smile and sucks on her straw. Nicky cuts a cookie in half and places it in her hand. She puts it to her lips. "Thanks, Nicky." When she says his name, he puffs out like a peacock. Maybe he's not a traitor after all. He's actually smiling at her.

Mr. Zeke comes in and takes Angie's hand in his. "Angie, do you mind if I pray with you before we leave?"

Angie sighs. "Mr. Zeke, you can do whatever you want." Angie Jett is the first person I ever hear call him Mr. Zeke to his face, except for Luka, who didn't know better.

And he doesn't say a word about it, just motions for us to close the door. "If either of you feel uncomfortable with this, you're welcome to wait in the hall."

Nicky clasps his hands, so I do the same, though I *am* uncomfortable, but what else is new?

Mr. Zeke clears his throat. "Father in Heaven, we thank you for sparing the life of your precious daughter, Angie, that she might accomplish your purpose for her here. Father, in your Word, you say, 'Even youths grow tired and weary, and the young stumble and fall; but those who hope in the Lord...'"

He pauses when a red-faced Leanne Morris slides through the door, clasps her hands, and bows her head.

"'Those that hope in you will renew their strength. They will soar on wings like eagles; they will run and not grow weary, they will walk and not be faint.'" Leanne recites the last two lines along with him.

Mr. Zeke continues, "Lord, your daughter, Angie, is hoping in you. Renew her strength as you have promised. Give her strength to walk again, to run, and to eventually soar with you. Let her know how much she is loved. In your Son's name we pray. Amen."

Everyone echoes the *amen*.

The line, *soar on wings like eagles*, echoes in my head. Mrs. Jett's, Angie's, and Leanne's eyes get all teary. Nicky backs out of the room.

Leanne rushes to the bedside. Angie glances up at us, smiles, and closes her eyes, looking exhausted.

Mr. Zeke bends down and kisses her head. He whispers something in her ear.

We leave the room with heavy hearts, immersed in our thoughts all the way to the parking garage.

Nicky breaks the silence, this time from the front seat, after Mr. Zeke pays the garage attendant. "I've never seen anything like that. She's really beat up. I mean, her life will be completely changed now."

It seems that Nicky is realizing for the first time the challenges that face Angie. Maybe I am, too. Seeing her so broken on the bed makes the situation much more real, and much more painful. I turn my head toward the window and will my eyes to stay dry.

"Her life will be different, no doubt." Mr. Zeke exhales slowly. "But Angie's one spunky spirit. She may surprise us."

LUKA, AS ONLY LUKA CAN, convinces me we *need* to go to tonight's party, despite the fact that she doesn't go to my school, despite the fact that I've already had one extremely VEMPy situation to deal with today, and despite the fact that we did what she wanted to do last night. Why I always let her steamroll me, I'll never know. Well, in this case, I guess I do. His name is Ben Chortov, and there's a part of me that would like to see him before Tuesday. And maybe it's a bigger part of me than I'm ready to admit to, but okay, it's there.

There is no question which house is hosting the party. Vehicles line both sides of the street leading to the house—or, to be more accurate, the mansion. A group of the *in* kids, now the Jettless Set, cluster around the back of a pickup truck across the street, looking guilty of something, but trying to act all cool about it. If I had to guess, I'd say one of them probably stole a bottle from their parents' liquor cabinet and is passing it around.

A long, circular driveway serves as a parking lot. I pull the Rover into an empty spot on the far end of the cul-de-sac—perfect for a speedy getaway if necessary.

"You didn't tell me we were slumming it, Verona. I think I saw this crib on TV—you know, *People who Have Way More Money than They Know What to Do With*." Luka winks at me.

Three stories of brick stretch out on either side of a massive, pillared porch. I stop counting windows when I get to twenty. Teenagers spill off the columned porches onto the yard and driveway.

I scan the scene for a sign of Ben or his pickup. If he's here, he's being stealth.

Luka jumps from the Rover. "Let's do this, girlfriend."

I follow, always the reluctant one. Luka saunters up the drive—looking all sleek and dangerous in black satin pants and a sequined shirt—with the confident stride of a woman twice her age. Faces turn to stare as she approaches. When they notice me, in a sweater dress and leggings behind her, they return to their conversations.

Susie rushes out the door, practically knocking us backward as we climb the steps. "Oh, good! You came." Then she shouts to the rest of the kids in the vicinity: "Nucleus is about to start their set. Come 'round back, everyone!"

Susie's brother's metal band, Nucleus, could be heard warming up in the backyard, which, based on the size of the house, I estimate to be approximately a half-mile away from where we are on the front porch. The steely guitar riffs climb up my back and clench the muscles of my neck like a vise.

Susie holds the door for us. Inside, two iron-railed staircases curve up from the base of the foyer and meet at a second-floor hallway. From where we stand, there are eleven different directions we could take. *How is that even possible?* Twisted maroon roping with large gold tassels forbids passage up each of the staircases. I look down at a dazzling mosaic tile design cut into the hardwoods at the entry. Luka grabs my arm and points up to the most majestic antique chandelier I've ever seen outside of the New York Met (the opera, not the museum).

We meander through a few rooms to a kitchen large enough that you could eat and lose weight simultaneously by doing laps around the mammoth island. Platters of taquitos and bowls of chips, salsa, sour cream, guacamole, and refried beans cover multiple countertops.

Leanne and Kolya converse across the center counter with Caitlin and Paris.

Kolya is reaching for another chip when he spots Luka across the threshold. He drops the chip. "Luka, you come to party. Awesome."

Luka groans, and points her thumb to me. It's her, *Aren't you forgetting someone?* look.

Kolya looks slightly embarrassed. "I happy what you come to party, Werona, and you take Luka."

Everyone laughs good-naturedly at Kolya's grammar and pronunciation.

"Don't think twice about these shrimp brains, Kolya," Luka says, in response to our teasing. "Your English is great for being here only three months. I've been tortured in French for two years, and if I ever needed a bathroom in Paris, I'd wet my pants before I could find the words."

We all laugh. Kolya smiles, but I doubt he has a clue as to what she just said.

We drift out the back door to join the crowd. The ragtag band is still warming up. I scan the folks sitting in lawn chairs and huddled around the cooler on a side porch. Still, no sign of Ben.

The Wythe's backyard slopes down a hill divided into several terraced levels, ending at a dock and boathouse, all of it overlooking the mile-wide James River. Each level has a unique, room-like setting, offering amazing views of the water. Some cheerleaders huddle on a distant patio amid columns covered with blooming rose vines that twirl around them. Fountains and statues complement the décor perfectly. Two levels up from the river, a gazebo overlooks a lily-padded duck pond.

Grabbing some Cokes from a cooler, we gather in a semicircle while the band launches into its first song.

Craig Hamilton—his fire-red hair is hard to miss under the torchlights—leans against a distant column, arms crossed. His eyes dart around the yard. I figure he's waiting for Ross to show up. One thing becomes obvious to me. Craig stands even further outside the social bubble than I do, though he's probably known everyone here for years. I consider going up to him, but his body language is so uninviting—make that repellent—that I decide to keep my distance. I tried to be nice to him at the lunch table, and what did that get me? Not even a smile.

Standing in the growing crowd, I fervently wish for two things: 1) that Ben would show up already, and 2) that my ears wouldn't bleed from the incessant attack on them.

"They're pretty good." Leanne looks to me for confirmation.

"Great," I deadpan. Luka chuckles. I shoot her a mean glare that says *you owe me.*

A group of football players emerge from around the house.

Ben twirls a football in one hand. I smile and wave.

He looks at me and pulls his head back, whispering to the heavy guy on his right. Oh, the heavy guy is Clyde Davis. Ben is clearly talking about me, but not in a good way. I look down. *How could I think he might like me? Moron. Moron. Moron.*

When I convince myself that showing up here is the biggest mistake of my life and get up the nerve to shoot a furtive glance toward him, I notice the tiny light glistening from his left ear.

I look to the ground, mortified. It's Alex, not Ben. Just my rotten luck to be attracted to a twin. Worse, an identical twin.

Inside I fume at Luka for convincing me to come. I fume at Ben for not being here when he's really the only reason I agreed to come; for being a twin, for being popular, and for making me think he might like me. And I fume at Nucleus, for their torturous excuse for music pulverizing us from two refrigerator-sized amplifiers.

I feel so alone in the middle of the ever-growing mass of swaying bodies. My jaw clenches, and I search the yard for a potential escape from the noise.

Luka is engrossed in stilted conversation with Kolya. This baffles me. How could they possibly communicate in this crushing din? Forget about their language differences.

I weed my way out of the rows of rocking bodies and meander through the garden, hoping no one will notice my getaway. I estimate that the gazebo stands about fifty yards from the Nucleus assault on our ears, but the sound travels just fine across the garden. Locating my iPod in the pocket of my purse, I shove the ear buds into place and search for my classic rock playlist and select shuffle. When the Eagles' "Peaceful Easy Feeling" erupts into my ears, I laugh. It's exactly what this eagle girl needs.

I position myself facing the river, with my legs bent on top of the bench. Curling wafts of burning tiki-torch smoke mixed with jasmine tickle my nostrils. Soft lights ripple over the water. One hand lifts my Diet Coke to swish the bubbly liquid over my tongue, and the other plays with the iPod volume.

A quick tug on my shoulder causes me choke on the soda. "Verona!" Susie's wide eyes glare at me. I hope she isn't going to yell at me for escaping the racket. I yank an ear bud out.

"Yes?" My eyes say this. I'm still coughing out Coke.

"Ben asked me to find you."

"Where is he?" I can't see him anywhere in the shadows of the yard.

"In the garage with my dad. Come on. I'll show you." She pulls on my sleeve. I follow her along a path that twists around the house to the four-car garage on the side.

Ben comes out one of the doors with a flashlight pointing up at the huge grin on his face.

"Thanks for finding her." He trains the light on me while I block my eyes. Ben looks like he has ridden here on horseback with boots, faded jeans, and crisp denim shirt open over a dark T-shirt.

"Luka talked you into coming." He turns the flashlight off and sets it under his arm. "I'll have to remember to pay her later." His light touch on my shoulder makes my knees feel wobbly.

I ignore his joke. "Did you just get here?" I ask coolly, turning toward the garden, with the not-so-hidden meaning that I thought he would've been here before now. That I've been waiting. I wonder why I'm upset about it. Then I realize what it is. Waiting for him makes me feel like I'm just another fan. It makes me uncomfortable. Like we're not on even ground.

"Sorry. I spent the last hour tearing my room apart looking for my cell phone." He touches my arm gently. "Can I ask you something? I'm pretty sure I left my phone in my locker at the stadium. Would you mind driving me over there so I can get it?"

I pause to consider my options. I could stay here, sit off by myself, or worse, mingle with the crowd and risk long-term hearing loss. Or I could go for a ride with the hottest guy I've ever met. Hmm. I may be stubborn, and I may not be able to tell the difference between the Chortov brothers, but I'm not *that* stupid. "Okay, but I'll need to let Luka know."

"I'll tell her," Susie pipes in. I forgot she was still here. She takes off like it's a done deal.

"This is some house, isn't it?" Ben whispers as we climb the steps to the front.

"Yeah."

"The first time I came here I asked Susie how many families lived with her. In Russia, a place this big could house two-dozen people. Putin's own house is smaller."

"Really?"

"Actually, he never invited me over." Ben nudges me.

Pulling the Rover out of the neighborhood, I think of something to ask to break the awkward silence. "Are you planning to break into the stadium? Won't it be locked?"

Ben slumps down in the seat to remove a lone key from his front pocket. He dangles the key in my peripheral vision.

"Where'd you get that?"

"One day last year I stole my father's key, drove down to Oryol's Hardware and made a copy."

"Devious. The man's devious." I cluck my tongue behind my teeth three times in mock disapproval. "Why didn't you drive to the stadium before the party to get your phone?"

"Your tone is accusing me of further deviosity." He feigns outrage, crossing his arms. "Therefore, I'll refrain from answering that question."

"C'mon!" I wonder if he knows that *deviosity* isn't really a word.

"Nope. Not until you apologize for sullying my character."

"Me apologize? For what?" I stop the Rover in the middle of the road. "I'm not driving one more foot until you answer my question."

"Okay, I just wanted to spend some time with you where we don't have to shout to hear each other." His smile tells me he's pleased with himself.

"Double devious." I step hard on the accelerator and he lurches back.

"Watch it, Danica!"

For a while neither of us says anything. I look for a way to break the silence. "You played well in the game last night. You made two important tackles, right?"

Ben smiles. "Thanks for noticing." I pull into the front of the school and park the Rover toward the end of the staff parking area closest to the stadium entrance.

"This should only take a few minutes. Want to come?" I consider remaining in the SUV, but decide I don't want him to think I'm afraid to break the rules. And I don't want to wait for him anymore.

"Sure." Tossing my purse into the backseat, I lock the doors and twirl the keys in my hand. From the front of the stadium, I glance toward the intersection where the accident occurred just one week ago.

"I saw Angie Jett today." Knowing he isn't a big fan of hers, I wonder how he'll react.

He closes his eyes for a second. "How is she?"

"Pretty much like you would guess—a mess. But she seems a lot different from how you described her the other day. She seems more thoughtful or something."

"I suppose being stuck in a hospital bed gives you time to think." Then his tone softens. "But why did you go to see her? You don't really know her, do you?"

"No. Mr. Zeke asked me to." There is no way I'm going to tell Ben about the crazy eagle visions. Not until I know him much better. Like golden wedding anniversary better.

"Mr. Zeke. Interesting. With your grades you don't need extra credit projects." When we reach the front gate of the stadium, Ben's grabs my arm. He bends his head down, puts a finger to his lips. "Do you hear that?"

I listen for a second. "I don't hear anything." That's not technically true. I hear a constant buzzing which I figure marks the onset of Nucleus-acquired hearing loss.

"Sounds like a car. I'll bet someone's making out in the auto shop lot. Let's sneak up on them." His eyes light up with a mischievous glow in the spotlight reflection.

I hesitate as several good objections formulate in my head. But, seeing as I've already stepped out of my goody two-shoes role by coming this far, I think I might as well go along with the adventure. Ben pulls me around the dark side of the stadium by the auto shop. We trek through the grass around the corner into blackness.

As my eyes adjust to the dark, the grayish outline of a car in the shadows emerges. I feel a tingly thrill at the element of danger. Of course, the tingly thrill might also be all about the guy I'm with.

The engine hums, but no lights are on, inside or outside the car.

Crouching close to the ground at the back of the car, Ben points the flashlight beam on the license plate, and then quickly turns it off. "It's Georgeson's Toyota." He pulls back. "What's he doing here? I thought he doesn't like girls."

"What's that supposed to mean?" I say, with a bit of attitude. I like Ross and I got the impression that he likes me. Is it possible Ben knows this, and is trying to steer me away from Ross?

"I don't know. Some of the guys think he's gay. They call him *Boy George* and claim that Craig Hamilton is his ... you know, partner."

"What do you think? Do you join in?"

"Of course not." His whisper sounds hurt. "I don't care if he's gay or not. He's a nice kid. And he's a fine kicker. He should've stayed in the game."

"Well, let's see what's going on. Maybe he's got a girlfriend and just isn't telling anyone." We stand up slowly by the side of the car—Ben in front. He directs the light through the window. "That's weird. No one's inside."

"What's this thing?" I maneuver the flashlight to show the hose wrapped in duct tape extending into the rear window on the driver's side.

"What the—?" Ben shines his light into the front window and downward, where a body is sprawled across the front seat. He pulls at the door handle so hard I feel sure it'll rip off. I yank at the passenger-side handle. Neither budges. The doors are all locked.

He shouts to me, "Quick! Call 911! Georgeson's trying to kill himself!"

Ben wrenches the hose out of the window and the exhaust pipe with the same firm tug. He bangs on the driver's window with the flashlight. I feel around for my phone, and realize I've left it in the Rover.

"Break the back window!" I say. "Since it's already open a crack, it'll be easier." I clutch the keys in my hand and run toward the light at the front of the stadium.

I hear glass shatter behind me, and automatically turn around to look. At the same time, I trip over something hard and bulky. My new purple glasses fly off my face. My right knee pounds into the ground and the keys poke into my palm. The pain splinters out from both wounds, down my leg and up my arm. I groan, feel around the pavement for my glasses. When I can't find them, I pick myself up and limp toward the now-blurry light.

Rounding the front of the stadium, I lunge for the Rover. I mutter a "thanks" to no one in particular for the automatic opener on my keychain. I've got seven keys on my keychain. Without my glasses, it would've taken precious time for me to locate the right key and insert it into the keyhole. I grope around in my pocketbook until I feel my cell phone. My fingers intuitively press the right buttons and a woman answers.

"Hello. 911. What is your emergency?" a woman's voice asks, calmly, matter-of-factly.

"We need an ambulance at the auto shop behind the Colonial High School stadium on Memorial Drive." I'm amazed with the calmness of my response when my heart is pounding through my chest.

"What's happened?"

"A kid is trying to kill himself in his car—you know, with carbon monoxide." I can't believe those words were leaving my lips. At the same time, the vision of the demon Mammon flashes in my mind. That vision of the black-hooded murderer toggling into the huge leathery demon has been lurking in the dark recesses of my mind since we first spotted Ross' car. But I don't have time to think about that now. It's *irrelevant*.

"Are you with him?"

"No, I ran to my car to get my phone, but I'm heading back there from the faculty parking lot now."

"Help is on its way."

Sirens blare through the night air. A police car skids past the oak tree corner, correcting its direction on the straightaway.

When the driver sees me shuffling clumsily along the sidewalk in front of the stadium, he slows down. I point in the direction of the shop parking lot.

"That was fast." I hang up, and ignore the pain shooting both up and down my leg while crossing the parking lot toward the police car, and Ben. Something crunches under my left boot. It takes my brain a moment to register that it's my new glasses, but since it seems insignificant in light of what's happening, I keep moving.

An ambulance races past me. I hobble on to the blurry cars with their red and blue lights. Ben has pulled Ross onto the pavement and is pressing on his chest with bone-crushing force.

A bearded paramedic pushes Ben out of the way, and continues pounding on Ross' chest. A squat female paramedic with a spiked crew cut rushes to the other side of the limp body. Ben steps backward until he's next to me.

"Thanks for calling." Ben turns away toward the dark stadium. "I hope they can resuscitate him. I couldn't." I wonder if he's crying. I want to. I think it would be a relief to cry, but I never cry in front of people. My knees shake. I hug myself, sticking my hands under my armpits to keep them still.

The EMS team—mostly the man—hoists Ross' body onto a stretcher and into the idling ambulance. They've got an oxygen mask strapped to his grayish-green face. In a stupor, we start back toward the stadium.

"Hey, you two! Don't go anywhere." A policeman, with tight black curls and a bowling pin physique, appears from behind Ross' car. "You need to answer some questions."

He leads us to the police cruiser with the flashing blue lights. His partner, still in the passenger seat, opens the door. Officer Morris, Colonial's top cop—or at least that's what everyone calls him—looks up, a phone at his ear. He glances at Ben and me, but continues listening to someone we can hear barking expletives on the other end.

"What are your names?" The bowling pin policeman retrieves a pen and notepad from his pocket. He rests his backside against the side of the squad car.

"That's Ben Chortov—Colonial's linebacker," Officer Morris interrupts, cupping his hand over the telephone.

"Verona Lamberti," I volunteer, when Officer Morris doesn't introduce me. I suppose it's good that I've never met him personally. Before now.

"Verona, Ben. I'm Officer Pollock. Tell me everything from the beginning. Why were you here? How did you find the car? What did you do after you found it? You know—the relevant stuff."

Ben answers the questions systematically.

"Let me see if I've got this right. You came here to get your phone from your locker? Is that correct?"

Ben nods. "Yes, sir. That's right."

"How did you plan to get in?"

I looked up at Ben's contorted face, curious as to how he was going to answer this one, when Officer Morris closes his phone, and lets him off the hook. "Ben Chortov is Coach Chortov's son. The coach has got a key." Then he climbs from the cruiser, secures the phone on his belt, and walks to the Toyota.

"Of course." Officer Pollock writes down our cell numbers, and hands us each a card with the precinct's number. "Call me if you think of anything else that might be important."

"Is this yours?" Officer Morris returns with Susie's flashlight.

"Yes." Ben takes it from him.

"You can go now. Be careful. Thanks for doing the right thing."

"Do you think Ross will pull through?" I ask.

Officer Morris looks at the ground. "I hate to say it, because I don't want to believe it myself, but I'm pretty sure young Georgeson is dead. They'll try to revive him in the ambulance and in the ER, but it doesn't look good. Usually by the time they are that color, that cold—" He shakes his head. "Such a waste. He was a good kid."

With those words, I go numb. It starts at my fingertips and spreads to my lips and scalp.

"You feeling okay?" Officer Morris shines his light in my face. I blink fast, then blackness closes in all around me. Ben catches me before I hit the ground.

"Where are your glasses?" Ben asks when I come to. I'm still shaking—scenes from the vision of Ross being forced to stay in the car overwhelm me. I want to tell someone, but it's too wacky. That, and my mouth won't work.

I point in the general direction of the place where I fell. Officer Morris shines the flashlight there. Next to a mysterious dark object, the object that tripped me, are the shattered remains of my purple frames.

Officer Morris retrieves the items. I know from experience my glasses are beyond repair. The mystery object turns out to be a book-laden, black backpack. Exactly where it was lying in the latest eagle vision—the ACV vision.

"Yours?" Officer Morris asks us, holding the pack in the air.

Ben and I shake our heads, no. He digs around and finds a notebook with Ross Georgeson's name Sharpied across the cover. He dumps the backpack into the police cruiser's trunk and slams it shut.

"Can you drive?" Officer Pollock asks.

"I have a pair of glasses in the SUV." I'm appalled at how shaky my voice sounds.

"She can't drive. She can barely stand." Officer Morris looks at Ben.

"I'll drive, sir." Ben wraps his arms around me. I couldn't fall if I wanted to.

When we reach the sidewalk, I break from his embrace. "I'm fine now. I can drive." I concentrate on steadying myself, but the streetlights along Memorial are whirling around me, and with them, images of my flight, and the evil Mammon pressing a gun at Ross' face, Ross' red-rimmed, beautiful blue eyes pleading. And the note with the rose petals telling me to watch out… I feel incredibly weak all of a sudden.

"Really, Verona, I want to drive. I know you could, but would you please let me?"

"Okay." I hand him the keys and climb into the passenger side. He adjusts the seat as far back as it will go.

I stare out the window, willing my eyes to stay dry. The only time I've ever seen a dead body was when it was on display in a casket, and even then it was only one—my Newpa—my mom's father. I was five and he was sixty-five, looking dead, but dapper, in his dark-gray tuxedo, lying in a red-velvet-lined casket. Still, it was unnerving to see. At one point, when my parents were huddled around Newma and some visitors, I disconnected myself, unobserved, and went to see him. I wanted to tickle Newpa like he always tickled me, to see if I could wake him up.

When tickling his side didn't budge him, I touched his pink cheek, cold as the ice rink at Rockefeller Center. I pulled my hand back and squealed. My dad lifted me in his arms, but my Newma took me from him, reassuring in her melodic Irish accent, "Deary, that man lying there isn't really your Newpa. That's just his shell—like the one covering the hermit crab in Mrs. Bean's class."

"Will I lose my shell too, Newma?" I remember being afraid of roaming around without my body.

"Not until you're much older and it doesn't fit right anymore."

This time it's the dead body of the only kid from the jock table who bothered to go out of his way to be nice the day Leanne introduced me. And he didn't die because his shell didn't fit him anymore. He's been murdered. And I may be the only one who knows. I hunt through the glove compartment for tissues for my nose. I pluck out my nerdy John Lennon glasses, and set them on my lap.

When we're on Monroe Highway, Ben reaches for my hand. "You did really good back there." He squeezes gently. "Most girls would've freaked."

"Thanks. I can't believe you did CPR on him. Too bad it looks like we were too late." Too little, too late. But what if I'd told someone? Could I have prevented this?

Ben continues to hold my hand. His hand is warm and comforting and strong wrapped around mine, and once again I'm reminded of my Newpa—this time a memory from when he took my hand at the beach. I was equally frightened and fascinated by the pounding and receding motion of the waves. It felt like they were playing with me, but could I trust them? My Newpa promised he'd never let the waves hurt me. He promised he'd hold on. That's how I feel now.

At any other time it would have unnerved me to be touching Ben. But now all I can think of is Ross' lifeless body. The blur of the passing lights makes this moment surreal—another overused word, but at this moment, it really fits. I rub my swollen knee with my right hand and keep my head down.

The Rover slides to the side and Ben lets go of my hand to put it in park. I glance up. Ben parked in the same place we pulled out of an hour ago. So much can change in such a short time. I'm reminded of the skyline from this morning. Talk about déjà vu.

Two eagle visions.

Each predicting tragedy.

Both tragedies come true in less than a week's time. Coincidence? Math isn't my strongest subject, but I know that it is statistically improbable that these things are not somehow related.

"Wait. I don't want to go in yet." I glance at Ben and down at my nerdy glasses again.

"Look at me." Ben brushes his thumb on my cheek. "It's going to be okay. I'm with you."

I smile at him and feel a jolt at the concern in his eyes. "What are we going to say to everyone? Luka knows me too well. She'll sense something is wrong." That last part is totally true. But what I don't say, what I can't tell him, is that everything is wrong, really wrong, and it's Luka I need to talk to—alone.

Ben's fingertips tap a nervous rhythm on the dashboard of the car. I look over at him. "Do we really know for sure he's dead? Maybe we should cling to the slim chance that Ross can be revived. Maybe we should call the hospital."

"We could. Let's figure out what we'd say. I don't think they'll release that kind of information to just anyone." Ben continues his tapping as if it might help him think.

"We never got your phone." I dig through my purse for my phone.

Ben taps my arm. "Look. We're not going to have to say anything." He points to the driveway.

I throw on my glasses in time to see Mr. Sams and Coach Chortov conversing all the way to the house—probably formulating a strategy for making this awful announcement, the second in one week. This announcement will shock Colonial High even more than Angie's accident.

"I bet Officer Morris called Mr. Sams from the scene. Then Mr. Sams called Coach." Ben gets out of the car as the men enter the house. "They wouldn't be here if Georgeson was still alive." I clutch my stomach, knowing he's right as I follow him out of the car.

Nucleus continues to torture Susie's neighbors.

I think of the redhead misfit waiting alone for his friend who will never meet him anywhere again. "What about Craig Hamilton? Do you think we might find him and tell him separately?" If something happened to Luka I wouldn't want to find out about it in a crowd—especially one that couldn't be trusted to be supportive.

"Hamilton's here?"

"He was around back when we left."

"We could." Ben takes my hand again. "Mr. Sams will probably talk with Susie's parents before he tells everyone else. Let's run around the back and find him."

"You run—you're a lot faster than me. Bring Craig to the garages where we met earlier." I push him on.

Ben considers this plan, nods, then runs down the driveway and disappears around the side of the house before I can limp up to the place where the side driveway spins off of the circular one. I stop once to lean on a car and then move down the stairs, using the railing to keep as much weight as possible from my hurt knee. I rest on a low wall by the entrance to the garage door closest to the path leading to the back yard. Moths dance around a spotlight that highlights beds of orange chrysanthemums.

Ross Georgeson is *dead*.

I clip one of the orange blossoms off in my fingers and flick it. Dead. It hasn't sunk in yet.

Will I be able to tell Craig about Ross' death? The *apparent* suicide.

Suicide. Cold, wet icicles drip down my spine at that word. I shiver. The horrible questions that gush from that one word will flood this school, this community. Could we have known? What could we have done to stop it? And, of course, the tsunami of all questions: why?

But what if it isn't a suicide? What if he was murdered, like in my vision? A murder made to look like a suicide?

Craig, clutching a can of Stewart's root beer, follows Ben around the path. He eyes Ben warily, and then looks at the ground.

"What's up?" Craig looks confused when he sees me, but takes a sip of root beer in an effort to appear cool. "Someone said Mr. Sams and Coach Chortov are here, and now *you* want to talk to me?"

"Yeah, we do." I jump down from my perch in the shadow of the bushes, almost falling to the ground when my knee gives out, but Ben steadies me.

The band stops playing mid-song.

I can't find the words, so I look at Ben, and signal toward Craig. "Tell him."

Before Ben can say anything, Mr. Sams' voice rings through the night. Craig shifts his weight from sneaker to sneaker, scowling at us like he might be missing something in the back yard.

Ben claps Craig on the shoulder and for the first time I see, really see, how much bigger Ben is than the average-sized kid. At Ben's touch, Craig's eyes dart around like a caged animal looking for a gap. "Craig, listen to Mr. Sams. And dude, know that we're here for you."

Craig narrows his eyes at Ben, wriggles out from under his grip and turns toward the backyard.

Ben stops him. "Please."

"Students of Colonial High School, come closer to the patio. I have an important announcement to make. I would like the football players to follow Coach Chortov into the house, and the rest of you stay out here with me." Murmurs and shouts.

"What about us?" one of the girls calls out—probably a cheerleader not wanting to be separated from the team. Ben rolls his eyes.

"You stay here." We hear thumping up the backstairs mixed with chatter.

Craig starts kicking the wall. "This has something to do with Ross, doesn't it?" He raises his drink at Ben. "He said he was coming tonight even though you football players all act like complete morons. You know what I mean."

Ben looks down at his boots, grimaces, and decides not to wait for Mr. Sams. "Yes, Craig. It's about Ross. Ross is dead. I'm real sorry, man."

Craig's face turns pallid, making his freckles really stand out. "He's not dead. He can't be. I was with him three hours ago. He was fine." He hurls the soda can at the wall and backs up. "You're lying."

Ben's mouth opens like he wants to defend himself, but doesn't know what to say. I put my hand on Ben's arm, in an effort to persuade him not to say anything.

Mr. Sams' authoritative voice sounds again. Craig freezes in place, his face hardening in disbelief, then anger, as the principal gives a sterile summary of the death.

"You know what I think? I think *you* killed him." On the word *you*, Craig pushes all his weight into Ben, reminding me of the time Danny pushed into Dad when he first learned of our parent's impending divorce. Craig runs up the driveway, leaving Ben with his mouth open. He didn't move, but he looks surprised just the same.

Wide-eyed, I look up at Ben. "Catch him. He can't drive like this." Ben doesn't wait for me to finish; he bolts in linebacker fashion after Craig. "Don't hurt him," I whisper to myself, hobbling up the incline in his wake.

Craig, all angles and slippery, squirms with such ferocity that, despite the considerable weight difference, Ben is having a hard time keeping his body pinned to the grass.

Frenzied, Craig lashes out. "Ross would never kill himself! Admit it! You killed him!"

Ben looks to me for help.

I think of something that might work: "Craig, Ross was the nicest kid I met from the football team. He is the only one to even acknowledge my presence. I really wish I was able to get to know him better. I can see why you liked him so much."

Ben flashes a confused look my way that easily translates into the question, *What about me?* I wave him away. He turns back to the distraught figure under him.

"Do you think he liked *you*?" Craig shoots that barb in my direction.

"Let me take you home." Ben eases up a bit, but still holds Craig under his weight.

"I want you . . . to leave me . . . alone." Craig's voice sputters.

The front door opens. Mr. Sams jumps from the porch to the two boys sprawled in the yard. "What's going on?" He leans over the tangled bodies.

"Hamilton wants to drive, but I'm afraid to let him. The news about Ross hit him real hard." Ben stands, wiping grass off his shirt. Craig curls into a ball, hugging his knees.

"That's understandable. You and Ross were friends for a long time." Mr. Sams bends down on one knee to address the mute Craig. "You're coming home with me, son. We'll get your grandmother's car in the morning." He helps Craig to his feet and puts his arm around his shoulders as they head to the cul-de-sac.

We watch them for a bit, then I pull on Ben's arm. "I need to find Luka. She's got to be wondering what happened to me."

We start toward the front porch when Ben notices my uneven gait. "I forgot about your knee."

"It's nothing—hey, what do you think you're doing?" He lifts me up and folds me into his arms like a small child.

"Hush." *How Southern*, I think. "I'm taking you inside where I can have a look at the injury."

Two conflicting feelings wash over me at once: mortification at my helplessness, and comfort, as Ben curls me close to his muscular chest. I inhale the clean cotton aroma tinged with musk and cinnamon.

At the open door, Susie is giving a solemn farewell to a couple of seniors I don't know. When she sees us approaching the steps, me in Ben's arms, she asks, "What happened?" Not waiting for an answer, but seeing my bloodied knee poking through my ripped leggings, she steers us into a room to the right of the foyer. Susie turns on the lamps of a two-story library.

My mouth falls open at the books; the books line floor-to-ceiling shelves. A tall ladder on rollers makes it possible to reach the higher shelves. This is a room I could fall in love with. "I fell. My knee is a little bruised—that's all. It's nothing. Really." Why do they care about a little scrape when Ross is dead?

Ben sets me down on the burgundy leather couch.

"I'll get some ice." Susie heads for the door.

"Get Luka!" I shout after her.

Ben kneels down, removes my boot and stretches my torn leggings over my knee. Propping my legs up on the couch, Ben places a pillow under my wounded knee. "We need to wash and bandage this. Then we'll ice it." Dirt is caked into the wound, but fortunately, the bleeding is minimal. I'm too emotionally spent to fight him.

Luka bursts into the room, with Kolya lapping at her heels. "V, where have you been? Susie told me—" She gasps in horror at my knee, then she glares at Ben, hands on hips. "What did you do to my friend?"

"It wasn't Ben." I sit up higher on the couch. "He's been a complete gentleman. Even carried me in here from outside."

"I'm going to go get something to clean it." Ben heads for the kitchen, passing Susie on the way.

Susie hands a bag of ice to me. "I'll be back." She leaves to take care of departing guests.

"Carried you across the threshold, did he?" Luka raises her eyebrows. "How was it?"

"Not now, Luka." I wince when the cold ice touches my skin. "You're not going to believe what happened to us."

"Wait. Before you tell me about your romantic interlude, did you hear about the kid who offed himself?"

I raise my eyebrows, expecting the light bulb to pop on in Luka's head.

"I think it might have been the kicker from last—" Luka presses her hand to her mouth and speaks through her fingers. "Wait. That's the one from your lunch table. Oh my—"

I nod. "We found him in his car."

Kolya looks curious, but confused, leaning against the windowsill and twirling his cell phone in the air.

Speechless for a second, Luka slumps down into a wing chair. "Wow. I'm sorry you had to see that." And then, because she just can't let me get down, she smirks. "I don't ever want to hear how boring Jamestown is again. Got that?" She looks at my face, hoping for a smile at least, but then pulls back. "Where are your new glasses?"

I make the thumbs-down sign.

"What's that—the eleventh pair this year?"

"Fourth," I say, louder than I want to.

"Fourth what?" Ben removes the ice, then places a warm, soapy compress on my knee.

"I'll get that." Luka pushes him out of the way and begins washing my knee.

From the open library door, I see the football players filing out the front.

Coach Chortov appears at the door. He looks at Ben, and wrinkles his brow. "We need to talk," he says in a heavy accent. His gaze falls on Kolya, then Luka washing my leg, and finally blazes into me. He never even hints at a smile.

"Can it wait until I get home?" Ben asks.

The coach runs his huge hand across the back of his scalp. "Don't be late." The door bangs shut.

"Whew, your old man's a creeper." Luka is not known for having a filter on her tongue.

"He can be intimidating. But his bark is worse than his bite." Ben looks at the floor.

"What means *bark worse than bite*?" Kolya asks.

We chortle, but Ben explains, "It means that he yells a lot, but that's about it."

Kolya nods with understanding.

"He's got to be taking Ross' suicide hard. Last night I overheard him arguing with Mr. Sams about Ross." Ben spins his pocketknife with a grimace.

"What about?" I can see that Ben is bothered by something.

"Ross wanted out of football—he took himself out of the game after his bad kick. And Coach—my father—was all for him leaving the team. But Mr. Sams said that Ross' father insisted he keep playing. At least that's what I gathered from Coach's end of the conversation, and his temper after."

"Why would his father insist he play when he didn't want to?" Luka places the bandage on my clean knee.

"I'm not sure—but I get the idea that Georgeson's old man is used to people pole-vaulting when he tells them to jump, and since he's head of the school board, Mr. Sams was caught in the middle—especially with budget cuts looming over his head."

"I wonder how Ross' father feels now." I swat at Luka's hand and affix the bandage.

We're deep in our thoughts when Susie bounds in. "Y'all can stay as long as you want. I'll be in the kitchen."

"We'll let ourselves out." Ben and Luka help me to my feet. Luka carries the ice and my boot while I limp out, my arms draped around the cousins' shoulders. When I'm safely in the driver's seat, Ben gives me a gentle hug. His eyes look faraway, sad. I'd give anything to know what he's thinking, but there are too many people around to ask.

When I pull out of the neighborhood, Luka turns to me like she wants to say something. She's been quiet for several minutes, an uncharacteristically long time for Luka.

"What? You want to say something. What?" I figure she wants to chew me out for leaving her at the party for so long—that's what I'd probably do in her shoes.

Luka swallows. "I don't want you to feel bad about this question. But I've got to know. Was it like the ACV—the vision you had in art class?"

I inhale. I didn't want to go there yet. There are too many feelings attached to these visions. The number one being guilt for not doing more to try to stop it. My mouth trembles and it's too hard for me to say anything, so I nod.

Luka sighs. "I think this is beyond the point where you need to tell someone besides me."

"I know." I take another deep breath and exhale. "The problem is, I don't know who I can trust. Who's going to believe that Ross didn't kill himself—he was actually murdered by some gun-toting demon?"

"You've got a point; but there has to be someone who'll believe you. Did you tell me the demon's name was Mammon?"

"Yeah, the greedy one. That's what the star lady called him."

"You know, I'm pretty sure there's a character named Mammon in the book I'm reading for AP Lit."

"You're kidding, right?"

"No, I'm serious. Paradise Lost."

"Milton?"

Luka nods. "I'd show you, but I didn't bring it with me. Too heavy, and I'm already several chapters ahead of the class."

"I'll bet my mom has it."

When we get home, my mom is waiting in her robe, ready to go to bed. I tell her I scraped my knee and broke my new glasses when I tripped. Of course she doesn't question it—just rolls her eyes—since my klutziness has been a running family joke for as long as I can remember. Revealing Ross' death and all that can wait until tomorrow. There's so much to explain, we'd be up all night. Also, I'm not sure how she'll react to my leaving the party to drive Ben to the stadium. Not good, I'm thinking.

Under the pretense that she needs it for her paper, Luka gets my mom to lend her Milton's famous book. "You're reading that heavy tome in high school?"

"It's heavy in more ways than one, Dr. Newman," Luka jokes. "But it's a college-level course."

In the privacy of my bedroom, Luka rummages through the pages, then hands the book to me, pointing.

I read:

> *Mammon led them on--*
> *Mammon, the least erected Spirit that fell*
> *From Heaven; for even in Heaven his looks and*
> *thoughts*
> *Were always downward bent, admiring more*
> *The riches of heaven's pavement, trodden gold,*
> *Than aught divine or holy else enjoyed*
> *In vision beatific. By him first*
> *Men also, and by his suggestion taught,*
> *Ransacked the centre, and with impious hands*
> *Rifled the bowels of their mother Earth*
> *For treasures better hid. Soon had his crew*
> *Opened into the hill a spacious wound,*
> *And digged out ribs of gold..*

"Holy streets of gold," I say.

"Nothing holy about this guy, V. This is your demon. He's leading someone, someone *human*, to murder," Luka retorts. "I think if we find the ribs of gold he's after, we'll probably find the killer. I'm gonna see what Google knows about this Mammon."

Why didn't I think of that? I Google-cheat everything else.

Luka flips open her MacBook Pro, and within seconds, she's got her eyes open wide. "Is this your demon?" She turns her laptop toward me, looking at my face.

The image, simply called Mammon, is a painting by George Frederick Watts from 1885. It shows the monster in my visions, gold crown and robes, fleshy face, and huge hands. He's sitting with bags of what can only be gold or money on his lap and by his feet. But that's not the worst of it. Under one bloody foot is the body of a young man, presumably dead. His hand rests on the head of a young woman, who is either dead or unconscious. I can't help but think of the two bodies as Ross and Angie.

My hand goes to my heart. I feel like it's skipped a beat. I kiss my silver cross.

"I take that as a *yes?*"

Feeling my eyes well up, once again I can only nod.

Sunday, September 20th
679 Days to Home Free

RAINDROPS BATTERING THE PLATFORM ROOF muffle my goodbye to Luka as she climbs the steps of the train. She's headed to Baltimore to spend the night with her elderly Aunt May before returning to New York tomorrow.

Back at home, with a fire keeping us cozy, my mom and I sit on opposite sides of the living room. My mom corrects student papers, while I pretend to read endless AP Human Geography handouts at the dining area table. Mostly I worry and wonder. *What is happening to me? Who should I tell?*

I look at my mom. One side of her mouth is pulled in like she's deep in concentration. *Will she even believe me?* She'll worry about me. The first thing she'll do is tell Dad, and then he'll worry about me, too. I sigh. Still, I need to chance it. If my parents worry, or I have to spend some time on a psychologist's couch, so what? If that's what it takes to keep someone else from getting hurt or killed, it's worth it, right? I take a deep breath and say, "Mom?"

The exact moment she looks up from her book, the doorbell rings.

"I'll get it." I trip over Max, catching myself before falling again.

Outside, a soggy Ben winks at me, his sad grin hiding something under its normalness, something that both intrigues and scares me. Water drips from his hair and cascades down his jacket. He is all wet and shiny. I resist the urge to touch him. "Can we talk out here? I'm soaked and I don't want to give your mom a reason not to like me."

I join him on the misty porch. Ben leans over and shakes the water from his hair like Max after a bath

"Hey!" I raise my hands to block the spray.

"Sorry." Ben looks down at his boots.

"How are you?" I tilt my head down to try to see beyond the long black bangs hiding his eyes.

He doesn't answer right away. Just puts his hands in his pockets and leans against the doorjamb like he's trying to find the right words. "The whole thing with Ross keeps playing over in my mind. I feel like there's something I could've done to stop it, but I'm not sure what." Did Ben have a prescient vision about Ross' death too? What if everyone has these weird vision-things, but no one talks about them? I immediately discount this theory. Luka would've told me if she had them or had ever even heard of them before.

"Ben," I say, putting my hand on his arm. "Don't be so hard on yourself. Even his best friend didn't see this coming—so there's no way *you* could have." But what if *I* did see it coming, and could've stopped it?

Now it's his turn to tilt his head. "No. I mean, when the guys teased him in the locker room…" He paused. "I ignored them. I thought the whole thing was stupid. If I'd known it would lead to this, I would've done something. I should've done something to stop it anyway. Maybe Craig's right. Maybe I killed him by not stopping the other guys." He swings his head back to move his wet hair off of his forehead and his fists clench. His eyes look angry—like he wants to punch something.

"Nothing you could've done would have stopped this from happening." I know in my heart this is true as it pertains to Ben, but I can only hope it applies to me, too.

"I want to believe that." He takes a deep breath and looks at his hand, examining it like he's trying to read his future. "But that's not why I wanted to see you." His brown eyes caress my face in a way that leaves me feeling all slushy-soft. "Do you have plans for lunch tomorrow?"

"No." It comes out before I have the chance to think. "Other than history homework."

"Can I take you to lunch at noon?"

"Where will we be going?"

"It's a surprise." Ben motions to my leg. "How's that knee?"

"Bruised, but the swelling is down."

"Good." Ben smiles at me and runs his fingers through his hair. "Now I need to drive Kolya to the airport. His mom's flying in from Russia."

I'm just going to ask Ben what he thinks about Luka and Kolya when he leans over and brushes his lips to my cheek. Then he jumps into the storm, yelling, "Noon tomorrow!"

My fingertips graze the surface of my cheek. It is getting harder to deny that he's interested in me. Not that I *want* to deny it. But this gushy, full feeling in my chest is new territory for me, completely different than my first encounter with a guy, and I'm not sure of the rules here.

Leaning against the door, I watch his truck lights disappear down the street. I gag at the memory of Tony Rubowski's sloppy-wet, banana-reeking kiss the day he pinned me against my locker. The whole thing caught me off-guard. I couldn't believe he would try to kiss me, not after I'd torn his note up right in front of him the previous year. That day, the drills we learned in self-defense class came to good use. I instinctively brought my knee to his groin. I did feel guilty when I saw the pain I had inflicted as he squirmed on the hallway floor, hands between his legs. But I got over it. The payoff: Tony Rubowski never tried to kiss me again.

I never told my mother about that incident—she would've overreacted. Probably call the principal and have Tony suspended, or worse. She would've made me read every news story printed on date rape she could find, and working at the newspaper back then, she could've found them all. She'd have enrolled me in tae-kwon-do.

Instead, I called my mother's mother, my Newma. She laughed, and then told me, "Good for you, darling! That *eejit* was asking for it."

That gave me the answer I was looking for. My mother isn't the right person to tell something like this: she's too close to me… and she overreacts. I take out my phone and look at the time, count the time difference to Galway, Ireland. There's still an hour before she'll be going to bed.

I sit on the porch chair and call Newma via SKYPE, hoping the rain won't get any harder. As it was, the tin roof above my head would make it difficult to hear.

The phone rang several times before she answered. "Hello? Verona, is that you?"

"Yes, Newma, it's me. Can you hear me?"

"Yes. Is everything alright? Your mum told me you're making friends, now. She forgets how hard it was…"

I knew I'd better stop her from steering the conversation away, or I'd never get a chance to tell her. "Newma, I need to ask you something, but first, you need to know it's a secret. Mom can't know."

"Secrets are my forte! I relish a good secret. Is it about that fella who plays American football?"

"Well, sort of. No, not really. I mean, he was there this last time. But no…Let me start at the beginning."

"That would be grand."

I tell Newma everything about the PCQ vision and Angie's accident, and then the ACV vision and the discovery of Ross Georgeson's body.

Newma listens, and then gets very quiet. She tells me she's got a secret for *me*. "If yer ma should find out, she won't let you visit me in November, or any other time, fer sure."

"Okay," I say, wondering how this secret could possibly relate to my prophetic visions.

"You know the story of your birth, right?"

I knew I was born in Galway when my mother rushed across the ocean to see her dying aunt, my Newma's sister, Claire. I came three weeks early. I told her what I'd heard: How at the precise moment Aunt Claire died, my mother went into labor. "My mother told me that I was born as Aunt Claire died." Meaning, it's no secret. Newma and her other sisters told her to name me Claire, but the woman with the normal name—Cheryl—thought it would be too creepy.

"Do you know what day that was?"

I wanted to say, *Who doesn't know their own birthday?* but thought it would sound too sarcastic. "November first."

"Well, of course you know the date. I'm referring to the day. It's a special Holy day."

Day? Date? What's the difference? I say, "I'm not sure what you mean, Newma."

"It's the feast of All Saint's. The second day of Hallowtide."

"You mean the day after Halloween?" Having my birthday right after Halloween meant that all my birthday parties were masquerades. My parents insisted that it made sense to combine the two, which meant where most kids' birthday parties meant balloons, candles, games, and presents, I got princesses, werewolves, witches, and ghosts. Instead of streamers, I got cobwebs and bats and spiders. When I pointed this out, my mother said I should be happy I wasn't one of those kids born on Christmas. Who'd want her birthday upstaged by someone who'd been dead for two thousand years?

"Halloween, the modern way to say *All Hallows Eve or Hallowmas*, falls on the ancient Celtic feast of Samhain. This day historically marked the end of the harvest, the end of the light days and the beginning of the dark days. It was a time to remember loved ones who had died, and a time to slaughter the beasts. But you were born early in the morning of All Hallows, which we now call All Saints Day."

"That's interesting, but not a secret. What does that have to do with my visions?"

"After you were born, you mother, poor dear, was physically, mentally, and emotionally exhausted. Not just because of your birth, dear, but because she so loved her Aunt Claire. The doctors gave her medicine to assure that she'd sleep like the dead. That's when I took you."

She took me? "You took me? Where? Why? I've never heard about this."

"I brought you back hours before she woke up. She never knew. If she did, there's no telling—"

"But, Newma. Why did you take me?"

"Darling, you were born on All Saint's Day. It's a known omen. Being born on a high holiday like that means you're special. I took you to be blessed, to be consecrated to God."

Now I know why this was a secret she had to keep from my mom. My mother and Newma had had many fights over religion. When I was only seven, my mother fired my Newma from babysitting me after school because, in my mother's words, she was filling my mind with superstitious nonsense. Newma and I were both brokenhearted, but my mother insisted she never try to influence me again. That's when Dad started working from home. "Where did you take me?"

"I bundled you in the hospital blankets and hid you under my mac. It was quite a circuitous route to the Cathedral, and it was storming so bad and you were such a wee thing, I prayed the whole way you wouldn't catch your death..."

"St. Nicholas' Cathedral?" I remembered passing this cathedral many times when walking from the shops of Galway to the waterfront to feed the swans.

"Aye. The priest, Father Burns, God bless him, died the following year after a terrible bout with lung cancer. But that's a story for another day. At the altar he waited, smelling like the bar he'd just come from, with one of the nuns who cleaned the church, Sister Agatha—or was it Agnes? Either way, the poor dear's face was a maze of scars—like she'd fallen into a fire."

"What did they do to me?"

"Well, I unwrapped you and handed you to the sister. I don't think you were sleeping, but your eyes were closed. She set you on the altar. Father Burns prayed over you, then dipped his thumb into the holy water and blessed your forehead. That's the usual way. But then he did something that made me think he'd gotten himself fluthered."

"Fluthered?"

"Drunk. No secret, the good father favored the Jameson." Newma got quiet, like she was remembering something and wanted to get it completely right.

"Yes? What did he do?"

"He dipped his forefinger into the holy water again and touched your eyelids."

"They don't usually do that?"

"No. The sister gave him a look when he dipped his finger, wondering what he was doing. Then he touched your eyes and made the sign of the cross over you. Your eyes flashed open, and at the same time, a great light beamed from an old quatrefoil on the wall, one that'd been there forever, but I'd never noticed. The light surrounded you, like you were cradled in it, embraced by warmth. You reached for something only you could see, and the light disappeared…"

"What happened?"

"Father pulled his hand away and Sister blessed herself, but we were staring at the quatrefoil on the wall. The source of the light."

"Why? What was it?"

"It was an eagle."

We both got quiet for a long time.

"What do you think happened?" I finally asked.

"Father Burns said it was a flash of lightening that reflected off the eagle quatrefoil. But when Sister pressed him, he couldn't explain why he'd touched your eyes. I remember the sister smiling like she knew something, but wasn't inclined to tell us. I was more anxious to get you back to the hospital before your mother woke up than to try to figure out what had happened. After all, it only lasted a second or two. I thought, maybe it *was* just the lightning. But now… these eagle visions. Verona, you're right not tell your mother. She won't understand. Find someone else to confide in—someone whose heart isn't closed to the supernatural. Because that's exactly what this is. Supernatural."

III

Eagle Feeding Habits

Monday, September 21ˢᵗ
678 Days to Home Free

I PRETEND TO BE ABSORBED in the scenery of the upscale neighborhood Ben's driving through, but secretly I steal glances at Ben, at his muscles flexing under a white T-shirt when he shifts gears. "Did your aunt arrive okay?" I steer the conversation as far from Saturday night as possible. Our first official date—quite honestly, my first date ever—and I don't want our time tainted with death and regret.

"It went great. Except for a few basic words, my Aunt Nadia can't speak English, so Kolya translated for me. She couldn't believe how much I'd grown, and how new and big everything is in America. Where she lives, most people don't even have indoor plumbing."

I grimace, thinking of running to an outhouse at night in the snow or heating up bathwater, then remember that that's where Ben's from, too. "Are you close to her?"

"Yes. Well, I used to be. Alex and I moved in with her and Uncle Vasa when my mother died. We were two. That's when Coach came to America. He found work as a mechanic, and put himself through college. When we were almost seven he came for us, promising we would visit Russia often. We never made it back, though—there was always football camp or money issues getting in the way. Through the years, Aunt Nadia sent us letters and cards and little presents."

"That's nice of her."

"Yeah, but it started to get hard. Alex and I both lost our Russian, and she can't speak much English, so we're kind of helpless without a translator. I know it makes her sad. So Kolya's agreed to help me relearn Russian."

"If you put your mind to it, you'll be fluent in no time."

"Then I'll also be able to talk to my uncle when he calls."

"Your Uncle Vasa? Why didn't he come with her?"

Ben's jaw tightens. "Uncle Vasa died two years ago. Aunt Nadia is my mother's sister, and Uncle Vasa was her husband. My other uncle, Oleg, is Coach's brother. He calls almost every Saturday. '*I talk to you father.*'" Ben wrinkles his brow, and adds a menacing Russian accent. I can't help but laugh. "I'm pretty sure that's the extent of Oleg's English. And Aunt Nadia's isn't any better."

Ben pulls his red pickup truck onto a gravel lot next to a weathered marina. Boats of different sizes and styles are moored to the docks, jutting into the James River.

Grabbing a quilt and basket, we head toward a strip of golden sand broken by a bald cypress with tentacle roots sucking at the waterline. The aroma of fish mingles with saltwater, and reminds me of long-ago family vacations at the Jersey Shore. Back when we were a family. And the salty sea smell reminds me of skimming the churning water as an eagle. Back when Ross was still alive. *Cut it out, Verona.* No death, no regret, remember?

I help Ben spread the blanket over the sand beneath the cypress and drop down on one side of it. "It's hard to believe this place is so close to home." *Did I just call Jamestown home?*

"I love it here," Ben says, then quickly adds, "when it's quiet. A lot of kids at school come down here to party."

"Do you like to party?" I ask.

"I tried it, but really didn't like it. I think there are better ways to get high than drinking beer and car racing."

"High?" I ask. Ben doesn't look like a druggie. His eyes are clear.

Ben laughs. "No, not drugs either. Unless you count caffeine. I prefer to get my kicks in simpler ways."

"Like?"

"I don't know." Ben looks uncomfortable. "Like being here. A picnic—you know, something simple. Beautiful."

Simple and *beautiful* are good words to describe this beach. Beautiful could also describe the guy on the blanket with me. Simple? Not so much. He's not matching up with any of the stereotypes I had of him.

"When was the last time you went on a picnic?" Ben asks.

Hmm. *Could he be prying?* "Does tailgating at a Giants game count?" I sift the cool sand in my hand.

"No. Not at all."

"What? How are the rising fumes of tar and asphalt, beer and burgers, mixed with New Jersey smog, so different from this?"

Ben laughs. "You saw the Giants play at the Meadowlands?"

"Many times." I pull out a perfectly formed seashell and hold it to my ear.

"That's funny. I wouldn't have taken you for a sports fan." Ben's bare feet rest on the sand past the end of the blanket. He hugs his knees.

"Then you would be perceptive. My dad and brother are the sports nuts of our family. Tom Lamberti—that's my father—writes for the sports section of the same newspaper where my mother used to be an editor, so I've been to more ball games than I can count. His specialty is baseball, but football is his next favorite." I throw the shell at the water. Naturally, it misses.

"Cool."

"Personally, I think cleaning my closet is more fun than baseball." I grin. "Anyway, two years ago I refused to do the *take your daughter to work* thing anymore. By then Danny was old enough to keep him company." I take my sneakers off, burying my toes in the sand, moist and cool from yesterday's monsoon.

"Danny?"

"My seven-year-old brother."

"You never told me you had a brother." Ben's eyes ask me to go on.

"You want to know about Danny?"

Ben nods. I never imagined a high school football star would give a whit about my little brother.

"Okay. The thing about Danny is, he's curious: 'Why is the sky blue? What would happen if all the birds die?' Normally his questions just make me laugh, unless I'm trying to actually *do* anything. When my family split last spring, we really split—male and female. Danny lives with my dad in New York. But we visit every-other weekend." I pick up a handful of sand and watch it sift through my fingers.

Ben nods like he'd like to hear more, but I don't want to go down that depressing road, picturing Danny's upturned face asking, *Why doesn't Mommy love Daddy anymore?* I change the subject. "You made lunch?"

"Homemade turkey sandwiches, chips, and soda." Ben hands me my food.

"This is so sweet of you, Ben." I wipe my hands on my jeans.

"Verona, guys don't like to be called *sweet*," he responds, with a scowl. "It's not manly."

"What would you prefer?"

"Cool. Talented. Brilliant." He looks at me, smiling and expectant.

"More like pompous. Arrogant. Spoiled." I'm certainly not going to pander to his overinflated ego just because he brought me a turkey sandwich. I take a bite and chew, staring at the river, wondering how I could've thought he'd be any different than this. Look at him! He is undoubtedly used to girls fawning all over him. If he expects me to be like one of the Amber-types, I'm determined to drop ice down his shirt—figuratively speaking.

Ben's eyes open wide. He sips his Dr. Pepper, looking hurt. "You're tough."

"Why? Because I won't kiss your feet like the cheerleaders do?" I respond impetuously, feeling my face redden.

"Whoa, whoa, slow down. Trust me—I don't want one of those yackers. Didn't I tell you the other night that I like you because you're not like them?"

"Yackers?" That's a word I never heard in New York.

"You know, the girls who spend all their time gossiping, scheming... I hate the drama. Most guys hate the drama."

"Your brother doesn't seem to mind." I roll my eyes.

Now it seems it's Ben's turn to get annoyed. He says softly, forcefully, "I am *not* my brother."

"I'm sorry. I didn't mean to imply that you were." I put my hand on his arm so he can see I mean it.

He wrinkles his mouth. "It's just that I'm always being compared to Alex. I'm tired of living in his shadow all the time—"

"It looked to me like *you* were the star of the game Friday night."

"A fluke," he says with a snort. "Most game days *he's* the one getting all the glory, which, by the way, is fine with me... Just sometimes I wish...like, next weekend, we'll be touring colleges around the state. Most of the coaches are way more interested in Alex than me. I guess that part hurts."

"How do you know that they're more interested in him?"

"A quarterback gets most of the attention—in the pros, they're usually the highest-paid player on the team. But I don't really want it—the attention or the money." He kicks the sand with his foot. "Arrogant? Really?"

I ignore his question. I haven't really decided what to think about him yet. I just know he's so impossibly gorgeous, it makes sense for him to be arrogant along with it. "What *do* you want?" I recoil when I think how leading that question sounds. I hope he doesn't think I'm flirting, asking if he wants *me*.

Ben is silent. He stretches back on the blanket with his hands behind his head, his elbows out to the side. His position affords me an extraordinary glimpse of his muscular chest and arms bulging out of his navy T-shirt. I avert my gaze and forced myself to focus on a sailboat in the distance.

"What do I want? Besides you not thinking I'm a pompous jerk?" He chuckles. "You'll laugh."

"No, I won't." I recline next to him. "Promise."

He takes a few deep breaths. I wait. "See those clouds?" he asks. "I want to fly through them. I want to fly higher, above them, where it's a different world."

I gulp. For the second time in two days, I wonder if he has visions of being an eagle, too. But that would be too weird. So I ask, tentatively, "How do you plan to do that?"

Ben rolls to his side. "By becoming a pilot." He smiles. "What were *you* thinking?"

"Oh, yeah. A pilot … of course."

"What do *you* want?" I can feel his gaze on me, but don't turn to meet it.

"Not so fast. I still have questions for you." It's way more fun learning about his dreams than talking about myself. Besides, what I want takes me back to New York, away from him. Telling the truth would release a freezing rain on our picnic.

"Can you learn to be a pilot at the colleges you're planning to visit?"

"No. I'd have to get a degree in something else."

"Then why don't you go to flight school?"

"Flight schools don't have football teams." Ben chuckles at the idea.

"So you want to play football in college …and then go to flight school?"

"If it were up to me, I think I'd go straight to flight school. But Coach is obsessed with Al and me playing football for some big college team."

"The same team? At the same college?"

"That's the plan that's been drilled into our heads."

"Don't you think that's a little …?"

"Controlling?"

"Yeah, *controlling* would work." I don't want to question Ben's father, but I'd always been taught to find my own way, chart my own course, pursue my own dreams. I'd hate it if my mother pushed me to be an editor, or my father insisted I go to college for journalism.

"It's the plight of being a son of Theo Chortov. We've definitely been coached into what he thinks we should be. I'm just biding my time until I can break free. Alex is different. He is forever looking for Coach's approval. Maybe that's the curse of the firstborn. I just want to rebel. Maybe that's the second son's job."

"Alex is the oldest?" I roll on my side to face him.

"By two minutes."

"You look astonishingly alike—even for identical twins."

"But you can tell us apart, right?" Ben frowns when I don't answer right away. I'm remembering my blunder the other night at the party, wondering if Alex told him about it. "I've got a good ten pounds on him," he adds.

You see a big-screen TV on the wall; are you supposed to be able to tell if it's a fifty-eight inch screen or a sixty-inch screen? *It's big either way, right?* But if you saw them on display next to each other… "If I saw you standing together, I'm sure I could," I say. "But do me a favor; don't pierce your ear, okay?"

"Alex only did that because Angie begged him to. I don't need my father calling me *gullaboy* too."

"Gullaboy?"

"It's Russian for the light blue of this afternoon sky." When I look completely flummoxed, he adds, "And it's slang, and not in a good way, for a gay guy. My dad called Alex *gullaboy* for a week after he got his ear pierced—even at practice. I'd just as soon not bring that kind of attention to myself."

"So *gullaboy* means gay," I shake my head. "My first Russian word. Too bad I can't use it without hurting someone's feelings." I cup my hand to my mouth, hoping Ben won't make the connection to the locker room jokes.

"You're thinking about Ross and Craig?" Ben moves a curl from in front of my eyes to behind my ear.

I nod, hold his stare for a second, and then plop onto my back, willing my heart to slow down. He's already reading my thoughts. Touching my hair. Am I ready for this? *Is anyone ever ready for this?* "How did you know that I was thinking of them?"

"Your face reflects your thoughts. And honestly, I was thinking about them, too. Coach—my father—often referred to Ross as *gullaboy*. He only said it at home, but Alex and his friends picked up on it." He grabs a fistful of sand. "And now Georgeson's old man wants these same guys—Ross' so-called friends from the football team—to carry the coffin."

"Are you going to be a pallbearer—that's what it's called, right?"

"Yeah, somehow I made the cut. I barely knew Ross Georgeson. I never tried to stop the harassing. It isn't right."

"What about Craig Hamilton?"

"He wasn't asked." Ben sits up and gazes out at the water. "When I questioned my father about it, he blew a gasket."

"Are you going to do it?" I rock up, hug my knees, and peer into the distance at the same boat whose sails hang limp in the still air.

"Do I have a choice?"

"We always have choices."

Ben brushes sand off his feet. "Verona, can I ask you something?"

"Okay." I hope I haven't trapped myself with that last statement.

"Will you be my date for the homecoming dance?"

This question is so off-topic that I clamp my mouth shut, struggling for a reply. When in doubt about what to say, always ask questions. A technique I learned from the indomitable Dr. Newman.

"When is the homecoming dance?" I'm not stalling or trying to be funny. I really don't know, because until this minute, I haven't given the homecoming dance a solitary thought.

"Verona Lamberti, you've got to be the only girl at Colonial who doesn't know when homecoming is." Ben flashes an adorable, one-dimpled smile. "That's another reason to like you." He touches my cheek. Just for a second. "It's a week from this Friday."

I look away. My cheeks feel hot all of a sudden.

"What's the matter? Don't you want to go with me?" I can't tell if Ben sounds incredulous or hurt—but since my last inference got me in trouble, I decide to go with hurt.

"It's not you. Really. I'd love to go with you. Here's the thing: First of all, I can't dance. I mean … I've never even *been* to a dance before."

"Well, that's a relief." Ben shakes his head.

"Why?"

"Because there's very little of what most people would call dancing that goes on at a Colonial High dance. Mostly a lot of bumping and grinding. I'm glad to hear that you're not into that." Ben grins mischievously. "It's fun to watch the chaperones freaking out, trying to keep the kids on the dance floor from becoming parents in nine months."

My eyes open wider than the rims of my glasses. "And you want to go to this?"

Ben shrugs. "I won't expect you to dance like that—in fact, I'd be upset if you wanted to. We'll just hang out with everyone, eat and sway back and forth to the occasional slow dance." He pauses for a minute, then says, "First reason shot down. What's the second reason?" His dark eyes are a sponge that absorb all the light from around them. I turn away.

"I'm supposed to visit my dad that weekend. I fly up to New York once a month. It's not written in stone or anything.

I could ask my mom if she bought the plane tickets yet. Can I tell you tomorrow?"

"Are you going to Ross' funeral tomorrow?"

"I don't know. You think it'd be okay to miss school?"

"Yes, it says on the school's website that students attending the funeral can have the day off. I wonder how many will go just to ditch school."

"I only met Ross the week before he, um, died. Still, somehow I feel connected to him, since we're the ones who found him. So, yes, I think I'll go," I say haltingly. *Was that my voice?* If I were to list the top ten places I never want to visit before I die, funerals would be right up there with hospitals.

"Good. I'll feel better knowing you're there," Ben says.

I recline with my head resting on my hands.

We stare up at the clouds and play the shape game. He picks out a dinosaur, the Frito Bandito, and a ghost. I ease my head back on the sand; point out a crocodile, a soldier, and Angelina Jolie's lips. Ben points out to a cloud, and says it's a bowling pin.

I say, "No, it's Officer Polluck," and he cracks up. He reaches for my hand, and I let him cover it in his. My hand feels delicate in his warm grip. For the first time since I knew my parents were splitting, I have a sense of security—like maybe things really will turn out okay in the end with someone other than me in control. It's like a part of me is floating high, up in the clouds. Surrendered and free. I wonder if Ben feels the same.

"Ben, look! A bald eagle." The mighty bird soars in circles high over our heads.

Ben squeezes my hand. "Wouldn't it be cool to hang-glide like that?"

I'd love to tell him about the time I was an eagle gliding over the stadium. Something inside me feels intimately connected to Ben by the sight of the eagle spiraling in and out of the clouds above us. Like it's a sign of some sort. Like both our deepest desires are somehow contained in the great bird's freedom of movement.

Ben's right. It's amazing how, in this moment, in the quiet afternoon, with the warm sun shining on us, the sand molding to my body, lying next to this hot guy, everything is so warm and tingly and perfect. I feel a kind of high. A marvelous, healthy sort of high.

And, as my rotten luck would have it, the perfect buzz is shattered by a loud horn blast. The eagle flies off straight across the river. Ben shields his eyes from the sun to get a look at the intruder.

"It's Alex." He rocks up to his feet. "Wait here. I'll see what he wants." Before I can even make it to my feet, he's halfway down the beach, sand flying from his bare heels. He slows down when he gets close to the driver's window. Ben leans on the driver door.

I don't know what to do. Wait. I hate waiting. And I hate it that the eagle got scared away and our moment together was ruined. Why did Ben tell Alex where he was taking me? The water caresses the shore invitingly so I decide to see how cold it is. I dip my toe, but yank it out quickly. The water's glacially cold.

Without warning, I'm hoisted off my feet, suspended a couple feet from the freezing river. "Put me down!"

"You want down? Here?" Ben loosens his grip as though he's ready to tumble me forward into the frigid river, but catches me before I hit the surface.

"Back there." I work to loosen my arms from his tight grip.

"Gosh, Verona. You're lighter than a football." Ben tosses me in the air to prove it.

"I am not amused," I say in my most severe voice, hoping I sound intimidating, but worried I only sound like my mother.

"Relax. I would never hurt you. Watch your sore knee."

As he lets me go, I glide down his solid body to the sand at the river's edge. A charge from his body sends a current down the length of my spine. I back up protectively. Out of his reach, I kick a clump of sand at him and run—well, more like hobble—back to the blanket.

"Home free," I say proudly, reminiscent of the games we played as children.

Ben looks down.

"Unfortunately, I do have to take you home. Coach called a meeting of the lucky pallbearers. He's probably worried we'll drop the coffin or something." He spins the keys in his hand. "That's Coach for you. He's going to drill us on gliding a box down an aisle."

On the drive home, I get up the nerve to ask him, "Why do you always call your father Coach—never Dad?"

Ben swallows. "Yeah, I guess it must sound weird. When we got to America, we never thought of him as Dad. To us, Uncle Vasa was our only *Papa*. We didn't call him anything. He asked why we didn't call him *Papa*—the Russian word for Dad. When we insisted he wasn't our Papa, this strange man who took us away from our family, our home, our village, said we could call him *Coach*. So that's what we did. It stuck." Ben pulls over in front of our townhouse. "You'll let me know tomorrow?"

I shoot him a confused look.

"*Homecoming Dance?*" He looks down and shakes his head.

"Right. Yes. Thanks for today." I push up my glasses.

"It was my pleasure." He grins at me. I catch the dimple and tuck it into a memory of a day I'll never forget.

"LUKA, WHERE'VE YOU BEEN?" I yell into the phone.

I just got home and had to charge my phone and debrief my mom before I could call you."

"Wait 'til you hear what happened."

"Wait 'til *you* hear what I heard!"

"Okay, then. You go first." I figure her news will be the short part of the conversation. What could happen in Baltimore with her eighty-six-year-old Aunt May?

"No, I can wait. You go first." *Luka could wait?* This I had to see.

"I'm going to get contacts," I say slowly, building suspense. "be…cause…*I've been asked to homecoming!*"

"No!" Luka shrieks. "Who asked you? Ben?"

"How did you know?" I guess it's pretty obvious, since the only other guy who's shown any interest in me since Tony Rubowski turned up dead the other night. I push the painful thought away.

"I told you he liked you."

"I guess this one time, you were right. The only problem is, I'm supposed to come to New York that weekend."

"Homecoming's the first weekend in October?"

"Yeah, but you know my mom. I doubt she's gotten around to booking the flight yet."

"Tell me how he asked. And I expect all the juicy details."

I comply, starting with yesterday's conversation on the front porch, and conclude with the bald eagle in the gullaboy sky at the beach.

Before I can finish, Luka interrupts. "The eagle! That's it! Aunt May says you're an eagle."

"What?" Confused, I figure she must've misheard me. "No, Luka, I said I *saw* an eagle. It's not all that unusual here—they nest less than a mile from the beach where we were. It's just that I'd never seen one before."

"I know what you said," Luka answers slowly, with bridled impatience. "What I'm saying is that after I told Aunt May about your wacky visions and everything that happened in your boring little town the past week, she told me that you may *be* an eagle." She then went uncharacteristically quiet.

I wait a few seconds, then ask, a bit harsher than I meant to, "What's that supposed to mean?"

Luka takes a deep breath. "She explained that there's this legend from ancient times that, at its core, comes from somewhere in the Old Testament. Aunt May thinks it's been around even longer than that. She said that some people, for no known reason, are given the supernatural power of the Cherubim to fight an evil force greater than them."

"What *kind* of supernatural powers?" I wrinkle my brow. *And what's a Cherubim?*

"Aunt May says that those people who become eagles are blessed with the gift of sight, or prophesy—they can see the future, either through visions, or just a keener insight than most of us possess. She said they have the ability to see the whole puzzle put together, when most people can only see random pieces."

"Don't tell her I said this, but your Aunt May is probably in the early stages of senility, because I have the worst vision of anyone I know. I'm half-blind. I'm not sure I'll even be able to wear contacts—my vision is *that* bad."

"That's what I told her—except for the senility part. She just said that God likes to confound folks by using the most unlikely people for His purposes."

"Her God sure is a joker, isn't He?" I laugh.

Luka turns serious. "Don't make fun, Verona. He's my God, too."

I recoil. "Are you saying that you believe this stuff?"

"When she said it, it made sense. But there's more. Aunt May suggested that you look for three other gifted beings: a lion, a bull, and an angel."

"I haven't seen anything even close," I chortle into the phone.

"Aunt May said you might not actually see these things, but you'll see the results of them."

"Hmmm. What results?" My heart speeds up. I'm getting curious, even though almost every logical brain cell in my head is laughing like crazy.

"She said the angel is a blinding light that takes the form of a person with a strong spiritual connection to God. He or she is given keen intuition and the ability to communicate. Sometimes the angel can be in two places at one time. The lion is a strong force that could overpower evil much larger than itself." Luka pauses.

"And the bull? You know that's what all this sounds like, right? *Bull?*" I can't believe Luka is taking this seriously.

"Be quiet! The bull will be someone who would be willing to give up his life for love. Think of the sacrificial bull people sacrificed to God in the old days. She said the bull is sometimes portray as a man to represent the sacrifice of God's son."

"That clinches it. I don't recognize any of those creatures," I say. But then it flashes in my head like a beacon, a light bulb, a star. The last vision, the one with Ross. Star Lady was a bright light. "Wait. Remember the last vision—the one I had in art. I told you about the Star Lady that talked, right? Could she—"

Something that sounds like the smoke detector rings out on Luka's end of the phone. "I've gotta go! I'll call you tomorrow!" I look into my phone, hoping there isn't a real fire. In the building Luka calls home, anything is possible.

I get on my mom's laptop and Google *cherubim*. Good ol' Wikipedia lists the biblical references, and the prophet Ezekiel describes cherubim as a tetrad of living creatures, each with four faces: a lion, an angel, a sacrificial bull or man, and an eagle. I feel a strange tingle in my fingers.

I'M JUST COMPLETING MY OUTLINE for the history essay due on Tuesday when my mother comes barreling backward through the front door at six o'clock, her briefcase slung over her shoulder, and a pizza held up with one hand. "I've got Giovanni's for dinner!"

"Great! I'll set the table." The sweet aroma of pepperoni and tomato sauce teases my stomach.

"I've got something to tell you," I say, as I gulp down a bite with a swig of milk. My mom wrinkles her nose at my preferred beverage and takes a sip of lemon water.

"Shoot." She wipes her mouth.

"First, I'm finally going to listen to you. I'm getting fitted for contacts."

"What happened to poking your eye out and all that?" Mom arches one auburn eyebrow.

"Well, I'm afraid my glasses won't look right with my homecoming gown."

"You're going to homecoming? With whom?" She drops her pizza on the plate. "The chemistry jock? Please tell me it's not the chemistry jock."

I lean back as though I've been hit. Then I find my voice, "You don't even know him. And his name is Ben! Not *the chemistry jock*. What makes you so prejudiced against him? Is it 'cause of Dad?"

"*Be*-cause! It *is* him! I knew it. You can't go," she blurts out. She immediately bites off a corner of her crust aggressively, as though that settles it.

I can feel my eyes grow rounder than the pepperoni. "Why not?"

"Because I've done a lit-tle in-ves-ti-ga-tion on Chortov—that's his name, right?" The way she shakes her head when she says *little investigation,* enunciating each syllable, makes it sound like she's found a smoking gun under his bed. She doesn't even look at me to confirm Ben's last name, but rises from her seat and dumps her crust in the garbage. Max whines.

"And?" I'm mystified at my normally rational mother's completely irrational reaction to my amazingly *good* news. I pick the crust out of the garbage and feed it to Max while my mother looks out the kitchen window.

"And you can't go." She turns sharply, arms braced, her butt leaning against the sink. I am caught so completely off-guard that I react without thinking.

Slamming my hands down on the table at either side of my plate, I rise from my seat. If it's unusual for me act to this way, I feel justified in that my reasonable mother has been replaced by a poseur, an imposter, a charlatan. A totally *unreasonable* poseur. And if this poseur wants a fight, I'm going to give her one. "Why do *you* say I can't go?"

"I, *your mother*, say you can't go, because—" She looks for help around the room, like the reason might pop out of the refrigerator. It is here that the Great Debater falters, but only for a second. Her eyes register a ready reason and she throws it at me, "You can't go because you're going to your dad's that weekend."

"The dance is next weekend, and I'm not supposed to go to Dad's until the following one," I lie, jutting my chin at her. I'm pretty sure she won't have any idea when homecoming is. I *go* to Colonial and I didn't know.

"See." My mom points at me repeatedly, a sure sign of desperation. "He waited until the last minute. You shouldn't go out with a guy who waits until the last minute."

"What have you learned, *Cheryl,* from your lit-tle in-ves-ti-ga-tion that predisposes you against him?" My mother's eyes narrow and her brow furls, more at my use of her first name than the question itself. I exhale loudly and some of my self-righteousness must have escaped with the air, because I add in a softer tone, "It's not like you, Mom. You've always told me to have an open mind."

My mom plops down in her chair. "A couple of girls in my freshman comp class graduated from Colonial last year. I asked them about your study partner."

"You checked up on him with kids you teach at the college?" My voice quivers. "And?" My hands grip the edge of my chair.

"Well, after they went on and on about how *hot* he is—notwithstanding the two-year age difference—they said you'd better watch out. He's a player."

"And how would they know that?" Obviously, calling Ben a *player* was not a reference to his time on the football field.

"Ginny Redmond said her sister—do you know Rachel Redmond?"

"I know she's a senior and part of the cheerleading crowd." And drop-dead stunning in a blond beauty-queen sort of way. All of a sudden, my stomach is not happy with the pepperoni-milk combo I just ate.

"Yes, that's her. Ginny told me that Ben Chortov broke Rachel's heart. And Rachel tried to kill herself over it."

My mouth opens wide, but I quickly slam it shut and cover it with my hand. Why didn't Leanne tell me about this?

"That's his reputation, honey. I'm sorry. I don't want to see you hurt." Mom reaches across and brushes a wayward curl from my eyes.

Still, there is probably more to the story than Ginny knows or told my mom, and I'm determined to find out for myself. "Mom, haven't you always told me that I demonstrated good judgment—that you admired the smart choices I made?" I play with my napkin.

"Well, yes," Mom stammers, "but this is different."

I shake my head. "It's no different. Will you please trust me to make good decisions now? I won't have the opportunity to learn how to make choices if I never leave the house." I speak in a quiet, but assured voice. Mom looks down and I tense, preparing for the verbal artillery sure to come my way for challenging her.

Instead, she smiles. "You're my daughter, Verona Louise." She pats my hand. "Get your contacts. I want final approval on the gown, though. No plunging necklines. If this Chortov kid *is* a player, you don't need to provide any encouragement."

I rush around the table to hug her. "Thanks, Mom."

Remembering my fib, I say, "Mom, I have a confession to make."

"Yes?"

"Ben didn't wait until the last minute to ask me."

"So, when did he ask you?" Mom's face looks stern again, like she might change her mind.

"Oh, he asked me today. It's just that the dance is really a week from next Friday. Can I please visit Dad this coming weekend instead?"

Mom looks down, scratches her neck, but I catch her suppressing a smile. "I suppose so. I can't imagine what your father's going to say when you tell him you're not going to be his date at the banquet."

I hang my head. How could I forget about the journalist banquet? It was all my dad talked about last time I was home. My uneasiness, discomfort, chagrin with the prospect of disappointing my dad is obvious, because my mom cannot conceal her grin. "You don't think *Cheryl* is going to tell him, do you?" She begins loading the dinner dishes into the dishwasher.

I put my glass next to hers.

Tuesday, September 22nd
677 Days to Home Free

LOCATING THE HISTORIC (and really, what *isn't* historic in this town?) Bruton Parish Church is easy. Its brick-walled exterior and seventeenth century gravestones are one of the many tourist magnets on Duke of Gloucester Street ("DoG Street" to the locals). This main thoroughfare is usually closed to traffic other than tourist-filled horse-drawn carriages.

Expecting a large turnout for the funeral, the parish has reserved space in a parking lot a block away. Leanne and I walk from there.

"You look like you're going to work as a lawyer in the city." I point to Leanne's navy pantsuit and lavender shirt.

"I wish." Leanne lets out a long breath. Then she turns to me. "Why do you think he did it?"

"Ross?" I look at the ground. "Do we know for sure he *did* do it?" I'm not ready to share my visions with Leanne, but why not throw the question out there?

Leanne grabs my shoulder. She swings me around so her eyes can bore into mine. "Are you saying you think there's a chance Ross Georgeson *didn't* kill himself?"

I want to start backpedalling fast, but something in Leanne's face encourages me to open up. "Leanne, obviously I didn't know Ross very well. And I know he was probably feeling pretty down after Friday's game. But still, Ross didn't strike me as the kind of guy who would do this."

"That's exactly what I keep thinking." Leanne appears relieved that we share the same perception. We weave into the line of people heading down DoG Street. "Ross would've gotten help if he was having suicidal thoughts."

"Maybe we should talk to someone about this? Someone grown up."

"The only teacher I trust is Mr. Zeke." We merge with the throng. "I bet he'll be here today. He knew Ross pretty well."

We cross the church threshold fifteen minutes early and yet, every pew looks full or overflowing. Leanne grabs my arm and drags me to the left, through the crowd, around a corner, and up a stairway to a balcony, where we nab seats in the front row just left of the center aisle. Somber strains echo from the pipe organ behind the altar across the church from us. My nostrils are bombarded by lemon oil and some spicy scent. I sneeze.

"God bless you." Then Leanne makes a low growly noise. "I can't believe Amber Claussen and her pack came." She nods to a pew of blond heads in the middle-left section below. "They've always been mean to Ross—joking about his friendship with Hamilton."

And they're not the only ones, I think. I say, "Alex Chortov and some of the other football players are pallbearers."

"I'd heard that," Leanne says. "It's ironic, but not all that surprising, with how much Superintendent Georgeson reveres football. He never misses a chance to tell people he line-backed for UVA. It's common knowledge that he pushed Ross to play football, as well as get the highest GPA possible."

After a minute, Leanne whispers, "What about Craig Hamilton? He's a pallbearer too, right?"

Still looking forward, I shake my head.

"Wow. He's got to be hurting." She exhales. "Wait. I see him." She nudges me. "Look below us—in the aisle." Mourners have taken to lining the center aisle, since there are absolutely no seats left. It takes me a few seconds to locate Craig. His hair doesn't look fire-red—more auburn in the shadows below. Even surrounded by other mourners, he appears alone, like there's some sort of force field around him.

A black-lacquered coffin acts like a fence between the altar and the people. I shudder, picturing the bright-eyed boy inside. Still, I know the finality of his death hasn't penetrated more than the surface of me. It's too impossible—too horrible. I can't bear to think about it longer than a moment, and even a passing thought is a sharp blade to my heart.

A middle-aged woman in a white robe with a rectangular gold scarf emerges from somewhere behind the casket. With her hands outstretched, she indicates for us to stand. The organ pelts the opening strains of a hymn. Most everyone flips through worn, red books to find the lyrics that sound more joyful than the occasion calls for. Leanne, with the same red book open, sings with the others.

Not wanting to inflict unnecessary pain on the ears of my pew neighbors, I keep myself busy by watching the multi-colored dust motes fairy dancing in the sunbeams. I imagine Ross is there—a tiny, dancing particle overlooking his funeral. It's better than thinking he's nowhere.

Leanne elbows me and nods at something going on in the aisle below. Despite never having seen either of Ross' parents, they are easily identifiable as they make their way toward the casket. Mrs. Georgeson clings to her husband so tightly it looks like he's half-carrying, half-dragging her through the crowd. Every eye in the pews is trained on them, and I can only imagine how raw they feel right now. Ross' parents stop at the right side of the coffin. Mrs. Georgeson bends down and kisses its cover. Her husband leads her into the front pew.

The music stops. I look up to see the female preacher climb an ornate wooden staircase to a raised podium to the right of the altar. She looks around the crowd. Her eyes settle on those in the front pew. "Reginald and Emily, Melissa and Mike, dear relatives and friends of the Georgeson family, we are gathered here today to acknowledge the lost life of a lamb. Many of us are here to support the Georgeson family in the wake of this horrible tragedy. Ross Elliot was too young to leave us. There was so much he had yet to offer the world. His engaging smile and tender personality will be missed by us all." Loud sobs bounce off the mahogany walls.

She continues: "Whenever a young person leaves us, we want to ask, 'Why, Lord?' Perhaps *Ben* Franklin can give us some insight. No, not the Ben Franklin who gave us insight into the nature of electricity and spectacles and so forth, but Benjamin *Malachi* Franklin who wrote this poem over sixty years ago."

Tears slip down Leanne's cheeks. Even the woman across from us pulls her wrap tighter, using a fringed corner to wipe her eyes. The preacher removes a sheet of paper from some hiding place in her robe, and recites the following:

> *My life is but a weaving*
> *Between my Lord and me;*
> *I cannot choose the colors,*
> *He worketh steadily.*
> *Oft times He weaveth sorrow,*
> *And I, in foolish pride,*
> *Forget He sees the upper,*
> *And I the under side.*
> *Not 'til the loom is silent*
> *And the shuttles cease to fly,*
> *Shall God unroll the canvas*
> *And explain the reason why.*
> *The dark threads are as needful*
> *In the Weaver's skillful hand,*
> *As the threads of gold and silver*
> *In the pattern He has planned.*
> *He knows, He loves, He cares,*
> *Nothing this truth can dim.*
> *He gives His very best to those*
> *Who leave the choice with Him.*

She pauses, and sets the paper down. "This is a dark-thread occasion for those of us who hold Ross Elliot and his family in our hearts. But I implore you to give up the search for *why* Ross left us so early, and instead, let God's embrace hold you in His generous and faithful love."

She smiles directly at the Georgeson family. "Our Lord said in the Sermon on the Mount, 'Blessed are those who mourn, for they will be comforted.'" Mrs. Georgeson blows her nose. So does the old lady next to us. I close my eyes, listening to the sound of sadness, the dark melody of suffering, and wonder how the preacher thinks a loving God could let innocent people suffer like this. From down here, under the tapestry, as she says, it makes no sense.

When I open my eyes, the preacher has left the podium. Mr. Sams, his eyes dark and puffy like he hasn't slept in days, moves to slightly right of the coffin. He clears his throat. "For those of you who don't know me, my name is Samuel English, commonly referred to as Mr. Sams by the teachers, staff, and students of Colonial High School, where I have the privilege of serving as principal. There are currently nine hundred fifty-two students attending CHS. Today I want to tell you why one of them, Mr. Ross Georgeson, will be sorely missed by me, his teachers, his classmates, his teammates," Mr. Sams pauses to smile sadly toward the family and continues, "and even by the cafeteria and janitorial staff." He glances to his right.

"Ross was one of those kids who stood out. He talked to everyone—always had a kind thing to say. Mary Burns from the lunchroom told me how he would try out a new joke on her almost every day from across the counter. Mr. Jackson, our head custodian, confided to me that Ross frequently suggested he stop working so hard so that the school would get condemned." Mr. Sams breaks into a small smile. He looks back at the Georgeson family. "Not a suggestion I appreciate, but I do appreciate the congeniality."

He scans the room. "Ross had a smile and a kind word for everyone. The first day of freshman year is the hardest day for most students. There was a student who'd just moved from Pakistan and knew very little English. He had no experience navigating the chaotic halls of an American high school. Ross risked being late for his own classes that day, in order to help this tremulous foreign student. I'm sure many of you have similar stories that demonstrate Ross' compassionate spirit. Here to share some of his memories of Ross is Colonial's football coach, Theo Chortov."

"This should be interesting," Leanne whispers, rolling her eyes. "Some kids at school are speculating that the reason Ross killed himself was that Coach Chortov replaced him after his kicking blunder in Friday night's game. That, and his father's refusal to let him quit."

I want to tell her what Ben told me, that Ross *asked* to be removed from the game. It's just that I'm not ready to reveal Ben's interest in me. What if he changes his mind?

Coach Chortov appears from the left—a section of the church hidden from us.

He removes a piece of paper from the inside pocket of his suit coat and says in a stilted voice, "Thank you, Mr. Sams, for the introduction."

Wow. His accent is thick. It reminds me Ben is Russian, like *from Russia* Russian. Not like Italian from Brooklyn.

"I speak for boys on team. Ross vas outstanding young man. Until end, he vork hard at football game. Like Mr. Sams say here, Ross always smile and help his friends on team. We—I and entire team—respect him very much."

"That's a lie!" The shout comes from below.

We lean over the edge of the balcony.

Craig Hamilton points his finger at the looming man on the altar. He looks as if he will add to his accusation, but just shakes his finger at the coach before returning it to his jacket pocket.

Coach Chortov's face flushes; his eyes shoot daggers at Craig.

Stunned into silence, everyone watches Craig wrestle past the other mourners and disappear under the balcony. The door closes with a *whoosh*.

Coach Chortov takes a deep breath and looks around the room. "I see zere is one who disagrees witz me. I am sorry." His blue eyes flash.

"Mr. Georgeson vas big help to football team, to school and to vorld. As we say in Russia on sad days like this, *Vwe ubyly moy nadejdy*. It means, 'You killed my hopes.'" He looks sympathetically toward the grieving family, and says, "I am sorry for your loss." Coach Chortov exits to the left, shoving the paper inside his blazer.

Mr. Zeke replaces him—dressed in a neat three-piece suit. His lips press in a straight line. He makes eye contact seemingly with everyone, just like he does in class. "I've had the pleasure of mentoring Ross Georgeson for six years as his Scoutmaster. It's customary for folks to laud an individual when he passes, but I don't think I've known a young man who deserves our admiration and respect more than Ross Georgeson." He places his hands on the coffin.

"Before I tell you about the accomplishments that this young man effected in his short life, I want to give you a quote attributed to the renowned author, philosopher, and Oxford professor, C. S. Lewis. Contrary to popular wisdom, Lewis said, 'You do not *have* a soul.'"

Mr. Zeke gazes around the room while some people gasp and others blurt other audible sounds of disbelief. When the noise subsides, he says, "You *are* a soul. You *have* a body." He has everyone's attention now; not a sob or nose blow interrupts the expectant silence.

"This handsome box holds the lifeless body of a remarkable young man." He taps on the wood. "But it cannot hold his soul. Ross Georgeson is still alive in every essence except in this limited physical world that we find ourselves in today. That's why this morning I'm going to refer to Ross in the present tense."

Mr. Zeke backs up the steps of the stage with the same ease that he navigates his classroom each day. "The first day I met Ross Georgeson he was wide-eyed and enthusiastic, with a string of freckles tracking across his nose. He entered the Scout meeting in full regalia with a single question: 'When do we go camping?' I didn't want to sink his titanic bubble by informing him that there was a lot more to Scouting than just camping, so without thinking, I answered, 'Next weekend.'

"Putting a camping trip together typically takes several months, so you can imagine my naïveté to think I could pull it off in six days." He pauses while the audience chuckles.

"We were able to reserve some cabins down on the York River, not far from here. I wasn't as blessed securing the recommended number of parent chaperones, it being such late notice. So I alone was in charge of seventeen beginning Scouts—most of whom didn't know each other because they hailed from five different elementary schools.

"Foolish? You bet it was. Would I trade it for the more sensible, well-planned outing? No way. Those of you with children of your own who have hit the ten to twelve-year mark realize that the typical boy this age is interested in action, sport, adventure, and little else. The seventeen boys I took camping were typical. We played games, fished off the dock, and built a fire surrounded by rocks where we told ghost stories into the night.

"What wasn't typical was the leadership displayed by Ross Georgeson. He helped me organize the kids into groups for cooking and cleanup. He was the first to volunteer for the unpopular job of cleaning the latrines. And he discreetly helped one lad who, let's just say, had an embarrassing situation in his sleeping bag."

Mr. Zeke pauses while the audience chuckles again. "Ross has a keen heart for the hurting, and befriended those individuals whom no one else wanted around. You know—the discards, the misfits, many not intellectually gifted enough to be classified as nerds. Mr. Sams already talked about the new boy from Pakistan. In that same vein, we had an eleven-year-old boy in our troop who suffered from Asperger's Syndrome. The stilted manner in which he talked and his awkward movements made him an object of ridicule with his peers. To try to be this boy's friend was a colossal challenge, because his behavior was so inappropriate that he would thwart the effort to the same degree the other kids would ostracize him.

"Nevertheless, Ross persisted in being his friend. He insisted this individual be included in whatever sport or project the group was doing. Ross persisted, despite not understanding the physical and emotional limitations of Asperger's. He persisted, despite the mocking he took from his friends. And his perseverance eventually paid off. Within months, the boys in the troop began to see this socially awkward boy as one of them. The three Scouts who went to this boy's school came to his aid when classmates teased him. He had a place at the lunch table. That troop became a cohesive unit largely because of the efforts of one freckle-faced twelve-year-old named Ross Georgeson."

Mr. Zeke removes a handkerchief from his pocket, turns around and blows his nose.

There is so much I didn't know about Ross. There is so much I don't know about Mr. Zeke. Seeing this strong, confident man tear up is almost more than I can bear. I feel my eyes welling up. I pinch the skin behind my knees to distract myself from thinking thoughts that will melt my resolve not to cry. Crying in public is never an option.

Mr. Zeke continues. I put my head on the balcony banister. It is obvious. Ross didn't kill himself. He was murdered. And worse, besides the murderer, I may be the only person in Jamestown who knows it. I've got to tell someone. But who's going to believe a sixteen-year-old girl who sees murders when she's flying around as an eagle? *Who can I trust?*

I lift my head and look down to where Mr. Zeke is still talking about Ross's Eagle Scout project. And I swear he looks directly at me and blinks. It feels like a "you're not in this alone" blink. I swallow. Somehow, I feel sure I have my answer.

"Ross," Mr. Zeke says, turning slightly toward the coffin, "your physical presence here is, and will always be, missed by the people whose lives you touched—and by all those you could've touched, had your life been spared. We look forward to seeing you on the other side of the curtain." Mr. Zeke returns to his seat as the organ sounds. The crowd is silent as the strains of a familiar song herald a time of prayer and reflection. The scent of lilies wafts up to the balcony.

The preacher-lady gives a final message, but I'm too absorbed in my thoughts to take in what she says.

"There's Ben!" Leanne speaks into my ear. Sure enough, the athletes assemble in twos on either side of the casket. They roll the casket forward. I wish Ben would look up, but he holds his head Marine-straight, his mouth tight. The others have the same serious posture as they exit below the balcony. I guess they've been coached well.

The Georgeson family follows closely. Superintendent Georgeson wears an impassive mask over his face, staring straight ahead. Ross's mother blots her swollen eyes and nose with a tissue. She carries herself with an air of strength leaving the church, unlike the beaten woman who entered an hour ago.

By the time Leanne and I weave our way down the circular steps and out the large wooden doors, most of the procession is in their cars. Some of the cars have their hazard lights flashing already.

"We'd better hurry! I'm not sure where the cemetery is," Leanne says, seeing the first of the limousines slowly worming out of DoG Street.

"What? Wait! We're going to the cemetery?" I feel the blood drain from my face.

"Of course. We have to. Ross is our friend."

Was our friend. Okay, assuming Mr. Zeke is right and Ross is alive somewhere—I really doubt he'd be hanging around to see who goes to his burial. If he *is* alive somewhere, I expect he's got more pressing things going on right now. This part is more than I bargained for. Funerals are bad enough, but when they drop the body in the ground, I don't want to be there to see it. I don't care if it *is* just a shell.

"You really think everyone is going?" I ask, as Leanne rushes me back to the Rover.

"Yes, they'll all be there. Haven't you ever been to an interment?"

"If by *interment* you mean when they drop the dead body into the cold ground, no. I try to avoid morbid experiences." Honestly, before today, I haven't ever tried to *avoid* an interment—I can't remember ever having the occasion to go to one.

"Well, it's not like in the movies, if that's what you're worried about. They won't even lower the casket into the ground while we're there."

I look at her suspiciously as I start the Rover. She works her stray locks back into her barrette. We make it to the end of the funeral procession.

"I wonder what Craig is going through right now?" Leanne gazes out the passenger window. "It was so not like him to yell out in front of the whole crowd. He must be heartbroken." She bows her head, staring at her folded hands.

"Judging from his reaction to Coach Chortov's little spiel, I'd say he's pretty angry."

"Anger is a normal part of grieving. Plus, I think he was reacting to the fact that most of the players treated Ross with anything but respect. And Coach Grimes is the only one who tried to stop it. From what I heard, Coach Chortov ignored it."

"Do you think Ben was one of the, ah—"

Leanne interrupts while I fish for a word that doesn't sound too harsh. "No, not Ben. He usually keeps to himself. Alex was in on it. But I don't put much stock in gossip—so who knows?" She pauses, inhaling deeply. "Well, since it doesn't appear you're going to volunteer anything, is it true Ben asked you to the homecoming dance?"

"For someone who doesn't like to gossip, you sure manage to get the scoop," I tease. "Yeah, he asked me yesterday."

"That is so awesome, Verona!"

"How did you find out about it if Ben usually keeps to himself?"

"On Friday, he asked me if I thought you would go with him. I said you'd be crazy not to," Leanne says. "I didn't tell him this, of course, but I think Ben Chortov is one of the smartest, coolest guys at Colonial. And that's not even because he's gorgeous and has a hot body."

"Leanne!" I say in mock surprise. Actually, it does sound funny coming from Leanne, and not Caitlin or Luka. "So, who's taking you?"

"I'll probably just go with Paris, Susie, and Caitlin if they don't get asked." She thinks for a moment. "Hey, you don't have a gown yet, do you? Let's go shopping this week for one, okay?"

"That would be great."

We pull in on the grass behind a white Chevy Blazer we've been following the entire serpentine route to the cemetery. A white tent with three sides open waits fifty feet from the road. The somber crowd makes its way to the tent. Leanne and I rush to catch up. From the back, it's hard to see anything, but the scent of white lilies makes it back far enough to tickle my nose.

A slender Boy Scout in full uniform holds a silver trumpet in one hand and looks at his feet. He raises the trumpet to his lips and plays a slow, sad tune. The crying and nose-blowing resume. I hear the female preacher's voice, but her words sound garbled from our position at the back of the crowd, so my focus wanders around.

Sensing a presence far to the right, I step back and look behind Leanne's mane—blowing wildly around her in spite of the barrette. A figure is leaning against the side of a weeping willow. I can only make out the shadows of the bottom torso and legs, but I know it's Craig Hamilton. The injustice hits me hard. This is Ross' best friend. He should have a place of honor with the family of the deceased—not be ostracized, relegated to the periphery.

The preacher concludes the ceremony by inviting everyone to join the family members at their home for lunch.

Mr. Zeke taps me on the shoulder. We step to the side. "Do you two want to join me for lunch at the Virginia Company Café in Jefferson Village? Some of your friends said they'd rather do that than go to the Georgeson's house."

Leanne and I don't even check with each other, but say in unison, "Sure!"

Mr. Zeke continues, "And Verona, there's something I need to give you after lunch."

As I open the door to the driver's side of the Rover, another tap on my shoulder makes me jump. I snap around.

Ben holds his hands up in self-defense. "Whoa," he says, the grin on his face causing me to relax. "I just want to thank you for coming."

"I thought it was the right thing to do." I don't want him to think I only came because I knew he would be here.

"Yeah, I know." He pushes the hair out of his eyes. "About the other day ..."

Here it comes. I brace myself for the inevitable letdown. Of course he's changed his mind. What was I thinking to believe that Ben Chortov wants to take me to a dance?

"Do you have an answer for me yet? About homecoming?" He steps in closer, his smell making it hard for me to find the words to answer him, despite the fact that my mouth is hanging open.

"Yes, I can come. I mean, I want to go to the dance with you." A car horn from the other end of the field honks.

Ben nods. "That's ...good. See you." He runs off toward the sound of the horn.

We're one of the last vehicles to leave the cemetery. As we're pulling out, Officer Morris, who has been directing traffic, signals for me to roll down my window.

"I need to ask you a question about Saturday night." He nods toward Leanne. "Did you find or see a cell phone anywhere around the backpack where you ... stumbled?"

"No, Officer Morris. I would've given it to you if I had."

"That's what I thought, but I needed to make sure."

THE VIRGINIA COMPANY CAFÉ is nestled halfway down a side street on the opposite end of Jefferson Village from where I live. Surprisingly, I have never been here before. Lively, acoustical guitar and the inviting smell of coffee give the room a relaxed feeling.

Leaning over the counter, Mr. Zeke talks to a matronly brunette in an apron sprinkled with sunflowers. It's clear they know each other.

Leanne and I take our place in line behind the other students, who turn to hug us—apparently part of the protocol for funeral-goers of all ages. Caitlin's face is a mess of mascara, but she doesn't seem to know or care. Paris twists her tiny braids in a way that makes her look younger. Nicky, unnaturally quiet, hugs me without his usual fanfare. We all sigh at the same time, causing smiles to form at the corners of our mouths.

Mr. Zeke breaks the awkward silence. "Order what you want, grab a drink from that bin, and come to the table in back. Don't even think about paying—it's taken care of." He heads in the direction of the back table.

Nautical charts plaster the walls covered intermittently by weathered wooden frames housing sepia drawings of early settlers—John Rolfe and Pocahontas, Captain John Smith and Chief Powhatan. A massive clock with a compass rose in the center says it's lunchtime.

I leave my spot by Leanne and follow Mr. Zeke to the back table. "Mr. Zeke, if you have time after lunch, would it be okay if I talked with you personally about something?"

"Of course. Do you mind telling me what it's about?" I glance back to the counter. Paris has just finished ordering but is waiting for Nicky.

"Remember the other day in class when I zoned out? It wasn't a seizure, but it was more than just zoning, too. I had this weird vision. You were in it. We were eagles. I saw—and felt—Angie's car wreck." My head lowers, but my eyes search for his reaction, expecting a hearty laugh, at the very least.

Instead Mr. Zeke looks stunned. "After Friday's quiz? Before the accident? We were eagles?"

"It's crazy, I know. And then I had one like it last week in art... about Ross." Mr. Zeke's eyes widen. He nods, but before he can respond, Nicky and Paris interrupt us.

"I'd better order." I leave him gazing at the floor over crossed arms.

When I return, I take the last available seat, at the far end of the table from Mr. Zeke. He breaks through the gloomy quiet. "Well, what do you think?" I'm not sure what he means. The funeral? His eulogy? Ross' death?

"I think the whole thing sucks, Mr. Z— Ezekiel." Nicky pushes his soda away and puts his elbows on the table. We all inhale quickly.

I don't know what to expect Mr. Zeke to say to that, but he surprises me. "Nick, I couldn't agree with you more."

Nicky pulls back, caught off-guard by Mr. Zeke's statement, which he takes as an invitation to continue. "Ross Georgeson was a great guy—I mean, *is* a great guy. If all that stuff you said about him is true, he's even cooler than I thought. I can't believe he would do the hari-kari because of one bad kick."

"Or because some stupid jocks made fun of him." Caitlin wrinkles her nose.

"First of all, the stuff I said is all true. I could've talked a lot more about Ross. Second, I'm with you on this, Nick. The whole suicide thing smells fishy to me."

A perky waitress delivers our sandwiches and chips in little baskets.

Paris sets a basket in front of Nicky. "What do you think happened, Mr. Zeke?"

"I've got no more information than you do, Paris."

"Wait, there is something more. Tell them, Verona." Leanne elbows me.

"What?" I turn my head to her. *Does she know about the visions?*

"You know—what Officer Morris asked you just now."

I exhale. "Officer Morris asked me if I'd found a phone the night we discovered Ross. That means his phone must be missing."

"He could've thrown it in the river, knowing he was going to kill himself," Susie says.

"What kid would drop his phone in the river? Besides, Ross had a sweet iPhone—he could've given it to me before—" The whole table glares at Nicky.

"That was just gross—even for you." Caitlin glares at him.

"Yeah, I know." Nicky looks up at the ceiling. "I'm sorry, Kicka."

"That *is* an interesting bit of information," Mr. Zeke says. "I've been told they found everything else—his books, notebooks, you name it—but no note and no phone. Ross loved his family, so I can't imagine him not leaving a farewell message for them—something to assuage their guilt." He looks down at his food. "Of course, I can't imagine he'd take his life, either."

"Mr. Z— Ezekiel, what do you think of Coach Chortov's talk, and Craig Hamilton's—" Caitlin searches for the word.

"Outburst," Susie says.

"Yes, outburst." Caitlin points to Susie.

"I'm not going to talk about another faculty member, but you need to keep in mind that Craig is hurting right now. He needs compassion—not judgment. Ross was his closest friend."

"Was Craig the Asberber's kid you talked about?" Paris asks.

"It's Asperger's Syndrome, Paris," Mr. Zeke says. "And, no, that Scout moved up to D.C. before freshman year. Craig has a difficult family life. We'll leave it at that. He and Ross had similar interests outside of school—video games, fishing, Scouting. Their friendship grew out of those things. The difference is that Ross could get along with most anyone, while Craig seemed satisfied to have just one friend."

After lunch, Mr. Zeke waves us off, but calls to me: "Verona, would you walk me to my car? Maybe Leanne could wait in yours."

After handing the keys to Leanne, I follow him to the Mercedes. Mr. Zeke shuffles through a folder in his briefcase on the front seat and pulls out the manila envelope. "Sorry it's taken me so long to get this to you. We needed some time to get to know each other."

"No, that's okay." I wonder what he means by that.

"Now, what did you want to tell me about Ross?"

"I had another vision in art class—I think on Tuesday—where I was an eagle again. You weren't in this one, but it was real scary. This amazingly bright star lady grew out of the broken glass from Angie's windshield and flew with me over the stadium to the auto shop. Ross' car was idling there. But there was this hooded demon the star lady called Mammon, pointing a gun through the window at Ross. The monster forced Ross to kill himself… and then Saturday we find Ross in the idling car…just like in the vision. Even his backpack was lying in the same place on the ground." My breathing becomes heavy, and I can feel my eyes starting to fill up.

Mr. Zeke nods for me to continue. "I don't know if it all means anything, but my friend Luka has this old aunt who's very religious, and she said that I could be an eagle of some sort—not like a *real* eagle, of course. Just a person with the power to see things." I push my glasses up and think how outlandish this sounds, fully expecting Mr. Zeke to laugh or at least make light of it. But his eyes get a faraway look, like he's thinking of something else, or trying to think of what to say.

I clear my throat, which provokes him to focus on me, and he says, "Have you told anyone else?"

"Just Luka."

"Good. Keep it quiet. In the meantime, you let me know if you have any more of these visions. By the way, have you ever had the experience of flying like an eagle while you were awake?"

"No. Just visions." *What a strange thing for him to ask!* Then I remember the note and unzip a pocket of my backpack. "Wait, there's something else." I hand him the note. "This came in an envelope with three dried-up rose petals."

"Can I have it? I'd like to have it tested."

"Sure." I guess a chemistry teacher has skills I don't know about.

"Do you have any idea who might have left it?"

"No. It was on my windshield right after you asked Nicky and me to visit Angie."

He still has that faraway look in his eyes, like *he's* having a vision. Since he doesn't say anything, I figure our conversation is over. Leanne is probably peeved that I kept her waiting for so long. "Verona." He rests a hand on my shoulder. "Tell your friends they can call me Mr. Zeke if they want. Just not in class.

I don't want everyone doing it."

I smile my assent, head back to the Rover, and mull over two of the words he said. *Your friends.* Plural. It doesn't seem possible. At the car, Leanne sits in the driver's seat, tuning the radio station. I yank the passenger door open, startling her.

"I'm sorry. Don't you want to drive?" She reaches for the door handle.

"Would you drive? I'd like to read this." I show her the envelope.

"Sure, but I've never driven something this big before." Leanne moves the seat closer, but it still looks like she can barely see over the dashboard.

"You'll be fine."

I open the folder and pull out the forms. I skim the standard reference questionnaire until I get to the written recommendation section. It reads:

To whom it may concern:

Verona Lamberti is the top student in the Advanced Chemistry class I teach at Colonial High. She is a bright young lady who holds a perfect grade in my class. She is prompt, polite, and hands in assignments on time. However, Verona's demonstrated leadership ability and service to others make her truly remarkable.

When another student was having difficulty grasping key chemistry concepts, Verona agreed to tutor him at night. In a very short time, the tutored student has brought his grades up dramatically, a direct result of Verona's leadership.

Another Colonial student suffered severe injury in a car wreck, including an amputated leg. Despite never having met this student, Verona visited her at the hospital an hour away. In a phone call to me this week, the injured girl reported that she had been very comforted by Verona's visit, and looks forward to seeing her in the future.

In conclusion, Verona Lamberti has proven to be an exem-

plary person and would be a true asset to your society.

Sincerely,
Mr. Curtis Ezekiel

"I don't believe this," I say, under my breath.

"What's the matter?" Leanne almost misses a red light, slams on the brakes, and has to back up a few feet.

"Oh, it's nothing," I say, "I'm just scared you're going to kill us."

WE MEET IN THE PARKING LOT of the College of William and Mary's library at the usual time, but Ben doesn't remove his backpack from his truck. "I'm pretty caught up in chemistry right now. Would you mind if we walk around the campus?"

"No, I'd like that. It's been a rough day." We head down a brick path, away from the parking lot.

"You could say that," Ben says. "Do you want to meet my Aunt Nadia?"

"Where's she staying?"

"Here on campus. The Russian House. It's a dorm floor set up like an apartment, with a kitchen and a living room, where the students primarily speak Russian. They had an extra room for visiting students."

While I've been to my mom's office, I've never been inside a college dorm. The path, wooded and hilly, welcomes us onward with the orange-yellow glow of old-fashioned wrought iron lights. It's romantic. More than once, girls do a double-take after glancing up at Ben, probably wondering why they haven't noticed him before. At the bottom of a steep path, we come to a clearing with a cluster of brick dorms. Climbing the steps of the nearest one, we head for a door in the farthest corner. Ben pushes the bell to the Russian House.

A gangly student with a heavy Southern drawl recognizes Ben and lets us in to the living room. A mural of the Moscow subway route covers one wall. "Your Aunt Nadia's in the kitchen cleaning up after dinner. That woman can rattle the pots and pans! We never had it so good." Ben introduces me to Clem Olson. We follow Clem to the kitchen, where the tantalizing aroma of onions and roast lingers from dinner.

"Vova! Vova!" A sturdy woman with deep-set blue eyes rushes at Ben. She clasps his face between her hands and brings it down to kiss both his cheeks. Ben turns a little pink, but it's obvious he likes the attention.

Aunt Nadia lets out a string of words that neither of us understand. Clem translates for us. "Your aunt says she is happy that you came, but Kolya has a late class today and won't be back until after ten o'clock. Would you like some tea?" We look at Clem.

"She asked that, not me." Clem points to Aunt Nadia.

Ben looks at me and I nod. "Da. Chai, pajalusta." I figure this means *yes.*

His aunt fills the teapot while asking Clem something in Russian. "She asks if this is your Verona." Clem winks at me.

Ben gives me a sheepish grin. "Tell her, *Yes, we're going to the dance next weekend.*" Clem's Russian accent is so convincing, it makes his heavy Southern accent seem like the foreign language.

Ben's aunt gets a serious expression on her face, and belts out a few more sentences in a harsher tone. "She wants to know if your father knows." Clem leans on the counter.

"Tell her he doesn't have to know everything." Ben looks at the floor. *Ben didn't tell his dad that he'd asked me to the dance?* The first person I told—besides Luka—was my mother.

We enjoy our tea with Ben's aunt through the very patient translation efforts of Clem, who insists that the practice is helpful for him. Aunt Nadia is maternally loving and straightforward. Her deep-lined face reveals a life wrought with hardship, yet her eyes twinkle whenever Ben smiles—the eyes of a mother reunited with her long-lost son.

On the way back to the parking lot, Ben speaks first. "I wish I remembered how to speak Russian. It's so frustrating to have to talk through someone else."

"Ben, why was she so concerned about whether or not you told your father about me?"

"I guess she knows how the coach is about women."

"What do you mean? Doesn't he like women?" I remember him eyeing Mrs. Cadella at the assembly.

"Oh, he likes women…a lot. He's not *gullaboy* or anything." Ben kicks a stone off the path. "It's just that Coach doesn't want Al or me to get serious with anyone. He's afraid it will hurt our concentration."

"Everything is football with him, isn't it?"

"That's an understatement. But it's more than that. Kolya told me that when Coach was my age, he had high hopes of becoming a soccer star in Russia—by my aunt's account, he was good enough. But then he met my mom, and not long after, we were born."

"It doesn't sound like you even want to be a football star."

"I don't know. Most days, like after practice, I never want to hear the word *football* again. But then there are moments, like when we take the field before the game starts, I'm so full of adrenaline that I can't think of anything else. But I do know what's expected of me. I am expected to be a star in college, and then on to the pros."

"That's a lot of pressure."

"I try to focus on the next step, which is to get admitted to a competitive college program."

"Like where?"

"Well, this coming weekend we're visiting some colleges to check out their programs—UNC, Duke, and then we'll stay for a camp at UVA in Charlottesville. Georgeson's dad played there. He's pressuring Coach to send us there. We're leaving Thursday, so I won't be able to study."

"I'm going out of town this weekend, too. New York." I try to keep things light, despite my heart pounding through my chest. In the parking lot, the light through the crepe myrtle blooms casts everything in a pinkish glow. "See you tomorrow in chemistry, *Vova*."

"Don't start calling me Vova. Kublai Khan is bad enough." He pulls me to him. I immediately tense up, but love the strong feel of his arms around my back. His finger lifts my chin and he brushes his lips against my cheek.

"Thanks for tonight. I feel a lot better." He hugs me, and then opens my door.

I drive away touching my lips, thinking, *Vova vavoom*, and I imagine his lips pressed on mine. Someday.

Wednesday, September 23rd
676 Days to Home Free

A GLOOM ENGULFS OUR CAFETERIA TABLE the next day, thick as the clam chowder Nicky stirs, but never seems to lift to his mouth. At the far end of the table, two empty chairs provide a reminder of the finality of the previous day's events. The gravity of Ross' death fouls the air and our mood.

"I guess Craig ditched school today." Leanne juts her head toward the empty chair. "Can't say I blame him."

"He's here," Paris says. "He was in first-block English."

Leanne raises her eyebrows. "How'd he look?"

"Like he was homeless and disturbed. And he smelled even worse."

"You think he's in trouble for what he said at the funeral?" Caitlin pushes her food away.

"I doubt it, Pringles," Nicky says. "Mr. Sams knows how torn up he is."

"We should do something nice for him." Everyone perks up at Leanne's suggestion. "If we had something positive to do, maybe we'd all feel better."

"Like what?"

"I'm not sure." Leanne rests her head on one hand, rearranging the vegetables on her plate.

"We could wash his car." Paris looks around.

"Hamilton doesn't have his own car," Nicky says. "His dad's in prison. From what I hear, his grandmother works two jobs, and drives a beat-up ol' Chevy. I don't know where his mom is." We all slump over in thought.

I have an idea. "We could get a card and all sign it."

"And we could invite him back to our table so he feels like he belongs somewhere." Leanne puts her arm on mine.

"He can have my seat so he doesn't have to sit across from Ross' empty one," Susie says.

Then I hear my voice addressing the group. "Let's all meet tomorrow morning outside Mr. Sams' office. I'll bring the card. After we all sign it, Paris can give it to him in first block." Everyone nods in agreement. I am amazed that I've suggested something the others think is a good idea. This is a first. I feel a little lighter.

LATER THAT DAY, I EXPERIENCE a minor mishap on the pottery wheel during third-block art class. At the last minute, the Grecian urn I've been envisioning for weeks inverts. In spite of my best efforts to reverse the damage, it needs to be rethrown. Consequently, by the time I arrive to fourth-block chemistry, I am peeved—as well as late. Mr. Zeke's door is closed.

I knock gently. He answers with a questioning look.

"I'm sorry," I whisper, rushing by him to my empty seat. Ben's wide smile—obviously teasing me for being late—doesn't improve my spirits. I glare at him. He mocks surprise.

I sulk for the entire period, pretending to be interested in chemistry while inconspicuously trying to remove sticky plaster from the creases of my fingers on a piece of paper under my desk. My hasty hand-washing after art left both my hands and my mood in a mess. When the final bell rang, I'm caught completely unaware when warm, cinnamon-flavored breath blows the hair next to my ear.

"I'm sorry you're upset. I was just glad that you made it to class. This used to be my worst class, but now it's my favorite." With that, Ben strolls out of the room before I can even collect my thoughts, much less my books.

My shoulders sag as I swing around my seat and load my backpack. Most of the kids have left the room when I look up at Mr. Zeke's form standing in front of my desk.

"I'm really sorry," I blurt out again, expecting a scolding.

"You're fine. You were only two minutes late, and you're not one to make it a habit." Mr. Zeke looks toward the door. "I want to talk to you about those visions. Unfortunately, I've got a meeting today." He walks me to the door. "Can you stay after tomorrow?"

It takes me a second for my mind to register what he's talking about. With my hands a sticky mess, it's easy to forget the mess the rest of my life has become. "I can stay for half an hour, but then I've got to go to work."

"Thirty minutes should be enough time."

"Oh, and thanks for the incredible reference, Mr. Zeke. I'm sure I don't deserve it."

"I'm sure you do." He nods me on.

When I turn down the hall, I'm surprised to find it empty except for one lone figure leaning against the lockers. I recognize Craig Hamilton more by his bent posture and red hair than by his face, completely hidden by his hair. I figure Mr. Zeke's meeting must be with Craig.

As I get closer, I think I should say something rather than pass by in silence. "Hi, Craig." I smile. A tentative smile—but definitely a smile.

He glares at me with a vengeance. A locker behind me slams, and I turn toward the metal reverberations. The next second, my foot lodges under Craig's outstretched leg and I'm flying through the air, backpack whirling up behind my neck, causing me to hit the ground with an unladylike thud—the fall broken by my palms, elbows, and knees. The knee impact sends a shooting pain up my leg past my hip.

"Watch out." Craig laughs.

The idiot tripped me! I will myself not to cry—my knee hurts so much! I pull myself up and adjust my glasses. My glasses, for once, have managed to stay attached to my head.

I turn to face him. "What did you do that for?" I say between gritted teeth.

"What? You tripped. You should watch where you're going," Craig sneers over crossed arms.

Mr. Zeke steps out of his room. "What's going on out here?"

"What is his problem?" I clench my fists.

"Craig, in the room." When Craig has rounded the corner into the classroom, Mr. Zeke puts his hand on my shoulder. "Cut him some slack."

LEANNE IS SYMPATHETIC WHEN I CALL to tell her what transpired in the hallway. She insists on buying the card, since we both agree that I might not be in the best frame of mind to select the right one at the moment, unless there's one with a salutation that began with *a* and ends with a word that rhymes with *mole*. In fact, every fiber in my being wants him to choke on the card.

After I rant about the injustice of it all for several minutes, Leanne says something odd, "Blessed are the persecuted because of righteousness, for theirs is the kingdom of heaven." I'm dumbstruck. Here is another of the *bless-ed* sayings, like the one the preacher spoke about at Ross's funeral. That one had to do with when people mourn—but there's even one for what happened to me in the hallway?

I guess I do feel like I've been persecuted. After all, I'm the one who suggested we get a card for him. But right now I don't feel like admitting that I have no clue what Leanne means, so I change the subject to the homecoming dance. We decide to dress shop tomorrow after I get off work.

On Wednesdays, my mom's light day at the college, we always eat at the Mexican restaurant around the corner. The food is plentiful and inexpensive, meaning we take home leftovers. So when I see her in a sleeveless black dress and heels, I'm perplexed.

"How do I look?" She roots through the closet for her jacket.

"Too dressed up for Casa Fernando."

"Oh, right. I guess I forgot to tell you." Jacket over her arm, she applies lipstick while gazing in the entry mirror. "I'm going out to dinner tonight."

"With who?" My mom has been so busy lately; I've been looking forward to some one-on-one time with her.

"With *whom*. A coworker." She smacks her lips together.

"A *male* coworker?" She is way too dolled up for a dinner with the girls. Besides, as far as I know, she hasn't made any girlfriends here. Not that she had a ton of them at home.

"As a matter of fact, yes, a man." Mom tosses her lipstick into a tiny purse.

"Isn't it a little early for dating?" The same despair from lunch clouds over me.

"I don't think there are rules about this, Verona. Once the divorce is final, all's fair." Still, she senses my dismay, rubs my hair, and kisses the top of my head. "I'm sorry if you're bothered by it, honey. It's just that I need to get out and meet people, and someone asked me. It'll probably lead to nowhere."

"But what about Dad?" I know as I say it that my question sounds ridiculous, in light of the divorce and all.

"I expect your father's been dating for a while. *He's* the one who wanted the divorce, remember?" Mom's reply crushes me; I feel my chest cave in. "And don't forget to tell your father about next weekend."

My dad? *Dating?* In a million years, I cannot picture Dad with anyone but my mom. Even after the divorce was finalized, he looked at her like a little kid standing outside the ice cream store counting his pennies and knowing he doesn't have enough. Why can't she see that?

To my relief, my mom's date doesn't come to the door to meet me. Mom waits on the porch. When I hear a car pull up, I peek through the shutters, but my mom blocks my view. His cherry-red BMW convertible tells me a lot. And she lectured *me* on dating a player!

I bang the front of my head on the window frame, but pull back when it hurts. *Blessed are those whose parents rip the family apart, for their job is to pick up the pieces.*

I decide to call Dad now and get it over with. Hopefully, he won't be too upset about me standing him up.

Dad answers and sounds genuinely pleased that I called. "How are you making out, V?"

"It's been a rough week," I answer. *And you should be here.*

"What happened?"

I tell him about Angie's car accident, discovering Ross Georgeson's body in his running car, and the funeral. I leave out the parts about being tripped in the hallway by the same jerk I was trying to help, as well as mom's date with Beamer Boy.

"Yeah, your mom told me about all this. I'm sorry you've had such a bad week, V." Dad exhales. "But I got the impression from your mother that something good happened this week as well. Your mother also mentioned that you have something important to ask me."

Might as well just come out with it. Get the disappointment over with. "Oh, right. Dad, a really popular football player asked me to go to the homecoming dance." I expect shock and awe at this revelation. "So can I come this weekend instead of next weekend?"

"Of course you can. And about this homecoming date—what position does he play?"

"I forget, but he sacks the other team's quarterback a lot."

"Probably a linebacker. Good for you."

"Why is that good, Dad? You don't even know him." What kind of father gives approval of his daughter's date based on the position he plays on a football team?

My dad laughs at my response. "I trust your judgment—what did you say his name was?"

IV

Eagle Grip and Letting Go

Thursday, September 24th
675 Days to Home Free

WE MET THURSDAY MORNING outside the front office as planned. Neither Leanne nor I disclosed Craig's hallway prank when we all signed the card and handed it to Paris. I so want to tell everyone what a jerk he is. Get some sympathy for the injustice of it all. I force myself to write something bland, not kind exactly, but not what he deserves, either. Consequently, at lunchtime, the still-empty chair at our table miffs me to no end.

"Paris, didn't you give Craig the card?" Susie taps the chair that Ross occupied only last week.

"I gave it to him." She sets her forearms on the table and leans in.

"And?" we all ask.

"He read it. All of it. And then he tore it into little pieces." Paris grabs a napkin and tears it slowly. "Then he took a piece and popped it into his mouth." She pauses, her eyes scanning each of us. We lean toward her center seat. "And every time Mr. McDonald turned his head, Hamilton reached in his mouth, removed a slimy wet piece of the card, and flung it at me."

"Eew." Caitlin scrunches her face.

Paris exhales. "Lucky for me his aim was off. The sicko pulled this stunt the whole period, whenever McDonald was distracted. By the end of class it looked like there'd been a snow squall under my desk. And the fool McDonald made *me* clean it up."

Leanne gives me a quick shake of her head when I look at her, sensing that I want to reveal how he tripped me. This makes me angry all over again.

"Try to do something nice for someone and look what happens." Nicky sighs.

"It just shows the degree to which he's hurting," Leanne says. "It was a great idea Verona had—Craig's just not ready." I appreciate Leanne's approval of my idea, because I'm feeling like it completely bombed. But then, I don't appreciate how she always wants to give people a pass. I want Hamilton to pay for being a jerk, loser, scoundrel. Or, as Dr. Newman would say, *miscreant*.

"I saw his eyes. Those eyes don't look hurting to me. They look dead." Paris pulls her sweater tight around her. "*Empty*. I'm staying far away from that dude."

I MAKE IT TO CHEMISTRY with two minutes to spare.

Ben's seat is empty.

When he doesn't show up before Mr. Zeke closes the door, I figure he's already left for the weekend. *Great.* Yesterday's class was my last opportunity to see him before his trip, and I blew it. I remember Ben's words as he walked out yesterday, and I spend the period feeling awful. I don't think I heard a word Mr. Zeke said all class, so I jump when the final bell rings.

When everyone besides me leaves, Mr. Zeke shuts the door. He leans against the front of his desk, thumbing through a folder. I sit on the desk in the first row, feet dangling over the side, with my backpack on my lap like a shield.

Pulling a pair of black-rimmed reading glasses from his inside jacket pocket, Mr. Zeke adjusts them on his nose. "Verona, your visions—and particularly what your friend told you—reminded me of something I heard at a seminar several years ago. Thankfully, I'm a pack rat."

"What did you find?"

He looks down at the notebook in his hand. "The lecture, titled *Heretics: Past and Present*, was facilitated by T. Gordon Blythe, a double doctorate—one in philosophy, and the other in divinity. Dr. Blythe hailed from Oxford. He professed to be a hardened atheist before converting to 'the Way' after a lifetime of extensive research."

"Can I ask a question?" I raise hand out of habit, and he smiles. "What do they mean by *the Way*? In the first vision, the one where you were an eagle too, you told me to *follow the Way*. Is it like Taoism?"

"I can see where you might confuse it with Taoism—others have. *The Way* is how the early Christian church and their persecutors described followers of Jesus. It comes from the book of John, chapter 14, verse 6, where Jesus says, '*I am the Way, the Truth and the Life.*'"

I nod my head to feign understanding. I don't want Mr. Zeke to go off on a tangent.

"The part of Dr. Blythe's lecture that pertained to eagles, lions, and so forth took no more than ten or fifteen minutes." He shuffles through his notes. He reads, "'In the year 1559, the local church pursued and persecuted a small heretic cult in a remote German parish on the Amper River. The group was comprised of individuals who claimed to possess divinely-instilled powers traced to the four faces of the cherubim in the book of Ezekiel.'"

"Ezekiel." I tilt my head. "I read about his vision of the cherubim online. It was described as a tetrad."

"He believed the cherubim too powerful to inhabit one individual, so their attributes fall unto a quattro of predestined individuals. Blythe calls these individuals *Transcenders,* but there really is no known name for this phenomenon. It's not directly referred to in the Bible, or any book I've been able to find."

"Transcenders? But why me?" My face reddens. "I don't want to be an eagle or a Transcender. And I certainly don't want to fight demons. I don't even believe in this."

"I'm not sure it matters what you want or even what you believe. Maybe you should just keep an open mind for now."

"Okay." I slide a hand under my thigh to keep it from shaking. "What kind of powers do they have?"

"As I think you know, the eagle is the visionary—the eyes. He or she can see things they ordinarily wouldn't. For instance, your vision about Angie in the accident proved true to what took place, and yet you had no earthly way of knowing it would happen." I slide my other hand under me. "Weird, huh?"

My eyes widen in agreement. "What about the lion?"

"The individual representing the lion façade is the strength. He or she grows fierce when opposing the powers of darkness. Blythe cites this example: 'From this 1559 band of Transcenders, a small—under five foot, approximately 100-pound German woman pulled a man weighing over two hundred pounds off the hanging scaffold. She ran with him dangling over her shoulders through a crowd of wide-eyed onlookers, depriving them of their weekend entertainment. And yet no one—not the sheriff, not the executioner, nor any of the throng, moved to stop this frail woman during the rescue. She had become frightfully strong. A priest at the scene attributed her power to the devil, but the whole time the lion woman insisted that the man she'd rescued was innocent, an angel.'"

"Angel—as in the *angel* Transcender?" *Luka's Aunt May was right.*

Mr. Zeke smiles his assent and continues reading from his notes: "'The angel man, on the other hand, had been convicted of witchcraft because he said that an eagle visionary told him the bishop killed several children, children who threatened to report the sexual abuse perpetrated on them. The angel man told them that at its core, the abuse came from the demon Asmodeus.'"

"If the bishop killed them, why did the angel guy say the demon was responsible?"

"Asmodeus is the demon of lust responsible for twisting a person's normal sexual desire."

"How could a demon make a man want to do that?" I think of all the news reports of children being sexually abused. *Is it possible that this demon could be responsible for this heartbreak even today?*

"I believe the man has to invite the demon or one of his minions into his being. With Asmodeus, maybe it's pornography that invites the demon. There are a lot of theories on this. We don't have time to delve into that now."

"This is crazy. I mean, how many demons are there?"

"No one knows. But many demons are said to have legions under them. They don't necessarily possess a person, but they are capable of infecting people with unhealthy, unnatural desires. These desires will eventually lead those infected to death. The seven deadly sins are, as they say, *deadly*."

"This would explain the Devine Donuts lady."

"Who?" Now it was Mr. Zeke's turn to be surprised.

"I didn't tell you because I didn't turn into an eagle that time, and no one was hurt or killed. A few weeks ago—in fact, the day after I had the vision with Angie, this donut vendor at the Farmer's Market looked at me and her face became all maggoty and gross, like she'd been decaying for months. I was able to see some awful things from her past. She was greedy and mean. But she didn't morph into Mammon."

"What you saw probably wasn't a full-blown possession like with Ross' killer—but a spirit was winning the battle with this woman. Let's focus on the good side, shall we? Remember the angel man that the lion woman rescued from the scaffold?" I nod. "Blythe contends that he was the heart connection to God—he could intuit divine will."

I swallow. "So what happened?"

"The clergy in Rome sent a team of authorities to apprehend the so-called heretics. When it appeared as though they had uncovered the threesome, a man came forward, claiming to be the eagle visionary."

"I thought you said the eagle was a woman?"

"No wonder you've got a perfect grade in chemistry. You're right. The man who came forward was hung for witchcraft, but the rest of the story was uncovered in 1924 in a tattered diary. Henrietta Weiss claimed to be a direct descendant of the real eagle: a woman."

"But why would that guy take the rap for her?"

"The diary revealed that the man who came forward was the eagle woman's closest friend from childhood; a clerk who was refused her hand in marriage by the woman's miserly father. The diary stated the powers associated with the eagle, the angel, and the lion. The woman asserted that her childhood friend became the sacrificial bull when he heroically traded his life for hers."

"So the bull—its power is suicide? That makes no sense to me. Unless… could Ross be the bull?"

Mr. Zeke shakes his head. "It's not the same as suicide. The mysterious key, the ultimate power, is found in the sacrificial love of the man. When this key is present, evil is defeated in whatever battle the Transcenders are engaged in. As far as we know, Ross wasn't trying to save someone else. From what you've told me, he was murdered. He was a victim."

I hug my waist with my arms, clutching my sweatshirt in my fists. "You believe this?"

"The facts in the diary were corroborated by old church documents which point to other cases." Mr. Zeke doesn't say whether or not he believes it. He looks at me while summarizing his notes. "In addition, Blythe discovered that the pope directed another investigation, after which Bishop Gustav was removed from office and excommunicated. One week later, he was found drowned in the Amper River. The eagle visionary recorded how the Transcenders' claims were authenticated by several children who came forward after the bishop had died."

"So the bull Transcender was found guilty of a crime he never committed and was killed. That isn't fair." My fists unclench.

"Fair or unfair, it's a recurring theme in the Bible, in literature, and in life."

That still doesn't make it right.

"And he had a choice. Blythe said that while the diary in this seventeenth-century account points to the fourth person of the man as the one who risked his life, sometimes the person of the bull is not as obvious, or even recognizable. He theorized that because humans are given free will, this face of the Transcenders may not materialize at all—it's a wild card. He cited the case of 1865, where Lincoln's assassination might have been prevented, as an example of when the sacrificial bull never showed up."

"There were more? Abraham Lincoln?" I can't stop my chest from pounding.

"Blythe contends that there are probably countless other Transcenders. He researched Native American legends promoting an eagle people, a lion people, and a spirit—what we might call *angel*—people. He said when you look for them, they're everywhere."

I gulp. I absolutely cannot believe my chemistry teacher is buying into this. "I have to get to work. Do you think I could borrow your notes?"

"You bet." He hands me the folder and I squeeze it into my backpack.

"I don't know anyone who could be thought of as a lion or an angel."

"I expect you'll find out when you need to. In the meantime, I'd like you to record your visions. You might want to add your thoughts and feelings as well. You've been through a lot these past few weeks." He hands me a journal, ornate and old-fashioned, with gold embossed over green vines and swirls on a deep burgundy background.

"Thanks, Mr. Zeke." I sprint out the door and down the hall, keeping a vigilant eye out for Craig Hamilton's leg.

A MAN WEARING A WHITE JUMPSUIT with a bold "Quality Extermination" patch displayed prominently on his right shoulder holds the door open for me as he leaves the Aquila's Artist's Emporium. I swallow a lump of guilt as I wonder how much my *gross bug* lie cost Mr. Stanworth.

"Miss Lamberti, you're late!" a shout resounds from the back office.

"Sorry, Mr. Stanworth!" I yell back. "I had to meet with a teacher after school."

He waddles out to the storefront. "I thought you were a smart girl. Are you having problems in school?"

"No, it's nothing like that," I say, searching for any explanation besides the truth—which is way too extraordinary to be believed, not to mention way too complicated to explain.

"Did you hear about the girl who lost her leg in the car accident a few weeks ago?" I ask.

"I saw it in the papers. Terrible thing to lose a leg—and so young. You know her?"

"Yeah, she's an artist—likes to paint. I visited her at the VCU Medical Center. I'm driving up tomorrow after school."

"I see. She must be pretty upset." Mr. Stanworth grabs a shopping basket from next to the counter.

"She's pretty torn up." Angie is torn up in so many ways.

Mr. Stanworth carries the basket to the paint section. I start unpacking a shipment behind the register. I hear some items drop on the counter above me.

"Miss Lamberti," he says in a soft voice, "Take these to the young lady. Maybe it'll take her mind off of..." I stand up and my jaw drops. There are two hundred dollars' worth of art supplies on the counter.

"Oh, Mr. Stanworth," I stammer. "Are you sure? This is really expensive."

He waves his hand back at me as if it's nothing, and waddles back to his office.

My mouth waters over the complete set of expensive oils, brushes, turpentine, palette, and set of canvases. Even a tabletop easel. I never imagined Mr. Stanworth to be so generous.

AFTER WORK, I HAVE FORTY-FIVE MINUTES to eat, give Max a romp outside, and fill Luka in on the day's news before meeting Leanne for our shopping excursion. I decide to tackle all three tasks at once: let Max torment a duck in the pond, wash a Quiznos Turkey-Bacon-Ranch sub down with Diet Coke, and converse with Luka between bites.

Luka's reaction to Mr. Zeke's research doesn't surprise me. "I told you! You're an eagle," she exclaims.

"If that's true, who's the lion? Who's the angel? And who's the bull?" I ask.

"C'mon, we both know who the lion is. Of course, he's an angel too! And that's no bull." The unusual inflection clues me that there's *something* she isn't telling me.

"Luka, what are you *tawking* about?" My impatience shows in my accent.

"I'm glad to see you can't take the New York out of the girl."

"I'm waiting," I say, tapping my fingertips on the phone speaker. "Is this about Ben?"

"You'll have to keep waiting. I'm sworn to secrecy."

"Luka," I scold. "Have you forgotten our oath? No secrets, remember?"

"But, V," she says, "I promised! I want to tell you—I really do! It's killing me to hold it in."

"You promised Ben something?"

"He made me."

"When have you been talking to my....uh, date?" I feel a tinge of jealousy at this idea. Luka *is* my best friend in the whole world, but still, what is she doing talking to my boyfriend behind my back?

"I didn't talk to Ben directly," she explains. "This was done through Kolya."

"If he made you promise and it was through another person, then it doesn't count."

"Oh, you're bad!" She laughs. "Wait. I have an idea. Remember when we used to play twenty questions? If you guess the secret, then no one can say I told you." She has a point. Besides, with Luka I usually uncover the answer before using up half my questions.

"Does the thing that makes Ben the man have anything to do with you and Kolya?"

"Yes."

"Does it have to do with me?"

"Sort of."

The clock tower at the center of Jefferson Village announces that it's almost five-thirty, and I need to get home to be on time to meet Leanne.

"Luka, I don't have time for this now. I've got to go dress shopping."

"Yes."

"You're saying it has to do with the homecoming dance?" I ask, hooking on Max's leash.

"Yes—and you wasted a question. That's four."

"Tell me!"

"Okay, but if you tell, I'll tell Kolya you sucked your thumb until you were ten years old. And you *know* he'll tell Ben."

"I won't tell." I tug Max away from his duck friends in the pond.

"I'm coming to your homecoming dance!" I hold the phone a foot away from my ear.

"You are? With who?"

"With Kolya, *duh*," she says, as though that part should be obvious.

"But Kolya doesn't go to Colonial."

"I know. That's why Ben is an angel. He got permission *and* two extra tickets."

LUKA'S REVELATION PUTS CAFFEINE in my cocoa for the rest of the day. Discovering the perfect dress tops it off. The minute the deep crimson dress falls down over my body, I feel like a princess. The red accentuates the green of my eyes and makes me glad that my new contacts should be available soon.

Leanne says there is no doubt this is *the one*. "Ben's mouth is gonna water when he sees you in that. The boy already thinks you hung the moon."

I smile, and scoot to the side so Leanne can look at her reflection. She pirouettes; the peachy satin strapless with flouncy lace at the hem makes her look like a ballerina. "What do you think?" I give it the thumbs up.

"What do you mean by *hung the moon?*" I've just gotten to the word *moon* when the charcoal taste fills my mouth. At the same time my fingers feel like thawing icicles, but at least I'm prepared for what's coming.

And it does.

In an instant I'm hovering over the dressing room stalls, and shooting out over color-coded racks of clothing, over a sales person so thin she's almost see-through, and out the door.

Unlike the two previous exits where I dove through glass, this time I have help. A young woman holds the door open for her mother with enough time for me to rush past. The older woman looks up, as if she feels the breeze from my wings, but otherwise no one seems aware of the bald eagle soaring out of Dee's Debutante Boutique.

No one in the parking lot notices the blinding spotlight glow of the angel, either. She precedes me, a beacon directing me to follow. The evening air has chilled, whipping against my face like a warning.

But I'm not afraid—I am exhilarated to be flying over the neighborhoods and streets of Jamestown. I know I *should* be afraid. These flights usually end with someone getting hurt or killed. But when I'm soaring, it's a rush like nothing else. I wish it could go on forever.

We move north from the James River, up Colonial Williamsburg's DoG Street toward William and Mary, over the Capital Building and the taverns, past the Governor's Palace on our right, and skim over the Bruton Parish Church where we'd attended Ross's funeral only days before. The air carries the faint smell of apple cider and the pungent smell of horse manure.

We cross low over the intersection dubbed *confusion corner* onto the campus, fly over the statue of Lord Botetourt—pronounced Bot-a-tot—close enough to the weathervane to set its 1693 flag spinning. Past the Wren Building and over the sunken garden, the angel banks right, simultaneously flying higher and faster. My wings pump hard to keep up.

She urges me onward over a heavily wooded area that stretches for miles along a four-lane divided highway that I'm pretty sure is I64—the interstate that passes Williamsburg from Richmond on its way to Virginia Beach. We begin our descent into an urban neighborhood, checkered with buildings rising next to postage-stamp wooded lots. All I can see are offices, apartment buildings, parking lots, and strip malls—but, unlike the skyscraper-filled skyline of New York City, none of the structures are taller than six floors.

The angel leads me down to a forested section of a quiet street connecting a four-lane avenue to several apartment complexes. I perch high in the arms of an evergreen. Fog spirals up from the ground and clings to the low places in the shrubbery. Except for the hum of traffic from a nearby road and the blare of a distant siren, the night is lonely and still. Even the leaves holding on to the highest branches aren't stirring. The air carries the heavy aroma of decomposing leaves and burned meat.

When we come down, so does my mood. The elation I feel soaring above is replaced by agitation and the obvious question: *Why are we here?*

"It is for you to see," the angel explains.

The words are barely spoken when a movement in the underbrush grabs my attention. My wings spread. I slide to a lower branch to get a closer look. The angel instructs me not to move any closer. Her luminosity reflects off the rising mist, but still the black-hooded man crouching low in the thick brush looks ominous. I can't help but think it's the same guy who killed Ross. The killer stands up and pokes through the leaves. He shouts something I can't understand, directly at me. *Like he can see me!*

What am I going to do if he attacks me? Poke his eyes out? I hear a noise from behind so I spin my neck around. I see lime-green glow-in-the-dark sneakers pedaling a bike too small for the rider. The rider slows his pace and glides to the side of the road, only a few feet from where I sit. Now, within the glow of the angel's light, I see the rider clearly. He's a gargantuan kid, with smoky-dark skin, short-cropped hair, and angry eyes. He stops at the curb, florescent-glowing feet planted on the ground on either side of the bike. He squints right at me. And the black-hooded guy from behind says something else in a garbled tone. Okay, he's not talking to me.

Whatever the hooded guy says incites the teen. I know this because the kid yells back—again it's something I can't understand—and throws first his backpack, then his bike to the ground. I am caught in the middle of the killer and the teen, but apparently invisible to both of them.

Black eyes blazing, the huge teen charges straight for me, fists clenched. Up close he is gargantuan, enormous, *dangerous*. I try to back up, but my talons cling to the limb.

As the boy sweeps away branches trying to get to the source of his fury, a strong vibration originates from behind. The vibration tunnels through my eagle abdomen. My stomach knots, but it doesn't hurt. It feels more like the rush of cold water going through me. Another vibration echoes though me, and I feel that same cold-water rush again.

I glance backward. The hooded guy has morphed into the giant demon Mammon, in golden robe and grisly evil expression. The smell of sulfur and decay chokes me.

Mammon knocks me off the branch with a back slap of his enormous hand like I'm a pesky horsefly. I rise up, and now it's not just the boy who's enraged, irate, furious. I want to dig my talons deep into his fat crusty head and peel off his horns with my beak, but, at the angel's telepathic request, I retreat, spread my wings and float to a lower branch.

I watch the black kid's eyes go wide. With arms held out to his sides, he tilts his head down, touches the big letter H on his gray sports jacket and brings his fingers to his mouth. Blood trickles from two holes spaced inches apart on his chest. He looks right at me, his face contorted, expressing pain, confusion, and sadness. Then his pupils roll to the side and his knees begin to shake, like he's going to collapse. A gloved hand shoots out, grabs the bloody jacket and flips the kid around to get a firm hold on the jacket's back collar. The boy's body is yanked back deeper into the woods. I watch as the florescent green sneakers disappear into the bushes.

Next to the bushes, a gleam of light reflects off a silver pistol lying in the fallen leaves. It's topped with some sort of extension, like a circus clown's gun—without the rainbow-colored flags. It's then that the realization of what I've witnessed washes over me like an icy rain. Mammon insulted the kid to get him to come closer. Then he shot him. The vibrations ripped through me, but didn't hurt my eagle body. I look for the angel—I want to ask her what we should do to help—but she's gone.

My mouth opens to let out a scream, but before my vocal chords engage, my eyes pop open. I'm on the floor, shaking, with Leanne's face swimming before my eyes—the knotted forehead telling me I've scared her.

When my eyes focus on hers, she lets out a huge exhale. "Hey, are you okay? What just happened? One minute you're asking what *hung the moon* means, and the next thing I know, you're on the floor."

I nod, and she helps me to my feet. Rubbing a sore spot on the back of my head, I say, "I'm fine, I think."

The anorexic employee sticks her head through the fitting room door and asks in an impatient, nasal twang, "Is everything alright in here?"

Leanne starts to say something, but I interrupt her. "Everything's fine. We found the dresses we want to buy. We'll be out in a minute to pay for them."

"No rush." And the head is gone.

"Verona Lamberti, everything is not fine! You'd better tell me what happened. If you're having seizures, you need to see a doctor."

"I am not having seizures. It's something else."

"I've seen seizures—and that looked an awful lot like a seizure."

"For now, you'll just have to trust me. It wasn't a seizure."

"Why can't you tell me what's going on? That's what friends do. They trust each other, but it's got to work both ways. I promise I won't tell anyone as long as it won't hurt you."

"Alright. Let's pay for the dresses and go back to my house. I'll show you as best I can what might be happening to me." As if I really know myself.

I LAY ACROSS MY BED, fingering the tulle underskirt of my new dress. When I finish explaining the Transcenders theory from both Aunt May's and Mr. Zeke's perspectives, Leanne is shaking her head.

"Mr. Zeke thinks this is real?" she asks. I nod. "But that means Ross' death probably wasn't suicide."

I nod again, and say, "Yup."

"And maybe Angie's brakes really were tampered with."

"Yup."

She rubs her temples. "But this last one, in the fitting room..." Leanne is starting to get spun up.

"FRV—fitting room vision," I say, trying for a little brevity.

"Whatever. Okay, FRV. What if there's some kid about to be killed?"

"I plan to tell Mr. Zeke about it tomorrow morning."

"What if tomorrow morning is too late?" Leanne paces the floor of my room, lackadaisically picking up dirty clothes and tossing them in my laundry basket.

"What can I do? Call 911 and tell them some red-eyed freak is going to shoot some big black kid and drag his body into the woods? *'How do I know, Officer? I saw it happen. Where? I'm not really sure about that—you see, I was in my eagle body at the time, following this really bright angel covered in eyes.'* You see the problem with this?"

"We can't just let some murderer get away with….um, murder." I agree with her, but can't seem to come up with a plausible way to alert the authorities.

Leanne types something in on her Droid. I'm worried she's texting someone about what I just told her. "I told you Mr. Zeke told me to keep it secret. I only told you because you saw…"

"Relax. I'm just googling *Transcenders*."

I berate myself for not thinking of it myself. I wriggle next to Leanne and peer at the screen. I can't see anything, so I plop down on my bed again. "Anything?"

"Transcenders is the name of some music production group in LA. Cool website—but no spiritual references."

Neither of us says anything for several minutes. Leanne puts her phone in her pocket, leans both arms on my desk and lets her head sink between her shoulders like she is concentrating.

"What's this, Verona?"

I look over to see what she means. "Oh, that's my calendar." Each month has different scenes from Central Park corresponding to the weather for that time of year.

"I *know* it's a calendar," Leanne snorts. "I mean, what's the countdown to home free. Like yesterday is 676 days to home free and today is 675. Tomorrow I guess will be 674. What's *home free*?"

"Don't you southerners play kick-the-can or freeze-tag? It's when…"

"I know what *that* home free means," Leanne says with a serious twang. "But we *southerners* don't mark it on our calendars like we're counting the days until we're released from prison."

I laugh. I guess in a way I did think moving here was like a prison sentence. "I've been counting the days until I'm back *home* in New York with Luka, and *free* of my parents and all their craziness—living on our own in the village."

"Y'all really don't like it here—do you?" Leanne's eyes meet mine.

"I like it okay. It was hard at first, but now that I have some friends..."

"It's tolerable?" She puts her hands on her hips and smirks. I've hurt her feelings.

I think of Ben's lop-sided grin and feel even guiltier. "I'm sorry—it's more than tolerable. It's growing on me."

"You have no idea how good you've got it. It must be comforting to have your whole future all figured out. I hope you can figure out what to do about that kid in your vision before he's as dead as Ross." Leanne grabs her bag.

But what *can* I do? I walk her to the front door, the space between us heavy with unspoken feelings as I close the door behind her.

I CHANGE INTO MY RED FLANNEL PAJAMAS, but my mind won't hold still long enough for me to sleep. I keep seeing the boy's face, angry, then confused, and then scared, like I'm the one shooting at him.

I flip on the light and then pull out the manila folder containing Blythe's seminar handouts. I place another pillow behind my back, and unfold the material onto my legs. Mr. Zeke's notes are scribbled on the opposite pages to the seminar outline. I skim through the first few pages of notes—much of which he read to me earlier—until I find what I've been searching for:

In early March 1865, Eleanor Kane, a young seamstress for First Lady Mary Todd Lincoln, told President Lincoln's bodyguard, Ward Hill Lamon, that she had a vision one of the residents of the National Hotel—whom she couldn't reveal other than the assurance that he lived there—plotted to kidnap the President following a performance. She described the vision, in which she had been transformed into an eagle, in great detail. It was the tremendous details that caused Lamon to change the president's plans and conduct an investigation. The investigators uncovered an assassination attempt thwarted by the change in venue.

Ward Lamon mentioned the vision and the results of the investigation to his daughter Dorothy. Dorothy confessed to both her father and fiancé at the time, Charles Augustus Leale, a Union Army surgeon specializing in gun wounds, that early on the morning of April 1st she had a horrible premonition that President Lincoln would be shot during a public performance. She'd spent all that day and half the night praying fervently for the president's safety.

At Dorothy's father's urging, the young couple met with Miss Kane in a restaurant close to the White House. Dorothy's journal entry of April 13th provides an account of that meeting. She wrote, "I'd never met Miss Eleanor Kane before, but it's as if we've known each other as children, or God forgive me, in a previous life. Charlie feels the same way. Sad our connection is over something so fearful."

Lincoln reported waking from a vivid dream on or around the night of April 1st. The dream foretold his death, with mourners all around his casket. This dream occurred precisely on the night of Dorothy's prayer vigil. Leading credence to the dream, during that time First Lady Mary Todd Lincoln had a disturbing premonition that something bad was going to happen to her husband.

Charles Augustus Leale attended Ford's theatre the Good Friday night of April 14th just to keep an eye on the president, so moved was he by his fiancée's growing angst.

We all know what happened to one of your most revered Presidents that fateful night. What you may not be aware of was that Leale was the first to burst through the barricaded door following John Wilkes Booth's jump to the stage. Numerous reports told of a man possessed by a lion charging up the aisle from the orchestra, knocking people out of his way until he reached the balcony. When Leale found Lincoln still alive, he did his best to resuscitate him, but to no avail.

Dorothy uncovered the spiritual connection borne from the cherubim. She wrote, "Eleanor is an eagle, Charlie is a lion, and I am an angel. Whoever was deemed the sacrificial bull—the completion of the four-part cherubim, didn't appear. I pray it wasn't my father, but in my heart, I fear it was."

It is my contention, along with Dorothy's, that her father, Ward Hill Lamon, Lincoln's bodyguard, would've been the sacrificial bull if he hadn't chosen to have a drink at a nearby pub instead of taking the bullet for the president.

Unfortunately, no details of the visions were written, so it is impossible to speculate which demon prince possessed John Wilkes Booth at the time.

I copy the key points from Mr. Zeke's notes into the back of my journal. If it's possible that the Transcenders were supposed to thwart the assignation of President Lincoln, could it be our role to stop the demon Mammon from killing someone else?

Friday, September 25th
674 Days to Home Free

I AM DETERMINED to get to school before the first bell, find Mr. Zeke, and unload the latest vision on him. Esther is parked in her usual spot at the end of the faculty parking lot, which means he's here. I hurry to the chemistry classroom, but it's empty, dark.

A classroom door is open across the hall, and from it, light spills into the hallway. The sign next to the door reads, *Ms. Kartal, Biology*. Having already taken biology in New York, I've never met this teacher. I take a step into the class.

A young woman, legs propped up on her desk, applies nail polish to a tear in the hose behind her knee. I start to back out, but she must have heard me. "Can I help you?" she asks, without taking her eyes off her pantyhose.

"Yes, please. I'm looking for Mr. Ezekiel." I don't know why I feel the need to be so formal when the woman is applying nail polish to the back of her knee.

"He's on break, first block," she says. "Try the lounge. Downstairs. Room 136."

"Thanks," I say.

I bound down the steps and around the school until I reach the lounge, but Mr. Zeke isn't there. He isn't in the second floor library, or the copy room. I check the lot again. Esther is still parked outside. I have built up a considerable sweat from running up and down the stairs, and the cool morning air is refreshing. Students have begun filing in, so I decide to go to his room after first block.

"Verona," the baritone voice bellows from behind. Mr. Zeke is standing at the door of Mr. Sams' office.

"Mr. Zeke! I had another vision yesterday. Another murder."

"Well, come in here." I have never been in Mr. Sams' office before. Or I should say *offices,* because it's actually two rooms—the first of which has a conference table with four chairs around it. Mr. Sams smiles at me from his desk in the adjoining room; a phone receiver is perched between his shoulder and ear, and he's scrawling notes on a legal pad.

Mr. Zeke closes the door between the rooms. "Now, what has your feathers so ruffled?" His eyes twinkle at the play on words.

"That is *not* funny," I say, shuffling through my books for the journal. I hand it to him, opened to the entry of the latest vision. He reads it quietly.

"I see," he says. "You don't know where you flew?"

"No. I only know it was past Williamsburg—I think on the way to Virginia Beach—and it was more of a city, but interspersed with woods—not like Richmond. No skyscrapers, more woods."

"That could be just about anywhere. Hampton, Newport News, Portsmouth. Did you go over any large bodies of water?"

"No. I saw the river, and there may have been a lake down on the right—and there was water, but it was a lot further away."

"Well that narrows it down to somewhere on the Peninsula." I shrug my shoulders. I haven't really explored this area enough to understand the geography. "You've never seen the bay before?" he asks.

I shake my head. He is taking me seriously, which scares me almost as much as the vision itself.

He clicks a pen against the table. "Was the hooded man in this vision the same one as the one with Ross?"

"I think so. With Ross, the angel told me it was some demon called Mammon. Luka and I researched it, and, from a painting I found, I think it *is* Mammon. The demon looked the same, but I never saw the man. I only briefly saw the hands in black gloves and the gun. The gun looked different. It had something that made it look long on the end—like a clown's gun."

"A silencer," Mr. Zeke says. He pulls an empty legal pad from the bookshelf behind him and starts taking notes. "What happened to the bicycle? Did the guy drag that back, too?" He looks up from the pad.

"I don't know. I snapped out of it when I realized the man shot the boy. I was scared. Leanne was with me and it scared her. I barely got any sleep last night."

"I'm sorry."

"Oh, and this didn't help," I say, handing him the folder. "I need to know: Do you really believe in the…?"

"Transcenders," he interjects.

"Do you?" I'm not going to let him get away with changing the subject this time.

"I'm not sure what to believe about what's going on here. Until we have more information, I'd suggest we suspend disbelief. It will help us be more aware of what is happening—or *could* happen—if we don't immediately reject any of this as impossible."

"Suspend disbelief?" It doesn't sound like something a chemistry teacher would suggest. "Is that scientific?"

"Absolutely. It's a key to discovery," he answers. "Otherwise, the world would still be flat."

SINCE I HAVE THE WORLD'S SMALLEST bladder, and in order to stay awake this morning I have downed enough Diet Coke to keep the Coca-Cola Company in business for another year, I run to the bathroom after lunch.

I'm drying my hands when the restroom door swings open, forcing me to the side.

"Oh, excuse *me*," says a voice, not sounding one bit like she cares whether I excuse her or not. I look up. I'm face-to-face with Amber Claussen, in a low-cut black sweater and skin-tight jeans. Her overwhelming, flowery perfume makes me cough. While she stands with her smirking face literally three inches from mine, three of her friends squeeze by, and watch us from the sinks.

Amber's asphalt eyes scan my body from the top of my head to my feet. "*You're* Ben Chortov's date?" The tone insinuates outrageous disbelief. Her stance adds to it, with arms crossed and chin high. My intestines knot up.

I force myself to meet her gaze. "As a matter of fact, yes." I slide past her and out the door.

From behind the door, I hear a mocking, "As a matter of fact, yes!" Laughter. Then another says, "As a matter of fact, I *am* from New York." More laughter.

In the safety of the hallway, I clench my fists, wondering what I've done to deserve this laughter gnawing away at my dignity.

THIS AFTERNOON AT THE VCU medical center, I ascend the parking garage stairway, walk past security, up the elevator and down the hall to Angie's room, loaded down with two heavy bags and an anxious, palpitating heart. So when I put one of the bags down to knock at the threshold, I'm only slightly more prepared to see Angie than I was last week.

It looks like I've come to the wrong room. Missing is the web of tubes, wires, and suspension ropes securing the wounded girl to her bed. Also missing is the wounded girl.

I confirm the room number, knock, and take a step inside. In the corner, behind the door, sitting with her casted leg propped up on a table, Angie appears engrossed in a little book with the big word HOPE splayed across its cover. Her raven hair is shiny, and she even wears a touch of makeup, concealing most of the yellowish-gray bruises on her face. Missing also is the flimsy hospital gown, and in its place, a navy sweat suit, one leg knotted below the knee.

"Verona! You came." Angie places the book on the stand next to her bed.

"*And* I've brought presents."

"I love presents!" Angie says. "But this is too much. You really shouldn't have."

"I didn't. Mr. Elliot Stanworth of the Artist's Emporium had me bring these for you." Angie unwraps the wooden art supply box, looking from the assorted paints and brushes to me.

"I don't know a Mr. Stanworth." She fingers the presents.

"He's the owner of the art supply store where I work," I explain. "When I told him I was visiting you, he insisted that I give these to you." I back up against the bed.

"Just like that—for no reason?"

"He feels bad about what happened."

"Wow." Angie eyes well up like she might cry. "You know, before this, I never thought twice about other people. I only thought about what I wanted, and how I was going to get it. Mostly I wanted excitement and fun—the more outrageous, the better." I hand her the other package. "But people have been so kind to me since—" She points to the knotted leg.

I can't think of anything to say, so I bite the inside of my lower lip.

"Oh, wow, an easel—and canvasses. I can't wait to paint!" Her eyes light up and she smiles at me. At that, I figure Angelina Jett is on the path to recovery.

I turn to rearrange some flowers on the sill to make room for the artist box when I see Mr. Sams walking briskly on the pavement below. I ask, "Was Mr. Sams just here?"

"No, not today," Angie replies.

"Well, that's him walking to the parking lot. I'm sure of it."

"I'm sure you're right. Mr. Sams stays here almost every night," Angie says casually, as though spending the night at a hospital an hour away from home is normal.

Angie smiles at my confused expression. "Mr. Sams' wife was admitted last week. She's getting chemo, and her blood count got too low or something. Her brother is a big shot in administration, so she's got her own room, with a bed for her husband. But now her numbers are doing a little better, so she can visit me. We've been doing this study on hope together." She picks up the book on the table.

"How do you study something like *hope*?" I always thought hope is something you either have or you don't have, depending on the severity of your situation.

"For one thing, you learn the truth about what you should hope *for*. When I first got here, I hoped I would die. I couldn't see a life worth living without my leg. But now I know I will walk again. It's weird, but I even have hope that my life will be better than before, somehow. Mrs. Sams has taught me so much."

"I can't believe Mr. Sams has been commuting this far every day and still running the school." For a second I think of all the assumptions I make by appearances. Mr. Sams usually looks and acts so calm and cool, like he has it all together, but he's dealing with heavy problems.

"Mrs. Sams has got stage four breast cancer, which by all accounts is incurable. But you'd never know it—she's the happiest person I've ever met."

"How's Mr. Sams taking it? Are they hoping for a miracle?"

"Mr. Sams is clearly concerned for her, but the few times he's come with her to see me, he stares at her like his eyes can't get enough. It's so romantic."

"Aren't they in their fifties?" I ask. I've always assumed that by then, most of the romantic flames have burned out, leaving a lifetime of cherished memories to hold you together... assuming you stayed together. My parents were barely forty when they bailed.

"Yeah, and they've been married forever." Angie sighs. "I want a man like him someday."

"Like Mr. Sams?"

"It's not like that. I don't have a crush on him or anything. What I mean is, I want a man who looks at me like that after being married for twenty or thirty years."

Angie's cell phone starts playing a seductive rap. "It's Tiffany. I need to get this."

I cringe. While I have never met Tiffany Green, I know she was one of the Amberettes laughing at me in the bathroom yesterday.

"Hi, Tiff. I can't talk long. What do you want?" Angie says, pausing as she waits for Tiffany's response. "Oh, she is? He did that? What a jerk."

I move toward the window and finger the unopened paints. From her room forty miles away, Angie Jett still has her finger on the pulse of the happenings at Colonial. She probably knows more about what's going on at school than I do.

"Verona Lamberti? He is? She did? What happened?"

My ears perk, and I turn.

Angie listens, winks, and flashes a knowing smile. Then she rolls her eyes at the caller. "Thanks for letting me know, Tiff. I've really got to go now. Later." She hangs up, the other girl's voice still yammering as she sets the receiver down.

"You've got a hot date for homecoming—Ben Chortov," Angie says. "Of course, Leanne told me last week. Tiffany loves to tell me old news like she's in the know. She did say that Amber tried her best to intimidate you at school. Tiffany said you didn't act scared at all. Good for you. Claussen's a bully who's nothing without her mob. Don't be afraid."

Don't be afraid. Don't be afraid. Don't be afraid.

"What?" I say, cupping my hand by my ear. "Say that again."

"Say what? *Don't be afraid?*"

"You're the one! You're the angel from my visions," I whisper, more to myself than to her. "It is definitely your voice."

"And you're starting to sound like that nit-wit Tiffany. What are you talking about?"

I explain the visions. She is intrigued.

"What I don't understand is, if this is for real, who would want to murder a nice kid like Ross Georgeson? He never said or did a mean thing to anyone in his life," Angie says.

"I don't know. I'm just as confused as you."

"Well, I trust Mr. Zeke to find the truth. He certainly has the skills."

"You mean as a chemistry teacher, he knows how to research?"

"I keep forgetting you just got here last spring. Before he moved here, Mr. Zeke was a detective in Milwaukee."

"That's quite a career shift, from detective to high school teacher."

"Yeah, I know. His son was killed by a mobster he had had arrested for murder but who had gotten off by intimidating the jury."

My mouth dropped open, and then I muttered, "That's horrible."

"Yeah, so he moved here, and within a year his wife died, too. I think he's got relatives back in Wisconsin, but he seems to like teaching chemistry."

"Besides Mr. Zeke and Leanne, I haven't told anyone about this. Please don't…"

"As one Transcender to another, I promise I won't tell anyone." Angie winks.

She's making fun of me. "Do you think this is my idea of a joke?"

Angie looks past the window to the cloudy sky. I wonder if she heard me, or maybe she is in a trance, when she sits up tall, and looks at me. "After the accident, I begged my mother to kill me. I was so low, I thought Hell had to be better. It's been only two weeks since the accident, but I can't wait to go home—they say I may get to leave on Monday. I can't wait to rip open these paints, and become the next Van Gogh." She laughs, but when I don't, she grabs her ear with one hand and points to her missing leg with the other. "Missing leg, missing ear—get it?"

I smile. "Crazy—isn't it?"

"Exactly. Life has taken on a new crazy for me. So maybe I can telepathically send you messages. Who knows? Crazier things can happen. Let's pray that Mr. Zeke stops the murdering demon before he kills anyone else."

Saturday, September 26th
673 Days to Home Free

LAST NIGHT, MY FLIGHT got into LaGuardia at nine-thirty. Dad and I stayed up past midnight letting Danny beat us at Scrabble. Honestly, I didn't have to try to let him beat me. He's memorized every two-letter word, as well as every word beginning with the letter Q, which we give him like a handicap. So, after two nights with too-little sleep, I'm less than thrilled that at 8:30 in the morning a feather-like object tickles my feet, and muffled giggles waft up from the end of my bed.

At least I'm in *my* bed. In my house. In my city. I'm home, if only temporarily. Not exactly free—I still have to report to my dad where I'm going and when I'll be home. I think about Leanne and feel a tinge of guilt. I think about Ben and feel a tinge of something that is definitely *not* guilt. But then I feel a tinge of guilt for thinking that sort of thing with my little brother in the room. And the tickling and giggling continues.

"Danny! I'm sleeping here." I throw my pillow at the red blob at the foot of my bed. It misses. Big surprise.

"Not anymore!" He throws it back at me. Hits me square in the face. "Strike!"

"I'm gonna *strike* you, you little runt!" I jump out of bed, adjust my glasses, and chase him down the hall.

Dad is at the hallway mirror fixing the collar on his polo. Danny hides behind him.

"Whoa. What's going on here?"

"The little runt woke me up." I try to catch him weaving around my father, but he's wiry.

"I'm glad you're up, V. I want to ask you something." My dad turns to face me. Even in my groggy-morning state, something looks different. "Would you mind taking Danny along with you today—a little brother-sister bonding time?"

"But Dad!" my brother and I whine in stereo. I say, "Luka and I are going to the Met. He'll hate it."

"Yeah, museums are boring. I want to go to the game with you. Besides, you said we were bringing candy."

"What happened to your mustache?" I interrupt. I've never seen my dad without his mustache. Never ever. His face looks… naked.

Dad's face turns an even brighter shade of pink than the razor burn.

"I thought I'd try something different." He starts down the stairs, with us in pursuit.

"'Cause Candy said she wants to see what you look like without it." Danny jumps on Dad's back. "That's really why, isn't it?"

So Candy is a *person*—a female person, obviously. I ask, "Who's Candy?"

In the living room, Dad drops Danny on the couch. "You," he says, pointing to the boy rolling onto the floor, "…are a rat. That was supposed to be our secret."

He looks at me. "Candy is a friend from work, nothing more." He heads to the kitchen.

"Then it shouldn't matter if Danny goes with you," I say, following. I haven't been to the Met in months, and Danny will just whine, "*How much longer,*" the whole time. I'll have Luka doing that already—I certainly don't need two of them.

"I just thought—" Dad exhales. "Okay, fine. Danny, get dressed. We're leaving in ten minutes."

SOME PEOPLE SAY that a cathedral or church is a place designed and constructed for contemplation, for thinking about the big mysteries of life. For me, that place is room 759 at the Metropolitan Museum of Art. Room 759 displays works by the Hudson River School of painters and specifically, Thomas Cole, my all-time favorite painter. I usually spend time in reverent awe with these amazing displays of color and genius before moving randomly around the museum, or intentionally visiting exhibits.

But, Luka, displaying her usual control issues, insists we do it differently this time. "Let's start on the first floor and work our way back and up the stairs so we eventually end up in room 759. You know, save the best for last."

"You know I always eat my Oreo from the inside out, right?"

"No kidding. But let's just do it my way for once."

"For once? We did it your way all last weekend when we went to the football game *and* Susie's party." I push her shoulder.

"Where you saw Ben both nights. The same Ben who asked you to homecoming. You still haven't thanked me for that." She pushes me back.

I grunt at her stubbornness, and decide to be happy she came to the museum with me at all. Museums are not her thing.

We go directly behind the main entryway into the Medieval Art section—a place I've always rushed through, since there's a good reason this era was known as the Dark Ages. It's gloomy and dark in here. No bright paintings—not even bright religious tapestries. Luka insists on reading every sign next to every little artifact. I'm scoping the room looking for something interesting, and inside I'm wrestling with the fact that my dad has another woman in his life. What kind of woman admits to the name Candy? It might actually be worse than Verona. I imagine some dim-witted blond in a—

"Verona! Come here. You are not going to believe this," Luka says, in what's supposed to be a whisper, but several decibels higher than what a normal-hearing person would consider a whisper. She grabs my jacket sleeve and yanks me over to a display.

"Don't rip my arm off."

She nods toward a section of artifacts attached to a wall in a display cabinet. I scan them quickly. Religious figures and mementos. Exactly what you'd expect from medieval art.

She points to a rectangular ivory frieze about the size of a small book and whispers, "Look! It's you—the Transcenders!"

My eyes adjust to see an ivory carving with a cross with a horse or dog or something in the middle, an angel in the top left quadrant, a lion with wings in the top right quadrant, a bull in with wings in the bottom left quadrant. In the bottom right, right where Luka's pointing, is an eagle.

My mouth goes dry. I don't believe it. It *is* the Transcenders. Luka reads the inscription next to the carving while I try to digest what I'm seeing. "*Plaque with Agnes Dei on a Cross between Emblems of the Four Evangelists.* Wow—it's old, from somewhere between 1000 and 1050 AD, and made of ivory from somewhere in southern Italy, probably Benevento."

"What's Agnes Dei?" I ask.

"It's Latin. I thought you'd be more curious about the Four Evangelists since they clearly are Transcenders."

"I *am* curious. That's why I want to know what it means. *You're* supposed to be the religious one."

Luka smirks. "I have a hard enough time with French. Latin would completely kill my GPA! We can Google it later. I'll take a picture." Luka whips out her phone and snaps a picture.

"You can't use a flash in here." Taking a step from her post by the door, an older woman with bushy salt and pepper hair, wearing a museum lanyard over a black suit, points to Luka's phone.

"Sorry. Hey, do you happen to know who the Four Evangelists are?" Luka never misses an opportunity.

After a quick look of surprise, the woman walks over. "That's just another name for the Gospel writers….you, know, Matthew, Mark—"

"Luke and John," Luka finishes for her. "Thanks. I just never heard them called that before."

The woman taps her knuckle on the glass enclosure. "See the books they're each holding?"

Luka and I shrug.

"They represent the gospels. This plaque originally covered an early church book containing the gospels."

"Do you know what these emblems mean exactly? Why is one an angel, one a bull—" Luka points to the different symbols.

"No, I don't know where they originated. Sorry. I need to get back to my post." She starts to walk away, but then turns to us and whispers, "The next room offers more displays with these symbols, if you're interested." She nods to an open doorway.

Luka and I look at each other with eyes opened wide, and shuffle toward the arch. The first thing we both see is an eagle sculpture. Luka whips out her phone.

"Wait. You heard what the lady said—*No pictures.*"

"Not, *pictures*—she said, *No flash.*" Luka adjusts her camera, motions for me to get in the picture and pushes the button. Nothing happens.

"Did it work?" I rush to her side.

"Yup." The picture comes out remarkably well, even without a flash. "Two eagles."

I hit her, then read the information plaque next to the eagle. "A Lectern for the Reading of the Gospels with the Eagle of St. John the Evangelist sculpted by Giovani Pisano, circa 1301, from the Tuscany region of Italy."

"So the Eagle is St. John," Luka murmurs.

"You know him?" I ask.

"All I know is he wrote one of the Gospels, some epistles, and the book of Revelation. He was the apostle who claimed to be Jesus' favorite."

"A bit conceited, wasn't he?"

Luka nudges me. "Does your father have a bible?"

I shrug. "I've never seen him read one—but he might. His parents go to church all the time. We can look for one later."

We wander around this gallery filled with religious artifacts, and I'm so confused. How could any of this be true? My mother's voice tells me it's only man's desire to know the unknowable—to place meaning to life. Newma, on the other hand, would tell me to listen to my heart. I'm not sure I know how to do that.

Luka heads to a sculpture of an angel with a lion growing out of its right side and a bull coming out of its left. "We have our answer. Look at this! This Tetramorph Pilaster, by Giovani Pisano. Matthew's the angel, Mark is the lion, and Luke is the bull. Cool."

"I wonder if Mr. Zeke knows about these guys." I touch Luka's arm. "Take a picture of this and send it to me. I've got to show him this on Monday."

BACK AT HOME, Luka finds a St. Jerome's Bible on a shelf in my father's office between *The Complete Collection of Edgar Allen Poe* and an even larger *Collection of Shakespeare*. I never realized that my dad is as much of a literary buff as my mom, but I guess it makes sense, as they met in an English lit class in college.

After Luka leaves, but before Dad and Danny get home, I start reading the Gospel of John, get completely confused with all his talk about light and some other guy named John, and fall asleep.

Just before midnight I'm dreaming about a lamb by a cascading stream when my cell phone plays Elvis. My first thought is that something's happened to my mother. I press the *send* button and say, "Hello?"

Nothing but an exhale. Thinking it must be a wrong number, I'm about to press *end* when a man's deep voice threatens, "Watch out. I *see* you."

"Who are you?" I yell into the phone. The caller hangs up.

I look at the number—it's a random number I've never seen before. But I know it's neither the Jamestown exchange nor the

Manhattan one. I want to believe it was a wrong number, but my dad taught me probability at a young age as it relates to baseball stats—and the probability is strong that the caller is the same person who left the note. And he means to terrorize me. First the note on my windshield, and now this phone call. He knows what I drive and has my cell phone number. This is definitely ramping up.

Eagle Healing

Sunday, September 27th
672 Days to Home Free

IT'S 4:30 SUNDAY AFTERNOON. Mom's picked me up from the airport and I've finally started my APUSH homework when the doorbell interrupts. I open the door to find Ben, hands in pockets, looking down at his boots. When he looks up, his dimpled grin pierces my heart. I can't believe how much I've missed him.

"Hey," he says. "We got back an hour ago. I hope it's okay I stopped by."

"C'mon in," I say. He steps in cautiously when he sees my mother reading. She looks up.

"Hi, Ben."

"Hello, Mrs. Lamberti." He realizes his error, "I mean, Mrs. Newman—I mean, Dr. Newman."

"You can call me *Cheryl*," my mom says, smiling. "Verona does." My mom rolls her eyes, recalling the argument we had over Ben.

"Let's take Max for a walk." I grab the leash from the hook. Max gambols around my feet, and I feel that my heart is gamboling around Ben in much the same way. I'm just slightly better at hiding it. I hope.

The rooftops to our west have just swallowed the sun, leaving a leftover glow at the edges. I pull my jacket tighter around me.

Ben takes a navy-blue UVA Cavalier cap from inside his jacket and hands it to me. "I brought you a souvenir."

"Oh, thanks!" He helps me put it on. "How were the football tryouts?"

"Good and bad." Ben chuckles. I arch my eyebrow. "Good, because I think Alex and I performed as close to our peak as possible."

"And bad?"

Ben's upraised hand stops me. "And good because it's over. I thought our father was the toughest coach on the planet. But honestly, all the extra drills he makes us do only prepared us for future torture."

"And that's not the bad?"

"What's bad is that Coach saw that even though we're big compared to the kids in our league, we look average next to the giants from Northern Virginia. And there are a couple of defensive tackles from Southside who weighed in close to three hundred pounds."

"You sound worried that you won't get picked."

"I'm not worried—but Coach is. The whole way home he rattled on about how they must be using steroids or something, and there has to be a way to bulk us up without getting caught."

"Oh, Ben. You don't think—"

"I won't let him pump drugs into me. The shakes and supplements are bad enough. I'm just thinking he's going to have us lifting every day even *after* practice… But what really got to me is that he looks at Alex and me like an investment—like we're commodities to be traded."

I can't think of anything to say to that, so I don't.

Max tugs toward a squirrel. I unbuckle the leash when we reach the bench overlooking the pond. A family of mallard ducks waddles into the water. Max runs over to play. The enthusiasm is not mutual.

"Verona, see those ducks?" Ben points to a duck family swimming away from the dog on the shore as we sit down on the bench. "That's what I want. Not a career tackling people for money."

"You want *ducks*?" Clearly, I've missed something.

He breaks into a grin. "I mean a family. See the mother duck, the father with the green neckband, and their ducklings?" His eyes get a faraway glaze. "I remember the time I lived with Kolya as being the happiest time of my life. I loved being part of a family. Living with Coach isn't like that. It's like we're business partners or something." Ben exhales, a frustrated exhale. "I don't know if I'm explaining this right." He throws a pebble into the lake.

"No, I get it. I do. This weekend at my home in New York, I missed my family so much. It's not the same when you're with the people individually, but never all together. Ever since the divorce, I can never be with my mom and dad at the same time anymore."

"Yeah, that's it. Does it make you feel like you're warped in some way?"

"Yeah, it does." We hold hands until the streetlights pop on.

"I'd better get you home." Ben pulls me up and pushes my hair back off my face. "Hey, something's different about you."

"You're just noticing?" I blink my eyes fast.

"Where are your glasses?" Ben holds me at arm's length and his eyes brush over my face. "You have amazing eyes." I close my eyes and he kisses my lids so gently I feel only the warmth of his breath like a promise of something good. Then he kisses me on the mouth. Soft at first, but then hard, hungry.

Ben pulls away, still holding my shoulders, and shakes his head. His eyes are smiling. "Wow!"

Monday, September 28th
671 Days to Home Free

"THERE'S A SPRING IN YOUR STEP today, Verona. Does it have anything to do with that Ben Chortov?" At least my mom isn't referring to Ben as *that football jock*. I grab a Diet Coke out of the fridge and a breakfast bar from the cabinet for the ride to school.

"I'm not saying a thing about that *Ben Chortov* until you come clean about Beamer Boy."

"Who's the parent here?" I go to kiss her, but as she puts the paper down, I notice a football player, front and center on the page she's been reading.

"Since when do you read the sports section?" Could this be a sign she's missing Dad?

"It's local news—not sports. A football player from Yorktown is reported missing. Their team is scheduled to play your school next Saturday."

I peer over my mother's shoulder at the picture. She hands the section to me. My hands start shaking so much I can barely read the article. It's him. It's definitely the boy from my last eagle vision. He is big, with dark-umber skin, and cropped hair. He looks happy in the picture—like his team just won. It's completely different from the angry-then-surprised expression he had in my vision. I melt to the tile floor to read:

> *Tyrone Blanchard, Benjamin Harrison High School's leading linebacker, was reported missing Friday night. He was last seen leaving the high school at approximately 5:30 p.m. following football practice. Shirley Blanchard, Ty's mother, told police her son usually heads for the public library for a few hours after practice, but no one at the York City Library could verify seeing him that evening. The police waited the usual 24 hours to file a missing persons report. They ask that anyone with information about this disappearance please contact . . .*

"What's the matter?" I ignore my mother until I get to the end. My eyes well up and I know there's nothing I can do about it. They aren't going to find him alive. It's too little/too late again.

"You don't know this boy, do you?" She drops to the floor next to me, putting her arm around my shoulder.

"No, that's not it." I search for an explanation that won't land me in a psychiatrist's office.

"What is it, honey?"

"Ross Georgeson told us about this kid the week before he—before he died," I hope that will satisfy her. As an added benefit, it happens to be true. Just not the *whole* truth.

"I see." Mom rubs my back. "This has been harder on you than I thought." She exhales. "Would you like to take a mental health day?"

In first grade, Mom and I made a pact. If I kept my grades up—almost always As—I could take one *mental health day* each semester whenever I feel I need to. She says that children need impromptu days off to just stare up at the clouds or curl up with a good book—same as adults. Funny, it's been a long time since I've used one.

"Thanks anyway, Mom." I pull myself together and up off the floor. "I'll be alright. I've got a quiz in chemistry today that I don't want to miss." This is technically true, but not the real reason I want to be in school.

IN MY EAGERNESS to tell Mr. Zeke about Ty Blanchard's disappearance and the threatening phone call, I arrive before the first bell. But Esther, his Mercedes, is missing from its usual spot at the end of the faculty lot.

Inside the front door, Mr. Sams is talking with Mrs. Hale, but touches her arm when he sees me. "Miss Lamberti, would you please wait in my office?" He returns to his conversation. I turn toward his office, which, as my luck would have it, is in the opposite direction of my first-block class.

"Oooh, Veronie Balonie! Wanted by *the man*!" Nicky struts alongside me, the lug nuts in his hair tinkling.

"Good morning to you, too, Nicky," I say.

"C'mon, out with it, girl. And look at you—no glasses! Can you even see me?" He jumps in front of me, walks backwards, and does a peace sign. "This should be easy for you, Woodstock. How many fingers am I holding up?"

"I'm not in the mood." I flash him my meanest look.

"Touchy, aren't we?" Nick jumps away from me and into a group of senior girls.

I step inside Mr. Sams' office, closing the door behind me. What a Monday this has turned out to be. I wish I'd accepted my mother's offer of a day off.

The first bell rings. I wait. And sweat. What does Mr. Sams want with me? I haven't done anything wrong as far as I know. Certainly, as far as Mr. Sams knows. Having a vision of someone being murdered isn't the same as killing him. And this time I told Mr. Zeke about it the very next day. So why do I feel guilty?

Mr. Sams bustles in. "Come to my inner office." He closes the outside door, affixes a "Do Not Disturb" sign, and motions for me to sit down. I wipe my hands on my jeans and sit with my backpack on my lap.

"I won't keep you wondering about why I called you in. Curtis—Mr. Ezekiel—asked me to tell you that the police found Ty Blanchard's body last night. He'd been shot in the chest." He looks at my face for a reaction. I hug my backpack tighter, and my teeth clench. I guess I knew it when I saw the newspaper report, but feelings of helplessness overwhelm me. I stare at a paper clip on the floor, imagine using it to somehow hold my jumbled emotions together.

"Mr. Ezekiel told me about the visions you've been having." My eyes shoot up at him in shock. Why would Mr. Zeke tell the principal when he was so adamant that I keep quiet about it? Mr. Sams reads my thoughts. "Don't worry. This is safe with me. He thinks Ty Blanchard may be the boy from your last vision."

"He is," I say, barely above a whisper.

"He what?" Now it's Mr. Sams who is surprised. "How do you know?"

"I saw the article about him missing in today's paper. It's definitely him."

"I see. Cur—Mr. Ezekiel led the York County Police to the body based on your description of the area. It was on a section of the young man's route home. As you can imagine, they're suspicious. He's being held for questioning, so we've hired a substitute for today."

"They think Mr. Ezekiel killed him?" My heart punches a hole in my chest.

"Don't worry. With his reputation on the force in Milwaukee, they'll figure out soon enough that he just wants to help."

"What if they don't?" *What if my latest vision implicates Mr. Zeke in this kid's murder?* "Mr. Zeke isn't the murderer in the vision—I know it isn't him."

"Did you get a good look at the gunman?" Mr. Sams raises his brows.

"No, but—"

"Then how can you know who it is or *isn't?*" Now I feel like I'm the one being interrogated.

How *do* I know? The answer comes to me. "The killer *wants* something real bad. I don't know what." I tell him about Mammon in Milton's Paradise Lost. "Mr. Ezekiel doesn't want anything—other than to give to others."

"I know Curtis Ezekiel didn't murder anyone. We've been friends for a long time." Mr. Sams folds his hands on his desk. "The police may want to question you."

My shoulders droop forward and I hang my head.

He says, "Don't be afraid, Verona." I've heard that before. But I *am* afraid. I am afraid of this so-called gift I haven't asked for. I'm afraid of someone who's got my number and knows what I drive. What if it's the killer? And I'm afraid I will burst if I don't get a chance to talk with Mr. Zeke today.

I PAINT THE RESTORED Grecian urn in third-period art while silently reciting the John Keats poem that inspired this latest art project, chosen partially because I like Keats' poetry, and partially because Keats is my teacher's name. I particularly love the last two lines from *Ode on a Grecian Urn*:

> "Beauty is truth, truth beauty — that is all
> Ye know on earth, and all ye need to know."

This notion soothes my head and my heart. I *wish* it were all I knew. I wish I didn't know about some demented murderer preying on high school students. I'm wishing these things while washing paint off my hands when Susie whispers to me from behind, "Your man is waiting for you in the hall."

I give her a confused look that asks, *What man?*

She says, "Ben Chortov."

I scope the room. Mr. Keats is bent over Amy Sedgwick's fallen chalice. I duck out the door, hoping no one will rat me out.

"Hey," Ben says. *Talk about truth and beauty.* The truth is, his sultry smile and twinkling eyes take my breath away. That's all I need to know right now.

"Hey," I say back.

He looks at the floor, then up into my eyes. "Let's ditch fourth block. Grumpy Trumpy is subbing for Mr. Zeke, so the quiz has been postponed. And there's something I want to show you."

I've never ditched class before, but I remember my mother's suggestion for a mental health day. "Okay." I can't believe I'm agreeing to this. "Where should we meet?"

"I'll wait here. If I'm not here, meet me at my truck. It's parked in the lot by the auto shop." He kisses my cheek.

I pull back. Surprised. Flabber and ghasted, with my feet on the ground this time. Ben flashes me a boyish grin. When I duck back into class, I feel relieved that my absence has gone unnoticed. Perhaps there are advantages to being the invisible new girl—although I have to admit my see-through self-image might need an update, at least when I'm walking next to Ben.

FIRST OUT OF THE CLASSROOM, I see Amber Claussen whispering in Ben's ear as though they are intimate friends. He stares at the floor, a smirk on his face. When I approach, his face lights up. He steps away from the cheerleader like she isn't there. Behind Ben's back, Amber glowers at me, then tramps away in the other direction.

"I don't think she likes me," I say.

"That's a good thing." Ben puts his arm through my elbow. He laughs. "If Claussen liked you, I'd think something was wrong with you."

I feel so self-conscious with our arms hugging and everyone looking at us, I wriggle my arm out, hoping he doesn't notice. We walk straight out the front entrance like it's perfectly normal for two juniors to leave school before their fourth-block class. No one stops us. Several seniors are leaving to go to jobs, or because their classes have ended for the day. Some rambunctious boys tussle with each other ahead of us. We follow them around the stadium, but they disappear into the front door of the auto shop near where Ben's truck is parked. He opens the door for me and I hop up, throwing my backpack over the seat.

I call my mother and leave a message.

"You called your mother to tell her you're ditching class?" Ben's tone is teasing.

"She asked me if I wanted to take a mental health day today."

"Mental health day?" Ben turns onto the Memorial. "Something I should know about?"

I poke him in the side. "It's something my mother lets me do once in a while. Take a day off just to *be*."

"That's pretty cool. Coach'd never do let us do that."

"Yeah, I guess." We turn down an unfamiliar road. "Where are we going?"

"One of my favorite places."

"Is it far?"

"No. I have to be back for practice." Ben turns onto an unpaved drive that winds around a hill, and then stops at the end of a field. We get out and start down a path through the trees.

"Is it alright if I hold your hand?" Ben asks. "You're not going to act like I have some disease, are you?"

"That's not it. It's just that I'm not sure if I'm ready for everyone to see us—you know, together. I mean…I don't know…" I don't know how to finish without sounding presumptuous.

"Are you asking me if we are *together*—like girlfriend and boyfriend?" Ben stops and pulls me in front of him.

I look at his face for a moment, ignoring the butterflies in my throat. "I guess."

"Do you want to be?" He pulls a strand of my wayward hair back from my face.

"You're the man." I feel like I can hear Luka saying the same thing.

Ben grins. "You won't let me get away with anything, will you?"

I flash a grin of my own.

"Okay, Verona Lamberti, will you be my girlfriend?" Ben's low, soft voice melts in my ears. I'd have to be an idiot to refuse him. So I don't.

"Yes, Benjamin Chortov. I will be your girlfriend."

"If you're going to be my girlfriend you should, at the very least, know my name."

"It's not Benjamin?"

"No." We continue on the gravel path.

"Benedict?" I wrinkle my nose at that possibility. "Like Benedict Arnold?"

He rolls his eyes. "Definitely not."

"Good—then just Ben?" I'm getting confused. I know a girl whose name is just Liz, and was constantly having to tell teachers not to call her Elizabeth.

"Remember when my Aunt Nadia called me Vova?"

"Yeah, but I thought that was just a pet name—like my Dad sometimes calls me V or *baby girl*. For all I know, Vova means Ben in Russian."

"Baby girl?" Ben teases.

"You'd better tell me your real name, or this will be the shortest relationship in history, *Vova*."

Ben laughs. "My real name is Vladimir Theodorovich Chortov. Vova is short for Vladimir."

"Vladimir Theodorovich Chortov." I laugh. "That doesn't exactly roll off the tongue."

"That's why my father started calling me Ben when we came to America, even though it doesn't match my documents."

We round a corner and come across an undulating meadow of blue flowers that ends at a rocky ledge over the James River. As we walk, ankle-deep in blue, I can see that we are at least fifteen feet above the water. Frothy waves crash into boulders below us—churning up rainbow crystals like ice glistening in the afternoon sun. Above us, a skein of geese flies in V formation up the river, and I remember my dad calling me V just this weekend and for some reason, even though I'm with the hottest guy I've ever known and definitely do not want to be thinking about my father, my heart twinges.

"This view is spectacular. I'd love to paint it," I say.

"I knew you'd like it here. It's a great place to think." I think I just discovered Ben's Room 759, his cathedral.

"What sort of things do you think about?"

He smiles and looks at me. "The last time I was here, I was thinking about asking a feisty brunette to homecoming."

"Important stuff, I see." I smile back at him.

"Yeah. Save-the-world kind of stuff." He tickles me. "Seriously, sometimes I come here to try to figure out what it's all about."

"What do you mean?"

"Life. Don't you ever wonder? I mean, we're born. We live. We die. Then what happens? What's it all for?" He removes his jacket and gestures for me to sit down. Ben's jacket is a lily pad in a puddle of brilliant blue. I sit down and make room for him. A yellow butterfly flits by.

"I didn't think about it much before," I tell him. "But since Ross died, there's a lot of stuff that's been on my mind." I consider telling Ben about Ty Blanchard and my suspicions about his death being related to Ross', but even though Mr. Zeke told Mr. Sams, I'm not ready to share my visions with Ben. Besides, I want to forget about all that now.

"Remember what Mr. Zeke said at the funeral? That we don't *have* souls—we *are* souls." Ben picks a blue flower, twirling it in his fingers.

"Yeah. So none of this is real?" I pinch the skin on my arm. It sure feels real.

"Sometimes I wonder if there is a reason behind all this." Ben waves the flower around. "Like our lives have meaning. Science teachers say that it's all a cosmic coincidence, random—but that doesn't seem right to me. I mean, look at this flower." He holds out the flower for me. I bring it to my nose. No discernable fragrance, but Ben's body gives off a musky cinnamon aroma that more than makes up for it.

"Exquisite," I say, thinking also gorgeous and adorable, and that these words pertain to more to Ben than the flower.

"Yes, but even more than that, it has all it needs to exist. You remember from biology—roots for nourishment and water, stems to carry the nutrients, leaves to convert the sunlight to food..."

"You must have had an easier time in biology than chemistry."

"Funny," Ben says. "But you do understand what I'm saying, right?"

"Yeah, I get the part about it not being a coincidence. But I still have a hard time with the idea of some God playing with our lives like we're pieces in a chess game. I mean, what's the point? If he's all-knowing, all-powerful and all that, why does He even care about us little people?"

Ben takes my hand and kisses it. "You're a little person, and I care about you."

"I'm not little. And you're not God!" I say, grabbing back my hand in mock indignation, and plop on my back. I chuckle, and bask in the warmth of the sun.

"You know I'm kidding. I'm not God, and you're not little. You're perfect."

He leans on his side, facing me. I can feel his stare, but my eyes are closed. He starts playing with the hair at the crown of my head, pulling it gently back from my face. It feels delicious. Ben may not be God, but if there is a heaven, I think I found it here with this guy on this carpet of blue flowers.

I shiver at the warmth of his touch. He runs his finger down the center of my nose and lightly across my lips and down my neck. I worry about what I will do if he stays on course, but he backtracks and traces a line around the edge of my lips. His touch is gentle, so light and gentle that it makes my lips tingle. All my nerves are on high alert, but in a good way that I've not experienced lately. Come to think of it, I'm not sure I've ever felt this way before.

A shadow passes over my eyes. I blink them open to see Ben's liquid brown eyes gazing lovingly at me. His lips part and I close my eyes while his warm, cinnamon taste melts into my mouth.

My heart threatens to spring from my ribcage when he pulls back. I clutch at his shirt and pull myself up to meet his mouth a second time. It's everything I've ever dreamed it would be—light and salty, like soaring over the river together, touching and twirling through the wildly blue sky. And, thank the stars, no bananas.

Too soon, Ben lays me back down and caresses my hair. Tears stream from the edges of my eyes. "Are you okay?" His finger touches my tears.

I smile and nod.

"You taste great." Winking at me, he licks his lips.

"Can we do it, you know, kiss again?"

"I'm always ready to oblige." Ben leans over with an eager look.

A twig snaps in the meadow behind us.

Ben twists around and yells, "Who's there?" There's no answer. We both spin to our feet. When my eyes adjust, I see red hair poking out from behind a bush on the meadow's edge.

"Hamilton," Ben says low. Then he shouts, "You want something, Hamilton?"

"You've taken what I want, Chortov." Craig backs up, then runs into the trees.

"Do you think he was watching the whole time?" I shake out Ben's jacket.

"I think he lives around here somewhere. One time, I saw Craig and Ross fishing from the river bank down there." Ben nods to a sandy strip below the cliff.

On the drive back to school, my lips tingle. Somehow this Monday, which started out so horribly, has catapulted into the most memorable day of my life.

Tuesday, September 29th
670 Days to Home Free

INSTEAD OF GOING STRAIGHT to the cafeteria, I stop by Mr. Zeke's classroom. He's writing something at his desk. His eyes have grayish lines under them.

"Please come in. Close the door behind you." Mr. Zeke motions for me to sit on a desk across from his.

"I heard what happened. Are you in trouble because of me?"

"Didn't Mr. Sams tell you I'd been a detective?"

"Actually, Angie told me first on Friday when I went to see her at the hospital."

"As soon as they cleared me with the folks in Wisconsin, I was no longer under suspicion."

"Good. What about me?" I say. "Aren't they a bit suspicious about a high school girl who dreams about a random murder in the next town?"

"You might find it surprising, but they're not. Some police departments have psychics on retainer."

"You're kidding me." I am stunned. *Am I a psychic?* I ask, "Am I a psychic?"

"No. Your visions are different. The gift you have is much more uncommon."

"That's a relief… I think." Then I look at the floor. "I only wish my so-called gift could've saved Ty Blanchard's life."

"Listen to me." Mr. Zeke positions himself so I'm looking straight into his bloodshot eyes. "None of this is your fault. It's the guy who pulled the trigger's fault. Your information helped us find the body before—well, let's just say Ty Blanchard's mom would've suffered more if it had taken longer to find him."

"Do they have any leads?"

"Not yet. The police are inclined to label it as a gang initiation or a vendetta involving a mistaken identity. They're having a hard time coming up with a motive. Ty Blanchard was an exceptional student—and to make it more complicated, everyone liked him. They haven't been able to find anyone to say anything bad about him." I immediately think of Ross Georgeson and the fact that people had to make up things about him, he was that good.

"What do you think?"

"I've never seen a street thug shooting with a silencer. They're rarely that sophisticated."

"They can tell there was a silencer?"

"No, but I trust the validity of your vision. The scene of the crime looked exactly as you depicted it. Blanchard was riding his bike home like he did every night. If, in fact, he was the intended target, the murderer had probably tailed him for some time. Also, despite it not being the best neighborhood, there's a busy roadway a block away, and the apartment complex where he lived is just a stone's throw in the other direction. A loud gunshot could've brought unwanted attention."

We both think about this for a minute. I decide this is as good a time as any to share my news from the museum. "I discovered something this weekend in New York…at the Met."

Mr. Zeke looks up. "Museum or opera?"

"Museum." I adjust my backpack, take out my phone and show him the picture Luka texted to me. "Religious art with Transcenders in it."

"The Evangelists?" Mr. Zeke smiles.

"You've heard of them?" I can see from his eyes that he has. "Why didn't you tell me?"

"As smart as you are, I figured you'd stumble on them eventually. Besides, I'm not convinced they had the same supernatural powers Blythe wrote and lectured on. That is, other than John—he definitely had visions. The whole last book of the bible, Revelation, is one. If there's a record somewhere of the others using these powers—I can't find it, and trust me, I've looked. Most of the symbolic literature on the Evangelists uses esoteric comparisons to the aspects of God—not real life ones."

"I'm reading the gospels—starting with John, since we may have something in common."

"Good. If you have any questions, maybe I can help. I've been studying the book for years." Mr. Zeke pats a black leather book on the edge of his desk. "There is something—no, two things—that nag at me about your visions."

I look up and he folds his hands. "It's the burnt charcoal you taste before a vision. That's not in any other record I've uncovered. Also, at this point, you're not a follower of the Way. I'm wondering if the charcoal is supposed to cleanse you somehow—like it did for Isaiah."

"I don't know. I mean, I don't know anything about Isaiah and charcoal."

"It may be a long shot, but it's the only thing I've got. As for Isaiah, here's the SparkNote's version: When God shows himself to Isaiah—a major prophet like Ezekiel, Isaiah is completely overwhelmed with God's glory. He falls to the ground, says, *Woe is me. I'm a man of unclean lips.* And a seraphim—that's another type of angel, different from cherubim—pulls a piece of burning charcoal up with tongs and touches his lips to cleanse them."

I touch my own lips, not knowing what to say, thankful that the taste isn't accompanied by searing pain. "It doesn't really burn."

"That's a relief, right?"

I remember Saturday night's threatening phone call and tell him about it.

"So whoever left the note on your car has also got your phone number."

"But I got his number, too." I hand Mr. Zeke a paper with the number on my cell phone.

"And it was definitely a guy's voice. Mr. Zeke, I'm afraid. What if it's the killer?"

Mr. Zeke puts the paper in the inside pocket of his suit. "Fear is like pain. It's meant as a signal that something isn't right. Listen to it, but don't let it consume you. You need to be careful."

He scribbles something on a piece of paper and hands it to me. "This is my cell number. Call me if you get any more threats. I'm going to relay this to the authorities." He pats his chest.

I take his number and stuff it in my pocket. I must have looked upset, because Mr. Zeke quickly changes the subject. "Thankfully, I have some good news. Angelina Jett came home from the hospital yesterday. She asked me to pass this on to you." He hands me a note on lined, loose-leaf paper.

This reminds me of the other reason I wanted to see him. "Oh, I forgot to tell you. Do you think Angie could be the angel, Mr. Zeke? The way she said, '*Don't be afraid*' to me at the hospital—sounded exactly like the cherub in my dream."

"I hadn't considered that," Mr. Zeke says with a laugh. "Angelina Jett, the angel. That would be something."

ON THE WAY TO THE CAFETERIA, I read Angie's note:

Dear Verona,

Thank you SO much for visiting me these past two weeks. I'm going home now and hope you'll come to see me. Please visit me as soon as you can.

Your friend,
Angie

P.S. I love the paints and can't wait to start my Van Gogh.

I read *your friend* over and over. Angelina Jett wants to be *my* friend. I stuff the note in my jeans pocket. When someone on top of the popularity totem pole like Angelina Jett wants to be my friend, I know the world has gone topsy-turvy.

I still have a few minutes for lunch, so I hurry to the cafeteria.

Nicky, Leanne, Susie, and Paris have exchanged ideas about Ty Blanchard's murder. They keep critiquing one another's respective theories.

"Chaser, that is so lame," Susie says. "He accidentally shot himself in the chest? Then what happened to the gun?"

"You don't know that neighborhood like I do. I'm telling you—some kids came by and stole the gun." Nicky bangs his hand on the table and we all jump.

"Why would anyone kill themselves like that?" Leanne interjects.

"Megatron was afraid of losing face against the Cougars—why else?" Everyone moans at Nicky's reasoning.

"I like Leanne's theory the best," Susie adds.

"Better than your own?" Leanne looks startled.

"Yeah, mine stinks. Alex Chortov couldn't have killed him—he was in Charlottesville last weekend."

"Verona, what do you think happened to Ty Blanchard?" Nicky asks.

"I don't know who did it, but I agree with Susie that it couldn't be Alex Chortov."

"I guess you would know," Nicky says. I glare at him, and he takes this as his cue to make an announcement, an announcement that is definitely nobody's business. "Did y'all know that Ben Chortov and our girl, Verona, are now official?"

"Who told you that?" I feel blood rising to my cheeks.

"Why are you embarrassed?" Susie puts down her fork. "Ben Chortov is the hottest guy at Colonial. I love those boots he wears."

"Cowboy boots?" Nicky wrinkles his face. "Those puppies are so *home on the range.*"

"He looks exactly like his brother," I say, ignoring Nicky.

"He may be the spittin' image of his brother, but Ben's the cool, thoughtful type," Leanne explains. "Non-conformist ... like, a little renegade."

"Y'all are hurting my feelings," Nicky says with a frown. "I'm hot. I could be a renegade."

BEN SLOUCHES LOW IN HIS SEAT, his *home-on-the-range* boots extended far beyond the desk in front of him and examines his study cards—the cards I encouraged him to make. It pleases me that he continues using this method even beyond that first chapter without further prodding on my part. Sneaking around to the back of the class, I whisper in his ear, "Did you know that you're the hottest guy at Colonial?" Before he can say anything, Mr. Zeke begins his lecture.

Within a minute, a note whizzes past my ear. I wait for Mr. Zeke to turn toward the board before unfolding it.

V,
I'm glad that you finally caught on. Was it the kiss?
I should've kissed you sooner. B

That egotistical—! I scrawl back:

B,
I'm not the one who said it. The girls in the lunchroom said it.
BTW, the kiss was OK. V

There, that should get him. I try to concentrate on class but keep listening to see if I can hear him writing. Finally, another note sails to my desk:

Only OK? We'll have to practice more. You'll get better with time. Are we on for tonight? B

I let out a disgusted New York humph, which causes the emoticon girl in front of me to glance over her shoulder. I clear my throat, annoyed by the low chuckle from behind. I decide to let him sweat out the rest of the class wondering about later.

ON OUR WAY HOME from middle school one cloudy May afternoon, Luka and I heard a baby crying. The sound was somewhat muffled, so at first we thought it was coming from inside the colossal church on 88th Street that we passed every day. We kept walking, expecting the crying to stop as soon as the baby was comforted. But the crying didn't stop. If anything, it became more desperate. We looked at each other, turned, and backtracked to the church stairs, where we realized the sound couldn't be coming from inside the church as all the doors and windows were shut. We rummaged around the shrubbery until Luka found the source of the noise. A dirty shoebox.

She lifted the cover and inside was a newborn—a just-been-born newborn—a clothespin on the umbilical cord newborn. The baby was covered in mucous and blood and ink from the newspaper it was wrapped inside, which just happened to be the same newspaper my parents worked for.

When word got out, reporters all over the city had a field day with the irony of the daughter of one of their chief editors finding, *The Apple Tribune Baby*. The kids at school had a field day with it, too. Major embarrassment. Shame. Humiliation. The teasing lasted until Jill Donnelley caught mono from kissing a high school kid and became the new target.

The image of that baby crying for its life flashes across my mind the minute I turn off my car and hear it. It sounds exactly the same, but one sound you don't expect to hear on a college campus is the wailing of a baby. I leave my backpack on the passenger seat and exit the car to listen to where it's coming from. Except for some empty cars parked closer to the library, no one is anywhere near the lot. Ben is late. I look at my cellphone. Actually, he's not late. I'm a few minutes early.

I follow the crying sound to the empty wooded end of the parking lot. Where the pavement ends, guardrails protect against a severe drop into a ravine, obscured with trees and underbrush. I pause at the top. Imagine the headlines: *William and Mary Campus baby found by English professor's daughter.* I really don't want to deal with the taunting again, not right after I've made new friends.

The crying becomes more insistent, almost frantic. I look down at my long skirt and flip-flops and shake my head. Nevertheless, I start down the steep hill, wrestling branches away from my face, grabbing onto thin tree trunks to keep from falling.

While my eyes adjust to the darkness, the cry sounds close and high-pitched. I slow my steps, looking before I place each foot, lest I step on what I am completely convinced is an abandoned baby. But I can't really see my feet very well—it's too dark and leafy, and I slip over a root, and slide on my bum the rest of the way, yelling, "Ow! Ow! Ow!" I rub my butt, assessing the damage. Probably a bruised coccyx. At least Ben didn't see it; a bruised ego would be worse.

I look up to discover the newborn baby image in my head is completely off. Tethered to a rope is the fluffiest orange kitten I've ever seen. The kitten, wide-eyed and trembling, backs away from a long, two-pronged fork, the kind of fork used to barbecue steaks. An older, lanky kid with tattooed shirtsleeves covering skinny arms and ball bearing ear gauges, uses the fork to poke at the kitten. Obviously he heard my less-than-graceful descent down the hill, because he's turning around.

A shorter kid with a cobalt blue Mohawk over a shaved scalp pulls on the rope. I'm relieved it's not a newborn baby, but still, what is *wrong* with these guys?

"What are you doing?" I yell. "Let it go!" Grimacing at the pain shooting down my legs, I work to stand up, trying to look tough.

The sickos face me with the dumbest looks on their faces—like they can't believe this girl has the audacity to interfere with their perverted amusement.

The taller kid scowls. He rubs the side of his neck with the blunt side of the fork, and I notice he's rubbing a crusty edged tattoo of a shiny cobra slithering up his neck. "*You* gonna stop us?" He laughs, exposing teeth that have been whittled to points.

"GIVE. ME. THE KITTEN!" The strong New York attitude in my voice surprises me, probably more than it surprises them. Unfortunately, it's going to take more than a big attitude to intimidate these morons.

Cobra Tattoo, licking his blubbery lips, rotates the barbecue fork back and forth in his hand and steps in my direction. "You want it?" He swings it like a baton so now it's pointing at me. Like I've become the meat he wants to skewer.

I arch my back, clench my fists, and inhale deeply in an attempt to appear taller, more threatening. "Get away from me!"

Cobra Tattoo laughs, then turns and grins at his accomplice. Mohawk moron stands there holding the rope, looking unsure of his part in this new game, but showing definite interest in it.

"Well, it's either you or the pussy." He nods toward the kitten, then tilts his head the other way, licking his lips. "And, darling, I'm sure you'd be a lot more fun."

"You're a… a bully!" As I say the words, I know it sounds cliché, cliché and ridiculously weak. I look to Mohawk moron for help, but the side of his mouth lifts into an evil grin. He's not going to help. At least he's not going to help *me*.

Cobra Tattoo lunges for me. Jumping back, I trip on another root, falling into the magnolia branches, and scrape my eye on a leaf. I twist away from the spot where I expect him to land. He lands on the ground where I would've been if I hadn't tripped. Holding a branch, I twist to my feet and kick him with as much force as I can while he is getting up. It doesn't seem to faze him, so I kick harder, which hurts my toes far more than it hurts him.

Everything has gotten all blurry; must've lost a lens in one eye. I close the blurry one in order to see. Bet I look real threatening with one eye closed and one hand rubbing my sore butt.

Cobra Tattoo keeps getting up. He spins around and faces me. While he may have had some other nefarious pursuit in mind before, now I see murder in his beetle-green eyes.

A piercing holler that couldn't possibly come from either a baby or a cat blasts past me. Through my good eye, I see what looks like a WWF event, only in fast motion. Some hunk of a guy lifts the bullies up and knocks their heads together. The hunk tosses them to the opposite side of the clearing and tosses the barbecue fork into the shrubbery next to me.

The hunk turns around and brushes his hands together. It's Ben, and he didn't even break a sweat. "Are you alright?" We hear the bullies crashing through the thicket, scuttling to get away from us. At any rate, away from Ben.

"I lost one of my contacts—that's all." I wipe my hands on my skirt, and then comb the grass for my lens. With my track record for breaking glasses, I guess I shouldn't be surprised to lose a contact once in a while. "Where did you come from?"

"I heard you screaming from the parking lot. You sounded *angry*. I wasn't sure if I should risk coming until I heard ... well, the rest." He lifts me up and kisses me full on the lips.

"I'm glad you did." Giving up on the contact lens, I search around in the bushes where the kitten was moments ago.

"You think your contact lens could've jumped that far?"

"Those sickos were torturing a kitten. We need to find it."

"Here kitten! Here kitten!" I say. Nothing.

Ben disappears into the bushes, making some sound like, "ksss, ksss."

I continue calling in the other direction.

"I found him," he yells. I head toward his voice, shielding my one good eye from the branches. The rope is tangled around some bushes and the kitten is yanking hard. Ben uses his pocketknife to cut through the rope and he hands me the fuzzy tangerine that I had mistaken for a baby. I let it snuggle under my neck, where it relaxes and starts purring.

"I want him." I close my eyes, and enjoy the softness, the contented purr.

"I'm all yours," Ben says, with twinkling eyes.

I pinch him in the side with my free hand, which isn't easy since he has no fat whatsoever to grab hold of.

"What do we do now?" Ben asks when we get to the parking lot.

"Let's take Khan home," I suggest. "We can stop by the pet store on the way."

"Khan? Are you teasing me? I rescued you, so now you're taking me home? *Cool.*" He grins really wide.

"Nice try. I'm naming this little guy after the big guy who saved him."

After Khan falls asleep on his new PetSmart pillow, Ben and I stroll to the Aetos Diner, located a few blocks from my house across from the JV Theater. The rest of the evening Ben and I study for the chemistry quiz, which Mr. Zeke rescheduled to the week after the homecoming frenzy. At the diner, I discover Ben loves French fries with mayonnaise, and cheeseburgers with just about everything on top. He discovers I love grilled cheese, and chocolate milk, and kittens.

Friday, October 2nd
667 Days to Home Free

ONCE LUKA ARRIVES we spend hours straightening, curling, and braiding our hair, applying and reapplying make-up, and dancing awkwardly around my bedroom in strappy high heels.

"You know, Verona, all the girls will take their shoes off and leave them in a pile at the coat check so they can dance all night without getting blisters," Luka informs me when I complain that my shoes squish my toes together.

"I don't plan to dance. And I don't want Ben to have to bend down so far to talk to me," I say. "Plus, I paid good money for these silly shoes, and I plan to get my money's worth out of them."

"Okay, but no whining that your feet hurt."

"Fine," I say, looking in the mirror. "I can't believe I'm doing this."

"Doing what?"

"Going to a dance with Ben." I see Luka in my reflection, pinning up my rather ornery curls. "Do you think he'll like how I look?" The sides of my hair wind up and around, but the tresses in back spiral down my back. "I mean, I love what you did with my hair. But what if he doesn't like this look? Or this dress?"

"What's not to like? You're a Greek goddess."

I hand her another stray curl. "I hope he won't think it's Medusa."

Luka half-heartedly backhands me with her brush. "I was going for Athena," she says, smiling. "Stop worrying. The man's mouth is gonna water." I throw my lip gloss at her.

"I love that lavender dress on you. I can't wait to see Kolya in his gullaboy purple tie."

"Shut up!" Luka hurls a stuffed teddy bear at me. We hear a growl from under the bed.

"Oh, baby, come here!" It was a classic love-at-first-sight the moment Luka saw Khan.

The doorbell rings. Luka and I hold each other and jump. "They're here!"

"How do I look?" she asks with a twirl.

"What's the Russian word for *wow*? You'll be hearing that all night."

We lean over the banister and watch my mother welcome our dates into the foyer.

"Do what I do," Luka whispers. She has only been to one formal dance in her life, but in her mind, that entitles her to the role of expert. I have to admit she displays runway-like grace swishing down the stairs. Kolya breaks into a huge smile when Luka kisses him on the cheek.

Choking on a giggle, I try to emulate her sashaying hips. Ben rushes around the banister, reaches for my hand, and eases me down the last few steps—his eyes twinkling with amusement. He looks amazing in a black suit, white shirt, and crimson tie. *Is this hottie really my date?* He places a crimson rose corsage on my wrist while my mom snaps the requisite photos.

THE FACULTY REPRESENTATIVE on the homecoming dance committee chose this year's homecoming theme—famous couples in literature and drama. Movie posters of these couples flank every available wall.

"We had no choice." Caitlin rolls her eyes. "English lit Czar, Mrs. Peachtree, thinks it's romance at its finest."

"It's got to be the lamest homecoming theme in the world," Luka whispers to me, pointing at Romeo and Juliet, Antony and Cleopatra, and Scarlett and Rhett. "What about all the kids here as just friends?"

At the coat check room, I refuse to kick off my shoes. Besides, Ben seems compelled to keep his arm around my waist, which actually helps steady me at this high altitude. He leads me down the corridor at about half my normal pace, as I can't move normally without toppling over.

The entrance to Colonial's gym is covered in a black and white balloon arch. On a stage set up for the occasion, a tuxedo-clad DJ plays loud dance music. We peer in, but Susie, adorable in a pink baby-doll dress and ballet slippers, stops us. "Y'all look gorgeous! But before you go in, you'll need to get your pictures taken." She points to a line of couples that disappears around a corner. We take our place at the back of the line.

"I want picture witz Luka." Kolya pulls Luka to him and kisses her cheek.

Alex Chortov appears from around the corner, blinking his eyes tightly. When he passes Ben, he gives him a soft one-two punch in the arm. Amber Claussen, in a skin-tight fire-engine-red dress that matches the red circles on her cheeks, follows closely, grimacing and complaining about something. She looks miserable. Alex ignores her, and seems bent on putting distance between them.

Ben whispers, "See, it's not you—she's not a happy person. It doesn't matter who she's with."

"Why do you think that is?"

"This is on the QT, but I know Alex is planning to cool things with her after the dance. Maybe he already told her, or maybe she senses it."

"Why?" I ask.

"I guess he finally came to his senses." Ben grins, pulling me close to him. "Have I told you that you're the most beautiful girl here tonight?"

"You've only seen a few girls so far." I finger my pocketbook, wishing we were somewhere less crowded. Seeing Amber makes the hair on my arm stand up, and I hate crowds. There is an astronomical amount of VEMP potential here. Plus, my tongue has become a tumbleweed in the desert of my mouth. It's that dry.

"Why would I waste my time looking?" His eyes burn into me, and I feel color rushing to my cheeks just in time for the pictures to be taken.

Leanne bubbles up in her taffeta peach gown, which accentuates the red streaks in her auburn hair. She tells me all about Angie's personal homecoming while Ben goes looking for drinks. Luka and Kolya disappear with him.

When Ben comes back with a Diet Coke for me, we cross under the balloon arch into the gymnasium that's been transformed with colored lights, lighted potted trees, and a disco ball. Round tables and chairs are set up at the edges of the room. In the center is a huge dance floor.

Parched and nervous, I drink the soda fast and struggle against the subsequent burp.

Ben tries to suppress his laugh. "I can dress you up, New York, but I can't take you out."

I pinch him. "Let's find Luka and Kolya."

"Are you sure you don't want another soda?" he says directly into my ear. It's impossible to have a normal conversation, but no one else seems to mind. The dance floor sways with gyrating bodies. Various hues—primaries and pastels—outlined by dark pants flash in the blinking strobes and twirling spotlights. The super-stimulating combination of the audio and visual distortions makes me dizzy. But at least I'm no longer parched.

"You wanna dance?" Ben asks. "I see Kolya and Luka out there."

That figures. Luka never passes up an opportunity to dance.

"Would it be okay if we sat for a minute first? I need a moment to take it all in."

Ben finds us a couple of seats at a table in the back of the room next to a cutout of Rhett Butler carrying Scarlett up the long staircase. I sip what is left of my soda. Ben moves his chair close and puts his arm around my shoulder.

The DJ plays a slow song and Ben lights up. He looks at me expectantly.

"Okay, but don't blame me if I step on your toes." I raise my brows.

"No worries. I wore my steel-rimmed boots as a precaution." I glance down at his feet for the first time. Sure enough, he is wearing new-looking black cowboy boots with a metal band around the toes.

Ben leads me to the edge of the crowded dance floor. He lifts my arms behind his neck and wraps his own around the curve of my back. Even with the benefit of three-inch heels, I barely reach his shoulders.

We sway in time to Peter Gabriel's *In Your Eyes,* losing ourselves in each other's eyes—the light and heat of the moment makes it feel like we're alone on a beach under starlight. The light and shadow dance across Ben's face, and I am mesmerized. Basking in his clean linen smell as he pulls me closer, I rest my head on his chest. This is a dream.

When the music lets up, Ben gently holds me away and lifts my face. He bends down to kiss me on the lips. My heart races as my lips respond, even while my mind clamors for a reason to make him stop. The thought of being one of *those* girls—the ones who make out at their lockers—repulses me to the same degree that this gorgeous guy attracts me.

I yank away.

Ben looks confused. His eyes ask if I'm okay.

My heart is pounding. I turn away and breathe slowly to calm it. I give Ben a weak smile to let him know I'm okay. But am I okay? Truth is, I don't know if I'm okay, if this swept away, out-of-control feeling is normal. At this moment there's only two things I know: One, I have fallen past the danger of losing my heart to this Ben Chortov—I am already in over my head. Two, if I don't make it to a bathroom soon, I'm in danger of some serious embarrassment. I excuse myself, but Ben catches my arm.

"I need to go…ladies room."

"Mr. Sams is ready to announce the homecoming queen. Please stay for that."

Homecoming queen. I really don't care who wins—especially since it isn't going to be Angie. I assess the danger of waiting, the fact that I have a young and healthy bladder, and decide to make Ben happy. "Okay, but I need to go right after they announce the winner." We take our seats.

Ben chuckles and asks, "You want another drink?" At his taunt I rise from my chair to leave, but he yanks me down on his lap. "I'm just kidding." I jump over to my chair next to him. If it turns out I can't wait, there is no reason we both have to be embarrassed.

Kolya and Luka join us, glistening. "This dance is awesome." Luka turns to Ben. "Thanks for getting us tickets."

"*Spaceba, moy brat!*" Kolya says. *Thank you, my brother.*

"*Neechevo,*" Ben replies. *It's nothing.*

"Your Russian very much improved." Kolya slaps Ben on the shoulder.

"Your English needs work." Luka elbows Kolya.

Mr. Sams recognizes the dance committee members for their fine work, and then thanks all the volunteers. He compliments the dancers—the small percentage—who've showed *personal dignity* on the floor. The microphone is handed to the assistant principal, Mrs. Hale, to announce the runner-up couple, and then the homecoming queen and king. I feel a bit safer sitting down, so I try to concentrate on guessing the identities of some of the cutouts around the room. Lucy and Desi are probably my favorite.

I don't know the runner-up couple; they're not in my lunch block or any of my classes, but I recognize their faces from the hallway.

Ben, of course, knows them. "Trevor's a wide receiver, and Marcie's one of the nicest girls I know. I'm glad they won." I smile, chewing on my lip. So far, so good, but I can only hold my legs clamped together for so long.

"And the official royal couple of this year's Colonial High School's homecoming weekend is...." I start clapping, and get up to start toward the ladies room. "Verona Lamberti and Ben Chortov."

Ben holds on to my arm. "Hey, it's us!" He chuckles at my obliviousness.

"What?" I turn to see the whole room standing, staring, clapping and taking pictures of us; not just Ben, but of me. I feel my face turn a darker shade of crimson than my gown.

"Now it's unanimous," Ben whispers. Not knowing what he means, and numb from all the attention, I say nothing. Ben leads me to the stage, a good thing since camera flashes blind me.

Mrs. Hale fastens a sparkling tiara to my hair. Mr. Sams hands me a dozen crimson roses that could have come from the same bush as my corsage. "You look truly lovely tonight, Miss Lamberti. Congratulations."

Ben, his arm holding me protectively, whispers, "We're going to have to start a dance. Can you do it?"

"I think so." The first strains of Frank Sinatra's "New York, New York," beckon us. Mrs. Hale relieves me of the roses. Ben wraps me in his arms again. The difference is, this time I feel all eyes piercing us. My eyes have welled up; I'm overcome with feelings I can't even name.

"I told you earlier that you were the most beautiful girl here, didn't I? Now do you believe me?" Ben kisses my hair. He doesn't seem affected by all the attention—perhaps his football notoriety has numbed him to it.

"This can't be happening. Things like this don't happen to me." I lose myself in Ben's eyes, working to ignore the cameras and the crowd.

"Relax, and flow with it." Ben kisses a tear running down my cheek.

"I'm afraid to relax, if you know what I mean, and I could do without the flow suggestion."

Ben laughs. "I'll dance you over to the exit by the ladies' room."

"You're the consummate gentleman, Vladimir Chortov."

"Thank you, my dear," Ben says, imitating Rhett Butler. I'm just grateful that he actually *does* give a damn, and it isn't long before the dance floor is full.

While everyone clamors around to congratulate us, Ben masterfully swings us through the bodies toward the side exit. I make a quick escape. In my peripheral vision, I see Alex accost Ben as I walk as fast as I can without falling—eyes fixed on the floor. The nearest restroom has a line of pastel skirts flowing out the door. Since I'm a Diet Coke junkie and thereby am acquainted with every ladies room at the high school, I quickly proceed to the one at the other end of the corridor.

This has reached emergency status. I fling the door open, flick on the light, jump into the first stall, free myself of the numerous layers of fabric and… Ah.

I wonder how the tiara looks over the goddess hair Luka gave me. I wonder how I won in the first place. This is too amazing. My mom is never going to believe this. My dad will be so happy. Danny will—Danny will tease me relentlessly, no doubt.

The door to the hall bangs open so hard it smacks against the tile wall and shakes the metal stall doors. Someone else must have found the way around the long queue—my Newma's word for line.

"Hello? Verona? You in here? The girls and I—we all just want to congratulate you on your coronation." My heart caves in. The sarcastic tone tells me it can only be Amber Claussen. The giggles tell me she brought backup. I gulp.

Another voice says, "It's not every year an out-of-towner wins queen."

"C'mon out, Verona." Amber sings my name. Makes me hate my name more than ever. "We all want to see how great you look in your crown. Plus, I hear that this year, for you, they used real diamonds." At that, the Amberettes can't contain their laughter.

I rub my sweaty palms on my dress and flush the toilet with my ridiculously high heel. What's the worst that could happen? If she wants a fight, I'll do my best. I try to remember everything, something, *anything* I'd learned in ninth grade self-defense class. It's no use; I'm suffering from acute brain freeze.

"Are you coming out, or do I need to come in there?" She shakes the metallic door. "You're stalling," she says, and once again, her sidekicks break into laughter at the stupid pun.

As dry as my mouth is, I taste it. Burnt charcoal. Like someone lit a barbecue in my mouth. Now would be an excellent time to fly away. But the *"poof"* doesn't come.

With my finger on the cold lock, I consider remaining in the toilet for the rest of the night. If Amber tries to come under, I can kick; if she tries to climb over, I could bite. Eventually, Ben would miss me and come to my rescue, like he did with Cobra Tattoo boy. But, as usual, my pride gets the best of me. I remember Angie's admonition to not be afraid. Amber's just a bully. I release the lock and pull the door open.

"*Excuse* me," I say, crossing to the sink, where I proceed to wash my hands. In the mirror, I see three girls guarding the door. Tiffany Green wears an emerald strapless, and Rachel Redmond a pale-blue silk. At my gaze, their eyes fix on the floor like they'd rather be anywhere else. The third cheerleader, the one holding the door, is considerably larger—could probably hold up the whole CHS pyramid herself. And as ugly as her frilly black dress is—and it is spooky ugly—it ranks a distant second to the evil look on her face. She's enjoying this. Reminds me of the Mohawk moron.

I look at myself in the mirror for a second. It's only a second, but I see the glowing tiara, carefully placed on my hair by Mrs. Hale. I see my hair, lovingly arranged by my best friend. I see my green eyes, the same eyes Ben was just admiring on the dance floor. And in that second, I feel an overwhelming sense that I am loved. And that love somehow injects me with strength.

Amber stands uncomfortably close on my left, arms crossed like a parent waiting for a wayward child. She glowers in the mirror behind me. I risk a glance in her direction. What I see shocks me so much I recoil, but I can't pull my eyes away. The cadmium red from her low-cut dress looks like it's bleeding upward over her chest and up her neck, exposing putrid, decaying flesh crawling with black, mutated roaches or beetles and white maggots. And she smells like rotting flesh. I gag in horror, covering my nose and mouth, all the while reminding myself that it's only a vision. *It's not real. Not real. Not real. Not really Amber, but one of Mammon's minions egging her on.* At the same time I'm overwhelmed with the feeling that she, or the demon, or maybe both of them, wants something from me. I touch the tiara on my head. If I hand it to her, will she go away?

Amber's teeth are rotted and her tongue flicks between the gaps, licking decomposing lips that are crusted and peel away from her mouth. Her eyes are red and oozing a venomous liquid that I somehow recognize is deviant desire. The eyes bore into me like they want to steal my heart, my soul. I cover my chest. I want to run back to the toilet. It takes all my will to stay rooted and stare down the demon.

It probably only lasts a second or two, but for me, time stands still. The air is sucked out of the room while Amber's face is being devoured by the demonic bugs. I sense the demon is eating the girl alive. *And she's letting it!* The vision fades, but her real face brings little relief. Amber's eyes, back to the ice-gray color I'm more familiar with, narrow at me.

"Aren't you all that, *Little Miss New York?*" She unleashes the weirdest-sounding cackle.

I clear my throat, and exhale. Then I reach in front of her, rip a paper towel from the dispenser, and turn to face her while drying my hands. "This has been fun. Thanks for your congratulations, but I need to get back to my date." I meet her widening eyes, fling my towel into the garbage, and take a step toward the door. I feel a strong shove on my back. I almost topple to the floor, but my left arm grabs hold of the sink to steady myself.

"Turn your back on me, you'd better watch out, you stuck-up—" Amber grabs a chunk of my hair, yanking it back toward her. I twirl around, my eyes tearing up as the hair pulls tightly on my scalp, some pieces coming out.

I rush into her with all my weight, but she reaches for my arm and twists it hard. This stick of a girl is strong. Maybe cheerleading really *is* a sport.

She pushes me back. My forehead pounds on the edge of the sink before I topple to the ground. It is so hard to stand, much less fight, in these stupid heels. I now wish I'd listened to Luka and kicked them off earlier.

"What are you doing? You said you were only going to tease her!" Is that Tiffany or Rachel?

In my head, I hear the angel's voice—Angie's voice—instructing me to say something weird. Not having any other working plan, I comply. "Amber, I'm sorry about Ben. I didn't know you still had a thing for him." It's then that I realize what Amber wants so badly that she's being eaten alive. It isn't a what, but a *who*. It's Ben.

"What?" Amber yanks me to my feet, and shrieks in my face. "Did *he* tell you that?" I kick her in the shin hard enough to make her wince, but she doesn't let go. She knocks me back against the cement wall.

I think I hear my skull crack. I feel my brain rattling around inside, sending a two-toned ringing in my ears. Like church bells in a far-off valley.

"Did you say Ben? Amber, you—you like *Ben*?" Behind Amber, I see Rachel Redmond move from the door toward us. I remember she tried to kill herself over Ben. This must be quite a revelation for her.

"She's lying. I never liked Ben, only Alex." Amber squeezes the skin on my shoulders, her fingernails piercing my skin, and pummels my head into the wall. "You know, Rachel…I'm…doing…this…for you," she says, knocking my head against the cement bricks after each word, the rotting corpse Amber fading in and out of view. Each time my scalp hits, the pain ricochets around inside me. My stomach churns from the smell of her, and the room spins.

The roar of a jet engine bursts into the bathroom, pushing the two girls guarding the door to the ground. "Get away from her!" It sounds somewhat familiar, like Leanne's voice; Leanne's voice on major steroids minus her gentle southern manners. Hair flying in all directions, she knocks Rachel backwards into a stall.

"Leanne?" Amber's eyes widen first in confusion, then fear. She lets go of my shoulders and turns. "What the—!"

The taffeta in my skirt crumbles under me like I'm falling on a pile of ten thousand dry and withering rose petals.

"Leanne?" I whisper during my descent. "Leanne, the *lion*." Darkness swirls around me like a warm embrace. I'm lying on my back in a field of red poppies, with tinkling church bells echoing a sad song in the distance. The clouds, marshmallow white, form a silhouette of Ben's face. Then his arm, in a dark suit with a white dress shirt, reaches out of the sky for me to join him. I feel my face relax into a smile.

"SHE'S COMING TO! Verona?" Leanne's arm is touching my waist, which is lying on some kind of jostling bed. A female paramedic with short, spiky hair shines a light in my eyes. I blink my eyes open, but immediately shut them. The whirling lights and shaking movements make me nauseous. "Where are we?" I ask with my eyes closed, willing myself not to get sick.

"On the way to the hospital," Leanne explains. "You passed out, remember?"

"What?" I open my eyes and shut them again. "Where are Ben and Luka?"

"They're meeting us at the ER." Leanne holds my hand in hers.

I have a horrible thought. "Did everyone see me rolled out on this thing?"

"Not *quite* everyone. But don't worry. I fixed your hair and your dress. Caitlin Prescott said you looked like sleeping beauty—and everyone agreed."

"*Great,*" I say. I try to remember how many days are left until home free, the amount of days I still have to be with these people. The attendants unload me off the back of the ambulance and roll me past a nurses' station to a sterile patient room. Leanne hangs by my side, trying to cheer me up.

I try to sit up and it's like I'm riding the Griffon rollercoaster again. Colors are swishing by my face so fast.

"Stay down until the physician examines you," a husky nurse with an even huskier voice orders, and holds me down with a hand on my shoulder. "We're waiting for your mother to finish the paperwork." She takes my blood pressure.

My mother rushes to my side, followed by a svelte thirty-something Asian woman in a white coat, looking down and flipping through pages on a clipboard.

I try to sit up to show my mom that I'm perfectly fine, but the room twists off to the side. I drop my head back onto the pillow. "Hi, Mom." I manage a smile. "I'm fine. Just a little dizzy from hitting my head. They're going way overboard with all of this. Really overboard. It's nothing."

"A concussion is *not* nothing," the white-jacketed woman says. "I'm Dr. Kate Young. I'm going to examine you. Also, I've ordered a CT scan. You're not claustrophobic, are you?"

"No." My many phobias include, but are not limited to, heights and snakes and crowds. But not tight places. "Not that I know of." I look at my mom. She squeezes my arm.

"You're the best-dressed patient I've seen in a long time," Dr. Young says with a smile, as she blinds me with a little flashlight. Then she proceeds to ask me a million questions. She feels the bump on the back of my head, and orders the nurse to get a cold pack for when I get back from radiology.

Following the CT scan, an elderly woman wheels me back to the ER. I can sit up with only mild queasiness. Luka, Ben, and Kolya squeeze into the tiny, sterile room with Leanne. Nope, tight places don't bother me a bit. But the fact that my mother is missing bothers me.

"Leanne told us what happened. I'm sorry I didn't go to the bathroom with you." Luka hands me my pocketbook.

"Could someone tell *me* what happened? It's like I woke up from a weird dream with a really bad headache." I rub the back of my head.

"You don't remember?" Leanne asks.

I shake my head slowly. The nurse gave me Tylenol, but it's only beginning to numb the headache, and movement makes it worse. She motions to Leanne to hold the cold pack thing against the back of my head.

"Do you remember winning homecoming queen and dancing with me?" Ben asks.

"That really happened? I thought I dreamed it."

"Yeah, but then you left me—if I'd only known, Verona, I swear I would've followed you." Ben places his hand over mine.

"To the ladies' room?" Luka elbows him.

"If I'd waited outside the ladies' room, I could've stopped it," Ben says. "I had no idea Amber could be so vicious."

"Wait! I remember. Amber Claussen, Rachel Redmond, Tiffany Green, and some other big cheerleader ganged up on me." I should probably add *cheerleader* to my phobia list.

"That's Nellie Humphrey. I wouldn't want to be them after ol' Hailstorm gets done with them." Leanne uses the student's nickname for Colonial's assistant principal, Mrs. Hale. "Woman was madder than a mosquito in a mannequin factory. Kicked Amber off the cheerleading squad right in front of everyone."

"Great. Now they'll have another reason to hate me. Of course, I don't have a clue what their first reason was, other than that I'm from New York." I swallow.

"I'm going to kill them!" Luka pounds a fist on the bed. Kolya backs into the wall.

Then the reason comes back to me. I swing my feet off the side of the bed and hold on. I look sideways at Ben. "It had more to do with you than New York, I think. Does Amber Claussen have a thing for you?"

My mother slides in the door behind the others, slipping her phone into her pocketbook. Bet she phoned Dad, interrupting the banquet he's been talking about for months, the one I ditched for homecoming. I shake my head.

Ben's mouth molds into a frown—an expression I've never seen him wear before. He still looks adorable, especially with his tie askew, lopsided, crooked. My breathing stops. *Here's where he tells me demon girl was his first love.* I grip the sheets, bracing myself for his answer.

He says softly: "Before Angie's accident, Amber hounded me. I didn't do anything to encourage it. She wasn't ever my type, but she couldn't take a hint, even when I didn't respond to her texts. And she did it all behind Rachel's back when she knew how Rachel.... Well, anyway, I had to confront Amber—told her flat-out I wasn't interested."

"She didn't take it well, I bet," Leanne says.

"You could say that." As Ben ran his fingers through his hair, I got the impression that the memory made him uncomfortable. "I received hateful text messages for weeks, but when I threatened to show them to Rachel, Amber backed down."

"You could've told *me* about that. It would've been nice to know what put me at the top of her fecal roster," I blurt out.

My mom moves through the crowd and actually comes to Ben's defense. "Honey, I wouldn't blame him for not telling you. It shows discretion for a young man not to brag about potential conquests."

Ben winks at me. "Your mom's right. I didn't want to brag that someone as gentle and kind and generous as Amber Claussen was interested in me."

The room falls out laughing, but then I stop. *What if Amber's the one?* Mammon, the one who killed Ross? I look at Leanne and Luka. I wish everyone else would give us some time alone, time to unload my new theory on my girlfriends and get their take on it.

Before I can ask everyone else to leave, Dr. Young swoops in, hangs a slide on the screen next to my bed and flips a switch. "Everyone out in the hall, except Verona and her mother."

Ben squeezes my hand before he leaves, and shuts the door behind the others.

"See this spot here?" Dr. Young points to some spot on a gray x-ray indistinguishable from all the other gray spots.

"Yes," I lie. The thing that is supposed to be my brain looks like a walnut cut in half.

"You have a moderate concussion. The fact that you were unconscious for twenty minutes, together with the amount of vertigo you're experiencing, makes me to want to admit you overnight for observation. But I'll leave that up to you and your mother."

"I want to go home," I say forcefully.

Dr. Young looks at my mother, sees that mom is okay with that, and shrugs. "Okay, but you need bed rest for three or four days." She pulls down the slides. "You'll probably have a headache and feel tired. You need time to heal completely before you do *anything* strenuous. In the meantime, take Tylenol every four to six hours for pain—no aspirin, and no Motrin or Advil. Agreed?"

I nod. She leaves the room with my mother, and my friends file back in.

"Ben, Kolya? Would you mind if I have a minute with Luka and Leanne?" I ask. "Just girl talk."

Ben gives me a suspicious look. Kolya looks confused, probably wondering what constitutes *girl talk*, but they file out again.

"You've got our attention, girlfriend. What's up?" Luka asks.

"Do you think Amber Claussen could be Mammon?" I look from face to face, expecting them to break out laughing.

"If it's true, it's the other way around. Could Mammon be influencing Amber Claussen?" Leanne corrects me.

"Which means she would be the one who killed Ross, and possibly Ty Blanchard."

Luka chews on her lower lip. "Do you think she's strong enough? Ty Blanchard was a big guy."

"Believe me—she was plenty strong back in that bathroom. But I know what you mean. It seems crazy. It's just that she morphed into this grotesque creature before she attacked me in the bathroom. Add to that the way she said, *'Watch out!'*—like the creepy phone call and note on my car that happened right after I met Ben. Maybe she taped some guy saying, 'Watch out... I see you.'"

"And...if Angie's brakes really *were* tampered with, Amber certainly had motive. Once Ben was out of the picture, Alex probably started looking pretty good." Leanne takes a deep breath and continues, "But why would she kill Ross or, for that matter, Ty Blanchard?"

"Ty was a threat to Alex in the upcoming game. Maybe it was some freaky way to show her devotion to him," I suggest.

"But that doesn't pertain to Ross Georgeson." Leanne looks at me. "You know what, Verona, you shouldn't worry about this now. I'll tell Mr. Zeke your suspicions, but for now, you need to rest."

"And don't worry about Claussen. If she comes anywhere near you, I'll kill her and whatever demon she's got hanging around inside her." Luka laughs. "Let's let Ben in—give you some alone time before your mom takes you home. Ben's who you should be thinking about, not some demented cheerleader."

They leave and Ben comes up to me. "I'm not sure if you remember this, but you were the most beautiful girl at the dance. Thank you so much for coming with me." Lifting me off my feet, he holds me close. I clasp my arms around his neck and feel tingles run up and down my spine—not concussion tingles, either. He gently brushes his lips against mine…but then pulls back when I'm just getting warmed up. "We'll continue when you're feeling better."

"What? You are such a tease, Chortov." He swings me up in his arms and walks into the hall, like he's going to carry me to the car.

"Wait right there, mister!" the heavy nurse bellows down the hall. "Put her down *now*! She needs to leave in a wheelchair."

Ben lets out a low growl. Nevertheless, he slides me gracefully into the chair she's set up underneath us. To add to my evening's mortification, I'm wheeled out to the warm and waiting SUV feeling like an invalid. I'm *up* and *set, per* and *turbed, cha* and *grinned,* until I remember Angie—stuck in this obnoxious thing all the time.

BACK IN MY ROOM at home, Luka helps me undress—even insists on removing my make-up. "Are you going to go to the bathroom for me, too?" I ask with faux snideness, although I'm actually grateful.

"If I did that earlier, this wouldn't have happened, right?" She climbs into the other bed. "Let's talk about everything tomorrow—when you feel better." Everything good is getting postponed until I feel better. I don't feel that bad. But, admittedly, I *am* tired. I drift off, dreaming of slow dancing with Ben.

Saturday, October 3rd
666 Days to Home Free

MY EYES FLIP OPEN. The room is spinning, and I haven't even sat up yet. For the second time in twenty-four hours, making it to the bathroom on time has taken on emergency proportions. Like the first time, I make it. And like the first time, I get beat up.

No, Amber Claussen has not found her way into my bathroom. This time it's extreme nausea that leads to hurling. Meanwhile, the pain in my head intensifies from intolerable to excruciating. By the time my stomach is empty, I've given up on life. I'm sprawled on the cool bathroom floor. I think being dead would be better than this.

Contemplating my mother's reaction to the discovery of my lifeless body on the floor, two things become evident over the next few minutes: 1) lying down, the pain has reverted back to simply intolerable and 2) something or someone is scratching at the bathroom door. Wiggling the door open with my toes, I lay still while a fuzzy orange blur races across my sprawled body, attacking my face with its scratchy tongue. Khan settles in the curve of my neck. It makes no sense, but his soft purring brings the pain down another notch.

Feeling a smidgeon better, I place the kitten on the bath mat. I lift myself up to the sink. When I've downed a couple of Tylenols, I sit on the side of the bathtub with my head resting on the cool, porcelain sink.

A tingly sensation starts at the tips of my toes and my fingers. I'm sure it's just a symptom of the concussion or a side effect of the painkillers—until the grill-licking charcoal taste fills my mouth. Not a good thing after just getting sick. I manage to slump to the floor, startling Khan, before *poofing* out of my body.

Up by the bathroom light fixture, I look down to see my body in my red flannel dogs and Milk-Bone biscuit pajamas, lying there, staring corpse-like at nothing. Once again, I hope my mother doesn't find me like this.

Khan huddles in the small space behind the toilet, looking at me with big round scaredy-cat eyes—not the comatose me on the floor, but straight up, to the eagle-me treading air over the shower curtain. I have only a second to contemplate the paranormal capacity of kittens before I rush into the hallway, swoop down the stairs and dive through the round window above the front door.

Angie, my brilliant angel companion, waits outside, like a miniature sun lighting up the night. She urges me onward, saying telepathically, "Verona, don't be afraid. Everything works together for a purpose." I'm getting so tired of people telling me not to be afraid, especially since that assurance is almost always followed by something painfully tragic.

The night sky is empty; no stars or moon compete with the angel's light as we circle over the JV and turn in the direction of Colonial High. The angel speeds downward. I follow as closely as possible, executing a sideways flyby past the naked flagpole in front of the school. She stops over the tennis courts. My talons grip the top of the wire fence while I catch my breath.

The angel's light illuminates the back of a man in a khaki raincoat, following the beam of his flashlight toward a black mound between the two nets. It looks like the kind of tarp covering people put on their mulch to keep the rain from getting to it. But why would someone put mulch on the school's tennis court?

I notice the mound move slightly.

The man stops a few feet away from the shaking lump and calls to it. His voice sounds garbled, but I sense from his tone that the words are meant to comfort—much like my father used to try to console Danny when he'd cry under his covers.

The man turns the beam of the flashlight back on his own face, still mumbling something to the mound. He turns his head slightly, allowing me to glimpse a slice of his profile. It's Mr. Zeke, for sure.

Could the shaking lump be Craig Hamilton? I remember Craig lying in the fetal position on Susan Wythe's front lawn after discovering Ross was dead. There could be a person under some kind of dark covering. Is Mr. Zeke here to comfort him?

The black mass jumps up—confirming that it isn't a mulch pile, but an actual person. The figure stands taller and broader than Mr. Zeke—definitely not Hamilton. Craig is only an inch or so taller than I am.

Then the black covering sweeps away like a magician's magic trick, billowing down to the ground. A man, dressed completely in black with his back to us, is silhouetted on the court. He turns slowly, without moving his feet, and only the macabre red eyes appear from under the hood, the clown gun pointing at the court.

It's like everything happens in slow motion. Mr. Zeke mumbles something to the man, drops his flashlight to the ground, and reaches for something inside his coat.

At the same time, the black-hooded guy turns into Mammon, in his golden robe and crown, towering over Mr. Zeke. The demon's face is contorted, raging and focused on the man below him. He lifts his fist, and it looks like he's going to punch Mr. Zeke; but then he shrinks back down into the hooded man. His mammoth fist morphs into the clown gun. He shoots two bullets straight into my favorite teacher. The sound is muffled, but there's a red flash with each shot, matching the demon's fiery eyes.

The flashlight rolls along the court—its beam blinking on and off. Mr. Zeke drops sideways to the ground, clutching his upper arm. The murderer, toggling between the hooded villain and Mammon so fast I can't keep up, sweeps the dark fabric over Mr. Zeke's body.

The flashlight burns out completely. The only light comes from a dim streetlamp between the court and faculty parking. I look over my shoulder for my angel partner, but she burns out in front of me like the flashlight.

A scream sticks in my throat. I shove it back down—listening to make sure I didn't wake anyone. The clock on the bathroom shelf reads 4:13. I struggle to calm my breathing, struggle to sit against the bathtub, hug my knees and rock. Khan continues to hide behind the toilet. I pull him out and cuddle him to my chest. His steady purring brings my heart rate down so I can think. *What am I going to do?*

This time I absolutely have to do something. Mr. Zeke is in mortal danger. I have to warn him. Stop him from going to the tennis court. *But how?* Luka would be no help. She'll wake my mother. They'll both insist that I go back to sleep and call for help in the morning.

I feel strongly, no, I *know* somehow, that if I don't do something immediately, Mr. Zeke will be dead by morning.

It takes me mere seconds to compose my plan. Slowly and quietly, I stand up. My stomach churns, but I don't feel like I need to throw up. The Tylenol must be working. I sneak back into my room, swipe my cell phone from on top of the bureau, a sweatshirt from the chair, and my sneakers from the floor. The door creaks as I close it. Luka mumbles something, then rolls over. I wait to see if she'll get up. Nope. She's probably in some far-off, romantic place, dancing with Kolya.

Safely ensconced in the bathroom, I search for Mr. Zeke's cell phone number. It's not here. I must've forgotten to press done! There's no time to search for his number. Who knows where I put it?! Plan B. I push the button for Ben's number. The phone rings three times, and Ben's sleepy voice answers, "Verona?"

"Ben, it's me."

"Are you alright?" I can picture him sitting up in bed, and running his hands through his straggly hair.

"Yes, err—no. I mean, I need your help."

"What's wrong?"

"Mr. Zeke's in trouble. I need you to come get me. We don't have much time," I whisper.

"Verona, you're supposed to be in bed—remember? Besides, what makes you think Mr. Zeke's in trouble? It's four in the morning. He's probably in bed copping z's, like you should be."

"I don't have time to explain. Are you picking me up or not? If the answer is no, I'm driving there myself."

"Where?"

"I'll explain when you get here." I hate resorting to an ultimatum with Ben, but the seriousness of the circumstances warrants it. I really hope he doesn't think I'm a drama queen because of this.

"You can't drive!" With a frustrated grunt, he consents. "I'll be there in ten minutes." I can hear him rummaging around.

"Pick me up in the alley around back. I don't want to wake my mom or Luka."

"I should call your mom and tell her what her crazy daughter's up to." But I can tell by his tone there's no will behind that threat.

"I'll never talk to you again." I think I might actually mean it, too. I hang up and gulp down another Extra Strength Tylenol. I hide Khan in Danny's room and shut the door. The real trick will be sneaking out of the house without Max waking up my mom, as his bed is right near hers.

I tread lightly down the carpeted stairs. Stop and listen. Tread again. Stop at the bottom. Max snores like an old man from inside my mother's room. A nightlight from the bathroom allows me to feel my way to the kitchen. When the room takes a little spin, I steady myself with my palms on the granite countertop.

This is insane, and I know it. But I don't care. Mr. Zeke could die, and I would never forgive myself if I don't do something to stop the murderer.

Determined, I turn the key in the deadbolt on the back door. The click echoes through the house. The icemaker turns on with a noisy crunch followed by a hum. I jump. Then freeze, listening for movement from my mother's room. I hear a rustling, but it sounds like it's coming from outside the window.

The backyard, dimly lit by a neighbor's porch light, looks menacing, but I don't dare turn our light on for fear of alerting the neighbor's dog. I close the door gently—leaving it unlocked for my return.

Tiptoeing down the backyard path, I pull my sweatshirt tighter. I should have thought of grabbing a pair of jeans. Goosebumps are popping out on my legs under my flannel pajamas. The gate hinge gives me some trouble in the dark, but I make it through and wait under the narrow overhang at the garage door.

I step out from the shadows when I see Ben's truck approaching. He slams on his brakes. When he leans over to open the door to the passenger side, I glimpse a look on his face that is anything but welcoming. "Are you trying to get yourself killed? What is going on?" It's hard to tell if he's angry at getting woken up, or genuinely concerned.

"Ben, please." I do a short karate chop in the air. "Drive to school and I'll explain. We don't have time. I hope it's not too late already."

"You've got some explaining to do—that's for sure," he says, pulling onto the main road. "So shoot."

I take a deep breath and try to figure out a way to explain my visions that won't make me sound certifiably crazy. "Ben, I have these…um… visions, that sometimes predict the future. The only people who know about them are Mr. Zeke, Angie, Leanne, and Luka."

I can see his face contorting, but can't decipher the emotion behind it, so I continue explaining. "I dreamed about Ross Georgeson dying before he died."

"You didn't say anything when we found his body." His lips press together.

"Yeah, I didn't believe in all this yet." That isn't the best example—so I try again. "You know the kid from Harrison who was shot last week?"

"Ty Blanchard?"

"Yeah, Ty Blanchard. I had one of these visions that vividly depicted his murder the night he disappeared. Mr. Sams said it helped Mr. Zeke lead the cops to the body."

"Mr. Sams knows about this too? You told all these people about your psychic abilities, but you never told me?" Ben swats at the steering wheel as he slows down for a red light.

"Ben, no one's coming the other way. Please keep going." I put my hand firmly on his thigh like that might help his foot push down harder. "I just had a vision that Mr. Zeke was murdered by the same—um, guy."

He clutches the wheel hard as the truck jerks forward. I lay back and close my eyes, trying to keep my churning stomach calm. Neither of us says a word until we pass the oak tree.

"Pull into the faculty parking lot." My eyes scan up the naked flagpole.

"Where are we going?" Ben asks.

"The tennis courts," I tell him. "Look! Mr. Zeke's Mercedes. He's here already." Then I add, to nobody in particular, "Please don't let us be too late this time." My breathing accelerates as Ben pulls into the spot next to the Mercedes.

"Lock the doors and wait here," Ben says, perhaps believing that my visions may have validity, since Mr. Zeke's car is parked here late on a Friday night. Technically, very early on a Saturday morning. He opens the truck door.

"I'm coming with you." I push my door open. He jumps back into the truck and motions for me to shut my door.

I continue getting out. "What are we waiting for?" I ask between gritted teeth.

"Verona, if you're right, and there's a murderer out there, I am not going to let you risk getting hurt. I care about you."

"We don't have time. Mr. Zeke's in danger. I care about *him*!"

"You stay here, doors locked. Crouch down under the dashboard. You'll just slow me down. I'll run over to the courts. If I'm not back in two minutes, call 911." My mind flashes back to the last time I had to make that call. I do not relish the thought of doing it again.

"No," I say as firmly as I know how. "I'm not leaving you. I can run, too."

"You heard what the doctor said."

"I don't care. We need to go now!" I open the door and slide out, holding onto the side of the truck to steady myself. Ben rushes around and holds me close to his body, practically carrying me. A flash of light from the tennis courts stops us for a second.

"Don't stop!" I whisper. Ben hoists me higher, picking up the pace.

Sirens go off in the distance. I wonder if we shouldn't have just called the police from back in the truck. When we reach the courts, they're empty. Well, almost empty. It takes a second for our eyes to adjust to the dim light.

Ben puts me down, shielding me with his body. He pulls on the chain link fence door. It creaks and slams shut behind us. He yells at the top of his lungs, "Mr. Zeke?"

I rush around him to the net where the covered mound was in my vision and stop abruptly. It's here—a black silhouette of a human-sized form. The question of who is under it remains to be seen. Could it be the murderer? Or worse, the demon? Then I see the dead flashlight—it's rolled slightly further than in my vision. The flashlight lying there tells me it's even worse than either the murderer or the demon. The pulsing in my head and the pull on my heart tells me it's way worse.

"Oh, Ben! It's him. We're too late." I cover my mouth, and point to the black mound.

The scream of the sirens is closing in on us. I can feel my heartbeat in the pounding of my temples.

Ben looks at me and back at the lump, like he's trying to decide what to do. Looking like a gray specter in the dim light, he bends down on one knee and pulls at the edge of the plastic fabric. A chill passes through me and I grip my arms.

Ben peels back a corner, revealing the top half of Mr. Zeke's motionless body, lying on its side. One of Mr. Zeke's arms reaches over his head like he's raising his hand. Blood puddles on the court around his head and chest.

"Is he dead?" My voice echoes around my head. "Is he dead? Is he dead?" Thick blackness like liquid smoke caves in around me. I fall backwards into a hollow chasm. I keep falling down, spinning, reeling, tumbling, clutching for a hold, a rope, a beacon, a light, and reaching, searching the inky darkness for my companion, my comforter, my guide and finally, finally landing like a lullaby in loving arms.

Sunday, October 4th

PING... PING... PING... What *is* that sound? Eagle talons knock on the tin roof under my bedroom window trying to wake me. She sings to me in my Newma's voice. A song I remember from somewhere in the distant past: *Verona. Verona, the fish that ate Jonah. Only today the fish got away, my darlin', my baby, Come'n out ta play.* I sing it with her. *Verona, Verona, the fish that ate Jonah. Only today the fish got away, my darlin', my baby, come'n out ta play.*

"Verona?" But then the eagle has my mom's worried voice. "Darling?"

"Mom?" But Mom never wants to play. I try to speak, but my voice is caught somewhere in my throat. My eyelids peel apart. I close them tightly and reopen them, hoping the scenery will change.

This place is not my bedroom. My hands forage around the bedcovers and side table for my glasses so the blurry distortions in front of me will make sense. All the while, the *Verona, Verona* song keeps ringing through my head like a lullaby. "Newma?"

"V, you're awake," my dad says. They are calling me from opposite sides of the bed. Am I dreaming? My muzzy brain knows this isn't the bed I fell asleep in last night. Even without my glasses, I can see the rails of a hospital bed, just like the one Angie had been lying in.

"Dad?" I whisper through parched lips. Dad is in this strange place with me? I vaguely remember wishing my parents were in the same room together. But this doesn't have the feel of a dream. I clutch one of the rails and try to pull myself up. My dad takes my shoulders and pushes me back—a good thing, since the room does a Tilt-A-Whirl impression.

"Slow down there, young lady." My dad holds my hand in his. A blur that can only be my mother runs out the door.

"What happened? Where am I? My glasses?" I ask in a raspy voice. Dad adjusts my glasses onto my nose. I *am* in a hospital room. The humming comes from some machine I'm hooked up to from a line in my arm. The pinging is horizontal raindrops striking the window.

"I was hoping you could tell me that." My dad tucks a curl behind my ear.

I scour my head to recall what might have happened, but come up blank. "I don't know."

"What's the last thing you remember?"

"The last thing I remember is Khan purring on my bed. Luka turning off the light." I look around the room. "Where is Luka?" I'm feeling a little peeved thinking my friend is out with Kolya instead of visiting me in the hospital.

"Luka's plane left for New York this morning. She sat here all day yesterday hoping you'd wake up."

"Yesterday? What's *today*?"

"Today is Sunday. You've been out for thirty-six hours."

A man with a square face and old-school black-rimmed spectacles covering humongous bulging gecko eyes marches into the room with a clipboard under his arm. My mom trails him closely, her brows in a knot. "Honey, this is Dr. Briscoe. He's the chief neurologist on staff here," Mom whispers.

"Where is *here*?" I have questions of my own, and I'm too tired for some prying physician with his own agenda.

"You're at Williamsburg General. I'm Nate Briscoe." He shakes my hand.

"Why am I here?"

"Do you remember what happened to you?"

"I remember going to bed last night." I glance at my dad. "Or I guess it was Friday. I remember I had a concussion."

"Do you remember *promising* to stay in bed?" My mother does not sound happy. Dad shoots her a fierce look from across the bed.

Dr. Briscoe asks my parents to wait outside, says that he needs to examine me. A matronly nurse assists him by handing him funny-looking objects to smack me with.

"Did I just fall asleep and not wake up? Is that why they brought me here?" I ask, while Dr. Briscoe removes my glasses and shines a bright light into my watering eyes. He is quiet. When he's done prodding and poking various parts of my body, he summons my parents.

"It's not uncommon to experience amnesia when you've had severe head trauma. Your memory may return with time. You're a very lucky young lady. You didn't bleed profusely or develop serious complications."

"The MRI doesn't show anything we need to worry about long-term—some bruising. She should be fine in a few days, as long as she stays put. I recommend that she stay with us until Tuesday. In the meantime, she's to rest in bed. Get help going to the bathroom. Another fall or head trauma could be life-threatening." He stares into my eyes. "Do you understand?"

"Yes," I say. *What have I done?* I feel like I'm in trouble, but no one will tell me why.

"What about school?" Mom asks.

"School's out of the question this week. Your pediatrician, Dr. Gessler, can give you a better idea of when Verona should return to school. She'll need to follow up with him Thursday or Friday. In the meantime, I've ordered some pills to help her sleep," Dr. Briscoe continues. "Sleep is the main thing she needs right now. Keep visitors to a minimum. No schoolwork for a few days—just rest."

The doctor continues his instructions to me: "You need to eat what you can. It might make you a bit nauseous at first, but you need to eat to regain your strength." He pauses at the door, turning back toward me with a mischievous twinkle in his gecko eyes. A tray of food is brought into the room, and it does look like he magically made it appear. My body has two opposing reactions to the aroma: my mouth waters for the beef gravy, but my stomach lurches.

Mom and Dad stand on either side of my bed, trying to look casual while making every effort not to look at each other. Their obvious discomfort is rubbing off on me.

"Can I get you anything, V?" my dad asks, looking for an escape, like Nicky in Angie's hospital room. The only drink on the tray is iced tea. I've always hated iced tea.

"Would you mind getting me a Diet Coke?"

"Sure, honey." My dad seems eager to be able to do something.

My mom catches his arm. "I don't think the caffeine…"

"Relax, Cheryl," Dad says. "With the drugs they've got her on, a little caffeine won't make any difference."

Is that Dad? I don't remember ever hearing him contradict my mother in front of me. When he leaves the room, Mom slumps into the corner chair. Limp hair hangs around her face—she looks way older without make-up. Or maybe it's lack of sleep.

"Mom, I'm sorry," I say, not really sure what I'm apologizing for.

She sits up. "Do you remember anything?"

"No, but I can tell I must have done something I wasn't supposed to. I'm really sorry."

"Sweetheart, we're all tired—that's all." Her eyes well up. "I was so afraid you wouldn't wake up." She takes a deep breath. Then, gaining her composure, she turns and nods at the food, saying with a stern voice, "Now, eat."

I pick at the meat, but I'm only able to stomach the bread and applesauce. Dad comes back with my drink. The Diet Coke tastes like heaven. I use it to wash down a handful of pills the nurse hands me in a plastic cup.

Dad leans against the windowsill, while my mom slumps back into the only chair. I feel both of their eyes on me. The undivided attention is a bit unnerving.

"Where's Danny?"

"He's staying with Mima and Papa," Dad answers.

"He's going to be mad at me," I predict. Mima and Papa are my dad's eccentric parents who live in Brooklyn. Papa emigrated from Italy when he was twelve, and speaks with a heavy accent. Mima has an Italian accent too, despite being born and raised in Brooklyn. I imagine Mima torturing Danny with pasta, "Mangia! Mangia! *Eat! Eat!*" until his belly feels like it will explode.

"Where are you staying?" I ask Dad. The question has been on my mind.

"I've been here, mostly." He looks at my mother. "Your mother let me crash for a few hours in Danny's room last night, but that cat of yours kept waking me up."

IT'S NOT KHAN, but my demanding bladder that wakes me up later that night. I try to sit, but fall back onto my pillow. The impact causes pain to whip across the inside of my skull. Very soon, I am fully awake, remembering why I'm not in my own bed at home. The door to my room is open enough for me to see the number 413 reflected in the hallway light. The rest of the room is hidden in gray shadows.

"Mom?" I whisper.

"V? What's wrong?" Dad's voice comes from the direction of the chair. In a second, he is towering over me.

"Where's Mom?"

"I convinced her to go home and get some sleep. She hasn't slept since you got here." Dad brushes my hair from my face. "Can I get you something?"

"Can you get me a nurse?" When he doesn't rush out, I add, "I need to use the ladies' room."

"Oh, sure, honey. I'll be right back." He squeezes my arm and then adds firmly, "Don't try to get up by yourself." I don't really think that's an option, with my arm attached to a long pole. Also, the bed railings are in the way, and the room spins whenever I sit up. Of course, wetting the bed isn't a particularly appealing option, either.

Two minutes later, Dad returns—alone, but still determined. "The nurses have all left for the night." He starts fiddling with the railings.

"Really?"

"I'm kidding," Dad says. "But it sure seems like it. You'll just have to let me help you." The way he says it, I can tell helping his teenage daughter to the bathroom is not high on his bucket list. Probably not on it at all.

"C'mon, Dad! I'm sixteen."

"Well, who do you think changed your diapers?" He forces the railing down.

"Mom. Newma."

"Well, yes," he says. "But I helped."

"Really?" My eyes narrow as he pulls the pole around to the bathroom side of the bed.

"Once or twice." He sighs. "We can do this, V. I'll lift you. You hold onto the pole and wheel it into the bathroom. Then I'll place you on the john and stand at the door, looking the other way. You do your thing and, when you're done, I'll help you back to bed."

"Okay, I guess." It beats wetting the bed. Dad's plan isn't as embarrassing as I expected. When I'm settled back into bed with the cord of my line untwisted, we both exhale loudly.

"Thanks, Dad."

"You're welcome, honey." He plops down in the corner chair.

"Dad, I really miss you." A renegade tear runs down my cheek.

"I really miss you too, baby girl." And then I hear him say, quietly, like he's talking to himself, "I never wanted it to be like this."

I mouth the words, "Me neither."

Monday, October 5th

THE ONLY WORDS I can think of to describe Monday at the hospital are weird, weirder, and weirdest. It is great having both my parents in the same room with me. The weird part is their awkwardness with being together. The awkwardness makes it hard to breathe at times.

"Mom, have you seen my cell phone?" I work the bed remote to the sitting up position. Mom tilts her head toward Dad like he's done something with it.

Dad sighs, after returning my mother the *Thanks for throwing me under the bus* look. "V, your doctors told us it would be best if you just rested these next few days with as little interruption as possible. Of course, your mother and I agreed with their recommendation. We'll give your phone back in a few days, when we see that you're out of danger."

"What about visitors? I'm feeling much better this morning. Look, I'm sitting up and eating." To demonstrate, I take an extra bite of the cinnamon roll left on my half-finished plate. "Plus, my headache is gone."

"That's from the medicine, I expect," Mom chimes in. "We'll see about visitors—maybe tomorrow. Honey, we're really trying to follow the doctor's advice." She looks to my dad for help.

"We don't want anything worse to happen to you. You gave us quite a scare, you know."

I shake my head. "No, I really don't know. Please tell me what happened."

My head bobs from one face to the other. Mom speaks first. "Well, you know, you passed out."

"For a day and a half." Dad looks at my mother in a weird, conspiratorial way.

"I know about that part. But *how* did I pass out? Did I fall going to the bathroom in my sleep?"

"Something like that, honey." My mom's cheeks flush cherry-red, like they do when she drinks a glass of wine. That clinches it for me. They are holding something back from me.

"Who brought the chrysanthemums?" I ask, thinking maybe this is a question they *will* answer. I'm expectant, hopeful, crazy-hopeful that they are from Ben. I try not to get my hopes up too high, but my heart hurts to think that I have been lying here for three days now without so much as an attempt on his part to see how I'm doing.

"It's the strangest thing," Mom says. "The flowers were delivered earlier today, when you were still asleep."

Mom brings me the note card from the little plastic holder. It reads:
Verona, hold out hope that everything will work out.

"That's pretty cryptic," I say. Inside I'm wondering who would send me flowers and not sign the card? Every person I come up with: Ben? He'd at least put a B at the end. Angie—she relied on hope to get through, but she always signs her notes. Leanne? Mr. Zeke? They'd all sign the card.

My parents look at each other, rubbing their stomachs like they haven't eaten in a week. They leave to go eat at some restaurant across from the hospital. *Together.* The two of them doing something together is weirder than when they were acting all awkward. It's how I know my questions are getting to them.

I look back at the note. *Who is this from?* Then I think of the little book she was holding, and think it has to be Angie. She must've forgotten to sign the card.

A knock at the door breaks my concentration. I look up. Angie wheels herself in. Maybe I really *am* psychic.

"Angie! I was just thinking about you." I sit up higher. I want to hug her, but soon realize there are too many obstacles in the way. The pain ricocheting around my head forces me back against the cushion of the mattress. "Did you send me the flowers? Write this note?"

Angie shakes her head. "Nope. Wasn't me. How are you feeling?" Angie's eyes look puffy, causing me to wonder if her exuberance isn't partly a front. It has to be hard adjusting to moving around in a wheelchair. But other than that, she looks like her old self. The bruises are gone, or completely covered with makeup. She wears a long skirt, with only one casted leg protruding down to the metal foot prop at the base of the wheelchair. I imagine she is sitting on the other leg.

"I'm feeling better," I say, "but they're making me stay until tomorrow. Boring."

"I know what you mean. I've brought you a present." Angie holds something large and flat on her lap. She struggles to move the chair closer to me without dislodging the awkward item. "My first painting with the art set you brought me." She hands the canvas to me. "Do you like it?"

I shake my head, no. She frowns. "I *love* it! For someone claiming to have problems with colors, this is fantastic! I love the eagle and the cherub. Your midnight-blue sky is awesome."

"It's us from your vision," she says. "Did I capture it?"

"Well, yes and no. I mean, in my vision, I know I'm a bald eagle, but I never actually see myself. I suppose I might look like this—I'm just not sure. The angel looks familiar—like you were there."

"Seems like in some strange way, I was."

"Does my mom know you're here?"

"I've never met your mom," Angie reminds me. "But when Leanne told me that you weren't allowed visitors for a while, I couldn't help but break the rules. I know how it feels when no one comes. It's lonely."

"It's like I'm being shunned for some reason."

"That's not it, Verona."

"Well, what is it, then?"

"I think they just don't want anyone to upset you while you're healing, that's all."

"How is anyone going to upset me by visiting?" Since Angie looks uncomfortable, I decide to change the subject. "Hey, I've been wondering, did we beat Harrison on Saturday?" I can't believe I slept through the entire homecoming game when I was supposed to be queen. What I'm really asking, hoping she's intuitive enough to guess, is, *what's up with Ben?*

"My insanely paranoid parents wouldn't let me go to the game, but I heard we got crushed. Stomped on. I don't remember the score, but it wasn't even close." Angie frowns, examining her nails. "Harrison was so pumped to win. They dedicated the game to Ty Blanchard. Our guys were just too discouraged..." she says, then looks up at me and continues, "from losing so much ground in the first quarter." Is that why Ben hasn't contacted me? He's discouraged?

Since Angie isn't volunteering anything, I decide to come right out with my question. "Have you heard anything from Ben?"

"Only what Leanne told me from seeing him at the game. She tried talking to him afterward, but he acted all angry." Angie tries to sound positive. "I'll know more when she calls me after school. Do you want me to tell you what I find out?"

"Please. Call me on the hospital line—my parents confiscated my phone." I hope she'll be able to time her call during one of the rare moments when neither parent is in the room.

"I will." Then Angie feels for something in her jacket pocket. "I almost forgot. I promised to give you this." She hands me a small envelope.

"What is it?"

"Open it."

I open the envelope to find a card with the cutest puppy crying on the front page. The caption reads, "I'm so sorry." I look up at Angie. *What did she have to be sorry about?*

"It's not from me," she says. "Read it."

I read the note inside. "Can you ever forgive me?" It is signed in small, rounded script, "I'm so sorry for my part in what happened, Rachel Redmond."

"Rachel's not a bad person. She's just too much of a follower," Angie says. "She's real torn up by what Amber did to you."

"She should be," I say. "If Amber hadn't beat me senseless, I wouldn't be in here. Rachel stood by, watching the whole thing."

"She didn't expect Amber to get physical. I know Rachel—she's very sensitive. Amber convinced her that if you hadn't come on the scene, Ben would've eventually fallen for her."

"I heard that he had leveled with her last year."

"Yeah, he did, but she never lost hope that he would change his mind. You know how irrational girl crushes can be. I guess not *all* hope is a good thing."

"Angie, wait! I remember hearing your voice in the middle of the fight, like when you're the cherub."

Angie laughs. "Figures. Only *I* can get caught up in a fight I'm not even at. At least this one didn't get me detention. What did I say?"

"You said something like, *Tell Amber you're sorry about her feelings for Ben*. Did you somehow send me a message like that? When I repeated it, Rachel began questioning Amber."

"No. I knew that Amber had secretly hounded Ben. But, no, I never consciously sent any telepathic messages, if that's what you mean. But when Leanne texted me that you won queen, I had a feeling something was wrong. I sent her a text message asking if you were all right. That's what made her go looking for you."

"Wow! That's the weirdest thing. In the information file Mr. Zeke gave me about the Transcenders, the angel has got special power through prayer, so maybe this is what it looks like. I'll have to ask Mr. Zeke when he visits." Angie's eyes well up. "After I sent Leanne the text, I prayed for you." She wheels to my nightstand and blows her nose into a Kleenex.

At the same time, my parents barrel through the door. Their first impression is surprise that I have a visitor, but my father changes expressions fast. "Hello. I'm Tom Lamberti, Verona's father."

"You must be Angie. Verona's told me so much about you," my mom adds quickly, bending down to shake Angie's hand. Her eyes dart from Angie's Kleenex to my face, like she's looking for something. "I'm sure you girls have had a nice visit, but Verona is under strict orders to rest, and she's been awake since seven this morning."

THE UNMISTAKABLE PERFUME of roses tickles my nose as I ascend into consciousness later that day. I open my eyes to a huge bouquet of deep-red roses filling the tray-on-wheels next to my bed. I glance toward my dad.

"Your principal and assistant principal came by. The woman…" Dad says.

"Mrs. Hale," Mom fills in.

Dad clears his throat. "Mrs. Hale said you'd left these at the dance, and she wanted you to have them before they wilted."

"Mr. Sams said you were a stunning homecoming queen. I don't think I even congratulated you yet." Dad kisses the top of my head.

"It was the shortest reign in history. I *slept* through the homecoming game."

"Still, it shows that you've been accepted at your new school." Mom folds the newspaper on her lap. Dad's brow wrinkles, like maybe he isn't ecstatic about that conclusion.

"What about that sad-looking rose?" I ask. Next to the chrysanthemums on the windowsill, a single rose withers in an empty glass, clinging to only a few petals.

"I didn't notice that, did you, Tom?" My mother looks over her glasses.

"No. Probably left by the last patient. I'll throw it out." Dad grabs the glass. "There's an envelope." He hands it to me since it has my name on it. In that same, drippy red. I fight to keep my hands from shaking. I smell the envelope. I'm almost expecting the rusty metallic smell of blood.

"Who would give you a dead rose?" My mother asks. "That's just weird." When I stuff the envelope under the covers, she continues, "Aren't you going to open it?"

"It's probably Nicky pranking me." I roll my eyes. The contents of the note might upset my parents further. They're already acting weirder than normal.

My mother—the human polygraph—squints at me and opens her mouth, but before she could hammer additional questions at me, lizard-eyes Dr. Briscoe shuffles in.

"How is our patient doing today?"

Mom says, "As well as can be expected, I suppose." She gives me a look that says, *later.*

"When can I go home? I'm feeling fine."

Dr. Briscoe laughs. "Slow down. Let me take a look." He prods me with a hammer, blinds me with a tiny strobe, and then has me do some silly exercises standing up. The room spins, just a bit, but at least my stomach has ceased getting in on the action.

I think I pass the test. "Okay, I'll have the nurse remove your IV this evening. I'm recommending one more night here. You can go home tomorrow with your pediatrician's final approval."

"Dr. Newman, may I have a word with you outside?" he asks, after giving me an awkward smile. Mom follows him to the hall. I wrinkle my forehead and wonder what that's all about.

"Oh, I forgot to tell you," Dad says. "Your friend Leanne stopped by while you were sleeping. She brought your assignments. She said your teachers said to only do what you feel up to. You can catch up when you're feeling better." Dad hands me a notebook, which I place next to the roses.

"I wish you woke me up," I say. "I feel like a prisoner here."

"It won't be much longer, honey." Dad tilts his head toward the door where my mom and the doctor are still whispering. "You heard what the doctor said." *Tomorrow.* I think about crawling into my own bed in my comfortably cluttered room, with Khan sleeping by me.

MOM DRIVES DAD TO THE AIRPORT that afternoon. I convince her that I need some time to myself, and if she really wants me to rest, she'll go home. After days of trying to sleep in the uncomfortable chair across from me, she agrees—too worn out to argue.

As soon as they leave the room, I pull the envelope from under the blanket. The same ivory parchment stationery as the one left on my windshield the day I agreed to tutor Ben. So much has happened since then. It seems like a lifetime ago.

I work to open it—not so easy with trembling hands. When the delivery lady brings my supper tray, I shove the envelope back under the covers.

We chitchat about the deluge that isn't expected to end until Friday before she goes on to the next patient. Grabbing a knife from my dinner tray, I slit the envelope and shake it. Again, a dead petal drops out. I exhale.

This is something for Mr. Zeke, not me. *He's* the investigator. Or was, in his former career. Nevertheless, as Angie said, he's got the skills. The card seems stuck in the envelope, or maybe it's just my shaking fingers. I've almost extracted the card when the nurse comes in.

"Let's get you unhooked." I'm already unhooked, unraveled, unnerved. I give her a questioning look, like what's that supposed to mean?

She points to the IV drip.

"Oh, yeah. Thanks." When she rolls the IV out, I swirl my arms around, enjoying the freedom of movement, and get back to the note card.

I expect it to read like the last one; but this one convinces me that I'm dealing with someone who's come completely unhinged. More unhinged than me. The note says: *Roses are red. Violets are blue. You don't listen to me. Now I kill you.* An adult threat hidden in a children's verse. The icy tingles on my neck tell me that whoever wrote this isn't a child, and obviously is not playing around.

I push my food tray away, walk to the window, and fling the disfigured rose into the garbage. Listening to the pelting rain, I trace it sliding down the glass like big tears. I want to cry along with the rain. Who would do this?

The only person who comes to mind, the only person with enough motive, the only person that makes sense, is Amber Claussen. It has to be her. She probably saw me talking to Ben outside Mr. Zeke's classroom the day he asked me to tutor him, and rushed to put the note on my car. She gave me the concussion that put me in the hospital. She craves Ben so much that she's lost her mind, and now she's trying to get me to lose mine, too. I shake my head.

On the way back to bed, I pick up Angie's painting. I slide the wheeled cart with the food tray to the foot of my bed. Then I lean the painting against it so it faces me when I climb back under the covers. Pushing my glasses up my nose, I study the painting, starting with Angie's signature in the bottom left corner, a thin, lilac vapor in the stormy sky.

The eagle's eyes are chartreuse—like mine. The perspective is from the ground, but the tree outlines in the lower background suggest that the eagle is turning right. The crystal cherub is shooting light from a gazillion facets, like in my visions.

How many eagle visions have I experienced altogether? I reach for my notebook, find a pen in a drawer, and make neat columns on the page. I head the five columns from the left with: Date, Vision, Setting, Others Present (OP), Result.

The first eagle vision ends with Angie's accident. The date is easy to remember—September 11. Mr. Zeke guides me as an eagle. Instead of Angie assuming the angel role, I somehow meshed with the human Angie during the car accident. The actual accident happened the same night as that first vision, and from the information I've garnered since then—first from Leanne, then from Angie—the events match the vision precisely.

I had the second eagle vision in art class the following week. No Mr. Zeke. This time, Angie was the cherub. She led me behind the stadium to witness Ross being murdered by some hooded demon she called Mammon—a demon who influenced some real person to engineer Ross' murder to look like a suicide. A few days later, Ross was found dead in his car in the same place as the vision—an apparent suicide.

In my last eagle vision, this time while out shopping for homecoming dresses with Leanne, Angie—again a cherub—leads me to a wooded lot in York County to witness what looked like the random murder of Ty Blanchard, a football player for Harrison. Mammon was the villain in that vision as well. Ty Blanchard was found shot to death in a wooded lot, just as I'd described it to Mr. Zeke.

I search Angie's painting for something that will spark my memory and connect the events that have taken place in the past few weeks. Now the only connections are these irritating visions. Well, two victims were football players and one was a cheerleader. I suppose that could be another connection.

Like I told Leanne in the ER, Amber would want Angie out of the way if she'd been after Alex. Also, she might have killed Ty Blanchard so that Alex wouldn't have to worry about him in the big game against Harrison. If Amber was responsible, she must have hired someone. As strong as she is, and I have the headache to prove that she's plenty strong, I doubt she could have lifted Ty Blanchard with one hand, even with a demon helping her. And like Leanne pointed out, what would she have against Ross Georgeson? Alex and his friends tormented Ross, not the other way around.

If I had my phone, I would ask Mr. Zeke. I wonder if Leanne told him my suspicions. I wonder why he hasn't visited me. He trekked an hour to see Angie when she was in the hospital, and Williamsburg Regional's only ten minutes away from Colonial.

I flip through the notebook, checking for a note from him. I find the assignments written in Leanne's neat print. The only class with no assignment is chemistry. Nothing from Mr. Zeke. Even Mr. Keats included two articles on Native American pottery to read by next week, along with a handwritten note wishing me a speedy recovery. Mr. Tristan, who has never said more than two words to me, wrote a note saying I could read the next geography chapter *only* if I felt up to it. And crazy Mrs. Adler sent me back my paper with an A marked at the top along with a smiley face. Why is there no note from Mr. Zeke? Not to mention Ben. Even Leanne could have written me a note instead of dropping the book off and leaving.

I pick up the phone beside my bed to see if I could call information to get Leanne's number. I programmed my friends' numbers into my cell phone, and never thought to memorize them. The hospital phone is dead. I think about sneaking down to the nurses' station and trying to make a call, but chicken out. If they catch me and call my mother, she'd be here in five minutes, fussing over me the rest of the night.

I pull the covers up to my chin and focus my attention on the painting. What is the connection? If everything Mr. Zeke said is true, why was I given this gift? It hasn't helped anyone at all. Angie is missing a leg. Ross is dead. Ty Blanchard was brutally murdered—and, as far as I know, the police are still treating it like a gang killing.

Some images press forward in my mind. I focus on the angel lighting up the turbulent sky. I get the prickly sensation that there may have been something else. Another vision. Lost in the dark abyss.

I will myself to travel into the darkness of the canvas. A raw fear moves up my body from my toes to the roots of my straggly hair. My legs convulse under the blankets, and the painting quakes. Every nerve in my body tells me to stop, but I force myself to go there. I need to know the truth.

Under the angel, a murky vision of a darkened tennis court forms. There is a heap of black near the net. Reaching forward, I grab the frame in my hands, and then shake it like the truth might fall out onto my bed. But also, I fight the desire to turn the painting around—*fuggedaboutit*, as my dad would say. No, I want to know the truth more. More than feeling safe. Comfortable. I want to know the truth no matter how frightening it turns out to be.

I set the painting down and lean back, close my eyes and take a deep breath. My heart knocks against my chest, but I can handle this. This is what everyone is hiding from me, I know it—the truth about what happened to land me in here. I press my lips together, sharpen my resolve, and take another breath. When I open my eyes, there is a silhouette of Ben, bent almost to kneeling, on the tennis court. He holds up the edge of the fabric, exposing Mr. Zeke's lifeless form, lying in a puddle of blood that looks like rose petals scattered around his body.

This time my body goes completely numb. I sit staring, stiff as a board, unable to breathe because of a crushing pain on my chest, making it hard to breathe. The truth really does hurt.

Mr. Zeke is dead. That's the secret they are all working so hard to keep from me. I hear a faraway cry that I only vaguely recognize as my own, then a hollow clunk—the painting crashing to the ground. I roll over and bury my face in the pillow.

The memories whiplash from the back of my brain to the front.

The killer, Mammon, crouching under the tarp.

The shots fired from the gun.

Mr. Zeke's flashlight rolling, blinking, and, like his life, burning out.

We tried to stop it—Ben and I, but like with Ross, we were too late.

And then it hits me full force: Mr. Zeke was the one with the answers. He was the only adult who listened to us. The only one we trusted to *really* listen to us. I realize how badly I wanted him—needed him—to visit me. Now he will never come. He won't be in chemistry class. He won't be at graduation next year. He won't be able to make sense of this.

He is dead. He was our hope. Our hope is dead.

It clicks together like a completed trigonometry problem. It explains my parents' evasiveness. Angie's puffy eyes. Each realization erupts into another wave of lava-hot tears and hacking sobs.

"Verona!" Ben's arms scoop me up—his kisses cover where my hair sticks to my wet face. I smell him first. The cinnamon.

"Ben?" My wet eyes search between soggy curls. I fold into his arms. "How?" I start to ask, but sob into his shoulder instead. He just lets me cry for what seems like a very long time. Then he pulls me away and pulls a soggy strand of hair from my face.

"Uh, excuse me? *Hello?* Remember the cripple in the room?" I pull back from Ben's embrace to see Angie struggling to move her wheelchair closer.

"Sorry, Angie." Ben turns me to face Angie.

I wipe my eyes with the sheet. "How did you get in here? Visiting hours are over."

"Well, I've learned a thing or two about hospitals in the past month," Angie says.

"And it's rumored you've never been a stickler for the rules," Ben adds.

"That particular rumor is probably true," Angie admits. "So what has you so down, Verona? You looked much better this afternoon."

"I figured it out—what you and everyone have been hiding from me. And why my parents don't want me to have visitors. It's Mr. Zeke, isn't it? He's dead. Murdered."

Ben takes a deep breath, looks first to Angie, and then to the ceiling, and exhales loudly.

"We would've told you. It's just that we all wanted you to have a chance to recover first." Angie puts her hand on mine.

"You did tell me. At least, your painting did." Tears spill down my face.

"I'm sorry," Ben whispers. "I will never forget Mr. Zeke. He's the one who brought us together." He picks the painting up from the floor and places it on the windowsill.

I stare at the painting through blurry eyes. "Who would do this? What are people saying? Did they catch the guy?"

Angie clears her throat. "Seems like everyone with a mouth and half a brain is spouting theories. Caitlin says it's a gangster he put in prison in Milwaukee. Paris swears Hamilton went berserk and shot his Scoutmaster. Tiffany thinks Caitlin did it to get out of chemistry. The truth is—no one knows."

"Is there going to be a funeral?" Not that attending a second funeral this month is something I really want to do, but I need to say goodbye to Mr. Zeke in some way.

"The funeral is going to be in Milwaukee," Angie says. "Apparently he's got a sister there. But Mr. Sams scheduled a memorial in the auditorium for Wednesday during fourth block for kids who knew him. And they have counselors set up all over the school again."

"I hope my mom lets me come," I say.

"Now that you remember what happened, I bet she will." Angie pats my hand.

"I can't believe I snuck out of the house that night. That was *so* not like me," I say. "But if I have to do it again to make his memorial, I will."

"You're sounding more like me all the time," Angie says with a snort.

"Angie, I don't like it. Verona needs to get better." Ben twirls my curls through his fingers. "You don't know how hard it is to feel completely helpless when I got you into this mess in the first place."

"I'm sorry."

"Why are you apologizing?" Ben picks up my chin. "You were *unconscious*."

"I know. It's like I have these visions—but I still can't change what happens in the end." Then I wonder, *what did happen in the end?* "Ben, what happened after we found Mr. Zeke and I passed out?"

"I ran to you when you fainted, but was too late to keep you from hitting your head. The police pulled up next to the courts. Officer Morris said something about Mr. Zeke calling him, but he didn't get the message right away. Then an ambulance showed up. They put you on a stretcher. I went with you. I don't know where they took Mr. Zeke."

"It doesn't matter now," Angie adds softly.

Ben kisses my cheek. "I called your mother on the way. She showed up with Luka a few minutes after we got here."

"Why didn't you stay with me?"

"No one would let me," Ben says. "I'm not immediate family. Besides, I think your mom blamed me for kidnapping her daughter in the middle of the night."

"She would. I've never gotten in any kind of trouble before."

"I could've told you those Chortov brothers were trouble." Angie pokes Ben in the arm.

"You should talk." Ben swats her hand away.

"Give it a rest, you two."

"Hey, y'all," Angie says. "Since I was here earlier, I'm going to roll down to the coffee shop. That way you can have a little one-on-one time without a third wheel cutting in." She winks and pats the large wheel on her chair.

"I'll be down in five minutes to take you home." Ben holds the door.

Angie and I hold hands for a second. I mouth "thank you," to her before she backs up, and deftly rolls back and out. The door clicks closed.

Ben positions me back down on the bed. He touches a tear that has escaped and brings it to his lips.

I clasp my hands behind his neck, pulling him down to me. His lips skim mine, just barely touching, like the whisper of a promise. He backs up, lifting me with him. My breathing increases as the delicious smell from his warm chest and the cool feel of his damp hair between my fingers arouse sensations in me I've never felt before. I fall back on the pillow, his lips firmly pressed against mine.

Ben's fingertips stroke my naked back through the thin cotton gown, igniting gooseflesh tingles down my spine. These rippling sensations eclipse the dark thoughts. At this moment I want to forget everything, just give in to these incredible feelings. I cling to him tighter, losing myself.

He jumps back and stands at the end of the bed. My body follows his upward. "No, Verona. Not here. Not like this. Not with you..." he stammers, trying to catch his breath. My arms reach toward him, fall to the bed and my head drops back to the pillow. I grimace at the pain of impact. "Are you okay?"

I labor to control my breathing enough to mutter, "Yes."

"I'm sorry. I shouldn't have."

I laugh.

"You're laughing at me?"

"Yes."

"Why?"

"Because *you* didn't do anything. It was me. You're always blaming yourself."

"I almost lost control."

"And that would be bad ... *why* exactly?"

"Well, you know ... look at you."

"Oh, that's it." My mouth opens. I feel my face and finger my hair. "I should've known. I must look a mess! I always get so red and blot—"

"It has nothing to do with how you look! You look—you're the most—I mean, if you weren't in a hospital bed recovering from a concussion, and if I didn't have you-know-who waiting for me downstairs, I would prove to you just how hot I think you are."

"Hmmm," I say. "You're not half-bad either, Ben Chortov."

"I want it to be special with us. I want to wait until it's perfect."

"I'm getting out of here tomorrow."

"That's not what I meant. But good. I'll stop by your house. If your mother lets me." He kisses my lips gently. This time I don't hang on. He holds the door open briefly, with only his head peeking in, and says, "I'm crazy about you, you know." Before I can respond, the door swishes shut.

I am alone in the dark room. Alone and wide awake. Thoughts swirl through my mind, barely connected thoughts, sliding past each other. Thoughts like, Why did Mr. Zeke have to die? And Ross. And Ty Blanchard. For that matter, why did Angie have to lose her leg? Most people, people like my mom, would tell me not to look for a *why*—it's just random.

My Newma told me I wouldn't lose my shell until I was much older, but what if Ross Georgeson's grandmother told him the same thing and was wrong? Newma could be wrong. If it's random, I could die at any time. Which means this could be my last day to live.

If this is to be my last day, at least I won't die without being kissed. And not just once. The first time at the overlook replays in my mind. Ben holding a flower, saying it can't be random because it has everything it needs. It's too complex to be random. Do I have everything I need? I have two parents who love me—even if they don't love each other anymore. I have a hot boyfriend who says he's crazy about me. At home I have a best friend and a snotty little brother. And I'm making friends in this place, my new home. Friends like Leanne and Angie, who would say that life is *not* random—even when it seems to be.

It seems wacky, illogical. But then, where did logic come from in the first place if everything is random? Ben was right when he said Angie had a lot of time to think when she was stuck in the hospital. But all this thinking makes my head hurt. I need to sleep.

VI

Eagle Nesting

Tuesday, October 6th

ENTERING THE HOUSE through the back door, I am met with enthusiastic greetings from both Max and Khan. Max sits at attention, his tail keeping time on the woodwork. Khan rubs my legs with a diesel-engine purr. I nestle Khan under my neck with one hand while I rub Max behind his ears with the other.

"To your bed, young lady," my mother orders. "Consider it your home for the time being." I am so happy to be home and, frankly, so super-sleepy, that I don't even summon my usual objections to my mother's controlling command. My messy room welcomes me. My bed linens smell like the first day of spring.

"Aren't you working today?" I ask my mom when she sets a glass of water on my nightstand.

"I don't know. That depends. How are you feeling? Do you want me to stay?" My mom glances at her watch. "It's no trouble. There's a grad student teaching in my place. A few more classes wouldn't matter."

"No, Mom. I'm feeling fine. Really. You heard what the doctor said. I need to rest. I rest better when you're not fluttering all around me—no offense."

Mom laughs. "No offense taken. I guess I'll go do what I do best—other than fluttering around, that is."

I WAKE UP FAMISHED. The doorbell rings while I'm pouring milk into a glass. I jump, causing the milk to splatter across the table. Questions pop into my mind: Should I answer the door in my pajamas? What if it's the murderer? What if it's Amber? What if it's a murderer Amber hired? If I don't move, will she go away? If these are the sort of things I'm worried about, maybe I *do* need to spend some time on a psychiatrist's couch.

As I run the paper towels under the water, I hear a loud knock at the back door. I jump, and Max comes bounding in from the other room in full attack mode, but I can see through the door's window. It's only Ben and Leanne.

"Cute pajamas," Leanne deadpans. I'm wearing my red Milk-Bone dog biscuit flannels—a Christmas present from Aunt Gina.

"We brought dinner." Ben hands me a Chick-fil-A bag, and I lead them to the table, where Khan is busy licking up the spilled milk.

"I was just about to eat."

"I see you already have company." Ben grabs Khan, flips him over, and tickles his stomach. I finish mopping up the mess while Leanne sets out dinner.

"You look great." Leanne smiles, but it's obvious she isn't feeling great. Her normally chipper countenance is heavy, and her eyes swollen.

"Yeah, you do," Ben adds.

"I look like I just woke up." I run my fingers through my unruly curls, wishing I had taken time to fix myself up a bit.

Leanne bows her head over her food. She takes a bite out of a chicken nugget and puts the other half back in the box, chewing with a scowl on her face. "It tastes like plastic."

"Is something wrong with the food?" Ben asks. "We can take it back."

"Something's wrong with the world." Leanne sighs. "Who would want to kill someone as nice as Mr. Zeke?"

"What if it's the same guy that killed Ross and Ty Blanchard?" I pass Ben a napkin.

"I wondered about that creeper from your visions." Leanne sits upright and her shoulders get big, like Khan before he pounces. "It seems like the three people who were killed—if your vision is right and Ross *was* murdered—have one thing in common. They were genuinely good people. Everyone loved them."

"So what's the motive?" Ben wipes his mouth.

"Evil's motive is to do evil. Cause fear and misery. Chaos. If this Mammon character is influencing someone to kill, then why not pick the nicest people? The people who do the most good in the world," Leanne says.

"This demon's motive is greed—at least that's what the angel told me." I sketch a cartoon figure of Mammon on a napkin. It looks like something from an anime book. It doesn't make my blood curdle to look at a drawing—not like in my visions. "What would a demon want from a high school teacher and three students? It doesn't make sense."

"Does it make sense that Angie Jett's an angel and, timid, people-pleasing me, I'm a lion?" Leanne shakes her head. "And some greedy guy is on a killing spree. None of this makes sense."

I shrug and say, "We're still missing the wild card—the man or ox or bull or whatever it is."

"The one willing to die for love." Leanne rolls her eyes, and throws a play punch at Ben. "You'd die for love, right?"

"I suppose so." He shrugs and blushes. I take a drink of milk.

"So romantic. But seriously, we have no way of knowing if you're the bull. Meaning... we're missing a Transcender...from what you said, the bull was the key to the whole thing working right. What are we supposed to do about this?"

"I don't know." I squeeze Leanne's hand. "Mr. Zeke said to keep our eyes and ears open." I frown, and put down my glass of milk. "But he never told me how to get used to a world without a Mr. Zeke."

"Did your mother give you the okay to go to the memorial service tomorrow?" Leanne asks. "Maybe the killer will show up. You know, how they often come back to the scene of their crime?"

"I don't know. I haven't broached the subject with my mother yet."

"Where *is* your mother?" Ben tilts his head toward the back rooms.

"At the college. Tuesday is her late night."

"I remember her ban on boys in the house when she's not here." Ben stuffs the bag with napkins and wrinkled ketchup packages.

"Yeah, but Leanne's here too. That's gotta make it null and void."

"*Yeah, but* I don't want to risk getting any higher on your mother's fecal roster, as you so delicately call it. She's already mad at me for picking you up in the middle of the night. I bet she blames me for you landing in the hospital." Ben compresses the Chick-fil-A bag into a ball and tosses it into our garbage.

BEN'S TRUCK PULLS AWAY and I hunt for my cell phone. I don't have to look far. It is charging in the usual place on my dresser. I call Luka to update her on my life.

"Hey, 663 days 'til home free." Luka's voice is even cheerier than normal.

"Did you hear about Mr. Zeke?" I interrupt.

Luka sighs. "Yeah. I'm so sorry. Your mom's been filling me in on how you're doing. We kind of hoped your amnesia would last longer. It's just too—"

"It sucks." I emphasize the word *sucks,* knowing my mother hates it with a passion, but also knowing that Mr. Zeke gave it the okay when Nicky talked about Ross' death.

"Yeah."

"Yeah, what?"

"Yeah, you're right. Did they catch—"

"No, I don't think so."

"Was it the same guy who killed Ross and that kid from Harrison?"

"It was the same guy in my vision."

"Did you tell anyone?"

"Who should I tell? The only one I trusted to believe me, to try to do something, is dead."

Luka lets out a puff of air before speaking. "You know something, Verona? Mr. Zeke was murdered on day 666 of our count down. That's considered the devil's number in Scripture."

"Well, I'm through with counting down. Sorry, girlfriend. I missed an entire day in a coma." I think about how my calendar hurt Leanne, my growing feelings toward Ben, and all the days that Ross Georgeson and Ty Blanchard and Mr. Zeke no longer have to live in this life. How could I wish entire days away?

Wednesday, October 7th

BEN CALLS ME THE NEXT MORNING between classes. He sounds thrilled that my mother is allowing me to attend the memorial service for Mr. Zeke that afternoon. I am not thrilled with the stipulation attached—that she will attend with me.

"Seriously. I've heard so much about this man—I want to go."

"You'll be the only parent there." I know that line of reasoning never works with my mother, but for some reason I feel it's my duty to try it anyway.

Despite my prediction, my mother is not the only parent there. The auditorium can easily hold all 950-plus students who attend Colonial High, with room for faculty and staff. However, the room is overflowing, and despite the memorial being scheduled smack in the middle of a workweek, many parents show up, some in business attire, some in jeans.

Mr. Sams frowns as he takes the stage. I wonder how much of his agitation is due to the murder of his friend, and how much to the fact that this crowd is breaking the fire code. When the side aisles are full, he alerts the teachers in the back to send any latecomers to the cafeteria, where the sound will be piped in.

Ben sprawls out of the chair to my left, one long leg stretching into the aisle, and the other one playfully smacking against mine. My mother sits with legs crossed on the other side of me and pretends not to notice the smacking legs.

"The techies made a really neat PowerPoint about Mr. Zeke," Leanne whispers from the chair behind mine. "Oh, and Amber Claussen transferred to St. Martin's."

"Good." *She can terrorize the Catholic kids.*

Mr. Sams' eyes search the room before speaking. "Good afternoon, students, faculty and staff, parents and friends. We've come here today to pay tribute to the life of a beloved colleague, teacher, friend, mentor, and Scoutmaster, Dr. Curtis Ezekiel."

I didn't know Mr. Zeke had a doctorate. He certainly didn't flaunt it. Almost imperceptibly, my mother sits taller in her seat and leans down to me. "Your principal looks like Liam Neeson."

Mr. Sams continues: "Only last week, we mourned the passing of Ross Georgeson. Curtis Ezekiel gave a stirring eulogy for his Scout. He insisted, as many of you will remember, that Ross still lives. In a very real way, so does Mr. Zeke."

Mr. Sams turns his head and coughs. "In order to honor my good friend and colleague in the manner he would appreciate, I've asked you to come here to celebrate his life. Celebrate his life for the love he showed everyone with whom he came in contact. Some students have put together a tribute to Mr. Zeke, as I know some of you refer to him."

Chuckles break out around the room, lifting everyone's mood. "After the film, I ask each of you who has something of relevance to share in the spirit of celebrating the life of this respected man. Line up next to the stage in an orderly fashion, taking turns at the podium."

He signals the AV crew in the windowed room above the back of the auditorium. The screen in front of the stage lowers. "Seasons of Love," the song from the *Rent* soundtrack, flows from the speakers around the theater. Luka and I saw the musical on Broadway and loved it.

The tribute film is a compilation of photographs of Mr. Zeke and others—Mr. Zeke reading at his desk, talking with Mr. Sams, laughing with a group of students, hiking with Boy Scouts. There's a picture of Mr. Zeke talking to someone who looks like me on the bleachers at a football game, hugging a young boy that looked so much like him I figure it has to be his son. There's one of a young Mr. Zeke, all smiles, on his wedding day. I watch through watery eyes.

The film ends, the screen retracts, and the velvet curtain opens to expose a smiling portrait of Mr. Zeke in a tasteful gold frame. Mr. Sams gestures toward the painting. "This handsome portrait of Curtis was donated by Superintendent and Mrs. Reginald Georgeson. The portrait will hang on the wall adjacent to the teacher's lounge on the second-floor science wing."

After the applause, Mrs. Hale, first in line, replaces Mr. Sams at the podium. She talks glowingly of the man she hired to teach chemistry at Colonial High.

Following Mrs. Hale, one at a time, students, teachers, a cafeteria worker, and even some parents stand at the podium with a quote or an anecdote that, all together, paint a more vivid picture of this amazing man than the portrait. After each memory is disclosed, the audience claps. I look around the room, at teachers, at students, but there is no one who looks like they would harm this incredible man. In fact, most folks have tears in their eyes or running down their cheeks.

My body rises from the chair. Squeezing into the aisle past Ben, I glance down at my mother, expecting alarm; but instead

I'm greeted with a warm smile. With my arms hugging myself, I listen, smile, and even laugh at the stories as I wait in line for my turn.

Jeremiah Cleveland, a senior trumpeter from the marching band, goes before me. He removes a folded sheet of paper from the back pocket of his baggy jeans and reads:

The Lord is my shepherd, I shall not be in want.
He makes me lie down in green pastures,
He leads me beside quiet waters,
He restores my soul.
He guides me in paths of righteousness
For his name's sake.
Even though I walk
Through the valley of the shadow of death,
I will fear no evil,
For you are with me;
Your rod and your staff,
They comfort me.
You prepare a table before me
In the presence of my enemies.
You anoint my head with oil;
My cup overflows.
Surely goodness and comfort will follow me
All the days of my life,
And I will dwell in the house of the Lord
Forever.

Jeremiah looks up from his paper nervously. "The first time I heard these verses from Psalm 23 was down at the Virginia Company Café two years ago in December—one week after my mom died. Mr. Zeke introduced me to the Shepherd from this poem in that coffee shop. It became obvious that this particular Shepherd lived in Mr. Zeke.

"He was this Shepherd when he listened to me.

"He was this Shepherd when he taught me the best way to channel my anger.

"He was this Shepherd when he told me not to be afraid. He counseled me once a week for six months until I could walk on my own. And he has gone before me to the banquet. I know that it's only because of Mr. Zeke's willingness to *be* the Shepherd for me that I'll get an invitation to the feast when it's my time." Jeremiah takes a deep breath. "Save me a seat, Mr. Zeke."

My knees start shaking. *How can I possibly follow something like that?* As I cross the stage to the podium, all the saliva in my mouth dries up. Nevertheless, I hear my voice say tremulously: "A few weeks ago, I asked Mr. Zeke to fill out a reference for me. I wasn't expecting anything fancy, just something to say I got decent grades—that sort of thing. Well, the form sat on his desk for two weeks. During that time, he encouraged me to step out of my comfort zone in two completely different ways. Each experience challenged me and changed me in ways it would take me a long time to explain. When I got the form back, I was a different person because of him. Mr. Zeke will live in my heart forever." The audience applauds while I walk down the other side, joining my mom and Ben. Leanne squeezes my shoulder.

Salty tears run down my face. For once, I don't care what anyone thinks. It all hurts too much to care about impressions.

VII

Eagle Parenting

Friday, October 9th

WITH MY CANVAS, EASEL, AND PAINT BOX in the back of the Rover, I find the road to the overlook—the place where Ben first kissed me on the lips. Since I can't be with him in school, I want to feel his presence in a place where we have been together. The view from the rock is more spectacular than I remembered. Last time, I was distracted by the riveting view of Ben.

The flowers have turned into a baby's blanket of soft lavender. The sun's reflection on the river is a million sparkling diamonds. Across the river, a red barn is anchored in golden waves of grass.

I mount my canvas to the easel in the most secure place I can find. Of course, with my fear of heights, it's several feet from the rocky ledge, but close enough to get the full view. A tree stump makes a convenient table for my paint box. I massage the paint in the tubes so they will mix after months of lying dormant, while searching for the best focal point.

The familiar feel of the brush between my fingers encourages me on like an old friend. I imagine my palette is happy to be used again for mixing acrylic colors. How long has it been since I've painted anything for myself, just for fun?

A turkey vulture glides overhead, disturbing a river birch chock-full of crows. The birds weave upward in harmonious circular patterns, cawing loudly. As interesting as their symmetry is, their chatter agitates me. I search my pocket for my iPod, and select Steve Winwood's "Higher Love".

First the sky and the river take form on my canvas, then the trees and land hugging the far side of the river. Finally, the farm, with its out buildings on the side. After working for several hours—the sun is directly overhead now—my arms and legs beg for rest.

The Beatles' "Come Together" rings from my phone. It's Leanne. Retrieving a Diet Coke from my bag, I sit down on the sweatshirt I no longer need, and press Send.

"Hey, Leanne! Aren't you in class?"

"Where are you?"

"I'm painting. Why?"

"*Where* are you painting?" she asks. "Are you at home?"

"At the overlook. Why?"

"I know where it is. I'll be right there."

"What happened? What's the matter?"

Leanne pauses. "Nothing. I just need to see y'all." She hangs up.

She's lying. Something must have happened for Leanne to sound so stressed. My mind ticks off possibilities, but I can't come up with anything that makes sense. Maybe she's found a clue to what's going on. Or maybe she's found the bull.

Whatever it is, if I'm going to get any more painting done, I'd better do it before Leanne gets here. I set my Diet Coke at the bottom of the stump, replace my iPod earbud, and pick up the brush and palette.

"What are you doing?" From behind, the voice sounds more menacing than curious. Yanking out my earbud, I turn to find a kid my age dressed completely in black—boots, skinny jeans, and motorcycle jacket. Even his hair and the lines drawn around his eyes could have come from the same tube of Mars black. He isn't much bigger than me—and thankfully, much smaller than the demon from my dream.

"I *asked* you a question." He moves steadily toward me.

"I figured it was rhetorical, since it's obvious what I'm doing." I glare at him. Bullies back down when the victim holds her ground, right?

I turn my back to him. Pretending to add more color to the canvas, I know full well that if my shaking fingers allow the brush to make contact with the painting, my morning's work will be ruined. At the same time, I try to keep the stranger in my peripheral vision. From five feet away, he's circling around me like a vulture, tilting his head to the side, almost like he's looking at the painting from different angles. I'm not fooled. He doesn't have the look or feel of an art lover. My breathing gets faster and my stomach churns.

I take a deep breath and make a decision. Intimidation may be my only chance. Throwing my brush on the ground, I turn and face him with my arms crossed. "What do you want?" It's my most angry, intimidating voice. It sounds intimidating to *me*, at least.

Jumping back a little, his eyes widen, surprised. He puts a finger to his lips, considering the question. "Hmmm. What do I want?" he repeats. "Interesting question." He moves toward the paint box. "I'll show you."

With hands on hips, I stand my ground, waiting for an opening to bolt for the path, but he is wiry and cautious and wearing boots. I know I don't stand a chance of beating him in these ridiculous flip-flops. Note to self: wear sneakers next time you venture into solitary places. *Assuming there is a next time.*

"May I?" He points at my paint box, his expression pained. Something about his face is very familiar and yet different—darker. Meaner. Without waiting for a response, he rummages through the box, flinging paint tubes to the ground until he finds the one he's looking for. Black—*go figure*. He twists the cap off and squirts a big glob into the palm of his hand.

"You want to know what I want, Lamberti?" he says.

He knows my name! The voice registers in my memory. I imagine red hair instead of black. *Bingo*.

"Craig?"

His head tilts toward me. His eyes get real small. He shoves me to the side and slaps my painting with black paint. "I ...want you...and your idiotic boyfriend ...to suffer like you made Ross suffer. Like you hurt me."

With each progressive phrase, he blackens part of my painting: my sky, my river, my golden fields. I see my chance, back away, then turn and run for the path. I can always buy new paints, but there is no telling what this lunatic might do next.

But Craig is too fast. The push from behind sends me sprawling to the ground. My chin smashes on a rock, rattling the teeth in my mouth and unleashing a bolt of pain through my head.

I move my jaw to both sides, thankful it's not broken and I can still talk. "Craig, you're wrong. We tried to *save* Ross. We liked him—*really*." I lift my torso from the ground, realizing how futile arguing with a lunatic is. "Ben isn't like the others. He liked Ross." I grab at the weeds, trying to pull myself forward.

"Tried to save him? Sure you did. Do you think I'm an idiot? Ben texted him to meet at the stadium!" he shouts in my ear as he flips me over, smudging black paint all over my T-shirt and skirt. He smears the paint left on his hands into my face and hair with no regard for where it goes.

I close my eyes and mouth, but my nose burns with the stench of the acrylic in my nostrils. I throw weeds at him, but they only fall back on me, clinging to the paint on my face and getting into my eyes.

Craig's breath smells like rotting garbage, but worse. My stomach rumbles angrily. I am afraid I'll choke on my own vomit if I can't get away from him. *Ben texted Ross before he died? How could he if his phone was in his locker?*

Craig's face morphs into something repugnant and putrid; the same sort of decaying, maggot-filled rot that I saw in the fuchsia Devine Donuts woman and Amber Claussen when she was accosting me in the ladies' room. The horrible memories come as I stare into the putrefying face: I see a red-faced, red-haired man that can only be Craig's father lashing at a woman with a golf club, the woman crouching on a checkerboard floor between cabinets, pleading with outstretched arms. When the woman is beaten into a pile of gingham and blood, the father throws the club across the linoleum floor, where it lands by an open pantry.

Craig is balled up behind a huge bag of dog food. He stares at the bloody seven-iron amid his mother's dying moans. An engine starts, and a rusty clunker races past the open door. I see Craig as a boy, no more than four or five, as he climbs over the golf club, over to his mother, putting his hand on her hip, the only place on her body not bloody and raw. At the same time, somehow, I'm able to see how badly the older Craig wants Ross to like him, *only* him, how betrayed he feels when Ross flirts with me.

I feel his hurt, like a festering wound, in my heart. I'm now able to understand how he could be so deeply wounded. And yet, it doesn't stop me from wanting to live.

"Craig, listen, I liked Ross. Ben liked Ross. Why would we kill him?" I feel for a place to grip his leather jacket. If I get some leverage, I might have a chance.

Craig pulls back, like he's considering what I said, and his face is back to the new normal, the black-rimmed eyes and black hair. I watch as a shadow crosses his face, bringing the maggots back. "How many times have I come here planning to jump?" he spits at me, with breath that smells like rotten potatoes. I turn my head as far away from his face as I can, willing the contents of my stomach to remain where they are, and the contents of my brain to come up with an escape plan.

"But I've got a better idea." He grabs my wrists. Then he yanks me toward the edge of the cliff.

I struggle to clasp my feet on anything. My left flip-flop falls off. I twist to the sides, hoping to break his hold. My foot hits the edge of the easel and it topples over. I know we are only a few feet from the edge. I scream.

Craig laughs—a pitiful hollow bark that doesn't sound human anymore.

A lone crow caws in the distance. I make myself as heavy as I can. "Please don't do this. Craig, we didn't do anything to Ross except try to save him. You've got to believe me."

"Shut up." He stops at the edge to catch his breath. It looks like he's engaged in a battle in his head. I wonder if he's having second thoughts. I close my eyes and plead. I'm not sure to whom I'm pleading, maybe God, maybe the universe, maybe my Newpa. *I don't want to die. Please don't let me die.*

A voice, thunder-loud, rings out and reverberates around us. "Craig, you are *not* your father."

Could that be God's voice? I'm struck speechless. The roaring voice comes from the path, and it's like a violent storm descends on us. It doesn't make sense with the clear skies and all, but a ferocious sound, like a tornado in a hurricane, and the sound of thunder, are the only things that I can relate to the uproar.

Craig drops my hands. "Leanne? Jeez, Leanne! What are you doing? Let go!"

I don't wait for a second chance. I twist onto my feet and scramble for the path, kicking off the remaining flip-flop. The paint stings my eyes, but I keep them open just enough to see the ground immediately in front of me.

"WHAT DO YOU THINK YOU'RE DOING, HAMILTON?" It's got to be a megaphone of some kind. I turn to see how Leanne is making her voice sound so loud and threatening that it sends shivers down my spine.

Leanne is holding Craig by the lapels of his leather jacket inches from the cliff's edge. Despite not having taken physics yet, I know it isn't physically possible for Leanne's 90-pound body to hoist Craig's 150-pound body over her head. And yet, that's what I'm seeing. I rub my eyes with the hem of my tarry shirt.

"I was just trying to scare her. Really. They killed Ross—I know they did. Or at least Chortov killed him."

"You need to get help, Hamilton. You've completely lost it. Verona called 911. Ben tried to resuscitate Ross."

"But Ben texted him before that."

"Who told you that?"

"Ross did. He texted me. It's why he was late for the party. Leanne, put me down."

"Not until you promise me that you won't get within ten feet of Verona again. If you've got a beef with Ben, you need to talk to him directly." Leanne voice diminished. She was talking more like Leanne now. Her arm shakes a little under Craig's weight, and yet she has enough strength left to throw Craig twenty feet into a birch tree, where he lands with a thud. "And another thing, Hamilton, you reek! Brush your teeth!"

She walks over to me, wiping her hands together.

"Leanne?" I whisper, not believing my eyes. I'm not sure Ben could have thrown Craig that far.

"Y'all alright?"

My chin is leaking blood, my eyes sting like crazy, but at least I'm not at the bottom of the cliff. "Umm, yeah."

Craig scurries along the edge of the field and disappears up the path, but I can't take my eyes off of Leanne, can't process what just happened. Leanne, the lion in the ladies room attacking Amber, pales in comparison to this powerful high-speed train.

Leanne picks up my painting. "Shame he ruined it. Bet it was good." I shake my head in disbelief, wondering if I should follow her lead and ignore the fact that something completely unnatural just took place. Maybe she's embarrassed. Southern girls seem to be all about frills and femininity. I bet manhandling psychos isn't part of cotillion training.

"No big deal." I throw the paint tubes back in the box, and close it up. Leanne carries the easel and canvas. We walk side by side up the path while the last ten minutes replay over in my mind.

Leanne helps me load the art supplies into the SUV. "I'm driving you home, and don't even try to argue with me," she says. "You should see yourself."

I angle the side view mirror to look at my black and red, grass-covered face. "Are you kidding? After what I just saw back there, I won't *ever* argue with you."

I look at her and tilt my head forward. "How did you know Craig would be here?"

"*I* didn't know he'd be here. Angie texted me when I was in second block, said she knew you were in trouble. She can be pretty persuasive, you know."

"You should talk. You are definitely the lion. How does it feel?"

"It's like I have this incredible strength and on top of it, incredible confidence. I had to work at holding back so I didn't seriously hurt Craig. I knew I could've killed him right there if I wanted to. I didn't realize how strong being the lion made me that first time. When I threw Amber off of you, she hit the wall so hard she lost her breath and threw up. I was easier on Hamilton—he's been through so much. You don't think Hamilton would've thrown you over, do you?"

"I did at first. But he stopped at the end. I saw this battle raging inside of him…. Did you know his father killed his mother right in front of him when he was a little kid? I thought I heard you tell him he's not his father."

"Yeah, I know about that. But it's not common knowledge. Explains a lot, though, doesn't it?"

"Did Mr. Zeke know?"

"Mr. Zeke and Ross. Hamilton didn't know I know, and if I were you, I'd keep it quiet. It's not the sort of thing you want everyone knowing about."

"Yeah, but will he keep the fact that you have superpower strength to himself?"

"Who's he going to tell? Who would believe *him*?"

"Craig told me Ben texted Ross the night he was killed. You don't think Ben—"

"Ben? *Your* Ben?" Leanne hits me playfully. I grab my arm and massage it, convinced that if she ever really wanted to hurt me—she could. "Hamilton's crazy—everyone knows that."

Yeah, he's crazy, all right, and now I'm one of a select few who actually know why.

Monday, October 12th

MONDAY MORNING I DO MY BEST to meld into the background like normal, but just walking to first block I get accosted. "How's the queen doing?" and, "Glad you're back, *Queenie*!" or, "We missed you at the football game, Queenie!" *Queenie* is something you'd call a manicured poodle. I hate it. Why did I want to come back to school?

And then, as if the stars are listening, the real reason presents itself—or *him*self, I should say. He wears his dimpled, lop-sided grin, faded jeans, and scuffed-up cowboy boots. He looks so adorable I rush to meet him in the hallway outside of history.

Mrs. Adler sticks her frizzy white head out of the room. I'm so excited to see Ben I stop just short of planting a kiss on his lips. She groans and steps back into her room.

"Back 'er down there, darlin'." He hands me a small ivory envelope. It's the same colored stationery as the menacing note on my car, and next to the dying rose at the hospital. The same size.

"For me?" I gulp.

"For your eyes only." He squeezes my hand. "By the way, chem's been moved to Kartal's room across the hall."

RELUCTANTLY, I ENTER history class. I want to drop the envelope in the trash and run away, take the next flight to New York and live with Dad. What if Hamilton isn't all that crazy? What if the killer *is* Ben? It doesn't make sense in so many ways, but there's what Craig said about Ben texting Ross. He did ask me to go to the stadium with him. It was his idea to check out who was making out behind the stadium. Could he have used me as a cover for what he did? It did allow him to return to the scene of the crime. Maybe he only pretended to give Ross CPR? Nah, he pounded on Ross' chest too hard for it to be fake. But would it matter if he knew that Ross was already dead?

What about this note card? It looks exactly like the others.

Some kid with a mouthful of plastic braces yells from the back of the room, "Hey, Queenie, how are you and the Khan doing?" Then, the same moron decides to impress everyone around him. "Did y'all know that Khan means King? That's why they won."

I slump down in my chair. Mrs. Adler shushes the heckler. After we pass our homework up the rows—mine is three times as thick as the others with all the make-up work—I open the envelope and stick the note in my textbook. Thankfully, no rose petals fall out with it. Mrs. Adler is answering questions.

I steal glances at Ben's note while trying to give the impression I'm completely absorbed in the homework review. The note is in blue ink, not the red, blood-like ink of the others.

> *Verona,*
> *Would you do me the honor of being my date Friday night? I'd like to take you to dinner. Do you like Italian? I'll make reservations for 6:30. Let's hope that this time nothing will happen to spoil our time together.*
> *Ben*

At least it doesn't say, "Watch out." I relax a little. It's a coincidence that Ben's note is on the same paper. It's pretty standard-looking stationery—like you could get anywhere. Besides, why would Ben act like he likes me so much just to scare me away? It makes no sense, unless he's demented in some way.

And yet, even if he was demented, he couldn't have killed Ty Blanchard—he was in Charlottesville. And he certainly sounded sleepy and unhappy to be woken up the night Mr. Zeke was killed.

Leanne's right. Hamilton is crazy—I'd better stop thinking like this, or I'm going to start sounding like him.

I TAKE MY USUAL SPOT at the far table in the cafeteria. Leanne, Nicky, Paris, and Caitlin join me. Then Rachel Redmond takes the seat at the end where Ross used to sit.

"What's *she* doing here?" I whisper to Leanne.

"I invited her." Leanne shrugs one shoulder as if it's a natural thing to invite the enemy to eat with us.

"Why did you do that? Are you trying to get rid of me?" My voice rises above a whisper. Rachel glances toward our end of the table.

"She apologized. Said she's real sorry. You need to give her another chance."

"What if I don't want to?" My teeth clench.

"Then you'll miss out."

"On what?" I ask, incredulous. "Another concussion?"

"On having a nice friend like Rachel."

"I don't get you. She was with Amber, watching my brains get bashed in."

"When I came in, she was heading over to stop Amber."

"Well, she was too late." I feel my face flush. Leanne's eyes exude compassion. I know I owe her for saving my life not once, but possibly two times—but this is too much for me to handle my first day back.

The others at the table pretend to be engrossed in conversation, but it's obvious they're working hard to pretend not to be eavesdropping. The muscles at the back of my neck throb. I grab the remainder of my lunch, dump it in the trash, and storm out of the room; my feelings chafe from the pinprick stares and the *Queenie* comments.

My first thought is to retreat to Mr. Zeke's room, forgetting for a second that that isn't an option anymore. I pop an ibuprofen in my mouth and swallow it down with water from the hallway fountain.

My next thought is to go outside. Without being conscious of my destination, my feet take me to the bench outside the tennis courts. The scene is so different from my troubled memories. Instead of the darkness of night, the sunlight coaxes the yellows, oranges, pinks, and reds out of the chrysanthemums, carnations, and roses strewn around the court, a hundred stems weaved through the netting so only the blooms are visible from here.

It's hard to imagine that a week ago my favorite teacher was shot dead in this tranquil spot. It's like a really bad dream. I rub my neck and inhale slowly.

A soft voice startles me. "May I sit with you?" I look up and groan. It's Rachel.

"Sure." My tone is anything, but inviting.

"Verona," she says, pulling on the hem of her shirt. "I want to apologize for what happened. I was so jealous of you. It's obvious to everyone that Ben is crazy about you." She looks down.

I close my eyes tightly. From somewhere behind my eyelids, Mr. Zeke's smiling face gazes at me expectantly. I can practically hear him urging me to forgive her. No, it's a feeling more than a sound I can hear. I exhale heavily, and the tension in my neck muscles abates somewhat.

"It's okay," I finally say, after what must have seemed like an eternity to her. "I'm just having a hard time with all this." I swing my arm toward the flowers.

"I understand. I am too. Everything's so different now. It's like the whole world has dimmed without Ross and Mr. Zeke. I sure hope they catch the killer."

Killer? Not killers. I look at her and wondered if she suspects what I feel certain to be true. Mr. Zeke was murdered by the same guy that killed Ross. Or maybe she's just referring to Mr. Zeke. How could she know that Ross didn't kill himself?

"Yeah, me too." I pat the bench next to me. Rachel sits down and folds into herself, her arms wrapping around the legs of her jeans, her blond ponytail swinging. She must have dumped her lunch, too.

We sit together watching the colorful blooms sway whenever the breeze catches the net.

I COME ONE FOOT FROM CROSSING the threshold into Mr. Zeke's classroom, but Ben's arm wraps around my shoulders, steering me across the hall.

"Well?" he asks, an expectant grin covering his face as we unload our books.

"Well what?" I'm still thinking about Rachel, and how I feel lighter somehow.

"Didn't you read the invitation?" The grin turns upside down.

"Oh, yeah. I mean, I accept. I love Italian food. I should, I *am* Italian, at least half-Italian."

I notice Ms. Kartal look my way. Her eyes squint at me, one side of her mouth curving down. I get the distinct feeling she doesn't like me. She walks down the aisle and drops a handful of papers on my desk. What did I do—or better yet, what does she *think* I did—to her?

"Make-up work." She says this with unconcealed disdain in front of everyone. I feel my face redden.

Great. Well I know what I'll be doing for the next few nights. Make-up work. I wonder when it's due, but decide to wait until after class to ask.

It makes my heart ache even more for Mr. Zeke. Ms. Kartal's teaching style is the exact opposite of his. She is stern in some ways, but unconventional in others—like teetering on her chair to illustrate a point. She obviously didn't get the memo about my fear of embarrassment because she calls on me, a lot. Thankfully, I've read ahead and am able to answer her questions. But instead of delighting in my preparedness, she scowls at me, like she's purposely trying to trip me up.

Ben holds his pen so taut I think it'll break. By the time the bell rings, he looks like he's ready for a fight. We wait together, loading our backpacks, until the other students have cleared the room. Ms. Kartal erases the board on the balls of her feet, her stiletto heels like little spears, warning us not to get close.

"What can I do for you?" she asks without turning around.

Ben starts, "I want—"

Before he can finish, I grab his arm to quiet him. "Ms. Kartal, when is all the make-up work due?"

"I'm sure someone as smart as you will have no problem getting it back to me tomorrow." Since all the rebuttals echoing through my head sound trite, I decide to complete the work just to spite her. Ben is livid.

"That's not fair." Ben's face burns redder with each breath. "Verona—"

"I'm sure you've learned by now, Mr. Chortov, life is a lot of things, least of all, *fair*."

"But—" Ben starts...

Mrs. Kartal spins around and glares at both of us. "Ask Mr. Zeke if life is fair."

So was this it? Does she hold us responsible for Mr. Zeke's murder? Like Craig Hamilton blames us for Ross' death? Guilt by proximity to the scene of the crime? We *were* the first at the scene both times. And for Mr. Zeke, it was in the middle of the night, when normal high school kids are home in bed. And yet, only a few people know we discovered Mr. Zeke's body. If everyone knew that, Craig Hamilton would look sane at the same time Ben and I would appear awfully suspicious. Who would tell? Angie? No. Leanne? No. Ben? No...unless, he told Alex. Maybe Alex told his friends...and so on.

I tug on Ben's arm and he gets the message and follows me out, but he is steaming. His biceps bulge and his fists clench as we march out the front door. We don't say anything until we reach the front of the stadium. I propose a theory. "Maybe she liked him."

"You mean *liked him* liked him?" Ben looks incredulous.

"Yeah."

"There's got to be twenty years between them."

"That doesn't always matter. It's possible they had *chemistry*?"

Ben rolls his eyes. "Like this?" He kisses me full on the lips. The only thing wrong with that kiss is that it's over too soon. Too bad we both need to be somewhere.

"Wait. Before you leave, did you tell anyone that we found Mr. Zeke's body?"

Ben's brow wrinkles in the cutest way. "No. But when I got home, Officer Morris and some other detective came to my house and questioned me. It was getting light before they left."

"What reason did you give them for us being there?"

"I said you had a premonition. They both were satisfied with that."

"Did your father or Alex know they were there?"

"Not that I know of."

"Did you tell Alex about it after?" He did tell Alex about our picnic. There's no telling how much the brother's share.

"No. Why?"

"Don't you think it looks suspicious that we discovered both bodies—Ross and Mr. Zeke?"

Ben snorts. "I suppose. But I don't get the sense that we're suspects in any way, do you?"

"It would explain why Mrs. Kartal doesn't like me." I consider telling him about Craig's attack, ask if there was any way he texted Ross that night, but decide to wait until we have more time. I give Ben another quick peck on the cheek, and cross the street so he can run to the stadium locker room and change for football practice.

I sigh, thinking about Ben's kiss, and how happy being with Ben makes me feel. It is a great high. But then I turn to see the empty space where Mr. Zeke's Esther used to be parked, and I feel an overwhelming low. Why can't everything just be all good, all at once? I want to savor the feeling of having an awesome boyfriend and a cornucopia of new friends. But there always seems to be a catch. Something or someone ruins the party. Maybe life is like that. To echo Ben, "It just isn't fair." *But is it wrong to wish it were?*

Tuesday, October 13th

MY SECOND DAY BACK to school brings two new developments—at least they're new to me. The danger of being out of school for a week is that it's hard not to appear clueless at times. I notice right away that some people relish being exclusively in the know, while others are more forthcoming with information.

"Did you guys notice the man in black who seems to be everywhere? He was never here before, was he?" I ask, scanning the faces at the lunch table.

"That guy? That's just Officer MacLeod, Mr. Sams' beefed-up security." Caitlin brushes a long lock of blond hair behind her shoulder like it should've been obvious. Makes me feel foolish for asking.

Leanne is kinder when I ask about Craig sitting with the kids in black. "Yeah, Craig's been hanging out with the *emo-goth*s."

When I was in middle school, my friend Mary Pat started wearing black and got her tongue pierced. She told me she was going *goth* like her older sister, Mary Ellen. I told her I thought she was crazy. "You can get all kinds of infections in your mouth." She stopped hanging out with me.

"Which accounts for Hamilton's new fetish with black," Leanne whispers. "Most of the kids at that table are actually pretty nice, although a shrink would have a field day with some of them. See the spiked-hair kid on the end? The one who looks like someone dumped a fishing tackle box over his head and the lures stuck willy-nilly?"

He'd be hard to miss. I nod.

"Jeffery Smaya. Also known as Mr. Smee. Just got out of Merrimac—the juvenile detention center."

"He's bad news." Nicky has been listening to everything.

"Why is that?"

"His rap sheet started when he got caught torturing a five-year-old neighbor boy. Then they discovered he had killed several of his neighbors' pets. Psycho." Nicky whirls his fingers around his ear.

I shudder. Just as I am turning away, Craig notices me looking at him. His black-rimmed eyes narrow in a dare. I avert my gaze to my food and pretend to eat. Even if the scab on my chin has fallen off, the scare at the overlook is all too fresh in my mind. And now Craig has a psycho friend. *Fan and tastic.*

CHEMISTRY HAD BECOME MY FAVORITE class—even surpassing art—because I knew I'd see Ben. But after yesterday's embarrassing experience with Mr. Zeke's replacement, my shoulders tighten as I make my way to the room. At least Ben is already in his seat with a welcoming grin. I look around the room, but there is no sign of Ms. Kartal. Maybe they found a new substitute.

"Hey, are we on for tonight?" Ben whispers in my ear. I unpack my book bag from the seat next to him.

"Sure, but can we go somewhere different?" I ask.

"Are you a little spooked to go back to the college?"

"No, that's not it." I say. "It's just that I've never been to *your* house. I'm really curious about the place you call home."

Ben exhales. "It's not anything like your mom's place. Remember, three guys live there. It's more like a locker room than an actual home."

"I've never been in a men's locker room."

"Count yourself lucky." Ben winks at me.

"Please? Just this once." I stick out my lower lip, which almost always works on my dad.

Ben looks down, shakes his head. "Alright. You've been warned."

THE WHITE FARMHOUSE with a screened-in porch is tucked in a grove of trees down a quarter-mile drive off a twisting country road. The exterior may have been white at one time, but has taken on a grayish hue, the paint faded and dirty. At the end of the driveway, a barn serves as an open garage—two old cars inside, and rusty parts cover the overgrown lawn.

Ben meets me outside. "I told you it isn't much." He pulls me close for a warm kiss.

"It's just fine." I hope I sound convincing. "Do you work on those cars?" I ask.

"Alex and Coach are the mechanics. Other than changing the oil, I'm not much interested in cars."

Ben leads me in through an enclosed back porch with tilted steps. The mudroom definitely deserves its name. Soggy boots and sneakers are strewn everywhere. "Hold your nose," Ben warns, as he kicks off his brown cowboy boots. He doesn't have to tell me twice.

"Coach makes us take our shoes off here because that's the way they do it in Russia. You can keep your boots on if you want—they're probably cleaner than the floor."

The kitchen is in better shape. A candle on the counter emits a soothing vanilla fragrance, which works to smother the contrasting odors of onions and vinegar. In place of cupboards are rows of shelves filled with dishes and kitchenware. Chipped counters hold unopened mail, cereal boxes, a deflated football, not one, but three blenders, notebooks, a coffee pot, a plate with a half-eaten sandwich, and other assorted miscellanea.

The living room serves as the world's smallest theater. A mammoth flat-screened TV dominates one wall, and three red La-Z-Boy recliners hug the opposite wall, with old-fashioned TV trays set between them. Stuck in the far corner, a computer desk and bookshelf look snowed under files, books, and movies. I scan the titles. Every item's label has some reference to football.

"You weren't kidding about all the football—were you?" I try to grasp what it would be like growing up with an obsessed parent. Even with my sports-fanatic father, it's hard to imagine.

"Yeah, but it could've been worse. Some kids never see their father. Ours may never have been what you would call *nurturing*, but at least he was around a lot."

"Can I see your room?" I gasp, realizing how that must sound. "I mean, not hang out there... I just want to see it."

"Sure, but it's nothing special." Ben leads me down a narrow hall with two bedrooms and a small bathroom between them. The small room holds a single bed with a plain navy quilt and a lone nightstand. Posters of football stars, old and new, cover the faded wallpaper.

"It's not much, but I love the view." Ben steps to the window. There are no curtains or blinds in this room—or, for that matter, in any of the rooms I've seen so far. I guess that when you live this far from your neighbors, privacy isn't an issue.

"How do you block the sunlight without blinds or curtains?"

"What sunlight?"

"You know, weekend mornings? Like when you want to sleep in."

Ben laughs. "Chortovs never sleep in. We've got practice or work-outs, remember?"

"You never sleep late?" I cannot imagine never sleeping in.

"I wouldn't want to block this." Ben puts his arm around my waist, turning me around so I'm looking out the window.

At the yard's edge, a cluster of southern pines house about a dozen birdhouses and feeders shaped like Russian churches and cathedrals—each one unique from the others. Some cathedrals are attached to the trees at varying heights. Others perch on top of poles anchored in the ground. Bluebirds, yellow finches, cardinals, and other birds I can't name, gather together—eating, chirping, and swooping down to eat. Squirrels feed off what falls to the ground.

"Where did you get these amazing churches?" I ask. "Are they from Russia?"

"I made them."

"You did not." I give him a little shove.

He laughs. "No, really. Aunt Nadia sent me this book of famous Russian cathedrals and churches." Ben rummages under his bed until he finds the book with large colored pictures. He points to several cathedrals that match the ones outside.

"You made that city of bird-churches yourself?" I'm still not sure I believe him.

"You think you're the only one who's creative? Whittling is something I do to relax. I guess like you paint, and Alex and Coach tinker on old cars."

"But Ben, these are incredible," I say, not believing my eyes. "If you carved these, you have a rare talent. I've been to just about every museum and art gallery in New York, so I *know* an exhibit like this would be worth a lot. Nature interacting with art. This is...amazing."

"They could use some color. Look at this one." He points to an illustration in the book. "St. Basil's in Red Square. Look at all the colors in the domes and peaks. If I tried to paint this, I'd ruin it."

"Is that a round-about way of asking for my help?"

"Only if you want to."

"Okay, but now we need to study. And before I forget, can I see your father's idioms?"

"Sure." Ben finds the spiral-bound notebook in the mess under his bed. He hands it to me. On each page are numbered idioms, just like he described to me. Many of the quotes I recognize. I scan the list to find those familiar ones: Number 4—*The early bird catches the worm*; Number 19—*Like father, like son*; Number 52—*All that glitters is not gold*; Number 79—*The end justifies the means*. Others are completely foreign: Number 10—*East or West—home is best*; Number 54—*Every man is the architect of his own fortune*.

"Alex's personal favorite is Number 2—*The best defense is offense*. It's supposed to be *a good* offense, but Coach always says it wrong.

"Where *is* your father?" I ask.

"I'm sure he's out eating somewhere—probably with Coach Grimes."

When I spin around, I am struck dumb by the sheer number of trophies lining the shelves on the opposite wall. There are over a dozen football trophies of various sizes, as well as five or six karate trophies. "Impressive."

"Yeah." Ben rolls his eyes. We hear the screen door slam. "Alex. Boy is he going to be surprised. The only person who's ever been here is Coach Grimes."

"Ben, whose car's here?" Alex yells from the other room. We meet him in the kitchen, where he's rummaging through the refrigerator.

"Alex, this is Verona. I'm sure you've seen her at school." Alex nods in my direction.

"What did you eat?"

"Frozen pizza."

"Any left?"

"Nope." I imagine the food bill for these two must be astronomical. On the top of the refrigerator, huge bottles of protein powder promise impressive results with muscle-bound body builders. Alex proceeds to make a shake in one of the three super-sized blenders on the counter. We wait for the screeching to stop before we start on our homework. Alex takes his shake into the other room and switches on the TV.

"What's it like having a twin?"

"It's cool, I guess. We used to be a lot tighter. Things changed when Alex started spending more time with Coach. It's like their obsession with football and cars binds them."

"Does your father date anyone?"

"Not seriously. Don't tell anyone because I'm not really sure about this, but I think he may have an on-again-off-again thing with Mrs. Cadella. She helped him get the job at the school. But then he's been with other women, too. When we were up at UVA a few weeks ago, he hooked up with a receptionist at the hotel. We only found out when she showed up at tryouts decked out in pink jeans and high heels. Watching him try to ditch her was awkward."

"Didn't you stay at the hotel with your dad? *That* would be awkward."

"No, we roomed with the other players in a dorm so the coaches can figure out which guys will mesh with the team."

We work on our homework. Ben makes note cards to study for an upcoming test.

We are almost finished studying when we hear a car pull up the driveway.

"Coach is home." Ben's demeanor changes—like he's gearing up for something. The hair on the back of my neck tingles. The screen door slams, causing my stomach to jump.

Coach Theo Chortov is a foot shorter than his sons, but much broader—the kind of man people often refer to as an ox. He storms into the room like a gust of wind. I notice he's still wearing his shoes.

"Who's here?" His voice alone pushes me back. Before Ben can answer, Coach Chortov spots me. His mouth stretches in a wide smile like a switch just flipped on. "You must be Verona." He extends his large hand to me. "I am Theo Chortov, Ben's father. Maybe you see me at school?"

"Yes, and at the football game. Nice to meet you." I think it best not to mention Ross' funeral.

"You help Ben with lessons. Difficult thing—chemistry. I don't understand why he needs to know …" He waves his hand over the book. "Because you help him study, Ben now able to play football. Thank you."

"You're welcome."

"We're more than study partners. We're in a relationship." Ben's tone has a sharp edge to it.

"I see. Welcome to our home." The Coach's voice oozes friendliness. And yet, when he addresses Ben, the charm switch snaps off. "What are you doing? Get your girlfriend sometzing to drink."

"No, I'm fine. I drank a whole soda before I came." I put a hand on Ben's thigh. His face turns the palest I've ever seen it. Almost as pale as mine.

Ben's ox-of-a-father nods, then joins Alex in the living room-slash-theater and we can hear them watching—surprise, surprise—football. For the next few minutes we pretend to be engrossed in the work. Ben's hand over mine is warm, but I can tell by the pencil in his other hand beating on the notebook, the temperature in the house has taken a nosedive.

Afterwards, out at the Rover, Ben holds the door. "What happened in there?" I toss my backpack to the passenger seat.

"He's just weird about Al and me and girls. Like it's okay if we hang out with them, as long as it doesn't get serious. It's none of his business, but he thinks it is. He's just weird. Period. I'm sorry."

"Maybe he's afraid a serious relationship will hurt your chances at a scholarship."

"He needs to get over it." Ben's jaw tightens. "It's *his* dream—not mine."

"Relax." I clasp my hands around his neck to pull him down to me. Standing on my toes, there is still too much air between us. His lips tease mine, but I pull him closer. Cinnamon never tasted so good. I inhale deeply.

He pulls back. "You'd better go." He glances toward the house and exhales loudly. "I'll see you tomorrow." He runs up the steps.

Anger and hurt rise up in me. As I start the engine, out of the corner of my eye, I catch a shadow inside the window.

VIII

Eagle Launching

Wednesday, October 14th

TODAY'S DEVELOPMENTS:
1. We discover, via Nicky, that Angie has succeeded in persuading her orthopedic surgeon, pediatrician, and parents that she can handle school. She'll be returning tomorrow. Nicky has orchestrated a *welcome-back* surprise. Angie asked Nicky to ask me if I would drive her to and from school because I'm the only one with a car big enough to hold a wheelchair. Leanne and Nicky want to ride along for moral support.
2. Ben teaches me two new Theoisms:

Number 146. One fire drives out another. I'm guessing he heard this for the first time last night after I left, but I don't ask and he doesn't say.

Number 99. There's no fire without smoke. I'm not exactly sure what this one means, but he does go on to give me a smokin' good kiss in the parking lot. This kiss more than makes up for leaving me standing outside his house last night.

Thursday, October 15th

"IS EVERYTHING IN PLACE?" I ask Nicky when we turn out of Jefferson Village.

"Yup." Nicky smiles. "She has no idea—unless someone told Tiffany."

Waiting in the open garage entry, Angie clutches her backpack to her chest. Mrs. Jett put on a smile, but you can tell it doesn't go all the way to her heart.

While Nicky jumps out of the SUV, Angie's mom recites a list of things for her to remember: *Take your time, sugar. Don't worry about the work yet. Call me if y'all get tired.*

"Mom, stop! You're making me more nervous!"

"You sure you want to go back? It's so soon." Crevices that probably weren't there a month ago divide Mrs. Jett's forehead like a tic-tac-toe board. "You could wait, you know, until the prosthesis is in." Nicky lifts Angie's small frame into the front seat, deposits her wheelchair in the back, and then climbs in the back seat next to Leanne.

"Bye, Mom. Try not to worry. You'll get an ulcer."

Mrs. Jett waves enthusiastically, but her lips press tightly together, like she's trying not to cry. She follows the SUV into the street with her hands clutching her elbows.

"Go! Fast!" Angie commands. I step on the gas, but not so hard to cause Mrs. Jett to worry that my driving might be another hazard to her daughter. "Freedom," Angie mutters. "Another day with that woman and I'd be back in the hospital—in the psych ward."

Leanne defends Mrs. Jett. "Your mom's worried about you. You're lucky she loves you so much."

"I know. It's just that I need to get back to living my life." She lists everything she's missed out on by being at home—the homecoming, my romance with Ben Chortov, Amber being kicked off the cheerleading squad and transferring to St. Martin's, Mr. Zeke's memorial—until we pull up to the oak tree on the opposite corner from the school. Then she gets all quiet.

"Stop!" Angie's eyes widen when she spots the larger-than-life mannequin leg covered in flowers at the base of the tree. She gulps.

The trunk of the tree is wrapped with so many yellow ribbons it looks embarrassed. But at least the scar is covered. In front of it all is a painted wooden sign with a big, hand-painted announcement: "We miss YOU, Angie—not your leg." Nicky has gotten at least two hundred signatures on the sign.

Angie's mouth opens. A tear spills down her cheeks.

"Okay. This is *not* the reaction I was going for," Nicky says.

"Are you responsible for this?" Angie twists in her seat to look at him.

"That depends," he says. "Does it make you happy? Because right now, you don't *look* happy."

"It's the sweetest thing you could have done for me." I hand her a tissue. The light turns green, and we head down Memorial Drive.

"Angie, are you ready? We can wait a minute if you want," Leanne says.

"I'm more than ready, Leanne. But it really helps having you guys here with me." We don't have long to wait, as the car pool line is just starting to form.

When we get to the front entrance circle, Nicky retrieves the wheelchair, lifts Angie into it, and Leanne places Angie's backpack on her lap. She looks so small in the chair. Her eyes stare straight ahead—like she's willing herself to be brave.

"Wait for us!" Leanne tells her. I pull around to the student parking lot. We hurry to catch up with them at the front door.

Leanne and I hold the doors for Nicky as he pushes Angie through. The entrance hall is lined with teachers and staff. They clap when she comes through the door. Mrs. Hale holds a poster that says, *Welcome Back*.

THE CHEERLEADERS ARE PRACTICALLY doing back flips in an effort not to notice Angie being wheeled into the cafeteria. She whispers something to Nicky, and he parks her across from me. I'm the only one at our table not in line for lunch. Nicky joins the rest of them.

"How's it going so far?" I ask Angie, as she drops her backpack on the floor and maneuvers her wheelchair under the table.

"Honestly, it's harder than I thought it would be." I admire Angie's openness. She has incredible courage—I wish some of it would rub off on me.

"In what way?"

"Well, for one thing, all my so-called friends *who never bothered to visit me* in the hospital, or even after I came home…" She tosses her head in the direction of the jock and cheerleading tables, "…can't seem to *look* at me. Except for Rachel and Tiffany. But even they act weird—acting like everything's the same—which is pretty ridiculous, considering I'm missing a leg."

"Maybe they just don't know what to say." *Since when do I consider the other point of view?*

Angie snorts. "You sound like Leanne."

"And what would be wrong with that?" Leanne settles in across from us. Nicky returns with a tray containing two meals, and places one in front of Angie. She looks at him and something exchanges between them. Angie and Nicky? *No way.*

From my vantage point across from Angie, Alex appears to be engrossed in conversation with the guys at his table, but I detect several clandestine looks toward Angie.

"Nothing. I wish I was more like you." I respond to Leanne, and bite into my apple.

Paris and Nicky do their usual nod thing. Caitlin and Rachel plop down at the other end of the table, where Ross and Craig used to sit.

"Why do you want to be like Leanne?" Caitlin asks. "No offense, Leanne, since you are one of the nicest people I know. It's just that Verona's friendly, too. And…" she elbows Rachel, "I've heard Leanne has a pretty nasty temper lately."

Rachel jabs Caitlin lightly in the arm. Over at the cheerleading and football table, uproarious laughter breaks out, causing students at the surrounding tables to turn toward them. But when several faces turn to face Angie and look away quickly, it becomes apparent that whoever made a joke has done so at Angie's expense.

Alex looks over at Angie, reddens, and makes a great show of eating his burger. I'm sure Angie caught Alex's glance, since nothing gets past her. She shakes her head slightly and mutters, "What a wuss. I've had it with these people."

Angie backs up her chair. We are all dumbfounded—thinking she's had enough and plans to leave.

Nicky raps, low and lyrically, *"You love your friends, but someone shoulda tol' you somethin' to save you..."*

"That's that song by Drake and Rihanna, right?" Caitlin snaps her fingers like it's on the tip of her tongue.

Paris exhales loudly, "Take Care."

"I love that song."

Instead of leaving, Angie rolls over by the football players and the cheerleaders, angling her chair so she's visible to most of the students in the cafeteria.

The noise level in the room lowers to pin-drop quiet. All eyes are on the girl in the wheelchair.

"Listen up. Who's the girl missing one leg?" Angie asks loudly, dramatically, directing her question to the cheerleading table, but loud enough for the whole cafeteria to hear. "C'mon, Nellie, everyone knows this one." She punches the heavy-set cheerleader.

When Nellie shrugs, Angie answers for her. "Eileen!"

"Here's one you should know, Tiff. Who's the girl with no legs sitting on the beach?" Again the room is so quiet, you would've thought Mr. Sams walked in. Tiffany shakes her head slowly. "Sandy, of course! You guys are so lame." Angie cups her mouth in mock drama. "Oops! I didn't plan that one!"

Some of the kids stifle chuckles, looking to their friends to see if it is politically correct to laugh. A net-haired cafeteria worker swings out the kitchen door, wiping her hands in a towel—probably to see what's going on to make the room so quiet.

"Okay, Alex, try this one: What do you call the girl with no arms or legs sitting on the grill?"

Alex looks down, but Nicky can't resist answering from his chair at the other end of the cafeteria, "Patty?"

Caitlin, Paris, and Susie look back at Angie. Her eyes light up and she lets out a raucous laugh, the permission everyone is looking for. Giggles erupt around the room.

Alex stands at his seat, glares at Nicky, pitches his lunch into the garbage, and walks out. Angie glances at Alex's exit and shrugs.

"I guess not everyone appreciates a good joke," she says. "Okay, one more. Who's the guy with no arms and legs sitting on the grill next to Patty?"

Everyone turns toward each other whispering, but no one says anything. "Frank!" Angie sighs, like it should be obvious. "Now if you'll excuse me, all this talk of food is making me hungry." Everyone at our table applauds as Angie rolls back into her spot, taking a short bow.

Glancing at the cheerleading table, she says, "That should shut them up." The girls at the cheerleading table toy with their food. Several sullenly exit the room, and for the first time all day, Angie has a mischievous twinkle in her eye.

IF BEN WASN'T WEARING his scuffed-up cowboy boots, I would've sworn Alex has appeared straight from the lunchroom and into my chemistry class. He looks livid—no dimple or crinkles near the eyes.

"What's wrong?" I give his boot a little kick.

"Coach is what's wrong." He lifts his books, distracting me with his flexing biceps.

"What happened?" I force myself to stay focused on his eyes.

"He's taking me on an impromptu interview at Virginia Tech tomorrow. It's not even tryout weekend, and Alex doesn't have to go."

"Don't you have a game this weekend?"

My question provokes the dimpled grin that I love. "You call yourself a football player's girl? Our next game is a week from Friday."

I bow my head. "Sorry." I haven't ever called myself a football player's girl. Why tempt fate by saying it out loud?

"Don't apologize. Most girls act overly-interested in football when they talk to me. It feels completely fake."

"Well, you don't have to worry about that from me." I wink at him.

"I *am* worried that you'll be angry at me for standing you up… Our date, remember?"

Ms. Kartal's heels click into the room. All chatter ceases as she passes out unit tests.

DRIZZLE DOTS THE WINDSHIELD when I slide the Rover into the library lot. Ben leans against his truck, a windbreaker hood covering his head, and the pocketknife twirling in his right hand.

"Let's ditch studying tonight," he says, pulling me up for a cinnamon-sweet kiss. "I'm gonna miss class tomorrow, and I'm sure you've already done your homework. Do you mind if we walk around the campus some?"

"In the rain?" I ask.

"Will you melt?"

I swat him with my umbrella. "At least I'm prepared."

Ben reaches for my umbrella, opens it, and holds it over me.

"Which way do you want to go?" I ask. "Do you want to visit your Aunt Nadia? Wait. Kolya has class tonight, doesn't he?"

Ben smiles, raising his hand. "To answer your questions: I thought we could look for a bridge Kolya told me about. Second, Aunt Nadia moved out of the Russian House. She moved into an apartment with a Russian professor."

"Male or female?"

"Female, of course." Ben flashes me a look that says, *That's my aunt you're talking about.* "Kolya does have class tonight, I think."

Staying relatively dry means staying wrapped closely to each other. The air under our umbrella is redolent of lush leaves and moist earth. I tell Ben about Angie's comedy act in the cafeteria while his arm glues me to his side.

Meandering along brick paths on the old campus, where some of the buildings predate the Declaration of Independence, we come upon a misty, hollowed-out field with a wrought-iron fence surrounding it. The Sunken Garden. A number of descending staircases allow students to cross to the classroom buildings flanking the opposite side. I point out the Tyler Building where my mom works. We turn left where the back of the field disappears down into a wooded knoll.

"Kolya told me the bridge is in this area somewhere." Ben stops abruptly. "Do you hear that?"

"Hear what?"

"The sound of running water."

"You mean this?" I catch some drops in my hand and toss them at Ben.

"You'd better watch it. I've got you right where I want you." He squeezes me tighter.

I listen. "I hear it. It's coming from over there." Since the direction in which I'm pointing is thick with underbrush and trees drooping with water, we continue on the path, looking for a fork to the left. It isn't long before we discover one. Circling around a grove of holly trees, a path takes us to a charming wooden bridge called the Crim Dell. Below the bridge, black water tumbles over river rocks. Red maple leaves cast a pink haze around branches stretched across the creek.

An old-fashioned streetlamp lights our way. We stop at the apex of the bridge. Ben faces me, gently lifting my chin with his free hand. We pause to study each other's faces for a moment. Our lips meet in a hungry kiss that makes my knees wobble and my heart soar and, while I know I'm not having a vision, I almost feel like I'm flying.

This time I pull back first, putting my hand on Ben's chest. My heart is pounding through my chest. It beats so strongly I think he must be able to hear it because he asks me, "Are you okay?"

"I'm not sure. I mean—that kiss. When we kiss ... it's ...wow." I blush, realizing that I sound stupider than any fifth grader.

"I feel it, too. But don't worry. I'm not going to hurt you."

"Are you sure? Because this feels so incredible, so good, for the first time in my life, I think I *could* be hurt by a guy." I close my mouth quickly. I can't believe I have just admitted that to him. Note to self: *shut up!*

"You know, it's the first time for me, too," Ben says. He lifts my chin. "You're willing to chance it, right?" His liquid black eyes search mine for confirmation.

"Hmm. I'm not sure. Let's try that kiss again."

We kiss once more—slow and smooth this time—nestled tightly under the umbrella. Ben's free arm is locked behind my back, pulling me up to meet him and his delicious lips.

The swooshing, flowing sound of the water is interrupted by low voices coming down the path. We freeze with our backs to the side of the bridge.

The first thing I see is the blue Mohawk, tinged magenta in the rosy light, the same light that makes Cobra Tattoo boy look mottled and ghostly.

Ben sees them too, and pushes me behind him. The kitten-torturers must have recognized Ben, because they spin around and take off running.

"Let's get out of here." Ben starts us down the bridge's incline. "I doubt those two have friends, but if I'm wrong and they reappear with backup, I don't want you here."

Our parting kiss at the Rover is long, but not long enough. It takes everything in my power to break from his embrace. I sigh afterward—feeling weighed down by our impending separation. "I'll see you before first block tomorrow," Ben says, sensing the reason for my sigh. "But then, Coach and I are leaving for Tech before lunch block."

"Okay." I don't tell him I'll do whatever I can to be early enough to see him.

IX

Eagle Courtship

Friday, October 16th

MY ONLY CHANCE to see Ben is outside Adler's class before first block. I rush to get ready, skipping breakfast. But fate plays with my head again—Nicky and Leanne are ten minutes late. I try to hide my frustration, but Leanne picks up on it. "It's my fault we're late—I couldn't find my homework. Turns out my mother threw it out."

"Don't worry about it," I say, but all the time I'm thinking that if I don't get to see Ben I'm going to scream. I try to make up time by driving faster—but every light at every intersection turns red right before we get there, and I'm afraid Angie will freak out if I run a red light after what happened to her.

"Verona, you want to come over to my house tomorrow—maybe paint something?" Angie flips the visor mirror open to apply lip gloss to her already shiny lips.

I really don't have an excuse not to, but my nostrils flare at the memory of choking on black acrylic last week. I flinch. Angie must have read my mind, because she quickly adds, "I promise not to invite Hamilton."

"Hamilton? What's that Prozac case-study got to do with anything?" Nicky asks between bites of his breakfast bar.

"Nothing," we say in unison, eyeing each other surreptitiously.

"*Women*," Nicky mutters with a loud exhale.

Despite my attempt to live up to the comparison with Danica Patrick, we're late for first block, but excused on account of Angie. As I anticipated, Ben couldn't wait for me at Mrs. Adler's door without being late for his own class. Our schedules and the layout of the school mean the only time we usually connect is in chemistry—and by then, Ben will already be on the road with his father. Which means I won't see him until Sunday or Monday. Which means I slog through the day feeling like I need to borrow some of Hamilton's Prozac.

TO COMPENSATE FOR BEN'S empty seat next to mine in chemistry, I look out at the charcoal clouds and daydream of last night's rendezvous in the rain. While we are locked in that amazing kiss, the top of the umbrella Ben is holding spins like a helicopter rotor—slowly at first, then increasing in speed to the point that we're rising up off the bridge and into the night sky.

Above the misty treetops, the rain stops. Ben and the umbrella, looking like a particularly warped version of Mary Poppins, swirl off in one direction and disappear into the night.

I sprout feathers and wings. I'm an eagle, again. With wings outstretched, I scale the air currents, ascending higher and higher in an ever-widening arc.

I scan the darkening sky for the Angie, my angel compatriot. And yet, I feel an interior tug to fly to our high school. When Angie doesn't show up, I decide to just fly to the school myself. Maybe she'll meet me there.

On the two-mile ride, I marvel at the intensity of all I see: I can read even the small letters of the help wanted sign on the Exxon Station, the colors so bright you'd think they were neon. I can spy a portly man tugged along by his adorable Yorkshire terrier, and somehow know that they are best friends. I can spot a tan Nissan Acura come within inches of slamming into the back of a gray pickup, and feel the relief of the texting driver.

I glide over Colonial's student parking lot, then circle past the oak with the mannequin and the sign welcoming Angie. Then over the roof of the school, the yellower-than-yellow chrysanthemum petals floating in a large puddle on the rain-soaked tennis courts.

I land on my two human legs in the center of the football field—right on top of the painted Colonial Cougar head. My wings fold up and back into my body.

Four candles burn around the edge of the cougar's head. Ben saunters from the shadows of the end zone toward me—a smile on his face, and two crimson roses in his hand. I step forward to meet him, embarrassed. Embarrassed that he's seen my eagle body.

His eyes don't look the same. They look empty, far away. If I didn't know better, if I didn't trust him not to hurt me, I'd say that Ben looks like a zombie.

I freeze in my spot. I want to run, but my legs won't listen. I want to fly, but my wings are gone, and even my arms hang loosely at my sides.

Ben gestures like he's handing me the roses, but his expression changes. His jaw clenches. His eyes, instead of the empty zombie-black, flash hatred, red and raw. At the same time, the roses glint orange from the light of a candle. Along with Ben's eyes, the roses have morphed - into a long, jagged knife that he plunges upward, straight through my heart.

He pulls the knife out and holds it up between us. He seems fixated with its dripping blood. My chest aches where he has pierced me—a hollow feeling—like all my emotions have been killed. It's not the intense pain I expect with such a serious wound. I clutch my chest, stare at him with one question, knowing it will be my last, as I feel the life pouring out of me. *Why?*

Ben grins and the dimple melts off his face. Then his whole face melts and molds itself into the oozing green mask.

I scream loud and long. My eyes clamp shut. But with my eyes closed, I see the stands are filled with people screaming, cheering.

My eyes flash open.

The entire chemistry class stares at me. Nicky and Caitlin and several others are standing up.

Caitlin shouts, "Verona! *Omigod!*"

"You okay? What was that all about?" Nicky pulls back, but a grin is forming on his face.

Ms. Kartal bellows. "In the hall, Lamberti. Now!" The whole class snickers, then breaks into laugher that sends shivers up my back.

Looking around, dazed and confused, I wonder if this world is the real one. Some girls in the front row stop giggling when Ms. Kartal glares at them. I head to the door, leaving my books.

"Bring your books." Ms. Kartal holds the door open. "The rest of you, look over your notes." I don't take time to stuff my chemistry book and notebook into my bag, all the while desperate to control the quiver in my lower lip. Papers fall out of my notebook at the door. I endure more laughter and ridicule when I bend down to retrieve them. My eyes swell with tears that I can't, *I won't*, let fall.

Mrs. Kartal presses her arm on the closed door. "Do you have an explanation for screaming like a banshee in my class?" The hiss of whispers slide under the door. She rolls her eyes at them.

"I don't know what happened. I wasn't sleeping, *really*," I emphasize this because I don't want her to think I find her class too easy or too boring, "but it was like a bad dream. I'm sorry."

"Do I look like some kind of counselor? Go explain it to the nurse." And then, as I step away from her, I hear her mumble something that sounds remarkably like, "Hell, do I look like a flipping chemistry teacher?" I turn back, not knowing what to say. She waves the back of her hand at me. "Go on."

I consider going to the nurse. I really do. But then I play over in my head what I'll tell someone I've never even met before about my reason for being there. I come up with nada. Nothing.

So instead, I head toward the front door. Escape sounds like the best idea. Sneaking past Mr. Sams' office, I risk a glance in the window. He's in a meeting with Mrs. Hale and the ubiquitous security man in black in the outer office. I breeze by, hoping not to be noticed.

Before I make it to the end of the hall and the safety of the front door, I hear Mr. Sams' voice. "Verona. I'd like to talk to you. Are you on your way out for an appointment or something urgent?" His tie lurches to the side and his hair is all mussed up like he's been meeting in a wind tunnel. Perhaps Mrs. Hale really does have that effect on people. He beckons me into an empty classroom.

"Uh, no." I struggle to think up an excuse that won't make me sound idiotic.

"Good. How've you been holding up?" A simple question that requires a simple half-truth to fit in the expected sound-bite answer.

"I've been okay." *Except for screaming in class because my boyfriend stabbed me.*

"Any more visions?" *Does he know?* Did Ms. Kartal call him? But this last one isn't the same as the visions. At least that's what I try to convince myself. "You know—where you're an eagle?" I feel like I'll lose my lunch right on the hallway floor.

"Not since Mr. Zeke." My eyes go to the floor. I rub the tip of my boot, think of a way to turn the subject, and think of one. "How's Mrs. Sams?"

"It's one day at a time. Today's a good one."

I nod.

He wipes his mouth like he might say more, but instead mumbles, "Take care."

I nod again, and we both turn our separate ways.

Instead of heading straight for the Rover, I cross the faculty parking lot to the stadium, allowing myself just a quick glance at the yellow buds littering the tennis court and the empty space where Mr. Zeke's Esther should be parked right now, but isn't. I think, maybe if I go to the scene, I'll find a clue—something to alert me to the truth behind all the killings. And now this latest vision. Scratch that. *Daydream.*

At the front of the stadium, I try opening the gate. Locked. I continue walking around the side toward the auto shop, juggling my books from arm to arm. I almost bump into two boys running back to school, and drop my pen.

"Sorry," we all mutter under our breaths. I reach down to pick it up, but my notebook slides out of my other hand and opens to the table I made in the hospital—the one listing all the visions. The boys are long gone so I take a moment, crouching to the ground to examine the previous visions. *Was this latest one for real?*

"Let me help you with that." I freeze for a second, flipping the notebook closed.

"I'm good." After gathering my things, I stand up abruptly—face to face with the man in black. Not the black hoodie—the black trench coat. The man who was, just a moment ago, meeting with Mr. Sams. And now that I have a good look at him, I see that he's also the man with the rock and roll hair from the bookstore. It's just that his hair is shorter, no longer slicked back, but spiked up in front. How long has this creeper been following me? Could he be the killer? It certainly can't be Ben.

I turn to cross Memorial to my car, but he holds my arm—not roughly, but enough to get me to stop. "Verona—isn't it?" I remember his accent—kind of like my Newma's.

"Yes." I look toward the student parking lot, feeling my heart pick up its rhythm.

"I'm Officer MacLeod. I'm a friend of Mr. Sams." He holds his hand out for me to shake.

I shake and exhale. "I remember you from the bookstore. Your hair was longer then."

"Aye, yes. When I finished my book, I came off of sabbatical. This is my day job. Pays the bills, you know." He puts his hand in his coat pocket. "Did you ever read that book?"

"I'm almost done with it."

"Like it?"

I look into his face for the first time and see nothing scary—if anything, it's filled with concern. "Yeah. It's got a lot of good stuff in—*MacLeod*. What's your first name?"

"Kendrick." He grins.

I point to him. "So, you're the author? You wrote it?" If that's true, there's no way he's the killer. To write all that, to connect eagles with truths about life, there's no way he could be bad.

He smiles. "Right. I'll see you around." He turns, and heads back to the school.

I cross the street, cutting between the horse fence and cars, to the safety of the Rover. The whole time I feel the heaviness of eyes on my back. But when I open the door and scan the stadium to the school, Officer MacLeod, author Kendrick MacLeod, is gone.

I start the Rover and put in a Led Zeppelin CD. Their mournful, then lively, guitar riffs from "In the Evening" ease me out of my funk while I try to decipher what happened in chemistry. I open my notebook to the table and start to write this fifth vision—I'll call it the UHV vision, for either Ultimate Humiliation or Unbelievable Heartbreak—into the next space on the table.

This one was clearly different—unbelievable, really—so I stop. I rip out another sheet of paper from my notebook and rest it on my chemistry text. I list all the reasons this vision is different from the others:

No grill-licking taste.

No burn or tingles.

I was consciously daydreaming about kissing Ben on the bridge when the daydream or whatever started. All the other visions started from scratch.

Neither Angie nor Mr. Zeke made an appearance. One or the other has been in every prior vision.

Ben changes before my eyes in this one, and not into Mammon. That never happened before. The person Mammon possesses in the other visions always hid behind a masked or hooded killer.

Is this exercise helpful? Yes and no. The differences almost convince me that this one is different, but the fact that he stabbed me sends a prickly chill down my back, even though I know in my heart there is no way Ben is a murderous psychopath.

I wish once again that Mr. Zeke were still alive, teaching chemistry right now. I know I could confide in him without fearing he'd jump to conclusions about Ben. He'd know what to do—if anything—with this crazy daydream. He'd agree with me that this one isn't like the others.

AFTER UNLOADING MY FRIENDS at their respective homes, I'm grateful to return home, where Max and Khan besiege me, looking for attention in their own unique ways. Khan meows and struts by his empty food bowl. Max jumps like a pogo stick next to the hook with the leash on it.

"Calm down, you two. I'll take care of you." I pour Purina into Khan's dish, ignoring my mother's directive to limit meals to twice a day.

After attaching Max's leash to his collar, I lead him out the door for a walk. The stubborn sheepdog pulls me along our familiar route. With his leash fastened to a fence banister outside the Aquila Artist's Emporium, I replenish my black and cerulean blue paint. Mr. Stanworth beams with delight when I tell him that Angie is back in school, and we plan to paint tomorrow. Plus, she's already used the gifts he gave her for at least one painting I know of. He says he knows, she stopped in personally to thank him, and gave him a painting. He points to a glorious painting of an angel he's hung above the door to his office.

Max and I bound up the back steps around five o'clock. My mother left a message that she's going out after work; probably with *Beamerboy*. Great. I know it's wrong to think this way, but the fact that she has a date probably wouldn't bother me so much if I were still going to Michelangelo's with Ben.

I'm gulping down a glass of chocolate milk when my phone buzzes—a text message. I expect Luka, so I'm surprised to find Ben's number instead. His message reads:

Ben: Didn't have to go to Blacksburg after all. Can u meet me @the stadium @ 6:30? I have surprise 4 u.

It is hard to press the buttons for Ben's number with shaking hands. Surely, he'll be okay with meeting somewhere else if I ask him to. It's too freaky that he wants to meet me at the same place where...no, I am not going there. Back to dwelling on whatever happened in chemistry today, I mean. It wasn't like the others. It couldn't be real.

The phone rings six times before I'm dumped into Ben's voicemail. Hearing the friendly, normal—obviously not maniacal—voice on his message makes me feel foolish for my shaking hands and rapid breathing. I hang up. I send him a text urging him to call me and wait for the text back.

When he hasn't called or texted back in over five minutes, I consider my options. Standing Ben up is not one of them. I ponder the possibility of calling Angie or Leanne, but this anxiety about meeting my boyfriend—whom everyone loves—will only make them think I've lost it. Angie will laugh, crack a joke. Even Leanne will laugh. And today, I've been laughed at enough for a lifetime. Although he never said anything in the car on the way home, I'm pretty sure Nicky filled them in about my insane outburst.

So, to go, or not to go? I feel ridiculous, yet uneasy with either decision. Why does he have to say to meet at the stadium? He obviously hasn't left his phone there, since he's texting me from it. I try calling a second time, but once again, I'm dumped into voicemail.

I take a shower, hoping the warm water pelting my back will relax my shoulder muscles. It works for my shoulders, but my mind cranks out a million reasons why I shouldn't go—reminds me that the four other visions came true—some almost matching the prophetic vision exactly.

And yet, just last night, Ben promised he would never hurt me. When he said it, I knew he meant it. *So what is my problem now?* I resolve not to let a silly daydream come between us. Plus, I am curious to find out what the big surprise is. Maybe he got news of a scholarship.

Pushing my discomfort down, I text him I'll be there.

Dressing for the date that I thought we weren't having, I settle on jeans, a soft purple sweater, and my new black boots. I hope we're just meeting by the stadium for some reason, and that Ben has planned to go out somewhere else—like Michelangelo's.

PARKED IN ITS USUAL SPOT, Ben's practical, sturdy pickup reminds me that he is trustworthy and normal—not a psychopathic killer. I pull into a space in the student lot behind the trees lining Memorial, closest to the stadium. Flipping down the visor mirror, I apply lip gloss with trembling hands.

The clock on the dashboard reads 6:25, so I still have five minutes. I try to relax by turning on my favorite classic rock station and meditating on what I know about Ben. Elvis' "Fools Rush In" is playing, and I consider throwing the SUV into reverse and high-tailing it home. But my rational mind wins out, saying something like, *You seriously think, Verona Louise, that some higher power is using words from an old Elvis song to warn you? Get over yourself.* My rational mind always sounds like Dr. Newman talking.

The sun slinks below the treetops and night creeps up from the low places in the bushes. A black turkey vulture stares at me from the top rail of the horse fence, like it's daring me to go in. I want to throw something at it. Instead, I slam the Rover's door, hoping the sound will send the vulture flying. The vulture looks away.

I will soon be with Ben. That's all I need to know. I wish he wanted to meet me out here in the lot. If I only had time to tell him about the dream, he would've understood why meeting at the stadium is not a good idea. But he would have no way of knowing why I'm so squeamish. In fact, he has no way of knowing that I *am* squeamish. Squeamish is not something I want to be. I want to be strong and decisive.

Squeamish-me considers calling Leanne again, but still can't think of what to say that won't sound idiotically paranoid. Strong-me drops my phone in my jeans pocket and crosses the street at an angle toward the stadium.

Halfway across Memorial, my cell phone buzzes. *Be Ben! Be Ben!* I think.

No such luck. It's a text from an unknown number:

Unknown texter: Verona, I'm coming home. Wait for me, Ben

I rack my brain to place the number, but I'm pretty sure I've never received a call from this number before.

Ben's truck is parked right in front of me in the auto shop parking lot. He's got to be here. Maybe his cell died earlier so he called from a payphone on his way back, but the call came through late. This is the only explanation that makes sense.

The stadium door bangs against the brick holding it open. A scrolled note sticks out of the fencing. It looks to be on the same stationery Ben used to invite me to Michelangelo's. I unfurl the parchment.

Follow the rose petals. I'm waiting.

My eyes fall to the ground. Sure enough, there is a trail of crimson petals leading from the gate into the stadium. Blood-red against the charcoal gray cement. *Note to self: Tell Ben ASAP that red roses are now my least favorite flower.*

I look back at the Rover, remembering the warning note with the withered rose petals on the windshield, probably still hidden under the seat. The note at the hospital. Yeah. I should leave.

I look up and down the street. Memorial is empty in both directions. The stadium door grates against the brick like chalk on a blackboard. I wish Officer Morris would drive by. Of course, what will I say to him if he does? I glance back to the horse fence. The vulture has flown away.

Verona Louise, you're afraid of your own boyfriend? The words shake me.

Ben is warm and safe and everything good in my life. I'm being a coward. I take a deep breath, open the gate just wide enough to squeeze through, and then leave it there—slightly ajar.

I follow the petal path through the entrance and down the tunnel that runs under the bleachers. First thing I notice coming out of the dark tunnel—the sky. A few early stars twinkle in the midnight-blue expanse above the shadowed bleachers, but a thick wall of clouds is moving from the west at the far end of the field, their edges picking up a pink-orange glow from the candles glimmering behind Ben's silhouette. I gulp. He stands waiting for me, his head tilted slightly to one side, like he's wondering what's taking me so long. I look back, consider running back to the Rover, back to…and then, what? Have him break up with me because I'm scared of him?

I can barely make out his face in the flickering candlelight, but I can tell by the grin that it's all him. I force myself to proceed slowly and with each step, I mumble my new mantra: *The vision wasn't real. The vision wasn't real.* The candles mark four corners of a huge quilt that's spread behind him, covering the cougar painted over the fifty-yard line. In the faded light, I can clearly see he isn't holding either roses or a knife—neither the large serrated one, nor the small carving knife he likes to twirl when he's nervous.

Okay. Four candles—but no knife. As an added benefit, I don't have the embarrassment of switching from eagle to human to contend with. This is definitely different. *The vision wasn't real.* Strong-but-squeamish me is almost to him.

He doesn't say anything, just backs and folds his body down on the blanket, which makes me uncomfortable. Ben always speaks first. Plus, he's the one who invited me here.

"I thought you'd be at Virginia Tech by now." I stop at the edge of the quilt, unsure of what he expects me to do, wishing we would go to Michelangelo's or San Fernando's or the Aetos Diner or Quiznos, or anywhere else, really…

"The Tech recruiter I was supposed to meet cancelled. We were almost there." A basket lays on the ground behind him.

"What's all this?" I wave at the blanket and basket.

"I thought you might like another picnic. I forgot how crowded Michelangelo's gets on Fridays. You don't like crowds, right? This will be more…romantic." He rakes his fingers through his hair like he's the nervous one. And how many times has he been to Michelangelo's on a Friday?

I feel a little prickle on the back of my arms. *It would be more romantic if you kissed me instead of just sitting there.* I look down at his feet.

"I see you're wearing your black boots."

He looks down, grimacing. "I wanted to look good for you." Then he pats the blanket next to him, motioning for me to sit. Why doesn't he stand up to greet me? What's the big surprise? Is he going to break up? Is that what the vision was telling me? If he broke up with me now, after I'd been so vulnerable with him last night, it will certainly feel like he stabbed me through the heart.

"You hungry?" he asks, as I sit down next to him.

"A little." I don't want to disappoint him with the truth about my churning stomach. He passes me a chicken sandwich and a Diet Coke. I open the soda and take a sip.

I peer around the stadium for the first time. The bleachers are all in shadow. A breeze plays on the candle flames, making shadows dance around us. In the middle of the dark stadium, it's like we're under a dim spotlight.

"It looks weird in the dark," I say, after swallowing more soda. The cloud wall eclipses the stars in a straight line, like we're inside a large coffin that's slowly being covered. My hands start sweating.

In my peripheral vision, I notice Ben attacking his sandwich like he hasn't eaten all day. "I'll bet it's fun to play football under the lights." I work to make conversation with the quiet boy next to me. His silence is making me nervous. Like he decided to break up with me, but now that I'm here, he doesn't know how. But then, why would he go to all this trouble—rose petals, sandwiches...

"Yeah, it's a rush all right—most of us prefer the night games." Ben devours his sandwich in a few bites, then scowls at my untouched meal. I sip my soda and work to calm my heart.

"I thought you said you were hungry." He reclines next to me, a nervous smile flitters across his face, and props his head on his elbow.

"I guess I'm not as hungry as I thought." I roll down on my side to join him. He runs his hand down my hair and continues right down my side, but something doesn't feel right. There is no spark when he touches me.

"Come here, babe. Give me a kiss."

I shrink back. Ben has never called me anything but Verona.

He laughs. "You're a shy one." Then he pounces on me like Khan going after one of his toys. The kiss tastes of onion and mouthwash, and the sweet-smelling cologne makes me sneeze all over his face and all over me.

He grimaces as he pulls back just enough to wipe his face on a napkin. But he doesn't let go of me.

I wipe my nose on my sleeve, then squeeze my hands between us and push to get him off of me with all of my strength.

He keeps me pinned with his legs, but leans up a bit, sticking up the palms of his hands. "What's the matter?"

"Alex," I say, between gritted teeth. "How *could* you?"

He shakes his head. "No, it's me....Ben." He reaches for me. I can't see an earring in this light or even a hole, but he could have easily taken it out. It's too dark to know for sure.

"Save it." With a strong thrust, I wriggle out from under him, standing up quickly and steadying myself. I intend to leave the field, head held high, with as much dignity as I can muster. And as I'm turning, he yanks on my wrist, pulling me back down into his arms with such force I think my shoulder might dislocate.

"What if I *was* Alex? That would be cool, wouldn't it?" He rolls over, taking me with him, so his bulk is on top, pinning my hands to the ground. "Ben and I are pretty much the same. Same DNA. Plus, we share everything. I'm sure he told you about Amber?" His eyes twinkle.

I struggle to breathe under the force of him. His onion breath covers my mouth. I twist, trying to break free. He holds my hands and I feel trapped, déjà vu of middle school. Not thinking, I force my knee up hard. And, as it did with banana-breath Tony Rubowski, my knee hits its mark.

Alex groans and slides off me, hands between his legs.

This time I don't hesitate—dignity is way overrated—I scramble to my feet and bolt for the exit as fast as my boots will take me.

Each step convinces me more. It's Alex. It's definitely Alex. Alex is the hooded killer the demon used to kill Ross and Mr. Zeke and Ty Blanchard. It has to be Alex.

He wrote the warning notes, called me that night when I was in New York. The night after Amber and her friends made fun of me in the locker room. She must have told him. Maybe they're in on it together. Yes. Amber and Alex plotted to kill Ross Georgeson and Ty Blanchard and Mr. Zeke and tampered with Angie's brakes, trying to kill her, too. Others must have suspected him for Mr. Sams to question him about the brakes. *Shoot! Why does it have to be Alex?* It will absolutely kill Ben to know what his brother is capable of.

The candlelight fades to a blur of muddy shadows as I run in the general direction of the tunnel. Almost past the end zone, I crash into a wall or something, probably one of those big punching-bag-thingies football players push around to practice blocking. Stumbling back onto the turf, I jam my wrist in an awkward position under me. Rubbing it quickly, I wonder if it's broken.

Then I glance back to Alex, but he's on his hands and knees, barfing up the sandwich he'd just downed. Doubtful he'll be pursuing me any time soon, but I should get out of here anyway, just in case.

I turn toward the exit and go to get up, but notice the wall, or punching bag, or whatever I ran into, is alive, like a giant black ghost moving toward me. I get the distinctly eerie feeling the shadow is after me. It wants me. I spring to my feet, but the shadow kicks my legs out from under me.

"Ow! Hey!" I say, as I break my fall with that same wrist, which goes numb and tingly and then shoots sparks down to my fingertips. I cradle my hand against my stomach and peer up at the source of the kick. My breathing accelerates.

Closer to the candlelight, I'm able to make out that it is definitely *not* a wall or a punching-bag-thingie. As I scoot back and it comes forward, closer, I know what it is.

I swallow. And I know it wants me. Dead. I'm staring up at Mammon, the demon of my eagle visions, and his minion human murderer, dressed in black from the hooded sweatshirt to the sneakers on its feet. I can't peel my eyes from its face. I want to. Although obscured somewhat by the hood, the face is hideous, oozing pustules and scars exactly like in my visions. I crouch lower to the ground.

Angie's voice pops into my head, urging me to get away—fast. I inch on my side with my one good wrist like a caterpillar toward the center of the field, to where, by the sound of it anyway, Alex has stopped puking.

Mammon says something loud enough for Alex to hear. In my visions I never understand what was being said because it was all garbled. This time it's different, like a foreign language, but not French or Spanish or Italian; I think I would've recognized those. I'd even recognize the Irish my Newma sometimes speaks with her friends. This one I don't know, and yet it's vaguely familiar, like I've heard the cadence and accent before—but not that fierce tone.

Mammon's next sentence is clearly understandable. English. "Never send boy to do man's job."

Alex jumps to his feet and faces us, wiping his hands on his jeans. "Coach? What are you doing here? What's that you've got on your face?" Alex's brow wrinkles.

With a dramatic bow, Coach Chortov yanks off the mask to reveal lethal, stormy bloodshot eyes, eyes that pierce into me before moving up to take a stab at Alex. "You are no good son. You can't even scare a little girl."

"You were *supposed* to scare me?" I turn toward Alex.

Alex looks at the ground and clenches and unclenches his fists. "Coach thought if I fooled you into thinking I was Ben, but got real aggressive, you'd break up with him." Alex shrugs as he walks toward us. "I tried. Obviously, you didn't fall for it."

"You are in our way—mistake. Ben can't see this now, but when he's big star, he will understand. Be happy for it." Coach Chortov kicks me in the thigh—hard enough to keep me moving along the ground. "Mistakes can be fixed."

He reaches behind his back, and already I know how he plans to fix this latest mistake—meaning me. Sure enough, he's holding the gun. Alex shakes his head, like he thinks he might be dreaming.

I know it's real. I've see this gun, first pointing at Ross, then firing at Ty Blanchard, and two weeks ago, killing Mr. Zeke.

If I am to become his next victim, then my latest vision had the murderer and the murder weapon all wrong—only the location was right. It's not Ben with a knife in the stadium. It's Coach Chortov with a gun in the stadium. My wrist is threatening to give out as I creep faster on my hands and rump toward Alex—hoping for any distraction that will give me time to run to where I won't be such an easy target.

While I'm creeping away, I watch his eyes so I can quickly roll away if he starts shooting. For some reason, right now he's content just kicking me toward the fifty yard line. Through his eyes, I witness events from his past, simultaneous and layered, like time doesn't have to be chronological, but is, in fact, multi-faceted.

I see Coach Chortov as an eight-year-old boy running soccer drills in the rain, his father shouting from under an umbrella. I might not understand the directives, but I can tell they're punctuated with insults and curses… At the same time I see Coach Chortov as a teenager, creeping into a rustic kitchen followed by a very pregnant girl with high cheekbones and blue-black hair. His father—Ben's grandfather—rises from the table, drops an almost-empty bottle of vodka, and slams the young Coach Chortov in the head with his bare fists, knocking him to the floor… I see Coach in a different room, sprawled on a tattered couch, yelling at the same raven-haired girl—the twins' mother. She's trying to soothe two crying babies at the same time. Exhausted, she holds a baby against her chest and yells something back. He slips off the couch and grapples to remove the infant from her arms. The mother tilts her head, confused. She claws at him as he wraps the fingers of both hands around her neck and holds tight, shaking her head until her limbs hang loose at her side. When he lets go, her body slides to the crimson carpet, a carpet of withered rose petals.

I turn away. I don't want to see this. Ben was just a baby! *These are his parents!*

Coach Chortov slams his foot down on my chest, knocking me to the ground with such force that I bang my head on the turf and gasp for air. Amazingly, I don't pass out. Through tearing eyes, I see he's gotten bigger; the black hood's been replaced by a gold crown with the familiar horns, the gold bishop costume. The smell of sulfur and rot makes me gag. I feel so small and weak. *Oh God, if you're real, please help me! I can't do this without you.*

The demon toggles back into Coach Chortov, who waves the gun at his son. "For once, do something right. Get blanket. We won't stain my field with girl's blood." Then he points it at me. "Hold still!"

Now I see him in a black skullcap, examining a ruby-red jewel the size of a small plum in the moonlight. Desire for the money, desire for the status the money will bring, grows within him like bacteria, infecting every cell with greedy obsession. He covets accolades for his superior coaching abilities, the interviews, the headlines, the plum-red sports car—plum-red, in memory of the jewel, and voluptuous women dressed in rose-red, lapping at his heels. He can hear the applause of crowds. His tongue feasts on caviar and is tickled by the finest champagne.

Holding the jewel tenderly between forefinger and thumb, his skin holograms from shades of peach to greenish-gray, then dries and withers like an autumn leaf. In order to reach his dreams, he has allowed himself to become infested with Mammon. Of his own free will, he invited the demon in, and now the demon has taken over. Mammon has rotted Coach Chortov's heart until it is as cold as the plum-red stone and all the wealth he covets. And now, the image before me toggles back and forth so fast it blurs into one being. Black and gold, evil to the core.

My jaw drops. "The notes with the rose petals? The phone call? That was you?" I shake my head, wondering why I persist in asking rhetorical questions. *God, help me!* I don't want to die.

He snickers. "Roses are red, violets are blue, you see too much, little girl, now I *kill* you."

I cover my nose and mouth in an attempt to mask the horrible smell, twisting my head toward Alex. Alex, who only moments ago I was convinced was the killer, has now become my only hope.

He stands rooted in the spot just a few yards from us. He wipes his eyes, and then stares at Coach Chortov, and by the look of horror on his face, I think he might be able to *see,* or understand in some way, what's become of his father.

"You can't kill her, Coach," he stutters, putting both hands on his head and swiveling around, as if massaging his brain will help him process the fact that his father is a demon-infested killer.

Alex drops his hands. "Ben loves her. He was right; she's not like the other girls."

"Girl is dangerous. She *sees* things. I know. I see things, too. Be good son. Get the blanket. Now!" He shakes the gun toward his son to hurry him.

Alex's mouth closes tightly and his brow tightens at this request. For a moment he looks broken, like he can't decide what to do. But the very next moment, he swallows, and his face relaxes. All signs of tension disappear. Except for his eyes. His eyes dart around the field.

He nods back toward the blanket and smiles at me. He says casually, like he's sorry for a rude comment, as opposed to being an accomplice to my murder, "Sorry, Verona, but he *is* my father and my coach. I've got to obey him."

Coach Chortov lowers the pistol and waits for his son to follow orders. The pressure on my stomach is lightened a bit as the demon is once again hidden inside the man.

I feel a rush of adrenaline fill me with fury. I scoot to the right, waiting for the inevitable kick to follow. Then I latch onto his leg and bite it as hard as I can through the black running pants.

At the same time, in my peripheral vision—something I never had with glasses—I see Alex angle back, like he's going to retrieve the blanket, but before he steps in that direction, he turns. He sprints toward his father. A typical quarterback fake, and it works.

Alex looks fierce and big, with beady eyes bearing down on his father. He's the bull. In fact, he almost looks like the charging bull down by Wall Street. Except he's not a bronze statue, and he's really charging.

Caught off guard by the ferocity of his son's attack and the distraction of trying to shake me off his leg, Coach Chortov steps back, raises his arm, and fires the gun.

The bull is almost on top of us, so I let go and roll over. But the impact of the bullet stops Alex, actually pushing him back a bit. With dark-brown eyes wide open, Alex crashes into his father.

The Coach steps back to gain his balance and pushes his son off his chest.

Alex's face is one big question mark. He mouths, "You...shot...?" He coughs, looks down. Clutching his chest, he turns to me, and chokes out, "Tell Ben...love him...Forgive me..." He's coughing and sputtering so much I can't tell if he means for me to forgive him, or for me to tell Ben to forgive him, but it's clear that he's not talking to his father. He collapses on the spot, red liquid oozing through the fingers pressed to his heart. His right leg twitches.

The Coach lowers the gun. Taking a step closer, he stares down at Alex who, hand still pressed over heart, stops moving.

It's horrific, but it's the break I've been waiting for. I stand up, trying to back away. But as much as I want—*need*—to run, my feet won't respond. My traitorous legs stay rooted in the turf. Instead of making a break for it, I stare at the face of the man who shot his son, and force myself to breathe. I take in big gulps of air, and the adrenaline I felt surging through my body a minute ago drains away, leaving me feeling nothing, numb.

Coach Chortov blinks hard, a hard face-wrinkling blink. Like being roused from sleep, his entire body quivers. Finally his eyes stay closed and he turns away, rubbing the back of his head with the hand holding the pistol.

"You shot him." It comes out as a whisper. Catching my breath, I find the words and speak louder. "You shot your own son." I don't know why I should find this hard to believe. I now know he strangled his wife. "You killed your childrens' mother."

Coach Chortov turns to me, head tilted, like he's wondering where I came from. If I had to guess, I'd say Mammon has fled the scene.

I drop to Alex's lifeless body. "Is he dead? Did you kill him? Like you killed Ross Georgeson and Mr. Zeke? And Ty Blanchard? Like you tried to kill Angie?" I feel Alex's wrist for a pulse. I was never good at finding my own pulse, and I can't feel his now. I mumble to myself, "We need to call an ambulance." I open my cellphone and press 911.

Coach Chortov convulses again. It looks like he may pass out, and I hope he doesn't fall on Alex or me, but he takes a big step back to steady himself. "No. It is you what killed him." Then he calls out in exasperation, "All I want is best thing for him! Ben and Alex big football stars. Make lots of money. Why you people always get in my way?"

"Like Alex and Ben got in the way of your soccer career?" My feelings have returned, and I'm surprised to find I'm not afraid of him—the Coach or Mammon—any longer. I'm angry. Angry at the killer coach and angry at the demon. Angry at myself because I can't find Alex's pulse.

What is taking the operators so long? I stand up, turn around, and look at my phone. The easiest number in the world, and I misdialed. I punched in the numbers again. *Answer already.* The number's ringing once, twice…

I turn, getting ready to talk into the phone. But the long hollow barrel is pointed at the side of my face. I feel the cold edge on my cheek. We are so close there is no point in running. My only hope is to knock the gun away. I swing the arm with the phone toward the gun. I feel the hollow metal on the edge of my hand, the vibration when he pulls the trigger.

The phone flies from my hand. This time I may die. I'm too close for him to miss. Funny. I don't care about dying as much as I did before.

I feel a sharp pinch in my arm, under the same shoulder Alex almost dislocated earlier. It hurts so much I start to care again.

I grab my shoulder and start to collapse forward. Another bull-like man is running toward us from the shadows. Then a flash of white light blinds me. It must be another bullet. Maybe it hit me between my eyes and knocked out my vision.

But I'm wrong. A break-the-sound-barrier-loud clap of thunder tells me it's lightening. Meanwhile, a blanket of warm air catches me before I land on the turf. The swell of air lifts me into the night sky. The thunder fades into a loud crackling sound. I know it can't be real, since I'm on a football field, but it feels like

I've been swept up in a forest fire, the familiar charcoal burning taste filling my mouth and my nostrils. But this time it's warm and crackling and comforting, not hot at all. I close my eyes, relieved not to be burned alive.

"You are witch!" I hear the accent, faint through the rushing, crackling air. "I will *keel* you!" And then I hear a blood-curdling scream.

I am carried straight up at first, then backwards. My body is spun around, twirling through a stormy vortex. Then the crackling stops. I'm no longer spinning. I open my eyes to find I have leveled out horizontally over the field, face down, with white yard-line stripes moving underneath me.

I'm flying. *Really flying!*

Air *whooshes* past my ears. It's exactly like in my visions, but this is for real.

Either that or I'm dead and don't realize it yet. No, wait—I can't be dead. If I were dead, I wouldn't feel the burn pulsing from my shoulder to my elbow.

I force my eyes to stay open. They water from the rush of oncoming air. Hand grasping my wounded arm, I glance behind to see if I have grown actual eagle wings. Nope, nothing sprouts from my purple sweater. Landing on trembling legs, I tumble down onto the turf, rolling onto my left side in an effort to shield the wounded arm.

I look back just in time to see the second bull leap toward the coach. It looks like Alex has recovered somehow and is rushing at his father all over again. But a quick glance to the mound to their left tells me that Alex is still on the ground.

"You want to kill someone, old man? Kill me!" It's Ben. Ben's the bull, but now he's back in his own body. He jumps, knocking Coach Chortov to the ground. In the melee, a candle falls over. Flames erupt, spiraling up into the night sky, filling the stadium with an eerie red-orange glow. It looks like the two men, father and son, are wrestling in a ring of fire.

I hear a bullet hit the metal bleachers behind my head and my heart stops. Oh, no! Could Coach have shot Ben? He shot his other son…

Then I see something I will never forget for as long as I live.

Leanne bounds out of the tunnel at a pace that looks unnaturally fast for her short legs. She hurls herself high in the air and, in that moment, she is transformed into a lion, jumping into the flames. The momentum of her impact causes a mess of black and red and blue to roll away from the fire.

"Ow! Leanne! That hurt!" Ben's voice rises from somewhere under her. He wiggles out, like he's disentangling from a tackle, jumps up, and peels off his smoldering shirt. He stomps on it until it stops smoking.

Leanne sits on a mound that can only be Coach Chortov.

"Ben?" I stand on wobbly knees.

"Verona!" He runs toward me at full speed, bare-chested and shiny.

I rush to meet him, forgetting about the pain.

For a moment, it looks like the whole stadium is on fire, and I'm afraid we're all going to die.

But my eyes clear, and I see that someone has turned on the big overhead lights. In the lights, I see Ben almost to me, his hand gripping a bloody knife. I stop dead.

The knife doesn't look like the one in my vision—it's shorter, and not at all serrated. But right now, after all that's happened, it doesn't matter what the knife looks like. It could be a butter knife and I'd freak.

I back up, feeling a cold sliver of fear pass through my chest. I turn and run for the end of the field, holding my right arm to my chest above the elbow. Each footfall shoots a fiery streak of pain from the wound in my arm.

At the five-yard line, Ben overtakes me and tackles me to the ground, spinning his body under us to break my fall. I'm on top of him. He bundles me into his arms, holding on tight like I'm a football. I try to push off him, but I can't stop shaking, and he's too strong for me. And then I notice there is no knife in his hand. The only thing Ben's holding is *me*.

"Shh! Don't worry, it's going to be alright." Ben looks genuinely confused. "It's over. I don't know what happened. Coach must have lost his mind. I knew he was wound too tight, and it seemed to get worse every day. I guess he snapped." Ben keeps running his fingers around the edges of my face, saying, *Shh, it's all right*, and I think, *No, it's not going to be all right.*

I smell something metallic and raw over the cinnamon-musk.

I pull back to look at Ben. Blood trickles from a wound on his forehead down the side of his face in little rivulets. "You're hurt!"

"Bullet must've skimmed my hairline." He holds his hand over it. "It stings a little, bleeds a lot. Something to tell my grandchildren someday."

I lift his hand. A penny-sized spot of hair and skin are missing. The bullet must have nicked him and kept going. His hair, mixed with the blood, looks dark-purple. I nod toward my arm and lift my hand.

"I guess we both need to go to the emergency room." I show him the hole in the sleeve of my favorite purple sweater, the blood that's already drying on the edges, my swelling wrist. Then I figure I can't wait any longer. "Your brother saved me."

"No, Verona. See, you're confused. Probably the concussion hasn't completely healed. That was me. I distracted Coach with my carving knife, but then, Leanne—wow—did you see Leanne? I'll bet Coach's going to be hurting tomorrow. What's made him flip? Do you have any idea why was he shooting at you?"

"No. No. No." I shake my head back and forth. "Alex tried to save me and your fa—the Coach—shot him. Alex… Oh Ben. Alex has been shot." In all the commotion, Ben never noticed his brother lying parallel to the thirty-five yard line.

We turn back to see Nicky carrying Angie toward Alex's body, behind where Leanne kneels with Coach Chortov motionless beneath her hands.

Overtaking Nicky and Angie, three men, with guns drawn and raised, rush from the tunnel over to where Leanne has pinned Coach Chortov to the ground. One is clearly Officer Morris, who shouts at Leanne to move away from the body. He motions for her to move toward him.

Leanne scoots back, saying something to Officer Morris. He's got his pistol in both hands, aimed at the Coach. One of the men, with his back to me, picks up the gun with a piece of fabric or something and deposits it into a big baggie.

While Ben half-carries me over to Alex, I hear Officer MacLeod. His lilting Scottish burr orders Coach Chortov to get up slowly and put his hands on his head. Still, Coach Chortov doesn't move.

By the time we get to Alex's side, Nicky has already eased Angie down next to the lifeless body. She caresses Alex's face, and then feels his neck for a pulse. "Alex! Do you hear me? Don't die! You can't die!" She knocks Alex's big hand from the chest wound to his side. We hear a weird snoring noise, like something's clogging a sink drain.

Angie drops her ear to his chest, her cheek pressed against the bloody wound. Tears stream down her cherubic face. "I love you, Alex. God help me, I always did. Please don't die."

"Is he breathing?" Ben asks.

"I don't know." Angie keeps her cheek on Alex's chest. "That weird noise is coming from his chest. But with my cheek here, it's stopped."

"Is there a pulse?" Ben picks up his brother's wrist and tightens his hand around it. "I think I feel something, but it's faint." Ben's eyes move from Alex to me to Nicky, his brow knotted.

"We called 911," Nicky says. "We should wait for the paramedics." Nicky grimaces at the sight of Angie's cheek plastered against the bloodied chest of her ex-boyfriend, and grabs her shoulder in an attempt to pull her away.

"No!" Angie shakes Nicky's hand off her shoulder. "This feels like the right thing to do."

Feeling helpless, I turn to look at what's happening around Coach Chortov. Officer MacLeod holds his gun directly over the Coach's head, pointing down. Officer Morris, gun pointing at the Coach's heart, leans over, looking for signs of life. Off to the side, the third black trench coat-wearing man has his arms around Leanne, who appears to be sobbing into him.

I wipe my eyes and blink fast, thinking I must have lost a contact. Or maybe Ben is right about my concussion.

But no. My contacts are still in place. And the vision isn't changing. How can it be? The third man, looks exactly like.... Mr. Zeke?

Blackness closes in from the perimeters of my vision. Nicky—always the coordinated one—catches me mid-fall. He holds me there for a moment until my vision comes back. At least I don't completely black out this time. "Mr. Zeke?" My muzzy mind registers a hundred questions. But...I *saw* him get shot...I *saw* the blood. I *saw* his body.

"I see him too, Verona. Like he rose from the dead. That man's got some 'splaining to do."

Friday, October 23rd

COACH THEODOR ALEXANDROVICH CHORTOV'S BURIAL takes place on a breezy overcast morning. Only close friends and families are invited; the football team and Coach Grimes are notably absent, but that doesn't deter the media from filming the service. Competing news vans set up far enough away to not be physically intrusive, but close enough for us to feel their presence.

Looking adorable as usual, but like he'd rather be anywhere else in the world, Ben stands next to Alex. He's wearing his black cowboy boots, new-looking jeans, and a black sports jacket over a button-down shirt and tie.

Alex, recovered but still weak, leans on the back of Angie's wheelchair. For once it is easy to distinguish the brothers by the dime-sized scab that has formed on Ben's hairline. I wonder if the hair will grow back, or if a permanent scar will mar his otherwise-perfect face?

Secretly, I root for the scar; as such a prominent marker differentiating the twins could potentially save me from future embarrassment. Plus, he's perfect enough already. His large hand warms my free one. My other arm rests in a sling covering a removable cast for my sprained wrist and a big obnoxious bandage for the bullet wound in my triceps muscle.

For the benefit of Alex and Ben, Mr. Zeke and Mr. Sams characterize Coach Chortov as a rugged, independent man. Naturally, they leave out the allegations leveled against him, but regardless, those allegations frost over any kind things that are said.

When Ben discovered that his father had been charged with two counts of murder and three counts of attempted murder, he refused to attend the burial ceremony. He said he was glad the Coach died—that a massive brain hemorrhage was too good for him. He should have rotted in jail or fried in the electric chair.

Initially, Alex theorized that a slow-leaking hemorrhage had somehow changed the chemistry in the Coach's brain over the last few years. He admitted that his father had always been obsessively ambitious, but couldn't believe he'd resort to murder to eliminate competition or female distractions.

Alex's theory changed when Officer MacLeod showed the brothers Ross Georgeson's phone and a playbook, discovered under floorboards in their father's closet. Seeing detailed plans for each murder written in the same manner the Coach used to demonstrate football plays made both brothers look visibly sick.

Among other incriminating things, the playbook included a two-week calendar of Ty Blanchard's daily activities leading up to his murder, and a notation saying "potential alibis" under *tryouts in Charlottesville* and the hotel's receptionist. The brothers were forced to face the truth—their father was a cold-blooded killer, a sociopath. I will take that last vision of the Coach choking the life out of their mother to my grave. No child should have to live with that. Look what it did to Craig Hamilton.

But when Alex said that even if their father turned out to be a monster—he still was their father, and they should attend the funeral, Ben went to be there for Alex. I went to be there for Ben.

Aunt Nadia stands farther from the coffin than anyone, her body only partially under the canopy, her lips plastered together in a tight line. Kolya holds her arm and whispers translations in Russian. She looks pale, like she's afraid the man in the coffin might jump out and grab her. I know she is only there to support her nephews—there is no love between her and her deceased brother-in-law.

Following Mr. Zeke's final blessing—a blessing directed to Alex and Ben—we turn toward our cars.

Aunt Nadia gasps loudly, clutching Kolya tighter. *"Nyet!"* she bellows. The sound is unfamiliar, almost inhuman. Our gaze follows her finger, which points across the cemetery. "Nyet!" *No!* This time it is fully human and full of panic.

"*Chto*, Mama?" Kolya asks—*what?*

She blurts out a slew of Russian words, but by that time we've followed her finger. It points to a black Escalade on the other side of a news van. Leaning against the front door, Coach Chortov's doppelganger, in a black suit and wearing blue-mirrored sunglasses, inhales deeply from a cigarette he holds between his thumb and forefinger. When he realizes our attention has turned to him, he drops the cigarette, jumps into the SUV and speeds away, followed by a cloud of rust-colored dust.

"Is brother to your father, Oleg Alexandrovich," Kolya explains to Ben and Alex. "Everyone call him Chort—Russian for devil. He is much worse than your father. He killed many, many people. Hurt first." Kolya mimes like he is hammering his hand. Then he disfigures his joints like he is in pain.

When Mr. Zeke hears this, he pulls Aunt Nadia back under the canopy. He shoots questions at her via Kolya, flips on his Bluetooth, then rushes to his car.

The rest of us march to our cars in silence, conscious that every move we make is being filmed. Did they catch the Coach Chortov look-a-like? Imagine the confusion on the evening news.

"Was your father a twin, too?" I ask Ben, while he helps me fasten my seat belt. He doesn't answer as he starts the Rover. I wonder if he heard me.

Alex helps Angie into the backseat.

"I've read where multiple births are often genetic." I hope this will prompt a response from Ben. He opens his mouth to answer, but is interrupted.

"He was a lot of things, but he wasn't a twin," Alex remarks from the back. "Oleg is two years older."

"What a creeper." Angie whistles through her teeth. "And why wasn't he under the tent, if he's your uncle and all; that would've been the polite thing to do."

"Chortovs were never known for their good manners." Ben pulls away fast to escape the reporters rushing the SUV, and a bumper grazes one of their cameras.

"Didn't Kolya tell you?" Alex leans forward to touch Ben's shoulder. "Chortov isn't our real name. Coach changed it."

Ben swerved around in his seat. "What?"

Alex laughed. "Yeah, I know. He changed it when he came to America. Kolya said he was wanted for murder in Ivanivka so he created a whole new identity."

"Why didn't Kolya tell *me* that?" Ben shook his head.

"He only told me the other day when I was still in the hospital. He thought we knew already. Our real name is Zharkov."

MR. ZEKE RUSHES UP TO OUR TABLE and takes a seat just as the small party is finishing lunch at the Virginia Company Café. "Sorry, I'm late." He bites into the ham sandwich that's been waiting for him. We look at him expectantly. There is so much he hasn't explained yet, starting with the chase scene at the cemetery, and going back to his resurrection from the dead. "What? Can't a man eat his lunch?"

Mr. Sams breaks the silence. "It could be that we're all curious about why you flew out of the graveyard like a bat out of hell, and why you're sitting here with us when you're supposed to be dead."

Mr. Zeke nods—his mouth full. "Oh, that. You may be my boss, but I can't tell you. Top secret." Mr. Sams shakes his head with a smile, but Mr. Zeke continues. "I do have a question for you two." He looks at Ben and Alex. Do the words 'key tree' mean anything to you?"

Ben and Alex look at each other, then shake their heads no.

"Maybe your father had some sort of tree-shaped sculpture to hang his keys at home?" Mr. Zeke prompts. They shake their heads again. If we weren't talking about their father, the murderer, it would be funny.

Aunt Nadia whispers something to Kolya.

"In Russian, *keytree* is one word. Cunning or resourceful," Kolya explains.

Mr. Zeke's eyes widen. He looks at Kolya and asks, "What about the word *wishbone*?" Kolya looks at his mother. They both say, "No."

"Wishbone is an offense formation in football." Alex takes a swig of root beer. "It was one of the Coach's favorites. There's the usual Delaware T—or sometimes we used the I-formation. It has to do with the way we set up before a play—this would mean we were going to run the ball because the quarterback isn't as protected for a pass."

Mr. Zeke nods his understanding. Despite our best efforts to cajole more information from him, Mr. Zeke thrusts up his palm.

When Officers Morris and MacLeod show up, we know it is futile to pry down that path any further. But I see an opening. "Mr. Zeke, how did you fake your death? I know for a fact I *saw* you lying there with my own eyes. There was blood everywhere."

Mr. Zeke's eyes sparkle. "It wasn't a trick, if that's what you think. I *was* shot. Twice. Once in the chest—that's what sent me down, knocked me out—and once in the shoulder, which accounted for all the blood." He rubs his shoulder like it's still sore.

My hand heads to my wound, but it still hurts to touch.

Alex rubs his own chest. "Sucking chest wound?"

"No, ol' Shirley saved my life again. Bullet bounced off, but not before it knocked me out." Mr. Zeke pats his chest.

"Shirley?" We all ask.

"My old Kevlar vest from my last job. I call her Shirley from a favorite psalm: 'For *surely*, O Lord, you bless the righteous; you surround them with your favor as with a shield.'"

We groan.

Mr. Zeke smiles. "I put her on when I got the text from Ross Georgeson's missing phone. The text signed off, Craig Hamilton. Earlier, Craig had assured me that he didn't have Ross' phone. But now he had it, and said he was going to kill himself. Said I should meet him at the tennis courts. I smelled something rotten. Called Officer Morris." He shakes his head, then nods toward the officers and Mr. Sams. "At the hospital, we decided to use my demise to do two things: remove me from the hit list, and allow me to officially join the investigation."

"So you knew he was alive during the memorial?" Angie's eyes narrow at Mr. Sams.

"We needed him to be dead to keep him alive." Mr. Sams pats Mr. Zeke on his good shoulder. "You're not one to feel sorry for yourself, but if you ever do, come to me. I've got a great DVD showing how much you're loved at Colonial."

Mr. Zeke was alive the whole time—even when I was in the hospital crying for him. Could this be the answer to a question that's been plaguing me? "Mr. Zeke, are you the one who sent me chrysanthemums when I was in the hospital?"

"Did you like them? They're my favorite this time of year." Mr. Zeke winks at me.

Mr. Sams explains how they were able to get Aunt Nadia guardianship for the twins until they turn eighteen next February. Also, an anonymous donor paid the rent on their farmhouse for the next year and a half, until they go off to college. I chuckle at the coincidence. If I were still keeping track, I'd know exactly how many days until then, since it's the same time I expect to be back in New York.

Kolya explains that he's going to help his mother move.

339

Mr. Sams and Nicky follow him with Officer Morris and Officer MacLeod.

After they've left, Mr. Zeke tips his glass to the five of us—Alex and Angie, Ben, Leanne, and me—the Transcenders. "You kids did great... I know you've got questions. I'll do my best with what I know."

"How can there be two bulls? Is it because Alex and Ben share the same DNA?" Angie asks.

"I don't have an answer for that. All I can tell you is that the bull is the wild card—so I guess having any preconceived notions about how this is supposed to work is foolish."

"I have a question." Leanne puts her drink down. "What really happened?" When we give her a questioning look, she adds, "I mean, how did Coach Chortov really die? I don't for a minute believe it was an aneurysm. Do y'all know if I killed him?" She swallows. The look on her face makes it obvious that this question has been bothering her for a while.

"He'd been knocked down, stabbed, burned, and bitten. The autopsy was inconclusive as to the cause of death."

"Did he even *have* an aneurysm?" Angie asks.

"Yes. As I told Alex and Ben, it started as a slow bleed in the back of his head about a month ago—or that's what the pathologist thinks. He probably sustained some trauma there right around the time Ross was killed."

I think back to the vision I had in art class, when I attacked the back of the killer's hooded head with my beak when I figured out what he was doing. *Could the vision have translated into reality? Is it possible that the eagle me caused the aneurysm that killed him?*

As if he can read our minds, Mr. Zeke points to Leanne, and then turns to me. "There is no reason that any of you should feel any guilt for what happened. Coach Chortov had a choice at every juncture. He chose poorly. The fault is his." He stood up, resting his hands on the shoulders of both Alex and Ben. "Now the choice is up to you how you plan to live your lives." He squeezes their shoulders.

"Any more questions before I take off?"

"Is that it?" I ask. "Our work as Transcenders is done, right?" No more crazy visions embarrassing me in classrooms or dressing rooms or anywhere.

"I can't say for sure." Mr. Zeke winks at me. "But if something else comes up, I'm sure you guys will be able to handle it." My mouth hangs open. I was so hoping for a simple *yes*.

I look at this group: Angie whispering to Leanne. Alex and Ben elbowing each other. I have such a strong sense of belonging—belonging to this group, but even more, belonging to something bigger, more important. I close my eyes and mouth a prayer of thanks to God. After all that has happened, it would be more foolish for me *not* to believe in Him.

While I can't claim to know Him very well, I do know that this God shields and protects us. But He also gives us choices. And our choices sometimes lead to tremendous heartache.

AFTER LUNCH, BEN AND I STROLL through Jefferson Village, hand in hand, and deep in thought. I can tell by his clenched jaw that something's bothering him. I guess it would be normal for him to be upset on the day his father is buried. But as it's the first opportunity for us to be with each other since the *stadium incident*, I was hoping our time together might be more intimate, or at least, more relaxed.

Ben shakes a newspaper article out of his inside jacket pocket. "Have you seen this?"

"My mom read it to me. She was suspicious when it didn't exactly match everything I told her. But having been an editor, she knows how sometimes by the time a story gets to print, some of the details get reported wrong."

Ben snorts. "*This* wrong?" He reads the first paragraph:

An unnamed source has learned that a group of students gathered Friday evening at Colonial's football stadium to discuss a memorial for Ross Georgeson, when police officers arrived to arrest Coach Theodore Chortov for Ty Blanchard's murder. During the arrest, Coach

Chortov suffered a fatal brain hemorrhage, causing him to accidentally shoot his son, Alex Chortov, starting quarterback for the Colonial Cougars, as well as two other students. The students survived their wounds, but Coach Chortov succumbed to the aneurysm. Since then, he's been linked to the death of Ross Georgeson, as well as the attempted murder of two others.

I suspect Mr. Sams is the unnamed source. I predict that the exact verbiage will make it into the yearbook, and after we're graduated, into Colonial Cougar lore.

"An aneurysm? You heard what Mr. Zeke said—he'd been bitten, beaten, stabbed, and burned. Okay, I get why you might not want to broadcast that. But this one is too much. A group of students gathered to discuss a memorial for Ross Georgeson? The gunshots were accidental? That's not getting some details a little wrong—that's an outright lie." Ben throws the paper to the ground and runs both hands through his hair.

"The truth would have been a bit complicated."

"The truth is that Coach lured you there to kill you." He keeps looking down as he spits these words out.

I pull back and swallow. That's not exactly the truth. The truth is that Coach sent Alex there to scare me; Coach may have only stepped in to kill me when he saw it wouldn't work, when he saw I wasn't going to go away. We'll never know for sure.

But I don't know how much Alex told Ben about his part in it. Plus, Alex did apologize after he was shot protecting me for Ben. The brothers need each other now more than ever. How many other reasons can I come up with for not telling him all that happened before he came?

I decide to take the conversation down a different road. "I still don't get why the Coach killed Ross. *For what?* 'Cause he messed up a kick in a game?"

"Probably to get back at Georgeson's dad, since he wouldn't let Ross quit the team. The Coach had no love for Ross, but he hated Ross' father with a passion."

"I hadn't thought of that." And then I remember that Mammon was directing the Coach to kill. Maybe Ross' light shined too bright, and he wanted it extinguished for that reason alone. Maybe that was Mammon's goal with Ty Blanchard. I start to trip on a curb, but Ben lets go of my hand, grabs my upper arm and steadies me before I fall.

We come to the bench by the duck pond. The ducks are on the other side of the pond being fed by a group of children. I ask, "I wonder how they came to suspect the Coach?"

"Officer Morris told us the Coach became a person of interest when Mr. Zeke linked the deaths of Ty Blanchard and Ross Georgeson to what happened to Angie's brakes. It all pointed to Alex. That wouldn't have happened if you hadn't told Mr. Zeke about your visions. Without the visions, it looked like Angie lost control of her car, Ross killed himself because of the missed kick, and Ty Blanchard was killed by a random murderer."

When he says this, it's like a tumbler in my head clicks and the lock is open. For the first time, the eagle visions make sense. The visions serve as a tool for truth. A tool to root evil out of the dark, and into the open. It's my gift. Angie's gift is intuition and prayer. Leanne's gift is amazing strength. Ben and Alex demonstrated willingness to sacrifice for love. Each of us is given a gift, and we must use our unique gifts to work together for good to overcome evil.

I think of the demon Mammon—how he could've killed or hurt so many more people if we didn't work to stop him. "How did Coach know that Mr. Zeke was on to him?"

"In his play book, the Coach had a section listing questions Mr. Zeke had asked about Angie's car and where he was the night of Ross' murder. He started questioning the students who helped out at the auto shop. When Coach used Ross' phone to lure him to the tennis court with a text supposedly from Craig Hamilton, Mr. Zeke grew really suspicious. Like he said back there, he called Officer Morris and wore his vest. But since he'd told Craig to call him any time he needed to talk, and there was still a chance it *could* be Craig, he went. Obviously, it wasn't Craig."

"Mr. Zeke didn't know for sure, but the size and shape of the man who shot him led the investigators to the possibility of it being Coach. So they looked into where Coach had been the nights of the killings."

"But wait!" I put my hand on his arm. "How could Coach have killed Ty Blanchard when he was with you and Alex two hours away at the UVA tryouts?"

"Actually, it was that crazy receptionist my dad picked up at the hotel and then ditched at tryouts. She told investigators he'd said he had a meeting to go to for about three hours. When Mr. Chortov returned to the room later that night, there was a spot of dried blood on his arm. He told her he spilled ketchup on it at dinner."

"Then a speeding ticket on I64 in Newport News put him back in the vicinity at the exact time Ty disappeared." Ben runs a finger through my hair. "Thank God we were able to stop him before..." His eyes get all murky and distant, and I can tell he's feeling guilty again—so I try to change the subject off of me.

"What about you? Why did you come back from Virginia Tech early? You told me you were going out there with Coach."

"Coach Grimes ended up driving me out—said the Coach had more prep work for the upcoming game. Or at least that's what he was told. We now know he had a different sort of prep work in mind." Ben looks at me, raising one side of his mouth in a semi-frown. "I wasn't doing a good job hiding my anger at having to go. If you recall, I'd made other plans for that night."

"Our date, right?"

Ben nods. "On the way, Coach Grimes asked what was eating me. When I told him about having to cancel the dinner, he said, *Don't do it, man. If you want to keep her, she's got to come first.* Then he told me why he never got married. He was engaged once, but his fiancée called it off two weeks before the wedding. He never got over it."

"Why? He seems like a really nice guy." I remember him patting Ross Georgeson on the back after the missed kick.

"The day they were supposed to go shopping for wedding rings, he forgot, and met a bunch of his friends to watch a playoff game. She didn't want to be a football widow." Ben swallows. "I told him to turn the car around. When we were almost home, I texted you from his phone—I thought I must have misplaced mine before I left because I couldn't find it anywhere."

"Alex had it."

"Yeah. I found it in my truck the next morning."

"That explains a lot. Alex texted me earlier, and I thought it was you. But then later, when I got your text, I didn't recognize Coach Grimes' number, and thought that one was the fake." A green-necked mallard skims across the surface of the pond sending ripples to the shore. I figure I'd better keep him explaining before he asks me any questions. "But Ben, how did you know to go to the stadium?"

"We were half a block from my house when we saw Coach pull out of the driveway. He didn't see us—but he was driving real erratic—like he'd been drinking or something. I saw Mr. Zeke pull out from the next driveway to follow him. We were both shocked to see Mr. Zeke—you know, *alive*—so Coach Grimes didn't have to say anything. We just followed at a distance. From the end of Memorial we saw Coach going through the stadium gate. Then I saw my truck and your SUV in the parking lot."

"No wonder you were curious."

"We waited for a few minutes. When it was clear that Coach wasn't coming right out, I went into the stadium while Coach Grimes followed Mr. Zeke to the auto shop. I learned later that they had gotten a search warrant for the shop and the house." He shakes his head. "I wouldn't have believed it if I didn't see it with my own eyes." He swirls one of my curls around his fingers.

"What?" I figure he must mean his father shooting at me.

He does a flying motion with his hand. "You flying down the field higher and faster than one of Alex's passes."

"You saw that?" My stomach lurches as Ben corroborates what I felt happening that night, but with each passing day, find harder to believe.

"Yeah, it was pretty dark in there, but still, it looked like you were caught up in a tornado that sent you flying down the field. Of course, it would've been a whole lot sweeter if the man who was supposed to be my father wasn't shooting at you at the time."

"And you charged right for us. You were a bull. Smoke coming out of your nostrils and everything." I smile so he knows I'm kidding. "I only flew away because I was scared of you."

Ben clenches his fist and grunts. "Maybe you're right to be scared of me."

"You know I'm only kidding, right?" I open my eyes wide at him, trying to get him to relax.

Ben looks away.

I watch the ducks paddle away from the shore.

This incredibly gorgeous, but obviously hurting guy turns to face me on the bench. I turn to look into his eyes, eyes that hold so much emotion. "After all that's happened to you because of me, I know... It would only be right..."

I close my eyes, not wanting to see his face when he lets me go.

He bunches a tangle of curls in his fist, and I see his biceps bulging through his jacket. "I have a confession to make." Ben's warm, cocoa eyes dart back and forth from one of my eyes to the other, like he's still debating whether or not to tell me.

I realize that the main emotion I'm feeling emanating from him—is fear. I guess a big, popular guy like Ben *can* be afraid.

His fist is still clenching and unclenching a tangle of my hair.

My heart races in anticipation of another rollercoaster ride. I hold my breath, bracing myself for the worst, and blink hard to stop tears from flooding my eyes. But when he turns my face to meet his, all I see in his eyes is longing. Painful desire.

"I know I should leave you. Knowing me has caused you nothing but trouble. Only...I don't want to leave you. I'm not sure I could even if I did want to. The truth is... Verona Lamberti, I'm crazy about you."

For once, I love how my name sounds; I don't even mind the tears of relief spilling down my cheeks. *Verona Lamberti, I'm crazy about you.*

Using the grip he has on my hair to gently pull me to him, he presses his lips into mine. Our mouths search for comfort, and wholeness, and healing. I think how, in one month, he has completely plowed me over, captured my heart. And at least for now, he's not leaving. He's my boyfriend. My very own Kublai Khan.

I brush the hair from his face with my good hand, kiss the scab over the bullet wound, and whisper lines from one of my favorite poems into his ear:

> *In Xanadu, did Kubla Khan*
> *A stately pleasure dome decree:*
> *Where Alph, the sacred river, ran*
> *Through caverns measureless to man*
> *Down to a sunless sea...*
> *For he on honey-dew hath fed,*
> *And drunk the milk of Paradise.*

Ben brushes my cheek with his thumb. "I like that...*honey-dew*." He kisses me again, sweet cinnamon, hungry, velvet kisses. "Where did you get that?"

"Samuel Taylor Coleridge wrote it after an opium-induced dream."

Ben's lips part, melding his pleasure with mine. "Mmm, milk of paradise...Might as well be opium." He grins, showing off that adorable dimple, then moves closer for another kiss.

In Ben's embrace, I feel like I'm in paradise. Home. I am *Home Free*. And for this eagle girl, being home free sends my heart soaring upwards, through cerulean skies and wispy clouds, to heights I've never even imagined. High. So incredibly high.

And then, in only a matter of seconds, with a jolting yell, I'm cast down, grounded.

"Verona! Come over here this minute!" My mother stands on the sidewalk, not ten feet from the bench where I'm locked in Ben's arms. Her briefcase is looped over one shoulder, and her arms are crossed. She beckons to me with one curved finger.

Okay, maybe I'm not *that* free.

THE END

Dear Reader,

Early in the story, Verona finds a book called *The Way of an Eagle*, by Kendrick MacLeod, a book connecting various attributes of eagles to practices for a healthy life.

The following bonus pages contain excerpts from *The Way of an Eagle*, by Kendrick MacLeod.

Excerpts from *The Way of an Eagle,*
by Kendrick MacLeod

I. Eagle Perspective

The Kwakiutl Indians from British Colombia, Canada have a legend recounting how the eagle snookered another animal for its keen eyesight. Originally, the eagle had dreadfully poor vision, but because it could fly higher than all the others, the chief asked it to stand watch for the tribe against invading enemies. Wanting to help, the eagle persuaded the slug, which at the time had excellent eyesight, to trade eyes temporarily. The slug agreed, but in the end, the crafty eagle reneged on his promise to trade back the slug's good eyes for the eagle's bad eyes. The Kwakiutl legend accounts for both the slowness of the slug and the eagle's sharp vision.

Whether the origin of the eagle's keen eyesight was the result of this swindle with the slug or not, this majestic bird is capable of seeing small prey over a mile away, or fish swimming a thousand feet below them, while soaring or flying overhead. By comparison, it is difficult for most fishermen to see fish swimming right below the surface only a few feet from the boat.

Scientists estimate that while eagles' eyes are the same size as the human eye, they see four to eight times better than the 20/20-sighted human. Where the average adult human weighs approximately one hundred and fifty pounds, an adult eagle weighs up to fourteen pounds, yet the back of the eagle's eye is much larger and flatter than ours, allowing it to view a much larger image—compare the screen size of a movie theater to an iPhone, and you'll get the picture. Also, the cells in the retina that send images to the brain—the rod and cone cells—are much more concentrated in the eagle's eye. In the fovea (a section of the retina with an enormous concentration of vision cells), while the human eye has approximately 200,000 cone cells per millimeter, the eagle has about a million per millimeter...

Whether we are trying to achieve a dream or a specific goal, or simply trying to get through a crisis, we can learn a lot from the eagle by looking at our life from a heavenly or higher perspective. If we ascribe to the notion that our purpose in life is to glorify the God that created us, then our goals should advance His kingdom. Goals that grow us in some way, such as a good education, skills for a new job, or even a new hobby, may provide us with sharper tools that we can use to serve others.

II. Eagle Preparation

Eagles have approximately 7,000 feathers. For more than an hour every morning, an eagle will preen these feathers. This process can be likened to washing and waxing a car. The eagle sits on the side of its nest and passes its feathers through its mouth, steam cleaning them with its breath and depositing a liquid that serves at least two functions: It bonds the feathers together, making the eagle more aerodynamic, and causes the feathers to be water repellant, preparing the eagle for diving one to three feet underwater to catch a fish, or for flying through rain or snow…

This daily preparation on the part of the eagle is wise. In the same way it benefits us to prepare—for our day, for our future, for a rainy day. We preen every morning when we wash, use deodorant, and slather on sunscreen, apply make-up and perfume or cologne, dress for the weather, receive a manicure or pedicure, wax off unwanted hair, trim the mustache, exercise, and so on.

What about our spirits? In addition to our physical body, our spirit could use a little preening to ready us for the day's challenges. Many people wake up a little earlier than necessary to take time for this. Some people call this meditation or a quiet time, some don't call it anything—they have just developed the habit to preen their spirits.

For some people, carving five minutes of distraction-free quiet from their day can be quite a challenge. Some of us are so anxious to get to our to-do list, the thought of sacrificing time out of our busy day to preen our spirit seems crazy, counter-intuitive. I was like this at first, but you need to trust me here. The small sacrifice of time will pay dividends in what and how much you accomplish for the rest of the day.

III. Eagle Feeding Habits

The eagle diet is most dependent on locale and season. Because of their size, eagles require a large hunting ground—anywhere from 1,700 to 10,000 acres. The eagle can lift up to four pounds, but rarely attacks livestock or domestic animals—preferring fish, rodents, or snakes. Eagles living near water prefer fish. Further inland, smaller birds, small mammals like rabbits, and snakes make up the bulk of the eagle's cuisine, with slight variations depending on eagle species.

Some scientists claim that an eagle is a finicky eater. This means that, unlike the vulture that prefers dead meat, an eagle, given a choice, will take a live animal to its nest, kill it, and eat it while it is still warm. The eagle's preference for live food over dead protects it from disease, which may explain its life expectancy of up to forty years.

As the lion is considered the king of beasts, the eagle is considered king of the sky. As such, eagles are at the very top of the food chain. While this status makes them virtually invulnerable to attack from predators other than man, it makes them the most vulnerable to toxic chemicals, which grow in concentration with each ascending link. The historic decline of the eagle in the last century is attributed to the chemical DDT, which weakens the eggshell. When DDT was banned in the United States and Canada in the early 1970s, the eagle population rebounded.

We can decide to follow the way of the eagle by opting for healthy, life-promoting foods, both literally and figuratively. By banning unhealthy poisons from our lives, we are destined to thrive!

Feeding our Body: *The constant barrage of commercials and advertisement for food items heavily laden with sugar and/or salt and unhealthy fats, in addition to the convenience of eating these packaged, processed, or fast foods, tempts us to choose poorly. The excess of sugar, salt, and fat in our diets keeps us craving more, and is the cause of a multitude of disease and misery.*

Unless we're very young, our diet is a choice. When given a choice, we should choose to eat fresh whole grains, fruit, and vegetables. Choose fresh fish over red meat. Eat vitamin-rich vegetables at most meals. Many people are willing to pay extra for organically grown foods to avoid the pesticides used in commercial farming.

Feeding our Spirit: In the same way, our physical wellbeing is dependent on our food choices. Our mental, emotional, and spiritual health is affected by our choice of what we partake in experientially—the programs and movies we watch, the magazines and books we read, the video games and websites we visit. The little choices we make every day eventually become habits, and over time, develop into our character. They become life choices that determine how our life will go. For better or worse. When we choose to use our time wisely, intentionally, and in ways that lift our spirit higher, we reap the rewards. Let's examine how our choices feed our spirits:

IV. Eagle Grip/Letting Go

Eagles are raptors, from the Latin word *rapere*, which means a bird of prey that hunts and kills with its feet. Eagles have four talons on each foot: three regular talons that face the back, and a longer, hallux talon at the back of the foot that faces front. The talons are made of the same tough keratin (protein) as human fingernails or dog's nails.

The tremendous power of the eagle's grip comes from its leg muscles, tendons and bones. Once in place, ridges on both the tendons and the tendon sheaths can lock together, allowing the eagle to maintain a tight grip without any exertion on the leg muscles. This explains why eagles can sleep with their talons gripped around a branch and not fall off. It permits the eagle to carry its prey over long distances back to the nest without dropping it. It also explains why some eagles drown when the fish they've captured is too heavy for them, but they can't seem to let go.

Like the eagle, we humans seem predisposed to hold on to things that are harmful for us, when the wise course of action would be to simply let go. Once something is caught in our vice, whether a bad habit, an unhealthy attachment, or an untrue belief, it takes tremendous willpower and often help from outside sources to let go. And then we'll need to replace that habit, attachment or belief with something healthy. So doesn't it make sense to let go at the start? Or choose not to succumb to the temptation in the first place?

In the case of a lost relationship, whether by death, divorce, a break-up, a move, and so forth, many choose to find solace in our relationship with God. This is one relationship where it's impossible to cling too tightly.

V. Eagle Healing

Eagles enjoy a relatively long life and rarely get ill. When they do get sick, they climb to the highest place available and stare into the sun. Shutting their thick eyelids prevents injury to their vision, but staring into the sun seems to revive the eagle. In ancient Greece and Rome, Aristotle and Pliny the Elder claimed the eagle was the only animal capable of looking directly into the sun.

We humans do not have the thick eyelids of the eagle, and should heed our mother's warning: Don't stare at the sun, you'll go blind. So, what does the eagle's practice of sun-gazing teach us about healing?

When we're suffering, many of us take comfort in looking to God's son, Jesus.

We take comfort knowing that Jesus, as fully human and God, suffered greatly in his life. Jesus wept. (Jn 11:35 KJV). *The shortest verse in the bible depicts Jesus suffering emotional pain when his friend died. While none of us should ever take comfort from another's pain, I find perspective for my aches and pains and worries when I think about how horrifically Jesus suffered in the last hours before his death. And all for love.*

Most of us pray more fervently when in physical or emotional pain. And the need for healing is known to bring many folks closer to God. Often God demonstrates His strength through our weakness.

VI. Eagle Nesting

Once eagles choose a mate, they begin building their nest, called an aerie, high atop large trees, most often near rivers or coasts. The average aerie is about five feet across, but since eagles often return to the same nests each year, they can get enormous—some weighing up to two tons, with a diameter of nine feet. The eagle's nesting area is usually one to two miles, and the eagle couple is very territorial about it—not even permitting other eagles to nest nearby.

Initially, the male gathers the heavy tree branches while the female fastens these into the foundation for the nest. The layout of the branches under the nest determines whether the nest will take on a cone, disk, or bowl shape. Once the foundation is set, the male brings thinner branches, vines, leaves and grass for the female to further strengthen the nest's construction. Next, the female lines the nest with fur saved from animals they've hunted. Before she lays the eggs, she softens the nest even more with down from her own breast. While the female roosts on the eggs, the male shops the area for toys—shiny, interesting things like string or a shiny marble for the eaglets to look at, and eventually play with. If the female doesn't approve, the toy gets tossed over the side.

Before the first egg has hatched, eagle parents work together using their respective strengths to ensure the physical, emotional, and intellectual health of their precious eaglets. In an ideal world, human parents do the same. Two loving parents, unified in the purpose of preparing for a baby, ensure the most welcoming environment for their precious girl or boy to enter this world. In addition to equipping the nursery, ideally parents communicate beforehand their dreams (spiritual instruction, schooling, athletic pursuits, and so forth) for the new addition to their family with the purpose of unifying, wherever possible. They might use this time to define and unify parenting strategies, reading books, or attending classes on childbirth and childrearing. They might discuss expectations and divvy up care-giving responsibilities, like who's going to get up for the three o'clock feeding, change diapers, prepare meals, and so forth. This is always important, but becomes uber-essential in homes where both parents plan to continue to work.

Last, but perhaps most important, the parents should plan for and implement strategies to ensure the couple's relationship needs doesn't get totally eclipsed by the needs of the newborn. Some couples find a reliable sitter so they can enjoy weekly date nights. Or they agree to leave the baby with a trusted loved one for a night alone together. The best present the parents can give their newborn is the secure presence of a unified team championing his or her life. Parents who regularly invest in their relationship build the strongest foundation for their baby's nest.

VII. Eagle Parenting

An eagle *hatchling* weighs about three ounces. Its eyes are closed and its slimy yolk sac glues its downy feathers to its pink skin. In a matter of hours the chick's eyes open and its downy coat dries out.

Except for the first day or so, eaglets are ravenous. The *nestlings* scream for food every time they wake up, consuming more than their body weight every day. The eagle parents hunt almost continually to keep the family fed. Because the tiny eaglets are so vulnerable, one parent stays close to the nest to keep predators at bay while the eaglets sleep. Early on, eagle parents must shred the food and coax their eaglets to eat.

Like eagle hatchlings, a human infant is completely dependent on her parents for every basic need and safety. If she had psychologically healthy and loving parents she will come to expect their provision for her and trust that the world is a good place.

On the other hand, studies show if the infant's needs are not met lovingly and consistently during this critical time, the child will view the world through a lens of distrust and fear. If noone responds to his cries, the infant cries louder and louder, releasing the stress hormone cortisol, which can affect the infant's immune system. Without consistent nurturing, infants and children fail to thrive, up until the point of death. If there is abuse instead of care, often rage develops and the child is unable to form attachments to others.

Loving parents work hard to care for their young ones—night feedings, doctor visits, endless diaper changes, bottles, car seats keep the parents perpetually busy during this time.

VIII. Eagle Launching

One day, when the eaglets are between ten and twelve weeks old, the mother starts throwing all the interesting toys the father had collected over the side of the nest. A few days later, she rips out the down she had lain in the nest to make it plush and comfortable. The feedings dwindle until the eaglets think they're starving. Next, the mother removes the animal fur lining, the leaves and grass, until all that's left are sharp twigs that poke at the eaglets. They must stand on their spindly legs and flap their wings to keep from getting stabbed, all the while squawking at the injustice of the parents.

The father circles below while the mother flaps her wings hard from one side of the nest, the wind gusts forcing them to the other side. Then she pushes one over. It may get caught in an updraft and glide until it tumbles to the ground. Or it may just tumble and the father swoops under and returns it to the nest for another try. Eventually, through trial and error, the eaglets learn how to fly and eventually soar. They stay near their nest for up to another ten weeks, practicing flying and hunting until they can go out on their own.

Appreciate your parents if they've worked to teach you to delay gratification, respect authority, make goals and stick to them, and all the other character traits that enable us to soar to new heights as a fully-functioning adult. Human parents infuse character by always looking for examples to teach the wisdoms of life. Then they must trust their young one with increased, but measured responsibility, measured according to age expectations and the particulars of the individual child.

They must permit their precious offspring to fall at times—again, a measured fall. The pain experienced from falling produces a stronger desire to fly. With love, encouragement, and help when necessary, the young one will pass through all the necessary stages—from toilet training to career training—until they're ready to leave the nest. Too many adult-age fledglings in our world behave like turkeys because they've never been equipped, encouraged, or forced, if necessary, to fly on their own.

IX. Eagle Courtship

The eagle reaches sexual maturity from two to four years old. Once they select a mate, they mate for life, although if one of them dies, they may select a new mate. The selection process looks like fighter jets playing chicken in the sky. If there is mutual interest after these aerial acrobatics, the female dives down all the way to the ground with the male in constant pursuit. She finds a stick and climbs straight up to an altitude of about ten thousand feet, and drops the stick. The male immediately dives under the stick, catches it on his back, and brings it back to her.

She ignores him and dives for a larger, heavier stick and does the same thing. As long as he is able to catch the stick, the game continues, until she tires and accepts him as her mate. They have a ceremony where they fly with their talons locked together, swinging round and round. But if he should drop the stick, the game is over, and she looks for another male to partner with.

Why all the testing with sticks? The female eagle needs to know he'll be a dependable mate and father for her precious eaglets. If he can't catch a stick, how will he catch an eaglet when she tosses it from the nest?

In the old days in America and western cultures, long before Facebook's relational status—and even in some cultures today—men and women practiced what was called courtship. Courtship refers to the period of time between mutual interest between a couple, and a proposal of marriage. In that time, the couple would spend time getting to know each other to determine if they wanted the relationship to progress to marriage. The couple might go to a movie, a dance, get a bite to eat at a café, or just sit on a porch swing, talking. The main objective, other than having a pleasant time, was to determine if this man or woman would make a good spouse…and ultimately a good parent.

Today's woman and her future children would benefit by slowing down, waiting. Waiting to find out if the man is interested enough to pursue her. Waiting to discover what the man is made of. Good, solid stuff that goes well with your good, solid stuff? I'm not talking about sex here, but character traits, personality, and visions for the future. If you're not working toward the same vision—let him go!

Women could learn a lot about mate selection from eagles.

Acknowledgements

Thank You to my husband Tim for your amazing love, support, wisdom, and patience. *You're the best husband ever!* I'd like to thank my children: Billy, Johnny, Will, E, Sophie, and Katya for enduring my obsession with this book for years, with a special *You Rock!* to Ethan for being our first YA to read the book from cover to cover. And thank you, Brynne Valla Briskey, my journalist-major daughter-in-law who provided great feedback. A great big gratitude hug goes to my parents, notably my mother Bonnylin Jean Briskey, my sister Barbara Jean Briskey, and her awesome daughter Kate O'Keefe.

To my beloved friend, Beverly Bruce…thank you for understanding why I couldn't always be available to hang out. For Erin Bruce, my first true young adult beta reader: Your enthusiasm—*reading the entire five hundred page manuscript in twenty-four hours and then begging me to write the sequel*—kept me in the ring those times when I wanted to throw in the towel.

Sheila Shepard and Jenny Abel, my first editors—you taught me so much! Thank you, Lee Ann from First Editing for your insights, encouragement, and formatting and editing expertise. Nathalia Suellen at Lady Symposia…your cover design is perfect!

To the Williamsburg Writers—Marilyn Fanning, Mary Petzinger, Dawn Linton, and Vonnie Swope—your prayers and support were invaluable on this long road. To my avid reader friends in the Greensprings West Book Club—your combined feedback was helpful and encouraging.

I am grateful to Dick Woodward for his pamphlet, *As Eagles: How to be an Eagle Disciple*. If I'd read it when I was a young adult, I might not have made so many mistakes!

I thank God for *vesyo!*—Russian for "everything". But mostly, I thank God for His infinite Presence and eternal love, the greatest presents in all creation.

About the Author

Charlene Quiram lives with her cat, Boris Badanov, in Williamsburg, Virginia. She decided early on that Verona needed a longhaired orange tabby to love. Charlene's husband and their six young adult children tease her, insisting she loves Boris more than them. This is not true. Really.

Visit the author's website at charlenequiram.com for contests, book club questions, and information on upcoming projects. Or scan the QR code on your smartphone.

Made in the USA
Charleston, SC
09 December 2013